Discover other titles by Anthony J. Harrison:
(all titles are available at most online retail outlets)

Suspicious by Design – A Geneviève Benoit Novel

Obscure Intentions – A Geneviève Benoit Novel

The Irishman's Deception – A Conor McDermott Novel

Betrayed by a Scot – A Conor McDermott Novel

Redemption Denied – A Conor Mc Dermott Novel

Illicit Encounters

Published by Anthony J. Harrison

Cover design by

Damonza

http://www.damonza.com

Editing Services provided by

Cecily Myers at Red Pen Edits

http://redpeneditor.weebly.com

ISBN: 978-0-4633507-2-0 (Ebook version)

ISBN: 978-1-7324081-5-9 (print version)

This book is dedicated to:

To my aunts, Bridget Philomena Harrison, and Frances Sheila McNamee. Each woman was an inspiration to their families, and their communities. They gave of themselves without reservation or want, and remained strong and true to their faith until their passing. May they both Rest in Peace.

Prelude

The driver turned another corner, this time a little too fast as the momentum slammed Patrice Galant's shoulder against the side. The policewoman shifted her weight and slid herself upright, flexing her muscles to relieve the pain.

Blindfolded, her head covered with a hood, any sense of time or place had been taken from her. After what she guessed to be thirty minutes, the vehicle stopped and one of the two captors inside the van grabbed her arm. His hands, callous and rough, scraped against her flesh, as she felt the dried skin on his palms.

Since her confrontation with the three men near the mall, Officer Galant had been bound, gagged, and blindfolded. Her elbows were pulled behind her back, the ropes bound tight against her skin. Trussed-up like this caused her shoulders to ache. As the van door slid open, she finally had a sense where her captors had taken her.

The foul stench of the sea and shoreline filled the air. A mix of fuel oil, garbage, and marine life, along with rotten vegetation from beneath the waves, assaulted their senses. The putrid smell offered the undercover officer clues to her location. Patrice heard waves as they lapped against the hull of a nearby boat. *I'm somewhere along the waterfront*, she told herself. *But where?*

The gang members for Amed Gilles didn't speak as they pulled the woman from the vehicle. The driver, Yacine El Amari, came around from the front and motioned the other two towards the marina's entrance. Along with the fourth member, the driver grasped Patrice's other arm, and led her away from the van. Amed had entrusted Yacine to move the woman, and he was determined to succeed where others had failed.

Just days earlier, the gang leader Gilles learned from a trusted source the police knew the woman he'd kidnapped was somewhere in the Verduron quarter of the city. It wasn't long before he found out a foot soldier who guarded her had allowed the policewoman to be seen while he moved her between buildings.

While she was led from the van, Officer Galant feigned being ill, which caused her captors to support most of her weight. She trailed her feet along the pier as they approached the boat, each man with a tightened grip. The early morning silence allowed her to hear the water against the hulls, and a slight breeze caused masts of nearby sailboats to creak in protest.

"Get her into the boat," Yacine commanded in their native Berber dialect of Arabic.

The men nodded as one of them pulled Patrice over his shoulder. With one hand he steadied the woman, as he labored down the ladder toward the motorboat. The second man climbed down, and took the officer from his companion and forced her to sit at the bow.

Yacine soon joined them as the boat cast off from the dock. The whir of an electric motor filled the air as the boat ventured into the darkness. A helmsman steered the boat while he held a pair of night-vision googles to his face. The special optics illuminated the darkness in a fluorescent glow reminiscent of pond algae.

Yacine took the goggles, and scanned the horizon to the southeast. In the distance, he saw a series of flashes. "To your right," he gestured to the helmsman as he handed the goggles back.

Patrice began to shiver in her place on the bow as the moist, cool air assaulted her. With no jacket or long sleeve shirt, the time on the water led her to wish for the warmth of her former place of capture in the city.

Five thousand meters past the marina entrance, a luxury yacht rode lazily on the swells, the hum of its engine the only noise which echoed across the water. Onboard, three men strained to see through the darkness while they kept their sights on the breakwater and the smaller vessel headed towards them. One of them used a hooded flashlight to transmit their location by a triggered flash every ten seconds or so to the boat which wallowed toward them.

The yacht's owner swiveled in his captain's chair as he watched two men point off to their left. Grabbing his night-vision goggles, he swept the water's surface until he saw what caught the men's attention: a small skiff struggled in the open ocean, headed in their direction. Onboard, he could see the ghostly glow of four people.

As he watched, the owner instructed a deckhand to continue with his signals until the motorboat approached. "Get ready to take on a passenger," he ordered the crewmen who manned the deck ladder, which had a buoy tied to its side.

The owner took some pleasure in the activity as he looked down from the bridge. This detour in his feigned fishing trip would clear a €50,000 debt to the Maghrebis gang leader. Just for the act of transporting a woman onboard until she could be returned to Rabat and the man who would pay his fee. While the yacht swayed with the swells, he smiled.

Chapter ONE

The protesters had grown from thirty to over a hundred in just ten minutes. The *"yellow vest"* movement, which began on the streets of Paris, had filtered their way to the other cities throughout France. Instigators of the movement, easily visible by the lemon-yellow attire, urged their fellow citizens on against the police line established near the cathedral. Many of the younger members had their faces covered with bandanas or scarfs and armed themselves with stones. In the middle of the march, several held bottles at their side.

"Can someone please remind me again why this section of the city was chosen for a stakeout?" Detective Genevieve Benoit asked over the radio. She watched as stones arched through the air from the crowd, and tumbled near the officers. Closer still, several young protesters hurled rocks against the officers' protective shields, as their chants grew louder.

"Surveillance reports from Captain Soucy noted increased actions between tourists and drug dealers near the cathedral," Detective (Captain) Claude Lemieux replied. "It won't be easy to spot the suspects, but it's what we're paid to do," he added. "Keep your eyes open and stay alert," he declared while he tossed his coffee cup into a trash bin.

Sirens grew louder as the captain in command of the riot squad called for vehicle support. The growl of a large engine announced the vehicle to her left. Here, Detective Benoit saw the armored truck approach with an officer perched behind a water cannon already aimed at the crowd. As the attachment swung, a fiery bottle came out of the crowd. While it fell short of its target, the glass shattered and spewed its liquid before the police, igniting in a whoosh of flames and smoke.

Throughout the country, the yellow vest movement had grown more aggressive, which led towards more violence. The single Molotov cocktail would just be the start of a more brazen assault. Television broadcasts had led instigators to increase their encouragement to challenge authority when the protesters looked to gain the upper hand.

As she watched the police vehicle come to a halt, Benoit noticed three men gather on the corner. "Stand by, everyone," she said, pulling her ponytail to conceal the radio earpiece. "I think I've spotted one suspect," she muttered as she stole another glance at photos Captain Soucy supplied. One image stood out from the rest. Satisfied, Detective Benoit began to stroll towards them as she continued to talk.

"Which one? Where do you see them?" Detective Nicolas Berger asked, with a slow glance of the square.

"About 100 meters northwest of the cathedral's rear entrance," she replied as her pace quickened. "It appears they are alone, just in front of the protestors."

Hedy Fatah, a senior man of the Maghrebi gang in the La Joliette district, was unaware of the police and their surveillance. His two runners found a group of students from Barcelona, eager to buy their marijuana, and most important, they had cash.

"Remember, you take their money first before handing over the *hachich* (marijuana)," Fatah instructed the two younger men. "When you finish, meet me near the Italian restaurant on Quai du Port," he instructed before he sent them on their way.

Benoit saw the exchange amongst the three men as she moved closer. "Nicolas, if they move, you take the shorter one," she said. "I'll follow the taller one in the orange shirt. Captain, that leaves the last one for you," she added.

"I'm on the wrong side of the protesters to be of any help," Captain Lemieux replied as he hustled along the sidewalk, cut-off by the crowd. "What is he wearing? I'll try to get around into a better position." He thrust himself past a handful of women who shouted profanities at him.

"He's got khaki trousers and a rainbow t-shirt on," Benoit explained, describing Fatah's attire. "And he's got a small powder-blue bag slung over his shoulder too."

Fatah watched the protesters march along the boulevard as police stood at the western end of the cathedral near an American-branded hotel. While he turned away, he became lost in the chaos of protesters while he strolled towards the marina to rendezvous with his two drug dealers.

Detective Benoit watched her suspect meander in front of the church entrance. After five minutes, the doors for the 19th century neo-Byzantine edifice swung open as a group of tourists emerged. She saw the noise from the visitors catch the suspect's attention.

"I think I've got a transaction being made..." she declared over her radio. Geneviève skirted past several women, as she kept her focus on the suspect clad in a Paris-Saint Germain soccer jersey. Two teenagers broke away from the tour group and approached the drug dealer. Unfolding a tourist's map of the city, she continued to make her way closer.

"I need some help here," Captain Lemieux exclaimed over his radio as several protestors blocked his path. "I'm surrounded by four or five of the protestors," he added as he tried to reverse his path.

"Standby, Captain. I'm on my way," Detective Berger replied as he left to help the senior officer.

The Spanish teenagers stood on the promenade in front of the church with a blatant disregard for authority, while engaged the drug dealer. Benoit saw them clench a wad of cash in one hand, while the dealer produced the drugs. The young Algerian pulled a small plastic bag from his waistband, handing the marijuana to the teenagers as he took the money from their hands.

Benoit saw the hand-off. "We've got a buy," she exclaimed with a rush towards the trio. Two uniformed officers heard the trigger phrase, and appeared from the opposite side of the church behind the men.

The Algerian dealer saw Geneviève get closer. His second glance at the female officer allowed him to see the pistol she had concealed under her jacket as she drew closer. "*Vous êtes sur votre proper*," he uttered in French to the Spanish teenagers, as he told them they were on their own to deal with the police. The dealer stuffed the cash into his pocket, turned and began a slow trot towards the waterfront.

"I've got a runner," Benoit shouted, her weapon unholstered as she began her pursuit of the drug dealer. "He's headed south towards the marina."

The captain leading the surveillance team heard Geneviève's call over the radio. "You've no back-up," Lemieux said as he continued his retreat from the crowd.

"Well, send me someone," Benoit shouted, with purposeful strides toward the suspect. *The last time I ran after a suspect, I nearly broke an ankle in the process*, she told herself. She quickened her pace as the distance grew between them.

The Algerian disappeared from sight as Benoit struggled to catch up with him. With a glance over his shoulder, he noticed the woman no longer in pursuit. But he knew his contact would not appreciate if the police met them, if he didn't lose his tail.

Geneviève's legs burned and feet ached as she continued her search for the suspect. Afternoon crowds of tourists and families made things more tenuous along the waterfront. Geneviève rounded a corner, and spied the dealer in a trot along the marina's walkway as he dodged past vendors. With her lungs on fire and her breath coming in gasps, she continued her chase.

"Where are you now?" came the familiar voice of Nicolas Berger on the radio.

Geneviève weaved amongst the people on the path, before she responded, "I'm almost at... the ferry building... on Quai du Port," she responded, struggling to breathe and speak at the same time. Several small children pointed at her and her weapon as she ran past them.

The Algerian continued on until he stood across from the agreed location. Hedy Fatah saw the young man, now bent over with his hands on his knees. Crossing the boulevard, he approached his dealer, who he saw was drenched in sweat. "What's wrong?"

"A policewoman...she followed me here," the dealer uttered as he fought to catch his breath with a glance over his shoulder. "She's got a brown leather coat and beige slacks on I think."

As the men conversed, Geneviève made it past the ferry building and closed the gap between herself and her suspect. "I've a second suspect," she declared over the radio. "It's the man from earlier: orange shirt and khakis with the blue bag."

"There... that's her," the young runner said, pointing out Benoit.

Fatah saw the policewoman hustle past a family who struggled with a cooler near the ferry service entrance. Above the noise of boats motoring on their way out of the marina, and people calling out to one another, he could hear distant wails of police cars grow closer.

On the stone promenade near the marinas' end sat one of many transients who roamed the waterfront. Surrounded by bags stuffed with clothes, people who walked past gave little notice to the haggard and dirty person huddled under a threadbare blanket. The strands of oily and knotted hair hid an earpiece. The transient was actually Damien Favre, a member of Captain Soucy's gang surveillance team for this area of Marseille's marina. Favre heard the report of the drug dealer and waited to see if it would ruin his cover.

Fatah looked back, as Geneviève slowed her pace, but still grew closer to where he and his dealer stood. "Go... head towards the mosque on Rue de la Clovisse. Tell the mullah Amed Gilles has blessed you," he instructed, pushing the young dealer away. As he glanced over his shoulder, Fatah could see a police car make its way past the ferry building.

"My suspect is headed north away from the marina," Benoit said. "I'm staying with the other here at the waterfront; they might have passed something along."

Striding with more purpose towards the Algerian, Geneviève locked her eyes on Fatah as he turned away and walked along the crowded promenade. He didn't consider his tie-dyed shirt as an easy mark to track, but even amongst the tourists, it was like a solitary lantern in a dark cavern.

With a glance over her shoulder, Geneviève signaled the two patrolmen to follow the drug runner while she stayed behind Fatah. As she drew near, she saw the Algerian weave his way amongst tents and canopies of the daily market sellers. A crackle over the radio caused her to pause.

"Benoit... where are you right now?" Captain Lemieux asked, catching his breath.

"I'm near the ferry boat landing; across from the town hall," she replied, as she kept her distance from Fatah, but continue to track the bright colored shirt move amongst the crowd. "One suspect is heading north, but I believe they exchanged drugs or money when they met."

Fatah saw a chance to hide as a gate leading to a dock was left open. He scurried behind the tent of a trinket seller, and made his way along the dock to a yacht secured to the end.

Officer Favre saw Fatah climb onboard the yacht. It was the worst-case scenario for him, as he'd spent three weeks staking out the waterfront for signs the gangs were retrieving drugs from the yachts. This particular one, the yacht *Le Femme Fatale*, had proven to be his best encounter to date. And now, this man was about to ruin it for him.

Though Geneviève lost sight of her suspect, she knew the man would be easy to spot again once she saw him again. Out the corner of her eye to the right, she noticed him climb onboard the yacht. "The suspect is now on a motor yacht near the Grande Roue de Marseille," she exclaimed into her microphone while trotted towards the dock.

Fatah felt confident he had evaded the police while he stepped into the salon of the luxury boat. Looking through the glass doors toward the stern, a figure reclined on a deck chair surprised him. He made his way with measured steps down the stairs towards the forward cabin. Here, he found a closet to hide in from the police. For Hedy Fatah, this choice would be the last in his life.

While she made her way along the dock, Benoit walked with care towards the yacht, her weapon still in her hand. A commotion from behind caused her to pause. With a glance, she saw her partner, Captain Lemieux and fellow Detective Nicolas Berger, exit their car. A wave of her hand caught their attention as they made their own way through the gate.

In moments, Berger was at her side while Captain Lemieux directed a patrolman to man the gate. "What've you got, Geneviève?" Berger whispered, his own weapon in hand.

"I think the leader of those drug dealers made his way onto this yacht," she replied, with a nod to the vessel. "I saw him meet with another from the cathedral." A trickle of sweat made its way down her cheek. "It looked as if they passed something, but I'm not sure what it was," Geneviève answered as she stepped to the wooden stairs which led to the deck.

By this time, Captain Lemieux had joined his officers. "Is the suspect armed?" he queried as he unholstered his pistol, a slight tremor causing his hand to shake.

"I didn't see a weapon, but who knows if the suspect will find one on the boat," Benoit mentioned, as she took the first step. "I'll go to the back of the boat, you go to the front," she nodded towards Berger. "Captain, you've the upstairs, okay?"

As each of the officers stepped onboard, Geneviève made her way to the stern deck. Rounding the corner of the superstructure, she spied the reclined figure of a woman. Geneviève noticed the person didn't move as she approached and when she grew closer, she could see why.

The woman in her late 40s, clad in a stylish bikini, died where she lay. To a casual observer, it was easy to surmise the woman had been shot. But for Geneviève, she could tell the wound had been inflected at close range. The victim's bikini, reminiscent of a ripened lemon, showed a black-grey smudge surround at the entry point over her heart. Besides, there was no trace blood trail across the deck to the chair from the salon. What blood escaped the entry point was now a darkened mahogany, congealed under the sun. "Captain, I've one shooting victim on the back deck," she spoke into her radio.

Berger entered the lower deck, and made his way to the main cabin. As he pushed the stateroom door open, he saw Fatah's feet sticking out from a closet. "And I believe I've found our drug dealer," came the voice of Berger in reply. As he peered in, he saw the Algerian with traces of blood ooze from his nostrils and mouth.

Benoit heard a ruckus come from the dock. Captain Lemieux looked back to the gate, and watched the patrolman confront a transient. After a brief exchange, Officer Favre approached the stairway.

"Who are you?" Lemieux asked.

"Officer Damien Favre, Gang Surveillance," the officer said, his badge and identification held out. "I've been watching this boat for weeks. What's happened?" he asked just as Geneviève came around the corner.

"We were conducting surveillance on some drug dealers near the cathedral and one ran this way," Benoit replied. "He met a man we suspect was the leader handling them, and he boarded this boat." with a nod toward the salon.

"And now he's dead," Detective Berger added as he came through the salon doors. "I'm not sure how though; but there was blood from his nose and mouth."

"Show me where he is," Officer Favre asked.

Heading below deck, Berger showed the officer to the cabin where Fatah lay. Officer Favre bend down to inspect the body. "Well... this doesn't look good," he said. "You'll want to step back," he told Berger. Taking a pair of rubber gloves from his pocket, Favre pulled them on and retrieved a specimen swab from his shirt.

He reached back into his coat, Favre also produced a small vial and pulled the cork off its top. With a swab, he wiped it across some powder from Fatah's cheek. Sticking the cotton tip into the solution, he replaced the cork, and shook the vial. The solution changed from translucent to magenta.

"What is it?" Berger asked.

"Some type of opioid; probably Fentanyl. High quality and very dangerous," Favre said. "This is now a job for the Hazardous Materials Team." He backed away from the victim. On the stern deck, Captain Lemieux and Detective Benoit compared notes of the dead woman and her surroundings.

Lemieux took a step back from the victim in the chair. "This woman, she looks familiar... doesn't she?" the captain asked, as he glanced toward Geneviève.

Geneviève shook her head. "I've not seen her before," she replied as she jotted down what little there was of the woman's attire and belongings. "You've got to remember, I'm not one to waste time in front of the television or go to movies," she added.

"No. No, you don't, do you?" Lemieux answered. "Instead, you spend your time at the academy pistol range taking money off those poor cadets. How much did you take in last week?"

Geneviève put her hand up, shielding her eyes as she looked at the captain. Before she could answer, Berger and Officer Favre came through the salon door and back on deck. "Your suspect died from exposure to fent...." Berger explained, with a glance toward the woman in the chair as he struggled to pronounce the drug.

"What?"

"He was exposed to Fentanyl," Favre corrected. "It's the next step below heroin for addictive narcotics. But in concentrated form, it's twice as lethal." With a tug, he pulled his gloves off, and continued. "I've been on the promenade for three weeks trying to establish how the gangs were operating here and stumbled across several of them meet various yachts. This was the last one I noticed them have contact with the other day."

"I wonder what her purpose was, then," Lemieux expressed, nodding to the body.

Officer Favre walked around the captain and looked at the body. "I've seen this woman. Her name is... or it was, Yvette Segal. She's the actress who the French Film Academy honored last month in Nice if I recall."

"So... is it any surprise we've a dead socialite and drugs in the same place?" Captain Lemieux asked, with looks toward his two detectives.

"But why was she killed? Seeing her this way screams she knew who shot her," Berger said.

"You've made an assumption someone shot her where she lays." Lemieux pulled his radio out to contact the homicide detectives. "Who's to say someone, maybe the shooter, didn't plant her here to disrupt another crime. If you care to look, her skin hasn't begun to redden. Our victim hasn't been in the sun for very long."

Berger glanced at his watch. "Which would suggest her death happened in the last hour?" Turning to Officer Favre, he nodded toward the woman. "And you didn't hear or see anything this morning?"

“Not if it came from the dock, I didn’t,” Favre replied. “But there’s always movement on the water.” He pointed to several boats head out of the marina.

“But if that’s the case, Captain, where do we begin our investigation?” Geneviève asked.

“We don’t, Detective Benoit,” Lemieux replied. “This case belongs to Captain Trembly and his homicide department. But we need to find out why there is... what is the drug called again?” he asked, turning to Officer Favre.

“Fentanyl, Captain,” he said.

“Thank you. Our concern now is how the Fentanyl came to be onboard,” Lemieux replied.

“The news-types will have a field day when they hear about this,” Geneviève said, looking back at the growing crowd on the docks. Amongst them, a well-dressed gentleman noted the activity before he turned away, to lose himself amongst the tourists.

Chapter TWO

Meanwhile, in Marseille's western district of Verduron, two men sat down to meet in a small restaurant near Boulevard Henri Barnier. This was the fourth location Gregory Arsenault was directed to since his first encounter with Amed Gilles.

Gilles, a small-time criminal from Soustara district of Algiers now led a Maghrebis group in this quarter of Marseille. He'd gone from petty theft and pick-pocketing tourists near the marina to drug dealing, extortion, and money laundering. All this since his rescue with other refugees nine months ago. Gilles's earlier meetings with Arsenault was his attempt to intimidate the Frenchman into thinking he was someone who shouldn't be taken for granted.

Four weeks ago, Gilles learned of Arsenault and his police informant, and planned to bribe the Frenchman to keep his secret safe. After their initial meeting, Arsenault, a former Legionnaire, used his own resources as he tried to learn what Gilles knew, and how he got his information. But so far, Arsenault's attempt came up dry on the Algerian.

"As you see, Monsieur Richelieu, I've ample resources at my disposal," Amed declared, as another photo crossed the table. This one showed a policewoman outside police headquarters. Earlier pictures showed the same woman, but in various locations throughout Marseille. "I'm not interested in your relationship with her, just the information she can provide on the police patrols and their tactics," Amed added as he took another long, deliberate drag on his cigarette. A curl of smoke wafted skyward as he exhaled.

Gregory's expression went unchanged as Amed addressed him by his alias. He glanced down at the photo. The features were distinct. The woman's identity unmistakable. It was his sister-in-law, Claire Dubois, a sergeant who worked in criminal records. "So... you believe I have influence over this officer," he said. "And she'll tell me what you want to know about the police work?" Gregory asked, pushing back the photo.

"But of course, Monsieur... you can do this," Gilles replied. "And, pay me €10,000 to keep her from having, shall we say... a most unfortunate accident." He smiled; another trail of smoke exhaled to convey his devious, deadly intention. "Considered it her life insurance policy," His yellow-stained teeth were on display as he placed the cigarette back between his lips.

As Gregory endured the conversation with Gilles, his partner Louis Clement leaned against their car outside, watching several men stand opposite the restaurant's entrance. "Come on Greg, this is taking too long," he muttered while he drank from a water bottle. A few droplets trickled through his beard. As he turned to look behind him, Clement could sense the pistol on his hip push against his body.

Peering back at the restaurant, Clement shifted his weight, and instinctively reached down to massage the bullet wound he took from a run in with police. *All the years with the team and I never took a hit*, he told himself. The depression in his thigh was a reminder he wasn't immune to being a target. Moments passed before the men in front of the restaurant stirred. Something was about to take place.

Inside, Gregory kept his expression blank while he considered Gilles demands. *My first concern is Claire's safety*, he told himself. The second, determine how Gilles obtained his cell phone number and most disturbing, learn of his alias as owner of Papillion Transport.

"Have your informant get the patrol schedules for the Le Estaque and Saint Henri districts for the next month," Gilles demanded, while he stabbed the cigarette out before he got to his feet. "You have till the end of the week." As he turned to leave, Gilles paused and looked back at Gregory. "Oh... don't forget the woman's insurance payment either," he grinned.

Gregory gulped down his coffee as Gilles walked out of the café. Through the door, he saw four men scramble around the waiting car as Gilles appeared, one grabbed the rear door which allowed him to enter unimpeded. The others assumed their positions: a driver and two guards, while the fourth waved to an unseen group.

Gregory pulled €10 from his billfold and tossed it on the table before he got to his feet. As he shuffled through the door, he saw his partner stare at the vehicles race toward the boulevard. Striding up to Louis, Gregory leaned against the sedan before he spoke. “Did you get their tag numbers?”

“Oui, Gregory,” Clement replied. “This man, Gilles, he must think he’s pretty important, heh? Between the two cars, I counted eight men guarding him, each of them armed.”

Gregory shook his head. “Good. It should help us track him down, then. We need to find out how he gets his information though. Someone talked. What’s worst is he used my alias and I want to know who told him.” He tapped his hand against the sedan.

Clement walked around to the driver’s door and got behind the wheel. Glancing at his partner sitting beside him, he considered the many individuals who knew something about them and their operation. “You think it was Geno?” he asked, as he recalled the Italian Mafia member and pizzeria owner from Toulon they confided in before.

Gregory closed his eyes, and contemplated Clement’s question. “I don’t know,” he replied. “If Giuseppe talked, I’m sure it would be to save himself from whomever the Mafia don is he answers to.”

Louis steered the car into the afternoon traffic. “Could it be that bastard Aziz? He never sounded right in his head, if you ask me. And what about his source in Algiers?”

Gregory sat and listened. “You mean Khalid? He’d have the connections, and I’d suspect Amed Gilles is one of them.” As Louis drove to leave the restaurant behind, Gregory began to piece together a plan, not only to protect Claire, but to find Amed Gilles information source.

“Do you think Sophia is in any danger?” Louis asked, alluding to Gregory’s niece.

“I’m not sure, but it might be a good idea to contact Phillip and have him prepare to return,” Gregory replied, with a glance out the window. “I’d prefer to keep Sophia away, but we can better protect her here in Marseille than in Toulon.”

While the head of Papillion Transport and his friend drove back to their office and the other members, Captain Lemieux listened to his superior's brief at police headquarters.

"We have three injured officers in the hospital recovering from wounds suffered during the protests," Superintendent Chevallier read. "Likewise, there's reports that six civilians were also injured, most of them minor. The television footage shows protestors engaged in throwing debris at our officers. But it also shows officers who used their non-lethal weapons without regard against non-protestors," Chevallier continued, as he pointed his pen at the monitor.

"These protests will not subside if we continue to disregard our own policies," Chevallier continued. "I expect each watch commander to brief their staff. Am I being understood gentlemen? Also, until further notice, all extended vacations requests are suspended," he concluded.

Claude Lemieux heard the grumbles as the superintendent walked out of the conference room. Lemieux closed his notebook and strolled out, with a detour to the cafeteria before he returned to his office. Grabbing his customary large coffee, he stepped forward to the cashier and pulled out his wallet.

"Just the coffee, or are you ready to settle your tab?" the cashier asked.

"Both this time. This should cover it... right?" Lemieux answered, while he put twenty-three 10-euro bills in her hand to count.

The cashier looked over a small notebook kept next to the register. "Yes, it does. Do you want your change back or can we add it to next month?"

"Keep it; I'll be back later today," Lemieux chuckled before heading toward his office. Within moments, he squeezed past several detectives in the squad room as they interviewed a sobbing woman, a recent robbery victim.

Detective Geneviève Benoit sat, mesmerized by the content on her computer screen. In a moment, her fingers glided over the keys as she added several more details from her experience with the drug dealer, Fatah. "Nicolas, did we ever get a copy of the medical report?"

Detective Berger looked over his computer. “I think it was dropped off earlier from forensics,” he answered, gesturing to the basket atop the file cabinets. “It came in with the lab reports on the drugs found on the yacht.”

Benoit slammed her chair back against the cabinet. With her left hand, she reached over her head, felt for the basket until she touched the edge and tugged the in-box until it fell in her lap. “Ha, I’ve struck it rich!” she exclaimed as Captain Lemieux came through the door.

“Excuse me? What did you do?” he asked, his coffee balanced on the notebook as he closed the door.

“Just grabbing the reports.” Benoit waved the folders over her head. “Isn’t that your third cup this morning?”

“And what if it is, young lady?”

“You know, scientists say caffeine is just as addictive as any other drug,” Benoit replied as she flipped open the folder. She let loose a low whistle while she looked over the front page of the medical examiner’s review. “It turns out nothing would have saved the dealer,” she declared. “Based on this, the dose of Fentanyl ingested was enough to sedate a stable of thoroughbreds.”

“It was rotten luck for him,” Berger answered. “According to Francine, a gram’s worth would cause an overdose worse than heroin.” Nicolas had gotten a run-down earlier from the forensic technician who was also his current companion about the drug’s potency.

“Are you both done?” Lemieux asked, exchanging glances between his officers.

“Why, is there something of interest from the superintendent?” Geneviève asked.

While he took a sip, Captain Lemieux flipped open his notebook. “There is, since you asked Benoit. We’re down three patrolmen after the other day’s protest, besides catching several citizens in the crossfire. And to top things off, we’re restricted to normal days off and no vacation days.”

“Wonderful,” Berger sighed, his head bowed in defeat.

“You and Francine had plans to go somewhere?” Benoit asked.

"Yeah, as a matter of fact we did," Berger answered. "We planned to head to Lyon for a few days. I hoped to get her mind off of Patrice's disappearance. Don't you and your friend the director have plans?"

"My relationship with Hector Dupont is not centered around trips... at least not yet," Benoit replied, her cheeks warming as she blushed. "Besides, he's busy. You wouldn't want something dreadful to happen at the airport, would you?"

"No, I guess not," Berger conceded. "About Officer Galant; is there anything new on her whereabouts?"

Lemieux sank into his chair. The abduction of the undercover officer didn't fall into his department's work, but an officer absent struck a chord in all of them. "Based on the last briefing from Captain Soucy, their best clue they had was a sighting near a petrol station in the Les Olives district," Lemieux said, his eyes closed. The statement hung in the air. Each detective considered the woman's fate, each knew the passing hours and days led them to a conclusion none wished to entertain.

"And what of Guy's replacement?" Benoit asked, gesturing to the unoccupied desk. "Any word on when we'll get another officer to fill his vacancy?"

"Paris is still working on it." Lemieux tossed his empty cup in the trash as he got to his feet. "Until then, we'll do what we can. Have either of you heard from Homicide about the woman on the yacht?"

Berger dug through his in-box and pulled out a handful of papers about mid-way through. "Based on what Officer Favre said on the boat, Homicide determined Miss Segal's last public appearance was in Nice. She received a humanitarian award at a benefit dinner from the French Film Academy," he read. "She was honored for establishing shelters for immigrants from North Africa."

"It doesn't explain how she ended on a boat full of drugs though," Lemieux answered. Taking up the phone, he dialed a number from memory. "Let's see if Vincent can give us a clue." After a few moments of awkward silence, the senior officer reached his counterpart. "Bonjour Vincent, it's Claude Lemieux."

Detective Vincent Noel sat in a cramped room amongst several officers just over 200 kilometers away in the city of Nice. His department was similar to Lemieux's: understaffed and overworked since the yellow vest movement erupted three months ago. Noel cleared his throat before he answered. "What can I do for you today, Claude?"

"I won't bore you with details," Lemieux replied. "You heard about the death of Yvette Segal. You know, the socialite from the movies?"

"Who hasn't, Claude? It's at least the fourth or fifth story being broadcast over the news," Vincent replied, while he grabbed a report from an officer who entered his office. "But they're only telling half the story. She wasn't the *'Angel of Mercy'* they're portraying her to be."

Benoit and Berger sat quiet while watching the facial expressions of their captain. The casual demeanor Lemieux exhibited before had changed to one of serious concentration.

"Is there something we should know, Vincent?" Lemieux asked.

"Immigration officers have tracked the refugees who entered the country," Vincent said. "And they noticed Miss Segal's group was very selective with the women she offered assistance. Immigration filed their report two months ago, but Paris declined to act on it. They cited lack of substance or evidence."

"Can you give me the report number?" Claude asked as he grabbed a pencil. "Oh... and were there any concerns about drugs along with immigration issues?" he added. This question drew the focus of Benoit and Berger even more than the earlier conversation.

"Give me a second," Vincent replied as he pushed aside a folder.

In a minute, Lemieux jotted down a series of letters, numbers, and dates from his friend. He pulled the sheet off the pad and handed it to Benoit. "Get me a copy of these reports," he mouthed.

Geneviève took the paper and looked over the case number. Turning to her computer, she entered the digits and letters to search the police database. In a minute, she found three files labeled "*Segal, Yvette*" with the date Captain Lemieux provided. As she highlighted the reports, Geneviève hit the print button, and soon the files from Nice were in her hands.

She slid the pencil into her ponytail and scanned the transcripts. Officers from Nice identified seven incidents where Segal's group targeted young women between the age of sixteen and twenty who sought asylum in France from war-torn African countries.

"What so interesting?" Berger asked, looking at his fellow officer.

"According to this report, Segal's group was selective about who they helped," Geneviève explained, handing Nicolas the first report. "This one addresses the Nice officers tracking several immigrants who attended a black-tie event," she continued. "They were obviously well attired, considering they just arrived off a rickety fishing boat from Tunisia." She passed the officer a sheet with several images of the women.

"We've got them Vincent," Lemieux said. "If we can be of any help, call me. Bon chance, mon ami," he said, as he hung up the phone. "So, what's in those reports that will help us?"

"So far, nothing," Geneviève said. "Everything written suggests she was a front for a prostitution ring, but nothing about drugs." She handed Lemieux a copy of the second report. "Unless we can tie Miss Segal to the yacht owner and the drugs, it's not our concern, if you ask me."

Berger held his hand in the air. "There's a snippet about a quantity of marijuana found on one boat which transported immigrants here. And this one states they found a half-kilo of heroin on one woman when medical staff conducted their health exam," he added.

"That's not enough to warrant our involvement," Benoit muttered as she continued to twirl the pencil through her ponytail. "We've enough on our hands here in Marseille to keep us busy."

"You're right," Lemieux exclaimed. "But we have a woman who was last seen in Nice, found dead on a yacht in our harbor with several kilos of drugs worth millions of euros. And that young lady... is our business."

"Do you think our drug smuggler Remesy has something to do with her death?" Geneviève asked.

"Do we have evidence to show a connection between the two?" Lemieux retorted. Rotating his chair around, he tossed his empty cup in the trash as he stood. "While I get another coffee, I want both of you to determine who owns the boat and any connection with the woman." Benoit and Berger glanced at each other as the captain walked out.

"Nothing more enjoyable than being buried in paperwork," Geneviève muttered under her breath. "You take the yacht owner; I'll look into Segal's acquaintances," she added, glancing at her companion before she looked behind Lemieux's desk. *When will realize he can ask for help?* she thought, the coffee she knew was just the substitute for wine.

Berger slouched back in his chair as he looked at Geneviève. "I better give Francine a call and let her know I'm stuck here for the rest of the day," he huffed.

Chapter THREE

Stars still dotted the sky as the evening faded to morning on the Mediterranean Sea. The *Motor/Vessel (M/V) Joan of Arc*, with its blurred edges and indistinct shape, glided slowly through the mist, hugging the water as it approached Marseille. A solitary figure stood outside of the bridge, watching the shadowy outlines of two crewmen walking forward towards the ship's bow.

"Slow to steerage speed," First Officer Anton Huet called through the open doorway. Leaning forward against the rail, he strained to hear the approaching launch carrying the harbor pilot whose job it was to lead the 11,000-ton vessel to its berth.

"Pilot approaching, port side" came the shout from the bow.

Huet took several strides across the deck until he stood at the control console on the ship's port side. Staring over the edge, he saw the familiar shape and color of the harbormaster's boat, and more importantly, the harbormaster.

Joan of Arc's captain, Marcel Dupont, entered the bridge after the morning watch called down to the galley for him. "What is so important I couldn't finish my breakfast?" he asked.

"Captain, there's a call from a Monsieur Richelieu for you," the young man answered while handing over the phone.

Taking the handset, Captain Dumont answered. "Good morning, mon ami," he replied. "What gets you up at this hour of the day?" Gregory Arsenault was always available when ships of Papillion Transport returned to their home port.

"I wanted to let you know first-hand what to expect today," Gregory said. "The police have taken a special interest in our activities ever since the British encountered the *Bonaparte* in July," he explained, referring to the last illegal drug delivery by Papillion.

Dumont frowned at the news. "Is everything all right with Henri and his men?"

"They're fine for the moment," Gregory said. "But after you dock, minimize the men's time on the beach so the police can't establish any patterns." He went on to mention his concern after the police encountered Claudette at their former company office. "I'll have Julien bring you a parcel after they have cleared you at the docks," he added.

A clamoring on the outer ladder drew Dumont's attention as he noticed the harbormaster's portly figure appear atop the stairway. "The harbormaster is onboard, so I've got to go. I'll have Anton keep an eye out for Julien," he finished before ending the call.

As Dumont entertained the harbormaster onboard the *Joan of Arc*, Detectives Benoit and Berger sat at the latter's office and overheard the radio traffic. Setting a folder on the counter, the office clerk was just about to address their concern about the yacht *Le Femme Fatale* when Geneviève spoke.

"When will they confirm the dock for the freighter?" Benoit asked.

The clerk read the anchorage report. "The vessel will put in at Berth number 17 in the west basin," she replied. "Based on her manifest, the *Joan of Arc* will offload forty-five containers. Based on where they are," the clerk continued, glancing at the map, "I'd say you've time for breakfast before we tie them up and are ready for boarding."

Detective Berger got to his feet. "That's the best suggestion I've heard."

"We'll be back in an hour then," Benoit replied as she followed her partner outside.

"What about the information concerning the yacht?" the clerk asked.

"It'll wait for a few minutes," Berger replied.

As they wandered to the car, tiny droplets of mist from the early morning fog dampened Geneviève's hair. Dropping into the passenger seat, she turned to Nicolas. "Isn't Francine feeding you in the morning?"

"What...? No... I mean..." Berger stuttered trying to explain their situation. "We're not to the point of her making me breakfast," he said. "Besides, she's still fixated on Patrice."

Geneviève grinned as Nicolas stumbled to explain his relationship. But her playfulness turned serious as she recalled the night of Officer Galant was kidnapped. Francine LeBeau planned to meet her friend to pass along a few hygienic supplies. When Patrice didn't show at the agreed location, Francine called Geneviève for help. The ring of Nicolas's cell phone broke the tension.

"Hello?"

"Where are you and Benoit?" Captain Lemieux asked. He'd called earlier and directed the detectives to the dock to follow up on their investigation of Papillion Transport freighters and their role in drug trafficking. "I thought I told you to meet me at the harbormaster office."

Berger handed the phone to Benoit. "It's Lemieux. You talk to him."

"Bon jour, Captain. How did you sleep?" she asked.

The captain picked up on the tone of the woman's voice before he answered. "Never mind how I slept; where the hell are you and Berger?" The aspirin he'd taken earlier was slowly attacking the hangover from last night's Cabernet.

For the next few minutes, Geneviève relayed the information about the Papillion freighter the harbormaster's clerk supplied. "Since we were told it would be about an hour, Nic and I decided to grab some breakfast."

"Make it to go," Lemieux said. "I want you both back here in fifteen minutes." The tone in his voice suggested there was something important he needed to tell them. "And make sure you've got a sandwich for me when you get back."

Geneviève pulled the phone from her ear, looked at it with disdain before answering. "We'll see you soon," she ended the call, and gave back the phone to Nicolas as she broke the news to him. "Seems we're to get our food to go and add a sandwich for the captain." She propped her head against the window. "He sounds a bit agitated this morning, too."

"I wonder if it means he finished two bottles last night instead of one," Berger said, referring to the captain's increasing habit of excessive drinking. "Didn't Captain Duval talk to him about his drinking?" he asked as he pulled in front of a small bistro.

"I thought he did just after the altercation on Chateau Il d'If," Benoit replied as she slid out of the car. "But he needs to recognize the problem before he'll ask for help you know."

Berger shook his head. "I just hope it doesn't affect his decisions. You and I need to keep a close eye on Lemieux while we're on the street." After a glance of the menu, he placed his order, as did Geneviève, which included a sandwich for their captain.

Two harbor tugs pushed the freighter against the dock fifteen minutes ahead of the scheduled arrival. With a series of horn blasts, the tug operators held the ship against the dock. A dozen men swarmed below as the *Joan of Arc* nudged against the enormous rubber fenders. Lines were tossed from the ship as several men strained to wrap them around bollards, securing the vessel in place. After a few minutes, the roar of a forklift echoed between the containers as it moved the gangway into position.

The three officers leaned against the patrol car parked at the gated entrance to the dock, keeping a close eye on the crewmembers on the freighter. Deckhands scurried along the rail, preparing additional mooring lines at the bow, while two others climbed a ladder toward the top container.

"Looks like too much physical labor for me," Berger said while he bit into his sandwich. "But it could be one hell of a work-out though too," as he swallowed the bite before taking a swig of his sport drink.

Captain Lemieux heard the comment, but didn't respond. He kept his eye on two men along the rail on the freighter's bridge. One wore a hi-vis jacket, while the other sported a heavy knit sweater and cap.

Geneviève replaced the cap on her water bottle before she tossed it and her trash into a nearby barrel. "Did the officers in Toulon have time to question the members from the other boat?" she asked, as she watched the deck hands work.

"Now that you mention it, no... We got nothing from them," Lemieux replied. With his last gulp of coffee, he stepped away from the car and tossed the cup towards the barrel.

An electric golf cart sped amongst the stacked containers waiting near the dock, its operator maneuvering deftly around a tractor pulling an empty trailer away. In moments, the operator brought his cart to a halt near the police officers.

Recognizing the older officer, he stepped out of the cart. "Captain Lemieux? My name is Enzo Tasse," the man announced, offering his hand. "I'm head of the Immigration office. I understand you have an interest with this freighter."

Captain Lemieux shook hands, but paused before he replied. "How did you know we were here?" he asked.

Enzo thumbed towards the light stanchion behind a stack of containers. "I'm connected to the surveillance system," he replied. "Plus, the clerk at the harbormaster's office called me just after your officers arrived earlier this morning. We'll have your information on the yacht in the office when you're done here."

"If that's the case, then yes... We're interested in speaking with the captain and crew members onboard the freighter," the captain replied. "It's possible several, if not all of them, are involved in a major smuggling operation."

The crackle of a two-way radio in the golf cart interrupted their conversation. Enzo stepped over and grabbed the microphone, answering the hail from the harbormaster. After a brief exchange, he returned his attention back to Captain Lemieux. "They're done mooring the freighter," he said. "My people will begin their inspection, and if you wish, you can come aboard."

Lemieux turned to Benoit and Berger. "I'll speak with the captain. You find and question the first officer," he ordered, as he sat next to Enzo in the cart. A small utility truck with the harbormaster sped past them. "And make sure we speak with him later."

Geneviève and Nicolas watched the cart carrying Lemieux maneuver around the activity and past the security guard, who waved them through, before stopped near the gangway. "I guess it means we're walking," Nicolas said, heading toward the freighter.

Benoit followed her partner, but felt an uneasiness creep over her the they got to the ship. With a glance upward, she saw several deckhands taking turns looking over the rail at her. Geneviève soon realized she was the only woman visible on the dock, and paused as she reached the bottom of the gangway.

"You all right?" Berger asked as he noticed the policewoman hesitate.

With a deep breath and a firm nod of her head, Geneviève answered. "I'm fine," she replied, grasping the handrail and took the first step up the gangway. In moments, the officers stood on the freighter's quarterdeck.

With the arrival of Immigration, each member of the *Joan of Arc* took to their respective tasks. Here, F/O Huet stood by the gangway to greet anyone who came onboard, which he did for the two detectives. "Welcome aboard the *Joan of Arc*," he said, with a mock salute before he extended his hand to Detective Berger. "My name is Anton Huet, the first officer."

"Detective Berger," Nicolas replied, shaking hands with the seaman. "And this is Detective Benoit." He motioned to Geneviève as he flipped open his notebook. "We'd like to ask you a few questions about your activities ashore."

Geneviève didn't hear Huet or Berger. All she felt were a dozen pair of eyes as she stood on the deck. In moments, she went from a policewoman on the freighter to adolescent girl on the streets of Cherbourg. It was here she saw herself walk along Rue Dom Pedro, passed the Construction Mechanical Normandy (CMN) shipyard facility. Each day she would hasten through the area as she endured the stares, whistles, and foul language from the workers on their break. The leering from the younger men felt as if they stripped her of her clothes, and exposed her innocence. Each time she passed by the facility made her skin crawl.

"Detective, this way, please," Huet said, with an extended hand toward her.

Sensing the movement more than seeing it, Geneviève reacted on instinct, and grabbed the first officer's hand while attempting to twist it behind his back. Any other occasion would have found the policewoman in control, but not this time. Huet countered her action, his response came after years of training as a Legionnaire.

Geneviève's sudden response caught her partner by surprise. "What the hell, Benoit?" Berger exclaimed as he pulled her aside.

"I'm sorry," Geneviève said as she straightened her jacket. "Your actions… I didn't expect you to reach out; I apologize."

"No apologies needed, Detective," Huet replied. "I should be more mindful around someone with a pistol. Looks like a SIG Sauer nine mil; am I right?"

Geneviève shook her head. "No, it's a Glock. But I see you know your firearms," Benoit replied. "And it's a .40 caliber, not a nine-millimeter," she added.

The first officer smiled. "I've looked at and handled a few guns in the past," he said. "And I've seen one or two from the wrong end."

"Oh... when was this?" Berger asked.

"Besides the few weapons we carry on the ship for self-defense, it was several years ago," Huet replied, as he tugged open a hatch and motioned down the hallway. "I was once a member of the Legion in my younger days. This way to the crews' galley."

Chapter FOUR

With the entire morning spent on freighter crew interviews, Benoit and Berger now had to transcribe conversation for their files. The silence in the office was deafening as each detective toiled over their computer. Other than muffled sounds from other detectives and officers outside, the only noise in the room were fingers on the keyboard. Each officer worked on their version of the investigation centered on the freighter and crew onboard.

After making a scene on deck, Berger gave Benoit the secondary interviews, something that would be less intimidating in his mind. "How many men did they have on the freighter?" Berger asked, while he looked over his computer at Geneviève.

She shrugged her shoulders without looking up. "I don't know. We never got a manifest from the first officer," Geneviève replied as she filled in the blanks on her interview report for one deckhand. It wasn't a surprise to her that every junior seaman onboard told the same story. Either they worked on deck, stood look-out watches, ate their meals and slept when they can. It was all they could relate to while at sea. The facts changed little when they docked, as the routine included handling cargo on and off the vessel with little time ashore.

"Nic," Geneviève began, "do you think the DEA fellow, oh... what was his name again?"

"Ochoa," Berger answered.

"Yes, him," Benoit said. "Do you think he had information about who handled the drugs onboard the freighter and didn't want to share it because who it might implicate?"

"Maybe... I don't know," Berger replied as he stopped typing. "By the way, what the hell made you take a swing at the first officer, anyway? I mean one minute you're like a statue, and the next you've nearly got him handcuffed."

Geneviève kept her head lowered as she took a deep breath. She knew why she reacted how she did. But her partner didn't need to know the real reason. "He caught me off-guard," she lied. "Besides, he reached for the side where I holster my pistol."

Even though they'd only been worked together less than a year, Berger saw enough of the policewoman's actions to know she always approached her work with 100% focus. And was never get caught by surprise... ever. *I wonder if she's as worried about Patrice as Francine is*, he thought. With a shake of his head, Berger went back to completing his notes from his earlier questioning.

The speaker crackling in the office brought both detectives to a stop as a man's voice coming over the intercom system directed them to the Annex. "What do you think that's about?" Berger asked while he saved his report.

"Your guess is as good as mine," Geneviève answered before she put her jacket on and pulled her ponytail from under the collar. Leaning over her chair, she saved her work before following Nicolas out of the office.

Long shadows fell on the parking lot behind the police station as the officers scurried toward the dilapidated trailers affectionately known as the Annex. Geneviève made a motion towards the third one which housed Captain Soucy and the Gang Enforcement Task Force.

Geneviève reached the entrance, and pulled the door open, its screech of metal on metal an audible protest of age and poor maintenance. She and Berger walked inside, where Officer Favre met them. He still looked like the transients and panhandlers from the waterfront. From strands of stringy, dirty hair escaped his knit cap, while a stained shirt hung loose on his shoulders and torn blue-jeans were held up with a rope.

"You didn't have to run," Favre greeted the detectives.

"Who said we did?" Berger replied.

Favre just grinned. "The captains have something to share with you," he continued, with a motion towards Soucy's office.

As each detective maneuvered through tables and chairs, they found themselves outside Captain Soucy's office where Claude Lemieux sat back against a cabinet.

He raised his coffee to acknowledge the detectives. “Come in and take a seat,” he said, waving them in the office. “Captain Soucy has information to share with both of you.” He moved his feet aside so Benoit and Berger could step past before he closed the door.

“Is it about Officer Galant?” Geneviève asked as she slid across a two-drawer cabinet, as the top flexed in protest.

“You found her?” Berger asked, his eyebrows raised in curious intrigue.

“No, Detective, we’ve not found her.... yet,” Captain Soucy replied. “But we did learn a Maghrebis gang member was seen handling a woman in the Le Estaque district.” He turned his chair to point at the city map. A crimson-colored pin stuck out, denoting a specific location within the quarter.

Spinning his chair back, Soucy flipped open one of a handful of folders on his desk. “One of my officers accepted food from the Church of Estaque when he overheard a comment by a volunteer. They were discussing the need to set some food aside for the mosque,” he read.

“The church isn’t too far from the mall where Officer Galant was abducted,” Geneviève said.

Soucy looked up from the report. “You’re correct, Detective... it’s not,” he acknowledged. “But it is in the middle of a neighborhood becoming more hostile toward police. These suggest there’s a growing contingent of North African settlers who are... shall I say… aggressive and suspicious towards our patrols,” he added. “And when we have time to question someone, they become defensive, like we will deport them.”

“You mean gang members, not the normal citizens, don’t you, Captain?” Berger asked. “If that’s the case, who’s their leader?”

Before Soucy could answer, Geneviève pushed into the conversation with another question. “Do you only have the one piece of evidence so far?” she asked. “What about someone who donates more women’s clothes or toiletries, something to show an unusual activity?”

“My people, at least the ones who are close enough, have their eyes open for such activity, Detective Benoit,” Soucy replied. “This society of immigrants, however, is not the easiest to infiltrate. This does not differ from your efforts to find where the dealers obtain their drugs. Am I right, Captain Lemieux?" he asked, turning to his fellow officer.

Claude tilted back his coffee, finishing it before tossing the cup and sitting upright in his chair. "You're right on all accounts. But you still haven't told them the other part."

Captain Soucy cleared his throat. "No, I haven't, have I?" Turning to Benoit and Berger, he continued. "A highly reliable source informed one of my officers about a suspicious group of men last week near the sailing frigate, *Inga des Riaux*. This person mentioned seeing a van pull up to the dock and let three people out. The informant described one person with a hood over their head and arms trussed behind them." Both detectives exchanged a glance between them before returning their attention to the senior officer.

"Was your informant able to say what day it was when they saw this van?" Geneviève asked, eager for more information. "Did they see anything significant? Color of clothes, hairstyles, height, anything that could help?"

"That's enough, Benoit," Lemieux interrupted.

"It's all right, Claude." Turning to face Geneviève, Soucy continued. "Detective Benoit, with gang activity, I have four groups which need equal attention. The Maghrebi factions and Black African gangs formed an uneasy alliance which covers the city west of *Avenue Jean Paul Sartre*." He directed her to the map again. "The Italians and Corsicans have divided the eastern half of the city between themselves. Each group has unique challenges which need a delicate hand to manage."

Geneviève squirmed in frustration on the metal cabinet, her gaze shifted between the map and Captain Soucy. "But if you've gotten information on Patrice's location, why can't you act on it?"

Soucy forced a smile. "Detective, how many police members are immigrants or have ties to regions outside of France? My struggle is to recruit immigrant members to the task force able to enforce our laws. And most importantly, be accepted by their ethnic groups in the neighborhood controlled by the gangs."

"So, you're saying you lack North African or sub-Saharan officers who can infiltrate the gangs without raising suspicions?" Berger said.

"Yes, in simple terms," Soucy replied, as he slid his hands through his hair. The captain pushed away from his desk, tapping his pencil against the map before looking at Geneviève.

"To answer your question about acting on our evidence Detective Benoit, we have done so," Soucy said. "I've shifted two of my team to the outskirts of the Le Estaque quarter near the harbor. Keep in mind, Detective, we won't stop looking." Before they could continue the discussion, there was a knock on the door.

"Come in, it's unlocked."

An older woman appeared, a plastic bag in one hand and a feather duster in the other. "Excuse me, sir, just checking for trash," she said, while she exchanged glances with the others.

"You're just in time." Captain Lemieux picked up his cup, and the custodian just smiled as she held open the plastic bag.

Captain Soucy motioned the woman towards the side of his desk. As she slid past the detectives, Geneviève spotted the hastily-sewn name tag on the denim work shirt. The writing was in both Arabic and English: *Asiya Fatah.*

The woman bent down to take the few papers from the trash bin. Glancing up, she acknowledged Captain Soucy again. "Thank you, sir. I'm sorry for the interruption," she muttered as she looked over his shoulder at the map before nodding at the others as she left.

"How are the workers vetted?" Benoit asked, staring at the closed door.

"I'm sure there's some process or procedures...why?" Captain Soucy replied.

"What are you getting at, Benoit?" This time it was Captain Lemieux who asked her the question.

"Didn't you catch her name tag? She has the same last name as our dead drug dealer from the yacht," Geneviève answered.

"So? It's doubtless a coincidence," Berger said. "How many Benoits do you think live in Marseille? Twenty? Fifty? It's nothing. Don't read into something which isn't there."

"Berger's right," Lemieux added. "Don't chase after something without knowing what you'll end up with," he finished, getting to his feet. "Is there anything else you need to discuss with us, Jean?"

"No."

While the officers ended their discussion, Asiya continued to clean the outer rooms. She knew the importance of keeping her activities in the police building as normal as possible; it was what her cousin had told her to do. As she bagged another can of trash, she observed the woman and two men walk out of the trailer. At the last minute, the policewoman glanced back at her, each of them catching a glimpse of the other.

Detective Benoit walked out into the darkness behind her fellow officers. "I'm still concerned about the cleaning lady," she said. "She was watching us while we left the captain's office. Why would a simple custodian want to do that?"

"Maybe you remind her of her niece," Berger muttered over his shoulder as they walked up the stairs of the police building. "Or she likes your hairstyle, or maybe it's your jacket."

Geneviève shook her head. "What about the way Omar Khalid and Louis Remesy found out about our accommodation on Il d'If?" The detectives knew it was a contentious point of how the criminals learned about their colleagues, though the attempt to free one of them failed. The raid also led to the death of four criminals.

Captain Lemieux turned and stopped in front of Geneviève; his finger pointed at her. "Evidence, Benoit. We investigate because we have evidence. To prosecute a citizen because of their name or where they come from is a dangerous form of justice. And I won't tolerate it."

While the captain walked away, Berger shook his head. "I guess we know how he feels about that."

Geneviève just stood there. This was the first time since joining Captain Lemieux's group he'd shown any sign of frustration towards her in front of other officers. *Was this a symptom of his drinking?* she thought. She felt the need to explain herself, but kept quiet to avoid another lecture.

It wasn't a secret amongst the other detectives that Geneviève was placed on administrative leave for her actions at Chateau Il d'If. They'd all heard the story of her assault against the suspects, killing at least two of them. Since the altercation, she'd been particularly careful with her actions, always conducting herself within the directions Lemieux gave her. Yet, this outburst wasn't Lemieux's normal way of showing his displeasure.

Captain Lemieux quickened his pace as he saw the hostess prepared to put away the coffee service for the day. "Just a minute, if you can," he exclaimed, coming up behind the server.

The café attendant shook her head as the officer approached. "You're lucky, Captain," the woman replied. "I'm behind with clean up or you'd be out of luck." She set the urn down for him to use.

Snatching a large Styrofoam cup, he poured the still hot coffee. "Thank you," Lemieux said as he added cream and sugar. "I think I still have a few euros from this morning, don't I?"

"I'll see they adjust your account, Captain," the server answered as she placed the urns on the cart.

Slipping a lid atop the cup, Lemieux gave a mock salute while turning away. In doing so, he caught the eye of his supervisor and friend, Captain Julien Duval.

"And how many is it today, Claude?" Julien asked.

"I rarely keep track," Lemieux answered as they walked together. "But I'm sure you'd get an answer from Detective Benoit if you're curious." After a few steps, he turned and faced Julien. "Was there something you wanted to talk about with me?"

Julien Duval had known Claude for nearly fifteen years, from when they each were promoted as detectives. He also knew the pain Claude carried every day after he lost his wife Nadine to cancer.

"Superintendent Chevallier asked if we had any further update on the freighters used in the drug trafficking case," Duval said. "It seems the inspectors from Scotland Yard made a discovery on the potential buyer. He'd like to show them something from our investigation to prove we haven't given up."

"We've got surveillance on one of the other vessels," Lemieux replied. "I'll have Benoit or Berger put together their notes from our interviews to add to the reports. But we've yet to see the crew do anything that links them with others from the shipping company."

Julien nodded his head. "All right, then. Put together what you have, but I expect you to keep your team focused on this investigation, do you understand?" The tone of his delivery provided the needed urgency. "If something comes up with Officer Galant's disappearance, I'll see you're informed."

Claude's eyes widened, as he listened to Duval. "Who told you I spoke with Captain Soucy?"

"It doesn't matter, Claude," Captain Duval said, stopping at his office. "You worry about your cases; let Soucy worry about his." He entered his office and closed the door.

"Yes, sir," Lemieux replied as he turned away.

Chapter FIVE

The two men stood outside the bridge, looking out over the deck of the freighter. They watched the single crane methodically lift containers from the stacks onboard their ship, each container removed an act to maintain a balance like a child's teeter-totter. Each time the crane swung its load past the overhead lights, shadows danced across the freighter.

The first officer turned to his captain. "He's late," Huet said. "I guess we're lucky the second crane failed. If it hadn't, we'd be here empty just to wait for Gregory's delivery."

Marcel Dumont glanced at his second-in-command. "Don't fret, Anton. I trust the person being sent is taking precautions to keep from being suspected of their involvement with us." As the men on the *Joan of Arc* contemplated the whereabouts of the courier; across town, a man waited near a small market.

With an up-turned collar, Julien LeBlanc stole another glance down the street. *Where in the hell is Claudette?* he thought. It wasn't like the secretary for Papillion Transport to be late for a rendezvous. And all Gregory mentioned was Claudette had a packet for him to deliver. The envelope would read "Charts and Manifests" across the front, but its contents was more than nautical documents.

Brakes squealed as the bus driver pushed against the peddle. The screeching resonated along the street as the Metro bus came to a halt. During the evening schedule, bus service brought workers home from throughout the city back at five-minute intervals. In moments, another handful stepped off, scurrying along the sidewalk. Among them was Claudette Minot. With a quick glance, she spotted Julien who sat outside the market on the opposite side of the road.

Claudette walked toward the market with a purposeful stride and her head held high, dodging cars as she crossed the road, drivers blaring their horns in protest. She fluttered her hand at the cars, a typical response from most pedestrians to harried motorists.

"That wasn't particularly ladylike," Julien exclaimed as Claudette approached him.

"If I had a stone, I would have tossed it at his window," she replied, exchanging feigned kisses. "How are you today?" She stepped back to look at the young man as a relative would.

"I'm doing well," Julien replied as he glanced over her shoulder and up the street. "Though I'm not happy to look behind me every day." Two school kids passed, which allowed him to glance behind for any potential trouble.

Claudette slipped her purse from her shoulder and tugged the envelope free. "Gregory said you'd handle this. I still don't understand why I couldn't do this earlier myself."

Julien took the envelope from her. "I'm sure it has to do with Gregory's concern for your well-being, Claudette. Besides, I have a debt to settle with one of the crew." He tapped his finger against the small box which sat on the table.

Another Metro bus lumbered down the avenue towards them. The motor caught and then revved as the driver shifted gears to slow the vehicle. This caused Geneviève to lurch forward in her seat. Next to her, a young woman, hip-hop music seeping from her headphones, nudged the policewoman. Geneviève glanced through the front window and caught a glimpse of a familiar person on the opposite side of the street.

Like clockwork, the protest of brakes and escaping air from the doors opening announced another scheduled stop. A dozen citizens filed out, including Detective Benoit. As Geneviève stood on the sidewalk, she glanced in both directions, looking for gaps in the traffic to navigate through without being struck.

Still engaged in conversation, Claudette was the first to recognize the policewoman. "Do you have a way out of here?" she asked Julien. "The policewoman who questioned me just walked off the bus."

"Are you sure you saw her get off the bus?" he asked.

Claudette could see Detective Benoit slip past several students. "Yes, she's waiting to cross the street."

Julien slipped his arm around Claudette's waist and positioned himself next to her. "All right, then, let's pretend we just met for the evening and it's time to leave. Remember we're just another couple headed to dinner," he muttered as they strolled towards his car.

"You and I hardly look the part; I'm ten years older than you," Claudette said.

"Really? I've never been able to tell all these years," Julien said, nuzzling her neck briefly as part of the charade. "Don't worry, I'll have you safely away once we confirm the policewoman hasn't followed us." He pulled a set of keys from his pocket and led the woman closer to his car. "Here, this one."

Geneviève noticed Claudette, and kept her eyes on her and the gentleman beside her. She crossed the street and caught the couple begin to walk away from her as she fumbled for her cell phone as pedestrians bumped into her on the sidewalk. As she selected Captain Lemieux's number, she listened to the rings, and after the fifth one, the familiar voice of her captain answered.

"Hello?" Claude asked with a slight slur in his speech.

"Captain? It's Geneviève," she said. "Are you okay?"

"I'm fine. Why are you calling me?"

"The woman we questioned from the Papillion Transport, I just saw her; she's in my neighborhood," Geneviève said. "And she's with a man, but I can't tell if I've seen him before." With a glance, she noticed the couple get into a sedan.

Claude took another drink. "You called me just to say a woman met a man near your apartment," he said. "And what makes it a police emergency?"

Geneviève stomped her foot. "Didn't you hear me? I said she's the one from the shipping company."

"I heard you the first time," Claude replied. "And I'll remind you not to raise your voice at me. What am I supposed to do for you and this woman you've seen, heh?"

Frustration grew as Geneviève watched the sedan pull away. "Damn it," she groaned. "They're gone. They got into a white Citroen heading west."

Claude sat in his apartment, half listening to the young officer. After he drained the last of the wine into his glass, he sat the decanter on the table. "Now what?" he asked.

"What?"

"I said now what do you wish to do?" Claude repeated. "You saw someone and now they're gone. What do you think you should do next, heh?"

Geneviève fought to think. She saw a suspect in their case, and yet Claude seemed lackadaisical in his concern. *He's drunk, that's why*, she told herself. Stabbing the *END* button, she hung up on her captain and glanced down the street at an approaching cab. With a wave, she caught the driver's attention and as he came to a stop, slid into the back seat.

"Where to, Miss?" the driver asked.

Looking past the driver, Geneviève pointed towards the front window. "Follow that white sedan making the turn," she demanded, as she leaned against the front seat to display her badge. "This is official police business."

With a grunt, the cab driver turned away and put his car in motion, attempting to close the distance between them and Julien's car. As he reached the corner, he sped past a couple just as they stepped off the curb.

"There, three cars ahead!" Glancing left and right, Geneviève tried to note which road they were on now. Nearly five minutes passed as the taxi cab tailed the suspect. Each sign passed showed they were near to Saint Jerome University.

The Citroen held its speed while Julien maneuvered through the traffic. He kept his focus as he stopped the sedan just past the Rond Point Pierre Paraf interchange. "How did you find an apartment near the university?" he asked, with a nod towards the building in front of the car.

"It wasn't easy, but it helps to have friends in the Admissions office," Claudette replied with a smile. As she stepped out, she leaned in the open door. "Let Gregory and Louis know I'm okay, will you?"

"I'll let them both know," Julien said as Claudette closed the door. As he glanced over his shoulder, he saw a space he could pull into and gunned the sedan to join the flow of traffic. Behind him, the taxi carrying Detective Benoit pulled into the space he'd just left.

As the taxi parked, Geneviève watched as Julien accelerate away through traffic. To her right, she saw the woman disappear amongst the foliage which lined the walkway that separated the apartments.

"€26.85, madame," the driver declared to Geneviève.

As she collapsed back into the seat, Geneviève was lost for what to do next. She'd acted on her gut, knowing the woman she questioned might still have information to add to her investigation. But she failed to consider it might have been just a simple exchange between friends.

"My fare, please," the driver demanded.

Geneviève pulled out her purse. "All I've got is a €20 on me," she said as she handed over the lone bill.

"And what do I tell my supervisor when I'm short on cash?"

"Tell him to send the invoice to the department," Geneviève replied, as she slid out of the cab and slammed the door closed. She stared at the path between the apartments, but Claudette had disappeared from her view.

"Damn it," she muttered. As she stood on the sidewalk, the familiar ringtone from her phone signaled a call. "Hello?"

As he walked down the stairs of Geneviève's apartment building, Hector Dupont called his date. As he exited, a familiar, but stress-filled voice answered his call. "Where are you?" he asked.

The policewoman glanced to her left and read the nearest road sign. "I'm just past Saint Jerome University, near the apartment complex on *Rond Point Pierre Paraf*," Geneviève answered. "Where are you?"

"Outside your apartment. We had a date tonight, didn't we?" Hector asked.

Her shoulders slumped. "I'm sorry, Hector. I completely forgot about our plans." Over the next few minutes Geneviève explained seeing the suspects and tailing them. Geneviève had finally found someone she was comfortable being with, but the last few weeks had seen the couple's time together lapse into just brief minutes from what were once hours.

While Geneviève continued to explain her actions, Hector got into his car and proceeded towards the university. "I'm on my way to you. As long as traffic cooperates, I'll meet you in say…, ten minutes or so," he said when she was finished as he pulled into traffic.

"Okay, I'll be at the corner," Geneviève replied. As she paced the sidewalk, she pulled out her notebook and jotted down what happened and who she thought she'd seen. "Claude will want an explanation tomorrow," she muttered.

Across town at an intersection, Julien LeBlanc observed a line of trucks leaving the harbor terminal he was ready to enter. In the distance, he recognized vessels moored along the docks, some waited for their loads while others discharged their own cargo.

"Finally!" he shouted as the signal changed. Making the turn, Julien followed the signs to the dock where the *Joan of Arc* was tied up. He pulled into a vacant space and shut off the engine. Julien reached over to the passenger seat, grabbed the manila envelope, and the small box before getting out.

As a cargo vehicle passed him, Julien quick-stepped across the street. As he sauntered up to the gate, the security guard confronted him. The woman, whose rotund figure belied the lack of meaningful exercise, blocked his passage.

The shack that doubled as a guard post and its warped plywood needed a fresh paint job. While she placed one hand to a baton, the other grasped a radio. "What business do you have here?" she demanded.

The question caught the former Legionnaire off-guard. Julien gathered himself, and looked down the pier's length before he answered. "I've a parcel for the captain of the *Joan of Arc*," he answered, pointing to the freighter.

Already instructed by her husband, a member of the Maghrebis gang in this quarter, she knew there was interest in anyone who visited the vessel, in addition to the other three freighters calling Marseille home. It was for this reason the woman was especially mindful on who approached that she'd not met. "Let me look at your courier license," the guard demanded.

Julien wasn't prepared for the question. "I'm just dropping off…" he began to say when he realized what she wanted. "Just a moment." He placed the envelope and box between his knees. Next, out came his wallet. As he flipped it open, Julien slipped two 100-euro bills before showing his driver's license.

As the woman saw the money, she flashed a smile with several gaps in her teeth. "That wasn't too difficult, was it now?" she said, as she slipped the bills from the wallet. "What's in the box, though?"

"I need to pay off a bet," Julien said as he opened the cover. Inside sat a neat row of hand-wrapped cigars. "I picked PSG to win their match against Lyon," he smirked. "Who knew they couldn't score."

"Those Paris clubs are overrated anyway," the woman scoffed, selecting one of the Cubans from the box. "Go ahead." She nodded over her shoulder towards the pier.

"Thank you," the former Legionnaire replied, striding towards the ship, its faded paint a display of time spent at sea.

As the guard observed Julien walk towards the freighter, she retrieved her cell phone and made a call, speaking before the other person even answered. "A man came to the boat. His name is Julien LeBlanc."

The rising tide coming in gave a gentle rock to the freighter. Two men aboard the ship viewed the exchange at the gate from atop the bridge wing. As Julien neared the ship's gangway, they made their way to the main deck to meet their guest.

Julien stepped onto the metal walkway which led to the deck. With the box and envelope under one arm, he grasped the handrail with the other. After trudging up the steep incline, he finally set foot on the deck surface. "Fancy seeing you again," a voice came from behind him. Julien spun around to see his friend, Marcel Dumont.

"We'd see each other more if you didn't have to sail all over the Med," Julien replied as he embraced the captain.

"You should join us, it'll do you some good," Anton Huet added, shaking hands with the Legionnaire. "I see you remembered our bet."

Julien smirked as he handed them over. "Here, and don't smoke them all on the next voyage. Oh, and you're down one courtesy of the security guard. And for you Marcel," he added, passing the envelope to the freighter's master.

The captain grasped the envelope and slid it under his arm for the moment. "So, how much did the woman take from you?"

Embarrassed to admit she took advantage of him, Julien replied, "I gave her two-hundred," with a slight upturn to his lip. "Was it too much?"

"Who knows? We've never seen her man the gate before until this morning," Anton answered.

Marcel listened while he slit open the envelope. Inside he saw several bundles of cash, a letter, and a folded printout of a cargo manifest. "Looks like we're back in the smuggling business again."

The freighter's first officer looked at his captain. "Not with that camel's ass Aziz again," Anton exclaimed. "I'd willingly scrub pig shit off the side of a container than negotiate with him and his Algerian thugs."

"You don't have to worry about Aziz, I'm afraid," Marcel replied as he stuffed the letter back in the envelope. "Turns out Gregory has a new client."

"Who then?"

The captain looked at both men. "We're to work with the Carbone family. Again," Dumont announced, heading towards the superstructure. "Give Gregory and Louis my best," he said over his shoulder as he disappeared behind the hatch.

Chapter SIX

The ringing of the phone pierced through the clamor of the officers' conversation in the room. Sergeant Dubois reached for the handset as she kept her focus on the computer. "Central records, Detainee Processing. How can I help you?"

Gregory Arsenault knew it was a risk to call his sister-in-law at work, but the confrontation with Amed Gilles had forced him in another direction. "Bonjour Sergeant, I'm wondering if you could tell me if a Monsieur Richelieu is being detained?"

As soon as Claire heard the man's voice, she knew who the caller was. The surprise came when the gentleman used a name, one only she knew. "One moment and I'll check," Claire replied, as she put Gregory on hold. While she pretended to check files on her computer, the sergeant scanned her colleagues for signs one of them heard her call. "I'm sorry, but the system is awfully slow today. Can I contact you at a later time?"

The head of Papillion Transport could only imagine what might happen to the woman on the other end. He knew his time was limited, so Gregory gave her an option. "Can I call you back... in, say," he looked at the clock, "in five minutes?"

"Of course, Monsieur. Au revoir," she replied before she hung up.

Louis Clement came into the office, and spotted the scowl on his partner's face. "Bad news?"

Gregory glanced up. "No, I just hate having to contact Claire at her desk. It sounded like she'd forgot to get the schedules I asked about the other day." He grabbed his cup from the desk. "Do we have any more coffee made?"

Louis pointed to the outer office. "There might be a cup left in the pot," he answered.

Gregory emptied the pot into his cup. "You didn't want any more, did you?"

"No... I'm good for the moment," Louis said. "Speaking of good, did Julien get the package delivered to Marcel? I haven't seen or heard from him yet."

Gregory shook his head. "I haven't gotten a call from him or the ship yet. But I suspect we'll hear from Marcel once he reviews the manifest and examines each port he'll be sailing to." Before he could sit, his cell phone rang. "It's Claire," he announced, selecting the talk feature. "Bonjour, Claire."

Claire took another drag off her cigarette as she paced the loading dock and listened to the phone ring. "Come on, Greg, answer the damn phone," she muttered under her breath. As she heard his voice after the fourth ring, her face lit up with relief.

"Gregory... what took you so long to answer?"

"I picked it up on the first ring, why?"

"It doesn't matter now. Why did you call?" Claire asked.

Relieved, he let out a sigh. Gregory answered. "I wanted to know if you got the schedules I asked about."

Claire glanced as a patrol car left. As she dropped her cigarette, Claire ground her foot on the end which glowed. "I've got them. Where do you want to meet? Wait, I'll be off in an hour. Why don't you come pick me up?"

Gregory glanced at the clock. "How about I meet you at Carrefour near the small Italian café in, say... ninety minutes?" He took a sip of coffee, and the bitterness caused him to shudder while looking at Louis, waving the cup. A look of *"What is this shit?"* etched across his face.

Before Claire answered, she watched two officers leave the building and walk to the Annex. Near the exit gate, she noticed the security guard staring at her. The buzz from the exit door caught her attention as more officers walked out. "I'll catch you around 7 o'clock then," she muttered with a look at her watch. "I've got to go; au revoir."

Thumbing the *OFF* button, Gregory slid the phone onto his desk. "I'll be meeting Claire at seven o'clock tonight," he declared to his partner. "You want to join me?"

Louis shrugged his shoulders. "Sure. You're the one who wants to be more cautious around the city because of Gilles," he replied just as the office phone rang. He grabbed it on the second ring. "Hello?"

On the other end, Julien LeBlanc tried to navigate through traffic while he monitored the sport-bikes behind him. "Louis... it's Julien. Seems I picked up two friends after I left the docks," he exclaimed. With a flick of the steering wheel, his Renault sedan slid just ahead of a Metro bus whose driver blasted his horn to signal his displeasure.

The blaring horn in the background alarmed Louis. "Where the hell are you?"

"I just left the port and I'm coming into town on the A55," Julien replied, his tone calm. He gave Louis a quick description of the motorcycles and riders. With a glance in the mirror, Julien saw the motorcycles slide past the bus and several cars, and miss the lead car's bumper by less than a meter.

Louis looked at Gregory. "Seems Julien has some unwanted company. He's on the expressway toward downtown. What do you want to do?"

There's not much either of us can do, Gregory told himself. Not from their office at least. "Tell him we'll meet him on *Rue de Lyon* near the Gaz Ocean Shipping Service."

Louis relayed the directions to Julien. Once traffic slowed, he saw the exit from the motorway he needed. As the first rider neared Julien's car, he noticed the radio secured to the rider's helmet. "Great," Julien muttered aloud. He figured the motorcyclists were communicating with someone, and if they needed help, it wouldn't be far behind. As the gap between cars widened and the exit appeared, he slid the Renault into the gap.

The first rider thumbed a button on his handlebar to activate the radio. "He's getting off on *Chemin du Littoral*. Do we still follow him?"

Yacine El Amari listened to the rider for a moment. He mentally watched the exit the Frenchman headed towards on the motorway. The most senior member of Gilles's Maghrebis gang knew to have his men continue would lead to a sector under an Italian family's control.

"Riad... learn where he goes. But do nothing to him to provoke him," he commanded.

The rider acknowledged while he continued the pursuit, his companion weaving several cars behind him.

As he neared downtown, Julien felt luck was on his side. Each intersection he encountered was void of pedestrians, and the signals cooperated. As he headed north towards the city center and the rendezvous with his friends, Julien's phone rang. It was Louis again. "Now what?"

"How close are you?"

"Three blocks, maybe a little closer... What do you have planned?"

"After you make the turn, flash your headlights and come down the street. Gregory and I will handle it from there," Louis said. He caught his partner across the road tying off a length of rope to a pole just a meter above the ground.

Julien looked ahead for the street he would turn on. With a glance in the mirror, he watched the sport bikes approach behind him, still not close enough to cause problems. "Showtime, guys," he muttered, as he swung the sedan around the corner without braking.

The two riders watched the sedan change direction and followed. The lead motorcyclist, Riad, crept a few meters closer to the sedan. Riad's companion took this as a sign to close the gap and sped up till he was alongside Riad. While twilight descended, the road in the industrial complex had grown dark, shadows from surrounding buildings obscured sections of pavement.

Julien saw his friends huddled in the shadows on the roadside and flashed his lights briefly to alert them as planned. With a steady speed, Julien recognized the rope laid on the pavement. A cruel smile came to his face as he saw what his friends devised for the motorcyclists behind him.

While the car and motorcycles came closer, the two men took hold of the rope they'd rolled out. "Don't forget to let go when you feel them catch the rope," Gregory said over his shoulder.

Julien passed over the rope and took a glance in the mirror to watch his friend's handywork.

Riad and his partner were so focused on the sedan they didn't consider the ambush and were surprised as the rope which crossed the roadway appeared from nowhere. Any attempt to avoid it was futile as the rope snared the motorcycles across the handlebars, violently dismounting the riders.

As novice riders, the Algerians wore typical street attire: jeans, t-shirts, and a light jacket. They'd disregarded the need for gloves or boots, and their hands and feet would show gruesome results. Each tumbled across the pavement. Riad's partner put his hands out to break his fall with grisly consequences. The asphalt tore through his exposed flesh, leaving a bloody reminder to wear proper gloves.

Riad didn't fare any better as the pavement tore through his jacket and jeans, shredding his elbows and knees as he rolled along the ground. He spared his hands the fate his partner endured by keeping them tucked while rolling across the pavement. The only thing which spared each rider a more serious outcome from the fall were helmets. But the impact damaged Riad's radio, making it useless.

Across town, Yacine sat at the table attempting to contact his men. Keying the radio's handset, he pleaded. "Riad, can you understand me?" But there was only static. "Something is wrong," he said, looking at the next man in charge. "Go... take three men and see if you can find them, but do nothing to draw attention to yourselves."

Gregory and Louis rushed up to the riders, and pulled them behind a delivery truck. Julien had turned the sedan around to return, and pushed the disabled motorcycles off the street.

With little concern for injuries to the riders' neck or head, Gregory pulled off Riad's helmet. "Why were you following my friend?" he demanded, a pistol held in view of the Maghrebis gang member.

Riad looked up at the Frenchman, but saw only a black ski mask. "A man at the harbor offered us money to keep an eye on any visitors to a freighter. They asked me to follow who boarded the ship, and where they went, I swear by Allah," he replied. He could see Louis stand over his companion, his face covered and a pistol aimed at his head.

Gregory had a feeling Amed Gilles had upped the ante on his actions and was willing to leverage anyone associated with Papillion Transport to tilt things in his favor. "Are you associated with the Maghrebis gangs in the Verduron quarter?" he questioned; the pistol pressed against Riad's cheek.

Riad shook his head. "No, they gave me €100 to follow the man in the sedan. It's the truth," he stammered. The fear of dying began to overcome him.

Gregory grabbed the helmet off the ground and yanked the radio from its side. "Then who were you talking to on the other end of this?" he demanded.

Julien kept an eye on possible intruders and spotted a car turn down the side street. It slowed down; its lights extinguished as it drew closer. He turned and gave a whistle to alert his companions they had company.

Louis overheard the noise and turned back to Gregory. "Mon ami, we must go now," he warned, with a tug on Gregory's shirt.

Gregory glanced up the road and watched the car amble towards them. "Oui... Au revoir, gentlemen." He brought his pistol across Riad's temple and knocked the man unconscious. He knew Louis would dispatch the other rider in the same fashion. Looking at his watch as they walked away, Gregory noted he would be cutting the rendezvous with Claire close.

"Louis, you go with Julien. I'll meet you both at the office," he said. "But be careful and take your time."

"And what are you going to do?"

"I've just enough time to meet Claire to get the schedules Amed wants," he replied. "When I get back, we'll begin our plan to deliver them... on our terms."

Louis nodded. Both he and Gregory had spent enough time together to understand where the other stood on particular subjects. Louis knew his friend didn't take to being manipulated by others, and he wouldn't allow the Algerian to gain the advantage. Louis learned when his friend made similar statements in the past, they always led the former Legionnaire to place himself and those he led to a position of strength. "We'll be waiting," he answered.

Gregory climbed into his car and hesitated for a moment. “And Louis... give Romain a call, too. Let him know we’ll need access to some of his hardware.” With the door closed, he started the engine and headed to meet with his sister-in-law, in hopes he wouldn’t be late.

Chapter SEVEN

Detectives of the evening shift continued their paperwork and answered phones as twilight gave way to morning. They were a stark contrast to those from dayshifts. Those manning a desk and not on the streets shifted their attention between suspects and witnesses while taking down statements. Desktops showed the struggle of night work as half-filled coffee cups waited for their owner to return.

As Detective Benoit shuffled into the office, several officers gave her a cursory wave, while others didn't hide their expressions as she appeared earlier than usual. She sat at her desk, flipped on her computer, pulled out a notepad, and wrote down her recollection from pursuing Claudette Minot. In typical fashion, Geneviève noted time, location, and reasons behind her effort. *But who was the man?* With eyes closed, she did her best to recall the depictions of potential suspects associated with Papillion Transport.

"Nice to know someone from the day shift is willing to put in extra hours," a passing officer exclaimed.

"I'll do my best not to squander it needlessly, Pierre," Benoit replied as she recognized the voice. She returned to her computer and began to type. As she added her thoughts from the pursuit, Geneviève couldn't shake the notion of seeing the driver before. While she pondered where she'd seen the driver. Detective Berger put a fright in her by tossing his knapsack over her head onto his desk.

Geneviève flinched as the bag slid onto his chair. "Damn you, Nic!"

"Just wanted to make sure you're awake, Benoit," he chuckled. "By the way; why are you here so early?" Berger pulled the bag off his chair, and set it on the floor as he placed an energy drink on his desk. "Did you forget to put something into the interviews from the other day?"

Geneviève turned her focus back to the computer screen. “No. Getting off the bus last night, I saw the woman from Papillion we questioned,” she answered. “I tried to follow her, but she met a man and drove off together. But I noticed her get dropped off near Saint Jerome’s just as my taxi driver caught up to them.”

“So, this woman met up with her companion,” Berger said. He shrugged his shoulders, as he turned his computer on. “And what makes you so sure the woman was from the shipping company?”

Geneviève glared over her computer at Berger. “Since I was the one who questioned her, I’m sure it was the same woman,” Benoit replied. Touching the print key, her finished report was soon ready to be added to the case file. “But the man she met, the one who drove her away, I’d swear I’ve seen him before, though.”

“And where do you think you bumped into this man from the past?” Berger asked as Captain Lemieux entered the office.

“What man are we talking about?” the senior officer asked as he put down his coffee. “Let me guess, is it your gentleman friend Hector?” Lemieux chuckled. “Or does this have to do with the mystery woman you chased?”

The policewoman scowled at the two men. “No, it wasn’t Hector,” Geneviève replied with a huff. “Like I told Nic, the man from last night met Papillion’s secretary, so she’s not a ‘mystery’ to me.” She shoved the paperwork into a folder. “And I know I’ve seen the man before too; I just can’t remember where.”

The captain grabbed his coffee and drained it in one swallow. “Haven’t we put together photos on the Papillion members we’re following... hmm? Since this woman worked for them, you might find your driver that way.”

“I hadn’t considered those,” Geneviève admitted. Her cursor slid across the screen to a folder which she opened. “Well, it turns out we have two pictures so far.”

The photo from Immigration showed a man in his mid-forties stare at the camera. Dark brown hair and what appear to be blue eyes as the common features. Geneviève closed her eyes and tried to envision the man from last night, but her memory and the picture wouldn’t match.

"What we have on record doesn't match. It's not the man I saw last night," she huffed, as she grabbed her note book and got to her feet.

"Where are you headed?" Berger asked.

"Down to Archives to see if they've compiled last month's photos from the docks or warehouse," Geneviève said. She scampered past a pair of janitors who stood at their closet, carts piled with cleaners and toiletries placed in the hallway.

Geneviève passed an empty interview room with a plain table and chairs waiting for the next suspect or victim. "Excuse me," she said as she brushed by a patrolman outside the Detainee processing area. Glancing in the room, she noticed someone getting their fingerprints taken.

While Detective Benoit was in the basement, Captain Lemieux was again at the cafeteria for another cup of coffee. As he stood in line to pay, he felt a gentle tap on his shoulder.

"Mind paying for mine, too?" a charming woman in her mid-forties asked, her smile showing a hint of friskiness to it.

"No... no, I don't mind," Lemieux replied, not hiding his delight from the woman. "What brings you back to the station, Louise?" Claude asked, pulling €20 from his pocket for the cashier. "It's for her coffee as well. Add the change to my tab, too please."

As she stepped to the captain's side, Louise spoke. "Since you asked. Superintendent Chevallier asked me to have a talk with several officers in the Gang unit," she began. "He said they lost one of their colleagues recently. And he's concerned about their mental well-being."

Claude took a deep breath. "I'm aware of the incident too," he replied. "One of my officers was the first who determined Officer Galant was abducted. But doesn't it place you outside your principle field? I mean... you're a doctor working on forensics for drug interactions, right?"

Louise looked down at her coffee before she answered. *How do I tell Claude I'm here for him without betraying his trust?* she thought. "Captain, I'm one of several doctors at the clinic who also help others handle the mental strain of their jobs."

"So, you dabble in psychology and drugs?"

"*Dabble* seems amateurish," Louise said. "But I've taking a few classes at Universite Sorbonne Paris Cite-USPC to broaden my knowledge, you might say."

As the pair reached the detective's office, a courier walked up to Captain Lemieux. "Excuse me sir, but this was delivered last night," he stated, handing over the parcel and steadying a clipboard in his other hand. "I need your signature for the record."

Lemieux signed at the designated space and took the package.

"Seems you've work to do," Louise said.

Fishing out a business card, Claude handed it over to the woman. "Call me if you're free," he said. "It'd be a pleasure if you let me buy you dinner; maybe this evening?"

"I'll check my calendar and give you call," Louise replied before she left.

As he watched the doctor walk past Detective Benoit and disappear amongst the crowd, Lemieux felt a nudge to his arm.

"Wasn't she the doctor you met last month?" Detective Berger asked.

"Yes... yes, it was," the captain answered without turning to face the detective.

"And her name is Doctor Beringer?" Geneviève asked, approaching the officers in the doorway.

Captain Lemieux pushed past the detectives to his desk. "Yes… it is."

"What's in the pouch?" Berger asked.

"I don't know at this moment, but I will when it's open," Lemieux put his coffee down and grabbed some scissors. As he cut open the sealed envelope, he found several folders and a computer disc. "It seems my friend Vincent was true to his word." Lemieux pulled the disc out, and tossed it to Detective Berger. "Load this on your computer and decide what's in it we can use."

As Captain Lemieux tugged the folders out, Geneviève sat at her desk, and flipped through images from surveillance of Papillion Transport's office. Without realizing it, she was soon twirling her hair around her finger as she studied photos of potential suspects. Lost in thought, she didn't hear Berger call her name.

"Benoit, look at who we have here," he called, tapping his monitor. Geneviève stepped away from her desk to look over Berger's shoulder at images of a man and woman.

"It's our dead socialite," Benoit noted. The photo showed the movie and television star turned immigration advocate Yvette Segal lean against the yacht's rail. The image represented what most would consider a woman of substance: tall, tan, and graceful with styled hair, holding a champagne flute. Her clothes followed the latest fashion and her blouse bellowed from the breeze while her cobalt-hued slacks clung to her legs.

In the background, a man stood partially turned away from the camera. With little more than a side view, nothing stood out as a distinguished feature other than dark complexion and close-cropped hair. "But who's the man with her?" she asked.

"Don't know," Berger said. "Let's see if there's a better view."

"Open them all first, then we'll see which ones include any men," Captain Lemieux said, tossing his empty cup in the trash. "I'll be back in a few minutes."

Berger selected the files, and typed the command to change views. In moments, the screen filled with thumbnail images. "There's over 250 to review!" the detective exclaimed, as he pointed to the counter.

"Open the viewer program and start from the beginning then," Benoit suggested as she returned to her desk. "If you come across an image with a man, save it so we can give it to the technicians. They just might be able to match them to ones we have on file."

Dragging up the next series of surveillance photos, Geneviève came across one which showed Julien LeBlanc outside the Papillion Transport office. "It's him," she muttered aloud. "I knew I'd seen him before yesterday."

"You mean your mystery driver," Berger replied without looking up.

"Yes, I ran into him at the market near my apartment," Geneviève answered. Sliding open her bottom drawer, she dug through stacks of notebooks before she grabbed one from the middle. "I remember seeing him one day purchase stuff to dress wounds. It was just after I shot the drug dealer's friend near the docks."

Geneviève flipped through pages and soon found her notes on the encounter with Julien LeBlanc. She'd taken the time to write a description and what he wore, having suspicions about the purchase of medical supplies. "The store clerk mentioned he used to be a medic in the Army or something along those lines," Geneviève added.

"Here, come look at this photo," Berger said, pushing his chair back. "It's the guy from the photo with our dead starlet."

Benoit stepped around the desk and glanced at the screen. "It can't be him," she uttered. "When was this picture taken?"

"The date shows they took it the last week of May," Berger answered "Why...? What's so important about the date?"

"Why is what important?" Captain Lemieux asked, fresh coffee in hand as he echoed Berger's same question.

"This photo shows Hakim Talib with Yvette Segal, that's why it's important," Geneviève exclaimed while pointing at the monitor. "Based on the date, Nice detectives took this before the incident with the cruise ship steward." Geneviève straightened up, nibbling on her thumbnail before spinning around to face the officers. "His appearance with her could be our link to another drug smuggling activity."

While he sipped his coffee, Lemieux watched Geneviève pace back and forth. "Until your run-in with this man in Algiers, we had nothing to link him to drug smuggling though, did we?"

"No... not at first," Benoit admitted. "But we were more concerned about our suspect Laurent and his affairs with the Filipina steward," she added before she slumped into her chair. "Come to think of it, we didn't get any indication of his activities in Nice during the interrogations either. But we had him and Louis Remesy in Algiers, possibly at the same time. And the connection to Omar Khalid too," she added.

Captain Lemieux put his coffee aside and sat up. "Pull the transcripts and recordings from Chateau Il d'If. I want you to go over them again. Nicolas, I want you to go through the photos and files from Captain Noel; note every instance with this man and any other men he might have been photographed or identified being with."

"And what are you going to do?" Geneviève asked.

"I'm going to see Captain Duval about the replacement for Detective Masson. I've got a sense we'll need the extra body before too long," he answered, slurping the last of his coffee before tossing the cup.

Chapter EIGHT

"*Bienvenu au Algiers,*" the woman's voice said over the loudspeaker. The next announcement was in Arabic. Leaving a country was never difficult for Nazim Aziz until the meddling inspector from Scotland Yard had exposed his drug smuggling activity. Ever since he was caught on the airport surveillance, Aziz needed help from his mentor, Omar Khalid and an Italian contact in Naples to forge his new identity. This would be the third time he tempted fate by exposing it to authorities since he fled France.

"And what is your purpose here in Algiers?" the customs agent asked.

"I'm here to establish a business venture," Aziz replied.

"And what business is that?"

"I'm a broker in agricultural products; citrus fruits mainly, but I'm also trying to introduce a wider need for your country's date production," the drug smuggler said with a smile. Just as he and Gregory Arsenault used olive oil as a ruse to export hashish, he would use date produce the same way.

The agent held the passport in front of him and compared it to the man standing across the counter, and was satisfied they were the same. With a thud from his stamp, the agent approved Nazim Aziz's return to his homeland. "Welcome to Algiers, Monsieur Vignes."

And with that, Nazim took his passport, picked up his suitcase, and exited Customs. Here he pushed through throngs of families who waited for loved ones to exit. Nazim searched the crowd, and caught sight of a placard with his name. As he drew closer, Nazim noticed the woman who held the sign, but any distinguishing features were hidden under a black robe, her face obscured by a veil.

"Welcome to Algeria, Monsieur Vignes," Aisha said.

"Bon jour Mademoiselle," Nazim replied, as he recognized the voice. As she turned away and headed towards the terminal exit,

Nazim followed. Watching the young woman strut to the door, he wondered if she assumed a more prominent role in Khalid's criminal enterprise. As Aisha approached the curb, he saw the vehicle they'd be leaving in.

A young Algerian stood at the tailgate of a Mercedes 300 station wagon, and motioned for him to hand over his bag. The grey exterior was faded to a dull pewter, the chrome roof rack pitted. In keeping with the Saharan environment, drivers tinted their windows a smoky charcoal, to limit intrusion from the outside. Nazim slid into the back seat, and recognized the driver took pride in its interior. The leather seats were supple and luxurious. In the cupholder was a bottle of mineral water, condensation crept down its side.

"His excellency will greet you when we arrive," the driver said as he pulled the vehicle from the curb. Soon they entered the expressway which led towards Omar Khalid's compound. The drive gave Nazim time to prepare for his discussion.

The trip from the airport took just over twenty minutes. Aisha and the driver kept to themselves, this allowed Nazim to recall what he observed in Marseille. Since his unceremonious fallout with Papillion Transport and his failed attempt to free his cousin Hakim Talib from police, Nazim had taken it upon himself to reestablish contacts in France.

Earlier this week, Nazim's chance encounter with a Black Saharan gang member from Sudan led him to Marseilles' marina. Here, he watched first-hand at the polices' attempt to apprehend a local drug dealer. It was pure luck one officer involved was the same he'd encountered at Chateau Il d'If. And the one responsible for killing Hakim.

As the Mercedes entered the compound, Omar Khalid stood on the veranda steps. The head of an Algerian crime syndicate watched his nephew Nazim step from the car and approached him. "Welcome home." he said while he embraced the younger man.

"I'm afraid my trip was not as fruitful as I'd hope for," Nazim replied as he stepped back from Khalid. "But it was interesting to learn of your friend's efforts to abduct the policewoman, though," he added as they followed Aisha into the residence.

Omar led his nephew to the terrace which overlooked the city. Khalid gestured to a chair, while he sat opposite Nazim. "Tell me what was so interesting," he started as Aisha returned, free of her robe, now attired in linen pants and silk blouse. "Have refreshments brought out." With a nod, Aisha left them. "So, you were about to tell me how my friend Youssef failed," Omar said.

Nazim leaned back, and took his time. "You mentioned Youssef's contact in Marseille abducted this policewoman, Benoit, the week before last." He paused as Aisha returned with another servant. Nazim smiled while the women prepared their refreshments. "He said he was prepared to hand the woman over to you next week. That is what you heard, isn't it?"

Omar waited as Aisha prepared glasses of mineral water and the other servant laid out a plate of fresh fruits. "Yes, it's what someone informed me aware of," Omar replied once the women left the table. "But you already know this, Nazim."

The young French-Algerian gave a slight nod towards Khalid. "It's why I was so surprised when I noticed the detective make an arrest at the marina three days ago," Nazim declared. "So... it begs the question worth asking: did Youssef lie to you or has his man in Marseille failed and he's afraid of what Youssef will do to him when he finds out?"

Khalid wiped his brow with a napkin before taking a drink. He set the glass down, and studied Nazim closely. "If Youssef's contact doesn't have the woman, the one we've paid him to abduct, then who is this woman he now possesses?"

Nazim shook his head and shrugged. "I don't know. If I was in your position, I wouldn't transfer any additional money until you're sure the woman they abducted is the one who killed Hakim," he stated. Nazim picked up his glass, and drank, the icy contents allowed to temper his anger.

The elder Algerian sat back, in careful contemplation of his next step. He wanted this policewoman to pay for his nephew's death, just as Nazim did. However, Khalid wasn't prepared to attempt another foolish plan on his own, and relied on Youssef Raif and his connections to bear the burden. "Something of this nature can't be discussed over the phone. It appears I need to make another visit to Rabat," Khalid replied as he took up his own glass.

***

Earlier in the afternoon, Benoit and Berger toiled over their respective computers, examining case material. Berger studied photos of suspects, trying to link individuals to their case, while Benoit listened to the audio file of interrogations.

Geneviève removed her headphones and slumped back in her chair. "I've never heard something as boring as the same question asked twenty separate times," she exclaimed to Berger. "And it doesn't even pertain to our investigation."

"What was the question?"

Geneviève picked up her notebook and flipped the page. "How often did you travel to Algeria?" she repeated. "This so-called psychologist seemed to only have one concern," she added, pulling the ribbon from her hair and shaking her head. In moments, auburn tresses obscured her face as she flung forward and flipped her hair in the process.

"Damn, I never knew your hair was so long," Berger exclaimed.

"I don't have time to visit a stylist to have it cut," Geneviève replied as her cell phone chirped. Snatching it, she answered without looking at who was calling. "Bon jour?"

"Geneviève? It's Hector. Are you going to be ready when I get there?" her suitor asked.

"Oh... Hector. Hello, yes... I'll be outside in ten minutes." She pushed her notebook into the drawer. "We're not going anywhere fancy, are we? I'm not really dressed for it, you know."

Hector Dupont sat at his desk, and took a moment to imagine Geneviève undressed. The last three months had seen their relationship become more than just associates in the same field, but not much more. He'd normally never wait for a woman to make advances, but he'd usually had relationships where the woman showed more desire to be intimate. But this wasn't the case with Geneviève. "All right, I'll meet you in about ten to fifteen minutes," he said.

"Au revoir, then," Geneviève replied. Clutching her hair in one hand, she spun it around tight before she slipped a rubber band over the bundle. Next, she wrapped the ribbon over the band, to hide it. "There... that's better."

Detective Berger looked at her with a smirk on his face.

"What's so funny?"

"I've never seen you fuss over your looks before," the detective replied. "Come to think of it, I've never seen you with any makeup on or anything close to cosmetics. You always wear simple clothes. Nothing fancy or outlandish. It's like you purposely try to be inconspicuous to men who might find you attractive."

"There's nothing wrong with keeping to oneself is there?"

"No, I guess not. Now, Francine on the other hand... there's another story," Berger chuckled to himself.

Geneviève knew how much effort Francine LeBeau put into her appearance, especially for dates with Nicolas. The lab technician had become a fixture around the detective's office since she and Nicolas began to date last month.

"I'm just a simple woman with simple tastes, that's all," Geneviève said, as she grabbed her coat. "It's the reason I don't struggle to survive between paydays." She slid her coat on and freed her ponytail before she grabbed a small purse from her desk. Geneviève slipped off her holster, and placed her pistol inside, and checked her extra magazine before she secured the clasp.

"You carrying so you can persuade Hector to pay for dinner?" Berger teased.

"Of course not. Hector doesn't have any issues who pays for dinner," Geneviève replied before headed for the lower lobby of the station.

"Detective Benoit, do you have a moment?" a woman's voice called out.

Geneviève turned and noticed the question came from Doctor Beringer, who approached from the auditorium doorway, her hand up as if hailing a taxi.

"Thank you for waiting," the doctor said. "Can we talk about Captain Lemieux for a moment? In private maybe..." she asked as she glanced toward a space away from the foot traffic.

At the opposite end of the lobby, Geneviève noticed a custodian make her way towards them. Her gut twisted, sensing, something was not as it should be, but it faded as she returned her attention to Dr. Beringer's question.

"Why? Is there something wrong?"

"No... I'm had hoped you could give me a little insight to his mannerisms; you know, likes... dislikes... things he enjoys," Louise said. "He asked me to call him about dinner earlier today, and, well... I don't want to embarrass myself or say something to upset him," she added.

Geneviève let out a slight sigh, glancing at the clock over the information desk. "I was worried you would ask about his work performance."

"It wouldn't be ethical in this setting," Louise said.

"I've not seen him in any social events, it's always been work." Geneviève fidgeted as she calculated the time for her to meet Hector draw closer. "I know he's a widower, lives alone, doesn't travel."

Louise listened as the detective spoke. "Am I keeping you from an errand?"

"I'm sorry," Geneviève replied. "A friend of mine is picking me up for dinner and should arrive soon. My recommendation... just be yourself with Claude; you'll do fine." She patted the doctor's arm. "He's not the one who expects too much in my opinion."

Louise nodded at the reply. "Thank you, Detective, I hope you aren't late meeting your friend."

Geneviève waved before she headed out where Hector parked his Peugeot, its exterior gleaming like berries on a holly bush. Climbing into the passenger seat, she gave her suitor a brief kiss on the cheek. "You know you can get a citation for parking here."

"But I'm sure you could dismiss it, couldn't you?"

"I'm not that sort of officer," she replied. "Where are we going for dinner? I'm famished!"

"One of my supervisors recommended a small restaurant near the park off *Jules Cantini*," Hector said. "He said it was relatively new, but the service and food were good."

"Doesn't sound too awful, I guess," Geneviève said as she peered out the window.

With one eye on the traffic, Hector glanced at Geneviève. He could see she was lost in her thoughts. *Now's not the time*, he told himself. The last few dates they had, Hector sensed there was something Geneviève didn't, or wouldn't, share with him, which caused for some awkward moments.

Twenty minutes of silent driving resulted in their arrival at the recommended restaurant. "Looks like an office complex rather than an eatery," Geneviève noted as she opened the door.

"Well, Henri' didn't mention the appearance, just that the atmosphere and food were enjoyable," Hector answered, coming around the car to join her. In moments, they were greeted by a hostess who escorted the couple to their table.

Sitting at the table, the couple went through the motion of entertaining each other. Hector did his best to hold a conversation with Geneviève without bringing up work-related issues, knowing there was only so much she would tell him.

"You can tell Henri' I agree with his recommendation," Geneviève said, smiling while the server cleared their plates. "The location doesn't lend itself to a bustling business, but the food was very good."

"I'll let him know you approve, then," Hector replied.

After they finished their drinks, Hector paid the bill and they stepped outside where other couples waited to enter. The September evening air was pleasant, as most pedestrians strolled with nothing more on than light jackets or sweaters. "How about we walk off our dinner at the park?" Hector suggested.

"As long as we're not out too late," Geneviève answered.

Sauntering along the path, Geneviève slid her arm through Hector's. As she relaxed, the stress of Hakim Talib's earlier audio interrogation faded with each step.

Hector could sense she was more relaxed as the couple strolled through manicured shrubbery. Spying an empty bench ahead, he paused. "Can I ask you something?" he muttered. the tone in his voice softer than usual. As he sat next to Geneviève, Hector tilted his head from side to side, weighing choices on how to ask the next question.

"What is it?"

"I'm getting a sense something's been troubling you... and it's not police work," Hector began. "I sense you enjoy my company, but... there's something else."

Geneviève could see the compassion in his eyes, that Hector wanted to be of help to her. But she wasn't sure she was ready to share her pain. "Hector..." she paused to inhale, "I know you feel able to help with just about anything, but I don't feel ready to share my troubles with you." She scuffed her feet in the gravel. "At least not today…" she added under her sniffles.

Hector sat up a little straighter on the bench. Swallowing hard, he asked his next question. "I'm willing to help you, Geneviève... for as long as it takes. Whatever it is... I'm sure," he took her hand in his, "we can get through it together."

With her head leaning forward, the tears fell easily on her lap. "It's not so simple, Hector... it's just..." She swiped her hand across her cheek. "Besides, it happened a long time ago... I just need to handle it in my own way."

Hector looked at the young woman. "Whatever happened... whatever it was... it still affects you today," he said. "I want to spend more time with you without a need to watch what I say or do... Geneviève... I care about you and don't want to waste another moment of our time together over something which happened years before today. I can't believe it's something we can't overcome together."

Geneviève felt the pressure of wanting... no, needing to tell Hector everything, but she feared the outcome. The shame of the act still haunted her. And the scars, though faded and smooth, would always be there. Just the thought of the dockworkers who pushed her against the wooden pallet caused her skin to react where the nails punctured.

Hector could see Geneviève struggle with her thoughts. He slid closer and slipped his arm over her shoulders, pulled her close to him. "It's not that bad, we can get through it... you and me."

"It is awful," she stammered through the tears. "Hector..." Geneviève turned to look into his eyes. "Hector..., when I was younger, I... I was raped...." She drew her hands to her face, sobbing quietly as she leaned against him.

Her admission struck Hector like a sledgehammer. *It all made sense now*, he told himself. The times where Geneviève wanted to be closer, to show her feminine side and not of a detective became clearer to him. "We'll get through this... I promise."

Chapter NINE

The continued effort by the instigators of the yellow vest movement had taken more extreme tactics to gain attention. Protests near the waterfront where tourists congregated drew a stronger police presence, which also meant greater media exposure to their cause. Today, those who coordinated the protest focused their efforts near the marina in the L'Estaque quarter of Marseilles.

At the police station, Nicolas Berger and his companion Francine LeBeau tried to be discreet saying goodbye. As they embraced off to the side, other officers and citizens came and went outside the entrance. "I'll call you later today for lunch?" Francine asked.

"You know the job, I can't promise anything," the detective answered. "But I'll do my best." He gave her another peck on the cheek before leaving.

The encounter didn't go unnoticed as Geneviève waited stood across the street. Last night didn't end the way she expected after telling Hector about her assault. They spent nearly an hour on the bench as Hector held her. His embrace was a comfort, yet unobtrusive, like one offered while they kept their distance. She was glad for that. Geneviève still felt uneasy getting too close with anyone. But her trust in Hector grew with each moment they spent together. Trotting across the boulevard with other pedestrians, she approached Berger and LeBeau. "Your attempt at being sneaky isn't working," she announced as she walked up behind the couple.

Caught by surprise, Francine blushed while Nicolas pulled away from the technician's embrace. "What?" Berger asked in protest. "It's no secret we're seeing each other."

"Then why stand off to the side to say your goodbyes?" Geneviève teased. "Why don't you both just walk in like a 'normal' couple then?"

"Who says we're not?" The question came from Francine while Nicolas held the door open.

Geneviève followed her, shaking her head. "Ahh... Francine, you know how it looks. And you, Nic... imagine the talk you'll create amongst other women."

"You're jealous, Geneviève," Francine replied as she turned to the stairwell which led to Forensics. "And don't forget about lunch, Nic," she added as they went through the doors.

Before either detective could respond, Captain Lemieux emerged from dispatch, coffee in hand. "Perfect timing," he said, approaching Benoit and Berger. "Benoit, you're with me." as he waved a finger in her direction. "Detective Berger; did you finish reviewing the packet from Captain Noel yesterday?"

"Ahh... no I didn't," Berger replied before Benoit could speak.

Geneviève studied Lemieux and noticed his eyes first. They were clearer, allowing one to determine their color more so than in past weeks, and his voice was more distinct, with less of a slur. "Where are we going?"

"One of Captain Soucy's informants gave him a tip on the drug dealer we missed at the marina," Lemieux answered. Gesturing back to Berger, he gave the detective his orders. "Get the review of the surveillance done and ready for Captain Duval by the end of today."

"Of course, Captain," Berger replied as he headed for the office.

"Before you ask again," Lemieux said, "we're headed to the marina in the L'Estaque quarter," as he led Geneviève out of the station to his sedan. "Captain Soucy mentioned his man overheard a group of peddlers talk about alluding a police raid."

"Doesn't sound like much to go on," Geneviève said as they reached Lemieux's Citroen sedan. "Who do we have as a back-up?"

Captain Lemieux slid behind the wheel before answering. "No one unless we're lucky to catch a local patrol," he replied as he set his cup down and started the engine. "Besides, we're investigating the last known location of a drug dealer; we shouldn't need back-up." As he pulled the car into traffic, the captain deftly balanced maneuvers around vehicles while he drank his coffee.

Lemieux kept one eye on the traffic ahead as he took another sip. “I understand Doctor Beringer talked to you yesterday,” Lemieux said nonchalantly as he passed a cargo truck. “Anything come up I need to know about?”

Geneviève peered at her captain, trying to decide what to divulge about her conversation with the psychologist. She said nothing which wasn’t already known by most of the officers in the station. “She was just curious about you,” Geneviève replied behind a brief smile. “Why... did she mention I said something which concerns you?”

“No... no, she didn’t,” Lemieux said.

“We didn’t really talk too much,” Geneviève added. “I told her to just act normally and whatever happens would happen.”

Captain Lemieux smiled briefly as he recalled last night’s dinner. His conversations with Louise were pleasant, as was her company. They didn’t delve into each other’s work which they both knew of anyway. And they maintained pleasantries while each discussed generalities of their personal life. *Most important, Louise didn’t bring up how Nadine had died*, he thought.

The closer Lemieux and Benoit got to the marina, the worse the traffic. Rounding the bend of the expressway, they saw at least four Provost tour buses parked near the yacht club entrance. “What the hell is going on?” the captain muttered as he pulled his car into a vacant spot on the roadside.

“Something special we didn’t get word of, maybe,” Geneviève answered as she stepped out of the car. In the distance, they could hear echoes of instructions mixed with whistles and drums. “Sounds like another protest march is being formed.”

Lemieux shook his head. It wouldn’t be the first time Soucy had placed him and Benoit into a less than perfect situation. Reaching into his coat, he pulled the note from his fellow captain and unfolded it. “According to Soucy, our suspect was seen in the vicinity of the yacht club’s parking area,” he read before shoving the note into his pocket. He peered over his shoulder and strolled across the street, with Geneviève close behind him.

“What do these dealers have about marinas anyway?” Benoit asked as she caught up to her partner.

"People who can afford a boat most certainly can afford drugs, mon Cheri," Lemieux replied. "And if it's not buying drugs, then it suggests the dealers found a way to move it from offshore," he added, "which means avoiding the scrutiny of Customs officers."

Near the marina entrance, the drug dealer Ali strolled across the street and positioned himself near the car park. To the west, he saw the banners and heard the cacophony of noise the growing protesters made. Just as before, the "yellow vest" movement would provide the diversion and allow him to meet the client. The man owed the Maghrebis gang and it was time to repay his debt.

Huddled under his tarp, tattered edges evidence of constant use, Captain Soucy's officer surveyed people make their way along the sidewalk. He recognized the drug dealer Ali from the picture circulated amongst the others in his group. Using a series of informants trusted by Captain Soucy, he would inform the captain of his sighting. Now, all he had to do was sit and wait.

"Do you recall what our dealer looked like?" Lemieux asked.

"Yes... he's of North African decent; perhaps Algerian, Moroccan, or from Tunisia. And just shy of 2 meters in height," Geneviève replied. "If I had to guess, I'd say he's about 60 to 65 kilos, with a thin build. I don't think we'd be lucky enough to catch him wearing the same football jersey again."

Captain Lemieux heard Geneviève's comment, but kept his focus ahead of them. The closer they came to the yacht club's main office, the louder the protesters became. Off in the distance, he noticed several hand-made banners waving in the breeze. This would, designate the front of the protesters march. *They're getting close*, Claude thought.

Ali also recognized the protesters getting near the yacht club. As the Algerian returned his attention to the parking zone across the street, he noticed the passenger in a van pulling into a space. He knew his meeting's success would lead to being seen with favor by the gang leader, Amed Gilles.

The Mercedes van with side windows tinted, pulled to the curb. In moments, Ali stood curbside across the road and watched as the client's family got out, grabbing several bags and headed toward the gate and the docks. The client, a banker indebted to Amed Gilles, lagged behind to acknowledge Ali.

Geneviève spotted their suspect before Captain Lemieux did. The drug dealer had made his way across the street. "I've got him," she said. "He's across the street headed towards the parking area." As she skirted the fence that separated two parking areas, Geneviève caught sight of the family waiting by the dock entrance.

"Don't spook him," Lemieux said while he walked along the sidewalk. Scanning left and right, the captain kept his eye on the suspect and gauged the distance between himself and the protestors. *Dammit, this business getting too risky*, he told himself. Lemieux followed the lead members of the protest, and off on the side street, noticed two patrol cars.

Situated in a third-floor apartment, two men watched with great interest as Ali approached the banker. Amed Gilles had dispatched them to shadow the dealer meant to replace Fatah. "He's being cautious enough," Yacine said to his companion.

"The protestors will be a welcome diversion," the second man said, glancing to his right as the crowd continued their march. "I'm amazed at how foolish the authorities are not to have considered a means to separate the instigators from the citizens."

"It's to our favor, so we shouldn't waste it," Yacine said. "Come, let us prepare to meet Ali." While the gang members stepped off the balcony, they failed to notice the detectives' approach from the east toward Ali. They left the apartment and headed to the alley behind the building.

Across the street, Geneviève drew closer to Ali who was now 10 meters behind the banker and his family. In the distance, Captain Soucy's officer noticed the drug dealer, and behind him, Detective Benoit draw closer.

Captain Lemieux stood next to the Mercedes van the family had exited. Knocking on the driver's window, Lemieux flashed his credentials. "Let me look at your identification," he demanded as the window was lowered.

While Lemieux questioned the driver, Geneviève got close enough to study the man approach his family. He turned to face the street and the detective stopped cold in her steps. *It's Monsieur Reno*, who she recognized from Banque Palatine. As Reno escorted his wife and children to their boat, he greeted other members of the marina who stood by his boat. Geneviève approached the gate, and noticed the suspect had made it to the first dock and the water's edge.

"Good morning Ulysse," one of the men said as he tipped his cap at the wife and children. While the children scampered aboard the yacht, Ulysse Reno noticed a navy-blue satchel on the deck. So did his wife.

"Ulys, why is this bag here?" he asked, kicking the side.

"I must have forgotten it from my last fishing trip," Reno replied, and grabbed the satchel off the deck and stepped over the rail. "I'll run it back to the van. I won't be long." With a nod to the men on the dock, Reno headed for the parking area. The manager for Banque Palatine looked to the marina entrance, as Ali approached.

Ali was delighted to watch the Frenchman walk towards him with the satchel. *This will be easier than I hoped*, he told himself. Fixated on the banker, he did not notice Geneviève lean against the fence behind him. The noise from the protesters had grown as they neared the marina, which aided in distracting him from others.

Meanwhile, Yacine and the other gang member crossed the street ahead of the protesters. Their presence in the parking area surprised Captain Soucy's undercover officer huddled under his tarp. He shifted the camera and captured images of the men. Behind them, he watched Captain Lemieux walk away from the van towards the gate.

Movement in the corner of her eye caused Geneviève to shift her gaze to the right. Two men, whose attire showed they were not mariners, sauntered closer to the marina entrance. From her vantage point, she noticed their interest in her suspect than one of the luxury yachts.

Without hesitation, Ulysse Reno walked up to Ali and handed over the satchel. "Tell your Imam I expect my debt absolved or the police get a call," the banker declared.

Ali smiled. "I'll pass along your concerns," he replied in guttural French.

Observing the exchange, Geneviève saw the satchel get passed on and hopped the fence to move against the dealer and banker. "*Police!*" she shouted. "Stay where you are," Geneviève barked, her weapon pulled from under her jacket.

The gang member with Yacine looked confused. "What do we do?" he asked.

"Distract the policewoman and I'll grab the bag. Ali will be sacrificed for the good of our Imam," he said with a push. "Don't get caught."

The gang member moved towards Geneviève, but kept his back turned to avoid eye contact. In a few short steps, he'd made himself an obstacle on the narrow path which led toward the docks.

Benoit came up on the Algerian. "Police... move aside," she replied, using her free arm against the man. Feeling his resistance, she grabbed the man's arm and swept her leg against his, which caused him to tumble to the pavement. Stepping over him, she looked down. "I'm sorry," she muttered as left the prone figure behind.

Captain Lemieux watched Benoit scuffle with the Algerian, which spurred him to action. Nearing the gate, he pushed through a small group gathered near the fence to watch Geneviève's encounter. He also noticed three men stand aside on the dock, one of whom was their drug dealer.

"Give me the bag," Yacine demanded with his hand held out while meeting Ulysse and Ali. "Ali, head towards the eastern dock, go now," he commanded. "I suggest you return to your family."

Benoit and Lemieux both watched the exchange take place. As Ali left the group, she called out to Lemieux, "I've got the young one. You get the other."

Captain Lemieux waved. Forcing his way closer, the men had already separated, so he made the decision to follow the older Algerian. While Yacine increased his distance from the detective, Lemieux quickened his pace to catch up. "You... with the bag... stop where you are!" he shouted, as he displayed his pistol.

Yacine kept his pace, not wanting to force the detective to act irrationally. Turning to his right, he skirted behind a motorboat, which obscured him from Lemieux. In one move, Yacine tossed the satchel on to the deck where it slid under the bench.

On the opposite side of the marina, Geneviève was closing in on Ali. Ahead, she noticed the end of the docks, which would force the Algerian to the street and the protest march. She trotted up a gangway towards a gate to cut the young man off at the street.

Ali never noticed Geneviève's action. As he came closer to the marina's perimeter, he turned toward the street and safety. While striding up the inclined path, he turned his head to look for the detective, and let out a sigh at the absence of his pursuer. Turning his attention to the gate, he never saw the punch thrown by Geneviève.

Geneviève hid behind a message board and took her stance, braced to deliver her punch. Fingers flexed, she clenched her hand and delivered a single thrust. Geneviève's skill in self-defense were ingrained as she struck the drug dealer with a technique taught years before today. "I told you... to stop," Benoit declared, looking over Ali who collapsed on the sidewalk.

Ali brought his hands against his face, anticipating another blow from the woman, but it never came. Blood trickled from his nose as he blinked, trying to regain his focus.

Geneviève stood over him and holstered her pistol. In a single motion, she grabbed one of his arms. "On your stomach," she commanded. She clutched his wrist and rolled him over, secured his hands with handcuffs and yanked him to his feet.

Across the marina, Captain Lemieux had less favorable results. Making his way to the gangway where Yacine had turned, he failed to notice the satchel under the deck chair of a boat he trotted passed. He'd also lost his suspect. Lemieux stood atop the gangway; all he saw were protesters mingle at the end of the march. Yacine had disappeared into the crowd.

Chapter TEN

While Captain Lemieux and Detective Benoit handed over the suspect to officers for transport to the district police station, an unsuspecting witness took note of the exchange. "Take good care of him," Geneviève said, patting the immigrant's shoulder. "I'll see you again soon." Across the city, two senior members of Papillion Transport drove towards the Catholic cemetery on *Rue Saint Pierre* for a meeting.

An ambulance, its siren echoing through the neighborhood came up behind the driver's vehicle off a side street. The Peugeot pulled aside for the emergency vehicle to rush past. "You know, last time we were near the hospital, Hector caused an accident while you freed me from custody." Louis chuckled at the irony.

"Hopefully we won't need to do that again for some time, heh," Gregory replied as he turned towards Saint Pierre Cemetery.

Up ahead, a procession of cars approached from the opposite direction. Gregory slowed his sedan, pulled through the gates and waited for the column of vehicles to enter. As he observed the hearse, his hairs stood on end as he and Louis saw the tri-colors of their nation drape the coffin through the side window.

"Rest easy, comrade," Louis said in quiet reflection of the unknown member being laid to rest.

"Bon chance, mon ami," Gregory added.

Fifteen or so cars followed the hearse, with the last turning in the opposite direction of the procession. "Now to find Claudio," the head of Papillion muttered. Turning in behind the sedan which left the procession, Gregory steered as Louis called out the cemetery plot locations and pathways.

In a few minutes, they found themselves deep within the cemetery grounds, surrounded by crypts of granite and shadowed by a mix of towering trees and shrubbery. As they crested a mound, Gregory and

Louis came face to face with two men who approached from the roadway. Gregory recognized one from an earlier encounter with the head of the local Mafia.

One of the Mafia security members approached the driver's side window, which Gregory had lowered. "You'll need to turn around; there's a private ceremony ahead which no one can disturb," he told the driver.

"We're here to pay our respects to Don Carbone's family," Gregory replied as he handed over his license.

The guard took the identification and read the name. Moving his hand to his face, the man spoke into a small lapel microphone. In moments, he turned his attention back to the car and its occupants. "Monsieur Carbone will see you. Park your car behind the red Mercedes on the left," he directed as he handed back Gregory's license.

"Polite sonofabitch, isn't he?" Louis mumbled.

Gregory shook his head at the comment and parked his car as directed. As they got out of the sedan, both men straightened their jackets, Louis did so in hopes of hiding his pistol. Plodding between crypts, the men approached a group oblivious to their presence.

Claudio Carbone led a woman toward the final resting place of her son. With a small bouquet in her hand, she knelt and set the flowers on the granite marker. To her side, the priest from the family's church offered a small prayer. Gregory and Louis stood a short distance from the family, observing the service.

After the final blessing, the group began disburse towards their respective cars. Claudio Carbone saw the Frenchmen stand along the fringe of the gathering and approached them.

While the Mafia leader walked up to Gregory, his partner took a few steps back to give the men some privacy. "My condolences at your family's loss Claudio," he uttered as he held out his hand. "And thank you for agreeing to meet me on such short notice."

"Merci, Gregory. My younger sister's firstborn," Carbone replied. "For the advances in medicine, it still baffles me to see a child succumb to something as simple as an infection. And now... what is it you wish to discuss?" He moved from grief to business without skipping a beat.

"Amed Gilles."

The mafia leader shrugged his shoulders, an indifferent look to his face. "And what about him?" Carbone asked.

The former Legionnaire stood, hands grasped together, showed a sense of vulnerability to the mafia leader. "He's found out some disturbing information about my business," Gregory answered. "And he thinks he can blackmail me with this information."

"Really? Do you expect me to lend you money?"

Gregory shook his head at the remark. "No... I do not, Claudio. The money, I have. What I lack is the manpower to locate Gilles. It's something I'm not able to undertake. I need your help to find him so the odds are in my favor at our next encounter," Gregory replied. "Or at least in a neutral place of my choosing."

It was Claudio's turn to react to the appeal, and let out a chuckle. "You want me to use my people... my resources to find Amed Gilles for you?" He turned towards his car to wait for his driver, Gregory at his side. "Okay, let's say I agree... and I tell you where he is... 'most vulnerable' shall we say... then what?"

Gregory stopped. Claudio took another step before turning back towards the Frenchman. "Claudio, all I'll say is the two of us would have a conversation… as long as he is civil about the discussion," Gregory replied. "And if he refuses... then I'd say his second in line better be ready to negotiate."

"You could start a gang war with the Maghrebi," Claudio cautioned. "And with my family caught in the middle of it," the mafia leader added, the stern expression of concern openly displayed his concern. "I'm not sure I want to assume those risks."

"Claudio, all I ask is for you to point me in the direction," Gregory said. "If you agree, just leave a message at this number." He handed over his business card. The number led to a new cell phone which only he carried. "It's as simple as one of your family making a phone call. The rest I'll take care of."

The Mafia leader lowered his head, his hand rubbing the back of his neck. "I make no promises if or when the call will be made... agreed?" He extended his hand.

Gregory accepted the offering. "Agreed... and thank you, Claudio."

Claudio turned away and walked the last ten meters to his car in silence, leaving Gregory standing unemotional amongst the dead. Louis walked up behind his friend, observing the Corsican turn and leave. As they watched the Mafia leader depart, they made their way back to Gregory's car.

"Do you think he'll help us?" Louis asked.

"I'm not sure," Gregory replied as he unlocked the car. "But he's not wrong about a gang war erupting if Amed doesn't agree to our terms."

Louis sat down and closed the door. "And what are 'our terms' going to be with him?"

"Back off... and more importantly, don't try using family as pawns," Gregory said as he maneuvered through the winding path of the cemetery. "Did we ever get a response from Romain?"

"Not yet. My call went straight to his voicemail service."

"Contact Hector," Gregory stated, "and have him go to Romain's apartment to see if he's in town. Make sure Pasqual goes with him. After last night's fiasco with Julien, I don't want to take any chances."

"Understood, Gregory."

While the men left the cemetery, Detective Benoit and Captain Lemieux sat at their desks. Each were busy writing up their reports on the morning's experience from the marina with the suspected drug dealer.

Geneviève glanced at her notes. *North African decent, Algerian, 2 meters tall and 63 and a half kilos* was the suspect's description she typed in her report. "Captain, do you have a copy of the booking information? I need the identification number for the report."

Lemieux grabbed a sheet of paper and handed it over to the woman. "Here... and when you're done, place it in a folder," he muttered before turned to his computer to finish his version of the incident.

"Should I start a file on the banker, Monsieur Reno?"

"What will you put down for an offense? While we tangled with the drug dealer, he sailed away. We didn't question him or see what was being passed in the bag," Lemieux answered in disgust. He looked up the time. "Doesn't the interrogation team expect you downstairs about now?"

Geneviève glanced over her shoulder. "Damn it," she muttered. "I'll be back." Hurrying out of the office, she made her way to the stairwell, and scampered down the steps two at a time. When she reached Interrogation, she stopped to catch her breath before she continued inside the room.

A sergeant approached from the opposite end of the hallway, several folders in hand. "Here's the suspect's file," Sergeant Dubois said, as she handed the paperwork to Geneviève. "Please see it's returned after your interrogation, Detective."

"Glad to see you're on time, Detective," the watch officer proclaimed for all to hear as Geneviève entered.

Chastised by the sergeant for making him wait, Geneviève composed herself. "I had to finish my arrest report," she replied while she scanned the many video monitors and leafed through the files. "Which room is the suspect in?"

The sergeant pointed at the wall where the monitors hung. "He's in Number 4. And his lawyer is somewhat impatient." A haggard-looking man paced back and forth on the video screen.

Geneviève thanked the sergeant and stepped into the hallway and walked the few meters to the identified room. As she drew close, the officer who escorted her suspect unlocked the door to allow her to enter. "I'm Detective Benoit," she addressed the lawyer.

The lawyer faced the door. "About time someone showed up," he declared.

As Geneviève entered, her nose twitched at the faint scent of marijuana assault her nose. As she walked past the counselor, she could detect some waft off his crumbled jacket. Geneviève forced herself to stay calm while she made her way past the lawyer and his client, Ali, who sat quietly in a metal chair. She set her notebook down and took the seat across from him.

"I want the name of the officer who injured my client," the lawyer demanded as he pointed Ali's bandaged face. The skin color around Ali's eyes had changed as bruises began to set in and blackened. "And I likewise want to know what charges are being levied against him."

Geneviève smiled inwardly knowing she was the one who caused the injury. "Your client... what did you say your name was again?" she asked as her pen hung while preparing to write.

"My name is Ali..."

Geneviève held her hand, stopping the Algerian. "I already have your name. But I need his for the record," as she pointed the pen at the lawyer.

The public defender placed both hands on the table's edge and leaned toward the detective. "Trudeau. Alfred Trudeau," the lawyer spat. "Now, I want the officer's name who hit my client? I want him charged at once."

In the control room, Captain Lemieux had joined the watch officer. "This should be interesting," he muttered as he sipped his coffee. "Have we any record of this lawyer in our files?"

"He handles cases for the less fortunate," the watch officer replied as he handed Lemieux a worn-out folder, its contents haphazardly stuffed inside. "Most times they're immigrants, poor, and his fee paid by others." The captain took the folder and slid it under his arm as they turned their attention back to the video feed.

"How does your client know Monsieur Reno?" Geneviève questioned the lawyer.

"Who?"

"The gentleman I saw your client receiving a parcel from," Geneviève said. "His name is Ulysse Reno, a senior executive at Banque Palatine. How does a young Algerian immigrant become acquainted with someone like him?"

"What is she talking about?" Ali stammered a puzzled look towards his lawyer. "I went to gain employment on one of the larger boats as a deckhand."

"There, you heard my client," Trudeau said. He knew the session would be recorded, which made his job to clear the drug dealer a game of cat-and-mouse during the interrogation. "There's no crime in trying to earn a few euros." He finally took a seat next to Ali. "Once again, before we go any further... I want to know who assaulted him?"

Geneviève flipped a few pages in her notebook as she looked across at Trudeau. "For the record, your client is suspected of trafficking drugs for sale. And the officer's name involved in your client's arrest was Benoit," she grinned.

"And what's his first name?" Trudeau asked.

"It's Geneviève. I'll spell it out for you if needed," she replied.

A brief look of bewilderment crossed the lawyer's face before he replied. "A female officer did this...?" Trudeau motioned to Ali.

"Yes. And if you get out of hand, I'll show you how it was done," Geneviève said. "Now, I want to know how your client is associated with Monsieur Reno? How and when they met, and who directed him to meet the banker at the docks?" Geneviève's frustration grew, and it was evident in her tone.

Ali straightened up in his chair and looked at the detective's eyes. As he cleared his throat, he felt Trudeau's hand on his arm, which he pushed aside. "I understand Baumettes prison accommodations have improved and you've a few new cooks. I'm not telling you anything." He sat back in his chair. Ali was well aware his fate would be worse at the hands of Amed Gilles if he talked. *Better to rot in a cell*, he told himself.

"You still haven't declared what he's being held on," Trudeau demanded, trying to gain control.

Geneviève turned to the corner of the room. "Could you please replay the answer to Monsieur Trudeau's question?" she asked, looking into the small video camera. In moments, they heard her voice answer Trudeau's question; Ali associated with drug trafficking.

"He'll be held the mandatory time as part of our investigation. Afterward, he'll be transferred to Baumettes until his trial date," Geneviève declared, closing her notebook before she stood. "Now, if you don't have any further objections, Monsieur Trudeau, there's another issue I'd like to discuss with you."

Looking up at the detective, the lawyer shook his head. "Really? Like what?" Trudeau asked, confusion edged on his face.

"When was the last time you smoked marijuana?"

The question caused a stir amongst those in the control room. As he heard his partner ask, Captain Lemieux left and made his way to the room where the sentry allowed him to enter. The three occupants in the room looked over as the door opened. “Excuse me, Detective, but can I have a word?” Lemieux asked, and motioned her outside.

Geneviève walked around the table and past Lemieux into the hallway. As the door closed, she looked at her captain. “Is there something wrong?”

“Where the hell did your question about his smoking come from?”

“You can’t smell it? He reeks of marijuana,” Geneviève said. “I caught it as soon as I entered,” she added. “I was about ready to call the lab and have Francine issue a drug test.”

Lemieux ran his hand over his face. “You can’t just force a drug test on a member of the court,” he said. “At least not without probable cause. And your sense of smell is not acceptable in court,” he added with a shake of his head. Lemieux nodded to the sentry, and directed the officer into action. “Call the K-9 unit, have them bring one of the dogs down.”

After five minutes of standing outside interrogation, they heard the tip-tap of claws on the floor. Both officers turned to see the Belgian Malinois trot towards them. At the end of the leash was its handler, Officer Romain Neuville, the lead trainer for the K-9 officers. “You called for help?” he asked.

“I believe one of the men in interrogation has drugs on his person,” Geneviève explained, motioning to the room.

“You mean you suspect someone...” Lemieux corrected.

“Fine.” She folded her arms across her chest. “I suspect one of them in possession of marijuana,” Geneviève corrected herself, each word pronounced with greater clarity. “I won’t say which one... but I’ve my suspicions on who it might be,” she added.

“We’ll soon know,” Romain answered. “Hunter... stay. If you’ll allow me some room,” He stepped past Geneviève to the door. “You can stand in the doorway after I enter.”

Trudeau and Ali were sitting as Romain entered. “Hunter... seek,” was the only thing they picked up before the dog trotted in and began to sniff. Within moments, the canine was barking as it sat next the lawyer.

"What's going on?" Trudeau asked as he cringed with every bark from the Malinois.

Watching the dog alert for drugs, Romain put a whistle to his lips and blew three times. Understanding the tone, the canine laid down, its tongue hanging out of its mouth as it panted. "Good boy," the handler said, scratching between the dog's ears. "I'll let you do the rest," the officer said with a look at Benoit and Lemieux just as his cell phone rang. Romain saw the number and returned the phone to his pocket. "If you'll excuse me, I've got another matter to attend to. Hunter, come," he commanded, setting the canine in motion and out the door.

The detectives both looked down at the lawyer, with Lemieux speaking first. "If you'll be so kind as to empty your pockets, Monsieur Trudeau," he said. "Officer, take the suspect back to holding please."

Chapter ELEVEN

As the detective's office door swung open, Police Detective Guy Masson's arrival caught his fellow detective by surprise. "Did you miss me?" Guy asked, putting his backpack on to his desk. The expression on his fellow officer's face gave him the answer he expected to see.

"Long enough to realize I still hate paperwork," came Nicolas Berger's reply. "How was the return to school work?" he asked, embracing his friend.

"Bethune is more pleasant than you'd expect this time of year," Guy replied. "And the course work was a challenge but not so hard you couldn't complete it," he teased. "Where's the Captain, and Benoit?"

"Downstairs questioning another drug dealer," Berger answered.

Masson noticed the images on Berger's computer. "Who are they?" he asked, with a nod toward the computer.

"Those are gentlemen callers of the once infamous actress, Yvette Segal," Berger proclaimed. "Turns out the drug smuggler Geneviève tracked down in Algiers was associated with her at one time. Geneviève stumbled upon her during a drug bust. Seems Madame Segal found herself in the wrong place and time, since we found her dead on a yacht here in Marseille."

Masson let out a low whistle. "Such a waste," he replied, looking at the woman in one picture. He turned around as the door swung open.

"Guy," Geneviève exclaimed when she saw the detective. "When did you get back?" she asked giving him a hug, her smile the most genuine they'd seen in months.

"Well, look who decided to come back to work," Captain Lemieux exclaimed as he entered, coffee in hand. "How was your training?"

Over the next half-hour, Guy Masson retold his story of the sessions at Bethune. The detective gave his colleagues a rare insight to the mental work and physical training he endured in preparation for his new assignment with the National Police Force in Paris.

As Guy joked with Nicolas about the stamina test, as Geneviève's computer pinged with an incoming email. As she tended to the message, she logged on and read the notification.

"Something interesting?" Lemieux asked as he noticed her attention shift.

"It's an email from Inspector Haddad in Algiers," Benoit answered, shifting the mouse on her desk to enlarge the message.

"Isn't he the officer who escorted your suspect?" This time it was Berger who asked the question.

"Yes... and he's a good officer," Geneviève said while reading the email. "Sounds like he was alerted by Algiers airport security about our other suspect, Louis Remesy being sighted. And he's included images from the surveillance cameras at the terminal." She shifted cursor to the first image and tapped the button to open the file.

Captain Lemieux glanced over her shoulder as the picture emerged. "Which suspect? Doesn't sound like anyone under investigation, does it?" The man with dark complexion and glasses could lend himself to nearly anyone from the region.

Geneviève pulled the message forward, covering a segment of the picture Lemieux studied. "Karim said he suspects the man in these images is our drug dealer, Louis Remesy. But he entered the country under the name 'Jacque Vignes.' They were captured on their surveillance after a flight arrived from Marseille." The words trailed away as the realization of his presence in the city hit home. "It's possible the bastard was here, and we didn't know it?" she exclaimed.

"Guess you need to have another talk with your gentleman friend, Dupont," Berger uttered in a cautious tone.

With her eyes narrowing and the growing tension in her neck building, Geneviève stared down her fellow detective for making the statement. "Hector's not expected to keep tabs on individuals for this department," she declared.

"Nonetheless, it wouldn't hurt for Berger and Masson to visit and ask to review his surveillance tapes," Captain Lemieux pointed out. "Did this inspector offer any specifics on the photos? Do we know when they were taken?"

"The timestamp shows last Friday," Geneviève answered. "The day after we found our murdered socialite." She jotted down the information before she slumped in her chair.

"And speaking of the deceased Miss Segal," Lemieux started as he looked over to Berger, "how is your report shaping up?"

As Berger cleared his throat, he answered. "There were five instances where the former drug dealer Hakim Talib was with our deceased socialite." He flipped a page. "On three of the five they were alone, twice on the boat, once ashore. The other two times, however, there was a third man; a European by his looks, and well-dressed too," Berger added. "The date of the last photo of both Talib and Segal was taken two weeks before your encounter with him in Algiers," he nodded to Geneviève.

"Sounds quite innocent to me," Masson said.

"Not behind the scenes, though," Berger replied. "According to Captain Noel's officers, there was an altercation on the docks between Talib and two other men," reading the summary. "It happened the day after the last photo was taken. Witnesses reported the two men dragging Talib off the boat and a large bag thrown at him while he was pushed into the street."

"He either did something unpleasant or outlived his usefulness," Captain Lemieux stated. "And with both parties dead, we'll never know." He tossed his empty cup behind him. "Guy, what's on your agenda for today?"

Detective Masson recalled his plans, most of which would be informing the various departments of his return. "And I've some gear to return to the academy I signed for," he replied.

Geneviève only half listened as she stared at the photos provided by the Algerian police. *Remesy was here*, she told herself. *What was he doing back in Marseille and why did he return now were questions beginning to trouble her?* She grabbed a pencil, and jotted down the date and time from the photos to pass to Hector when she saw him.

The ringing of the phone interrupted her thoughts. "Benoit, can you get that?" Berger asked, tossing a wad of paper in her direction.

"What?"

"Your phone, it's ringing," the detective pointed out.

As she reached into her purse, the ringing ceased. Getting out the cell, she looked at the screen to see missed call displayed across it. She opened the call log and saw the original number and the name, *Unknown.*

"Who was it?"

"It was an unknown person according to the ID, but there's a number," Geneviève answered, displaying the screen to her fellow detective while grabbing the desk phone with her free hand.

"What are you going to do now?"

"Call the number, what else?" Geneviève punched in the number. In moments, the ringing began. Though the number was local to Marseille, the call was routed to a phone outside of France. After the third ring, a man's monotone voice answered.

"Hello, may I ask who's calling?"

"Bon jour Monsieur," Geneviève replied. "You tried to call me but I didn't answer quick enough. I'm sorry," she began. "Is there something you wish to discuss?"

"I called to let you know our time is not over," the man replied. "There are many things still needing to be addressed between you and me, Officer Benoit," he said, glancing at his watch before ending the call.

The coldness to his statement made Geneviève stiffen in her chair.

Berger noticed this. "What's wrong?"

"I don't know," Geneviève replied, holding the handset, the disconnected call echoing in the earpiece. "It was a man who answered. He said we still had things to discuss." Her voice was shaky, but quiet.

"Any idea who it might be?" Berger asked as Captain Lemieux returned with another coffee in hand.

"Who are you talking about?" the senior officer asked.

"Benoit just took a call from someone," Berger answered.

"He said we had things to talk about, but didn't say what they were," Geneviève added. "He mentioned our time wasn't over yet either."

"It sounds like the two of you've met before," Berger mentioned. "Another investigation, maybe?"

Captain Lemieux pulled out his chair and grabbed a pen to jot down notes. "He didn't mention his name. What about noises; anything to give you a sense where the call was made?"

Geneviève shook her head. "It was quiet. Surreal like, the lack of noise in the backdrop was almost deafening," she answered. "All I heard was his voice." A visible shutter coursed through her as she recalled the conversation. "Nothing about it made any sense, though."

Lemieux wrote out several more things he was pondering before he asked his next question. "How did the call come into the office? Did it come through our telephone lines first?"

"It was a missed call on my cell," Geneviève replied. "I dialed back on one of the office lines."

Captain Lemieux picked up the phone and dialed the number to the communications supervisor downstairs. "Sergeant, Captain Lemieux calling. I need a trace put on the last outgoing call made from the following extension." He recited the number Geneviève called from. "Let me know what you find out," he added before hanging up the phone.

"What are you thinking?" Geneviève asked.

Captain Lemieux sipped his coffee. "Well... we know you've drawn the attention of Omar Khalid," the captain answered. "And he's been in touch with the Italians as well. And now... your colleague in Algiers sends us the possible identity of a wanted drug trafficker."

The desk phone rang, interrupting the conversation. Reaching out, Captain Lemieux answered the call. "Drug Intervention, Lemieux speaking."

In the Communications department, the sergeant working on Captain Lemieux's earlier request called back to pass along what he'd learned. "The call was traced to a residence on *Boulevard de Beaumont*."

Captain Lemieux wrote down the information. "Thank you, Sergeant," he said as he hung up the phone. "They traced your call. It came from a residence in the Beaumont quarter. Come on, let's put this to rest," he ordered, motioning to his detectives.

After a thirty-minute drive through town, which included detouring recently collapsed buildings, the three officers came upon the residence in question. Parking at the corner, Captain Lemieux caught sight of a patrol car approach from the opposite direction. He waved it down and explained their plight, and establish the patrol's role as backup. "Let's see who your mystery caller is."

With deliberate and cautious approach, the officers made their way into the apartment building. "I'll take the stairs," Berger announced as she moved to his right. "I'll meet you on the third-floor." Lemieux and Benoit looked at each other as they entered the elevator.

"Any last thoughts?" Benoit asked.

"Just hope it turns out to be a crank caller," the captain replied. Maintaining his gaze on the door, he hoped the woman didn't notice the beads of sweat gather on his forehead.

Geneviève had noticed the captain sweating, but discounted it as tension of what's about to happen. As trickles of sweat inched their way down her neck, its movement caused her to shiver. As the doors opened, she and Lemieux stepped out and noticed Berger stand off to one side of the hallway.

Lemieux nodded to Berger and held up three fingers signaling which apartment they would enter. Staring at the door opposite the elevator, he saw they need to move to their left. "You lead, Berger," he directed the detective who'd already unholstered his weapon. "And you have our backs," he said to Geneviève, who drew her own pistol.

As they approached the location, Berger got to the door. Out of habit, he reached down and turned the handle, which spun quietly in his hand. Opening the door somewhat, Berger glanced over his shoulder at Captain Lemieux. "Shall we?"

Lemieux signaled for him to enter. As they stepped into the apartment, it was noticeably barren except for a table set against the far wall. Located on it was a single phone, its handset positioned on another device. “Berger, check the other rooms.”

Detective Benoit bent down to examine the phone and the mystery item which sat next to it. “What do you think it is?” she asked.

“If I had to guess... it’s some form of homemade transmitter,” Lemieux replied as he holstered his pistol. Taking a pen from his jacket, he slipped it behind a flap of cardboard and lifted. Behind it, a digital screen was visible, with numbers cycling in a random and haphazard sequence. “And it’s searching for a signal.” He exposed the digits for Geneviève to see.

Berger came back into the main room, and holstered his pistol. “This place is empty; there’s no sign anyone occupied this apartment in the last few months. Have you figured out what the gadget is?”

Geneviève continued to study the transmitter. As she stepped to the side, she noticed several wires connecting the transmitter to the telephone jack in the wall. “The phone is a decoy,” she declared, and motioned the others to consider her discovery. “Someone wanted to make it look like the phone was used.”

Captain Lemieux took a step back and glanced to his right. Through the window, he could see a telecommunication tower in the distance. “Best signals are always line-of-sight, aren’t they?” he said, pointing to the stanchion with its array of antennas.

Detective Berger joined his captain to see for himself. “It seems this apartment wasn’t chosen at random either.” The detective looked at Captain Lemieux before glancing to Benoit.

An expression of concern covered Geneviève’s face. Once again, the reality of being stalked by unknown people was cause for concern. “And it seems neither was I.”

Chapter TWELVE

Late afternoon sun filtered through dusty windows, casting a muted light behind the occupants in the room. The typical tone of a call unanswered emanated from the cell phone's speaker and filled the small office. "Still nothing," Hector said, hanging up. As he pushed himself away from the desk, he called out to his companion. "Pasqual, are you about ready?"

The Frenchman stepped out of the restroom shared by the three offices of Papillion Transport. "What were you saying Hector?"

"I was wondering if you were going to be in there all day," Hector Pichon replied, tossing keys at his friend. "You're driving."

Claudette Minot was the only woman with intimate knowledge of the members of Papillion Transport and their past. The head of Papillion, Gregory Arsenault, and Claudette's husband Jules were once business associates in Toulon. Four years ago, Jules was killed in a botched ambush by Corsican mafia when his car was mistaken for the rival gang leader's. After his death, Gregory vowed to look after the widow.

"Where are you going and how long will you be gone?"

"Gregory wants us to contact Romain," Hector replied. "We shouldn't be too long... maybe an hour," he added. Before he and Pasqual left the office, each checked their weapons, ensuring they were ready for possible encounters with the Maghrebis gang.

"You two be careful," Claudette stated as they left.

Both men walked out, making their way to the street. As casually as one can be, all while being suspicious of every passerby, the men climbed into Pasqual's Volkswagen. "Sometimes Claudette acts too much like my mother," he said, starting the car.

"She's just concerned for the men who keep her safe, you know," Hector said. "Besides, she doubtless has little social life since her husband is died."

As Pasqual pulled out into traffic, the men found themselves in the middle of afternoon traffic as people began to head home. As they made their way to the Saint Joseph quarter of the city, Pasqual soon noticed a vehicle make an attempt to keep pace with them. "We've company," he declared to his companion.

"Are you sure?"

"Same silver Renault with four men in it," Pasqual replied. "I didn't pick them up until after we crossed under the A55." His eyes shifted between the traffic ahead and the car behind. "Any suggestions?"

Hector pulled out his cell phone and opened the map function. "We can't go straight to Romain's apartment with them in tow. Make the next left turn," he directed his partner towards their new destination.

Pasqual stared ahead. "Where are we going?"

"We're going to see how interested these guys are," Hector said. "There's a police station on *Rue Odette Jasse* we can head towards. If they're still behind us, we'll park, go inside, and file a harassment report." He chuckled at the thought of being a law-abiding citizen.

"And what, tell the police they're part of the protests?" Pasqual asked.

"Hey, that's a good idea," Hector said. Next, he dialed a number from memory. In moments, the phone was ringing on the other end. "Come on, Romain, pick up," he muttered.

Several kilometers away, the police sergeant had just entered his apartment when the phone began ringing. Removing the leash from Hunter, he picked up the phone as the dog headed to the kitchen. "Hello?"

"Romain? It's Hector Pichon."

"Afternoon, my friend. What's the occasion this time?" Romain asked.

Over the next few minutes, the men discussed Papillion's plight, which included Gregory's eagerness to prepare themselves for the next encounter with the Maghrebis gangs. As Romain listened, the Belgian Malinois returned to his side and sat obediently at his feet.

"Hunter and I will be ready when you get here." He scratched the canine between the ears, getting a tail wag in return.

"We'll see you soon," Hector said, ending the conversation.

While the members of Papillion Transport made their way across town, Detectives Benoit and Berger filled out reports on their action surrounding the mysterious call received earlier.

"Did you notice the Captain's demeanor this morning?" Geneviève asked.

Berger shrugged his shoulders as he typed away. "Not really, why?"

"He looked... I don't know, more focused, even less lethargic," she said. "If I had to guess, I'd say he was certainly more sober than what he'd been in past weeks."

"Didn't he have dinner with the doctor... oh, what's her name?"

"Beringer."

"Yeah, that's her," Berger replied as he filled out his report. "Maybe he felt he needed to be on his best behavior and took it easy on the wine."

Geneviève sat and reflected on what Nicolas said. "Maybe he's finally ready to move on from Nadine," she spoke quietly. "I'm sure Doctor Beringer would agree." The phone rang on the desk and she grabbed it before Nicolas could and answered. "Detective Benoit."

In Forensics, Francine LeBeau just finished processing the mystery caller evidence from the apartment the detectives raided. "Geneviève? Francine here. Can you and Nic come down to the lab? I've got something for you."

"Be there in a few," Geneviève replied before hanging up and grabbing her notebook. Looking at Nic, she added, "Francine has something to show us downstairs."

"Let me save this file first," Berger said, hitting a series of keys before he got up only to find himself scurrying after Geneviève towards the stairwell.

As the detectives scampered down the stairs, Captain Lemieux sat outside the office of his friend and supervisor, Captain Julien Duval. Taking a sip of his coffee, his mind wandered between issues which might come up during their discussion. The young woman sitting outside the captain's door smiled politely when he entered, but avoided saying anything. He was left alone to ponder why he was summoned. The buzz from the desk phone broke through his thoughts.

The young woman spoke as she set the phone down. "Captain Duval will see you now, Detective." She got up to show Lemieux to the door.

"Thank you," he replied, dropping the empty cup in the trash bin.

Captain Lemieux froze when he caught sight of Doctor Beringer sitting to one side of the desk. Louise sat, notebook on her lap and what looked to be a forced smile on her face.

"Have a seat, Claude," Captain Duval said as he motioned to the chair before him. "That'll be all, Annette."

"I take it this doesn't have anything to do with our current cases?" Claude said, sitting down.

"No... it doesn't," Duval answered. He and Claude had risen through the ranks from police cadets and knew each other beyond work. He was the first individual Claude reached out to when Nadine was diagnosed with cancer. And he was there when she passed away in the hospital. Duval knew the next few minutes would be hard on his friend, but he accepted the outcome as part of caring for the man.

Before Captain Duval could begin, Claude turned to Dr. Beringer. "Was your acceptance to join me for dinner just your way of diagnosing me and my issues?"

Louise took in a deep breath. She'd heard the question before, its tone and delivery one of implied deception. "Last night had nothing to do with what your Captain wishes to discuss with you today, Claude," she said. "He's asked me to be present in an official capacity as part of protocol."

"Claude, several of the officers have noticed your demeanor and temperament...."

"Who?" Claude interrupted.

"Your fellow officers," Duval repeated. "Over the last several months, they've noted your appearance steadily decline, and they're concerned your letting your personal life interfere with your duties."

"I've never faltered once when in the field," Claude replied.

"For the most part, that's been true," Duval said. "But your actions last month with the suspects at Il d'If certainly caused some concern."

"I was caught up at the moment," Claude said in defense. "And nothing's happened since then." He shifted in his seat; the sense he was being reprimanded based on a single event weighed on his mind. "Has Benoit been telling you things?" he asked, knowing Geneviève voiced concerns about his personal life in the past.

"As I said before, your colleagues and fellow officers have all taken notice," Duval repeated. "It goes beyond those you work with in the office."

"Then why didn't they say something beforehand?" Claude queried his friend.

"I can't speak for their reason not to discuss their concerns," the senior officer replied. Duval sat back and looked at his friend. "Claude, you need to seek help and move past the loss of Nadine."

"We've had this talk before. As far as I'm concerned, it has no bearing on my conduct."

Dr. Beringer sat quietly as she jotted down her observation between the two men. *He's still hurting*, she told herself of Claude. She'd interviewed hundreds of patients in the past whose story was much like his. The loss of a loved one, the guilt of surviving or the inability to do more always the root cause of their anguish.

"You're functioning only because you've substituted coffee for wine," Captain Duval stated. "The head of food services mentioned you're running a tab exceeding most others by €150 a week."

"I have to drink something," Claude countered, shifting in the chair. "Since I don't like soda, it leaves me with coffee. And I always pay my bill when asked, or did he fail to mention that part?"

The planned intervention to his friends grieving wasn't going as planned, Duval thought. He didn't want to use his seniority on Claude, but he was beginning to see he wouldn't have a choice.

"Claude, I want you to submit a request for medical leave. Take the next two weeks off and work with Dr. Beringer's colleagues and get the help you need," the captain said. "She's willing to make the preparations for you."

"I'll arrange for you to see a colleague of mine at the hospital in Rennes," Dr. Beringer said. "I trust Patrick and his staff. And I wouldn't place you with anyone who wasn't capable of providing you with the best care."

Claude stood, looking at Louise before facing his friend. "And what about my cases? Who's going to manage the detective's workload in my absence?"

Duval put his hand in the air. "Claude, you've said Berger and Benoit are capable of working on their own," he replied. "And I've heard Detective Masson just returned from his training. And even though he's transferring, he'll still be with us until the end of the month. So, your team isn't as short-handed as you might think."

"And who will they report to in my absence?"

"Why, me, of course," Captain Duval said.

Claude slouched back into his chair, feeling somewhat betrayed by his friend. But he knew Julien wouldn't have taken these steps unless he was concerned. He glanced over at Louise and wondered if he'd be given another chance to see her after his two weeks.

While Captain Lemieux was with Captain Duval and Dr. Beringer, Berger and Benoit were pacing the Forensics lab listening to Francine recite her test results.

"This device, crude as it looks, scrambles the signal from cell phone towers, making a trace nearly impossible," Francine pointed out. "However, I was able to find part of the frequency code the person used to set up the signal."

"Which means what?" Geneviève asked.

"The line of code used for the signal contained a prefix used to establish the signal's origin," Francine replied. "And it was rather a surprise where the location is."

"Where did it originate?" Berger asked.

"Offshore," Francine answered. "More specifically, from communication equipment used on a ship."

Geneviève stopped pacing the room when she heard the location. "A ship? Can you determine which one?"

"What are you thinking, Geneviève?"

The woman looked at Berger. "We've been trying to nail down information on Papillion Transport. You and Guy were looking into the ship movements while Claude and I were pursuing leads on the owners."

"You think it came from one of Papillion's freighters?"

The detective spun gradually in the chair following Berger as he meandered around the room. Geneviève tossed her hands upward. "Do you have a better idea? We have one in port now, but where are the others?"

Berger continued to wander about the room. As he shifted his gaze between the women, he struggled to come up with an alternative to Geneviève's declaration. He shuffled passed Francine's desk and noticed a folder labeled *"Segal"* sitting open, and the thought struck him. "What about someone affiliated with Yvette Segal?"

"The dead socialite?" Francine asked.

"I'm not following… what about her?" Geneviève asked.

Berger grabbed the folder and began flipping through pages. "The signal originated from a maritime communication. Who's saying it wasn't from someone connected with the yacht?" Berger answered. "Yeah, we're working on something with Papillion, but the most recent is her murder on the yacht and the drugs we found."

Geneviève slid off the chair and pointed at her partner. "Or it could be the bank executive, Ulysse Reno," she recalled her surveillance from the other day. "Once we link him to the drug dealer we arrested, he'll have a lot of explaining to do." The door to the laboratory opened as she was prepared to continue with her argument against the banker.

"But we don't have any drugs linking the banker to the dealer, do we, Detective?" Captain Lemieux stated as he joined the conversation. "All we have is a suspected drug dealer in the vicinity of the banker and nothing more. And for the moment, we'll table this discussion. I need to have a word with both of you; upstairs, if you please," he said, pointing out Berger and Benoit before ushering them through the door. "If you'll excuse us, Officer LeBeau."

The detectives exchanged looks of confusion before Berger spoke. "What do you think it is this time?"

"I'm not sure," Geneviève replied as they followed their captain into the hallway.

Just outside the lab door, Asiya Fatah swept a mop back and forth along the corridor nearly tripping Detective Berger. "I'm so sorry, sir," she exclaimed with a bow of her head.

Geneviève bumped into her partner as he came to a stop. "Come on, Nic." She tried to push him aside before she noticed why he stopped. As she glanced around him, she saw the custodian with her mop. "Didn't we see you the other day in the Annex?"

The custodian looked past Berger and recognized Geneviève peer over his shoulder. "Yes, Detective," Asiya replied.

"Why are you here in the laboratory section, then?" Geneviève asked.

"I go where I'm told," Asiya answered, stepping aside for them to pass.

"Am I missing something?" Berger asked from a few meters away.

Geneviève shook her head, leaving the custodian behind in the hallway. "It's nothing," she replied, shaking her head. "I'm just being paranoid again."

"It wouldn't be the first time," Berger muttered under his breath.

As the detectives reached their office, Captain Lemieux held the door open, waiting for them to sit down. "This shouldn't come as a surprise."

"What is it?" Berger asked.

Lemieux straightened up in his chair, and glanced back and forth at each officer. "I've been asked to take a leave of absence," he said. "Captain Duval has noted my personal life is giving others cause for concern," he added without going into details. "Effective tomorrow, you'll include him on all your reports."

"How long will you be gone?" Geneviève asked.

"Two weeks... three at the most," Lemieux replied. "With Masson back from training, I'll expect you both to bring him up to speed on what's been happening."

"We won't let you down, Captain," Berger said.

Chapter THIRTEEN

The drive from the station to the docks took longer than usual. Between the protesters and crush of summer tourist activities, navigating the streets for police had become more of a chore. And the snail's pace of the tour buses wore on the normally calm Detective Berger.

"I'll never understand why the district can't get the bypass built for these damn caravans," Berger exclaimed. "Thank God I'm not trying to get to Francine's apartment to pick her up."

Geneviève smiled inwardly as she heard Berger mention his companion. "And how are things going for you two?" she asked.

Berger stole a glance at Geneviève as the light changed, letting them enter the dock's secure zone. Without shifting his attention, he answered, "Things are fine," as he slowed for a bus. "We're learning how not to agitate each other while on a date," he chuckled.

Geneviève smiled. She and Francine had spoken the other day when the technician let her know Nicolas's plan for their weekend trip to Lyon. "Sounds like you might have a steady woman on your hands, Nic," she said. Staring out the window, Geneviève caught sight of the Papillion freighter. "Just ahead, Pier 17," she gestured.

While Berger and Benoit made their way to the docks, the captain of *Joan of Arc* and the vessel's owner met onboard the freighter. The two men were discussing the next port-of-call.

"I thought we were with drugs and were trying to become a legitimate operation?" Marcel Dumont asked. "But this trip to Izmir? It's not our usual port to load cargo at. And what of Ahmet and his people? Is our relationship with them over or do they plan on moving across Turkey just for us?"

Gregory Arsenault looked at his friend. The deal he struck with Claudio Carbone to pass along information came with a price. "I've already contacted Ahmet and explained our situation," he began. "I still plan on doing business through Istanbul; we just need to add one stop on this trip to pay off the Carbone family."

"What?"

"The information which would force Nazim's hand went through, Claudio," Gregory replied. "Then, I made an anonymous call to the police about armed men trying to free a prisoner at Chateau Il d'If." He paused to take a drink. "The only problem was the police didn't kill or capture Nazim during the attempt to free his cousin, Hakim."

Marcel glanced at the nautical map on his cabin wall. "So, you're telling me I'm adding 400 kilometers to a voyage because you want to rid yourself of Nazim Aziz?"

Gregory looked at the freighter's captain before he replied. "It has to be done," he said. "If not, we risked being found out by the police."

A sharp rap on the cabin door disturbed Captain Dumont before he could speak. Both men looked to the noise as Marcel answered, "Enter."

A sailor stepped into the room. "My apologies, Captain, but Mister Huet needs you on deck. Seems the police are here and want to ask more questions," he said before backing into the passageway.

Dumont looked at his friend. "Any ideas why they came back?"

Gregory shook his head somewhat. "No. You're clean though, right?"

"Until we arrive in Izmir, we are," Dumont answered, grabbing his hat before he and Gregory left the cabin.

Detective Berger stood off to one side of the ship's quarterdeck as he waited for Captain Dumont's arrival. First Officer Huet leaned against the rail, his Cuban cigar clenched in his teeth. Geneviève paced the deck and watched deckhands work on one of the freighter's cranes.

The squeal of protesting metal caused everyone on deck to look towards the cause of the noise. Marcel Dumont stepped into the afternoon sun, and made his way to Huet and the detectives. "What is it, Anton?"

"This is Detective Berger," Anton replied, motioning towards Nicolas. "And this is Detective Benoit," with a nod to the lone woman. "They've come back to discuss our relationship with the owner, Monsieur Richelieu."

"Good afternoon, Detective." Marcel offered his hand to Berger. "What do you need to know?"

Berger glanced at Geneviève before looking back at the Captain and shook his hand. "Good afternoon, sir. We're investigating several instances of drug trafficking which originated here in Marseille and this vessel's possible involvement."

Marcel stood before Berger, his posture and demeanor reflecting a confident man. "I see," he replied. The captain pulled a cigar and lighter from his shirt. Taking his time to light the end, he sent a cloud of blueish-grey smoke skyward. "And you've evidence of this and where it happened?"

Geneviève heard Dumont's response and stepped forward to join the conversation. "This ship made a port call in England where several people died from drug overdoses. Scotland Yard linked those deaths to a crewman under your command," she stressed as she stepped before the captain. Above the deck, Gregory Arsenault listened from the shadow of the bridge.

"If the British authorities had such concerns, why don't they conduct this inquiry, then?" Marcel asked with a draw on the cigar, its end sizzling aglow. As he exhaled, the captain continued. "And if one of my crew were involved, what's his name? I'll be more than happy to hand the guilty party over to you, Detective." Dumont took another drag on his cigar.

"His name was Ochoa. And we're here as part…." Geneviève began before Berger cut her off.

Huet pushed off the rail, his full attention turned toward the detectives when he heard the former crewman's name. The erstwhile engineer, Guillermo Ochoa, had caused the freighter's delay in Hamburg when he instigated a fight with several dockworkers.

"Captain, as part of the investigation Detective Benoit alluded to, we're here to request your help in contacting the owners, not just a single person," Berger said. "We'd like to discuss the firm's dealings with several entities, here in Marseille and abroad."

"Any communication with ownership is done by telex and courier," Dumont answered. "I've rarely seen anyone from the board of directors, much less the owner themselves," he lied with ease.

"Then how do you receive your orders or pay the men under your command?" Benoit asked as she rejoined the conversation.

"Like most businesses these days, we're provided documentation via courier or payment electronically from the banks," Huet answered for his captain. "What with pirates plying the north coast of Africa, it'd be foolish to carry any sum of cash onboard."

Twenty minutes passed while Dumont and Berger sparred over the former's way of getting contacted by the owners. Berger fought to keep his demeanor calm as the captain gave vague answers to each question.

While the conversation progressed, Gregory Arsenault made his way to the main deck. Nearing the outer hatch, Dumont's cigar smoke wafted inside. Gregory stepped onto the deck behind Captain Dumont and his first officer. "Can I be of any help, Marcel?"

Dumont and Huet exchanged glances as they fought off surprised looks as their boss appeared unexpectedly.

"And you are?" Detective Berger asked as he glanced toward the man walking towards them.

"Monsieur Arsenault," Gregory replied, his hand extended.

Geneviève came to Berger's side, as she stared at the gentleman who joined their conversation. He was well dressed, which led her to guess he wasn't a member of the crew. The Frenchman didn't look nervous, not like the crewmen she interviewed the other day.

"What business do you have with this vessel?" Berger asked.

"I'm a commodities broker," Arsenault replied. "I work with several of the local businesses using the shipping firm," he added. "I can assure you these vessels are brokered to handle legitimate cargo between here and ports in the Mediterranean."

Geneviève stepped in front of Arsenault, coming between him and the vessel's captain. "And how can you prove this?" she queried. "Do you have the means to control precisely what Captain Dumont does on Papillion Transport's behalf?"

"Detective, all I'm saying is this freighter and its sister ships are hired to handle material shipped in this region," the head of Papillion answered. "And of course, I can produce the necessary paperwork to show each transaction I have brokered for you."

Geneviève stared back at him. *Confident, but not cocky or arrogant*, she thought. "I'm sure you'll be given a chance to do just that Monsieur Arsenault," she quipped while she glanced at her partner. "Detective Berger, I'd say we're done for now. Gentlemen, have a pleasant afternoon," she said before striding towards the gangway that led down to the pier.

Berger closed his notebook. "Once a woman makes up her mind…" he muttered to himself. "Captain Dumont, Monsieur Arsenault, we'll be in touch later this week." Stepping to the side, he lumbered down the gangway until he stood next to Geneviève on the dock.

"So, you're satisfied they have nothing to hide?"

Geneviève looked up at the freighter, spied the men watching them from above. "They're not telling the truth, Nic. Especially the fellow Arsenault," she replied. "I can't put my finger on it, but he's definitely hiding something." She paced back and forth a few steps. "And did you see their reactions when I mentioned Ochoa's name?"

"Your years of experience tell you this?" Berger joked. "We can't go to the magistrate and demand a summons on your feminine intuition, you know. And yes, I saw their reaction, but what made you mention him in the first place?"

"Scotland Yard identified Ochoa in Portsmouth and the German police had him in custody. And each time, this freighter was in port. But Captain Dumont didn't report him missing. Why not?" Geneviève asked.

As the detectives stood on the dock having their conversation, Gregory Arsenault stepped away from the rail before he addressed Dumont. "Marcel, I want you to be as courteous to the police as possible while in port," he said.

"Why?"

"You heard. They know Ochoa was onboard when we were in England," Huet said as he voiced his own concern. "What if he's their source about the drug shipments?"

A mischievous smile came to Gregory's face. "I've a plan to have the police help put pressure on Nazim Aziz and Amed Gilles," he declared. "And that female detective is going to be the one who helps."

"Don't you think it's dangerous letting them know your identity?" This time it was Dumont asking the question.

"Maybe," Gregory replied. "But I'll see that it's only me they look in to. Marcel, wait twenty minutes or so, then call my cell phone. It'll give me an excuse to leave them without looking suspicious," he added as he stepped down the gangway.

"All right, I'll give you twenty minutes," Dumont replied.

Glancing up from the dock, Geneviève noticed Gregory Arsenault make his way towards them. "We've got company," she said with a thumb upward. "What do you think he wants to talk about now?"

"Don't know, but I'm willing to listen."

"I'm glad you haven't left, Detectives," Arsenault began as he walked up to the officers. "I wanted to mention something before, but not in front of Captain Dumont and his men."

"And what might that be?" Geneviève asked.

Gregory Arsenault reached into his coat, pulling out his wallet. "Several months ago, actually it was around the beginning of April, I was approached by this gentleman." He handed a worn-out business card to the detectives. The name read *Louis Remesy.*

Detective Berger took the card and read the name before he handed it to Geneviève. "What about him?"

The name of the suspected drug trafficker on the card lifted the detective's spirits. "You've met this man?" Geneviève asked.

"Yes, just once though," Arsenault answered. "My first contact was by phone. During the call, he asked about ports the freighters could be expected to visit," Arsenault began. "He specifically asked about ports outside the Med. He wished to have cargo transported from the Moroccan port of Rabat to Naples."

"And what makes this man stand out?" Berger asked.

"I'm a businessman in the market to make as much money as possible, you understand," Arsenault answered. "But even I can tell when a transaction has the look of something illicit. During our meeting, he offered an additional €100,000 in exchange for my guarantee to transport his cargo without questions being asked."

"What did this man look like? How was he dressed, his demeanor…?" Geneviève probed, wanting to know more.

Gregory was right in thinking the female detective would be the key to have the police take up the task of hunting down his former partner, Nazim Aziz. He also could see she'd be just as enthusiastic in her effort to hunt down Amed Gilles and his gang members. But only if he played his cards right and not force her into something too quick in his haste for vengeance.

"We met face-to-face in April after the call," Gregory replied. "I'd say he looked like any other businessman; not dressed too fancy, nor plain in his appearance. But he did look preoccupied with another matter though while we discussed our business."

"Really? In what manner?" Berger asked.

"He kept checking his cell phone. Almost like he expected another call," Arsenault answered. "And after we were done, he asked how to get to the La Castellane district to meet someone. It seemed to me he didn't know his way around Marseille."

The detectives exchanged looks as the head of Papillion Transport discussed the encounter. "Do you mind if we keep this?" Berger asked as took he the business card back from Geneviève.

"No, not at all, Officer," Gregory replied. "I'm sure I won't have a need for it anytime soon," he added. "But if he were to contact me again, how can I contact you?"

"Of course," Berger said, handing over his own business card. "You can reach our office at this number."

It wasn't lost on Berger that Geneviève's demeanor changed when she read the name on the business card. He could see her focus return and she was more attentive when Arsenault talked.

"And how can we contact you if we have further questions?" Geneviève asked.

Gregory reached back into his pocket and handed over his card. "I can be reached at this number during the hours listed."

"You don't have a business address?"

"No, I work from my residence," Arsenault answered.

"Why do you work from your home and not an office?" Geneviève asked.

"I'm an independent broker, Detective Benoit. I work with several of the shipping firms, not just the one affiliated with this freighter."

"If that's the case, how can you provide proof of the freighters' voyages and cargo?"

Gregory paused and smiled briefly. "I keep very good records of each transaction I'm involved in," he answered. "It's my insurance policy in the event a company withholds my fees." Just then, his cell phone began to ring. "If you'll excuse me." He took the call and walked away from the officers.

Berger and Benoit both nodded and walked back to their police car. Nicolas glanced at Geneviève and could tell she was contemplating how to use the information they just learned. As they reached the car, he leaned against the fender.

"Okay, so what are you thinking?"

Geneviève looked over her shoulder at the freighter, the deckhands still clamoring about the deck and forward crane. As she turned back to Berger, she paused before she answered. "Arsenault wanted us to know something, but not what the freighter was involved in," she began. "And it was somewhat convenient it was information on the drug trafficker we're investigating."

Berger scratched his head. "I'd agree with you, but how'd he know?"

"Know what?" Geneviève asked.

"That we're looking for this Remesy guy," Berger replied. "It's not like we announced our visit to the freighter today. If anything, I'd consider this guy a suspect as well just because he had contact with the drug trafficker."

Geneviève scuffed her foot in the gravel. “Let’s say, for the moment, he’s a legitimate broker, though. How would you act on the information he gave us about Remesy?”

Berger chuckled at the question. “What information did he provide that we don’t already have? We know Remesy is a suspected drug trafficker based on previous information. And it was confirmed by your friend with the Algerian police the other day.” Berger pulled open the door to the patrol car. “I’m not sure Arsenault’s being truthful about the freighter either. How does he know what they do after cargo is loaded and they’re out to sea, hmm?”

Geneviève leaned on the car, her head resting against the rooftop. “He wanted us to know something more than that, though; I could see it in his eyes, Nic,” she uttered. Geneviève spun around and gazed toward the freighter, frustrated at the fact they’d been given clues, but no direction which led to a conclusion.

Chapter FOURTEEN

"What were you thinking, Gregory?" The question came from Arsenault's friend and colleague of Papillion Transport as the men sat in the office. Louis Clement had sat quietly at the conference room table while Gregory retold the encounter with the detectives onboard the *Joan of Arc*. The information nearly floored Louis as he found out Gregory not only addressed the officers by his proper name, he also gave them the alias of their former partner.

The head of Papillion leaned against his desk, a confident look on his face. "I'm sure Claire could eliminate any records leading to anyone associated with Papillion," Gregory replied. His sister-in-law's position with the police had proven useful in the past. So long as he took care with what he asked Claire to undertake. "I figured with the problems we're having with the Maghrebi gangs; it couldn't hurt to have the police look for Aziz."

Louis sat, head in hand for a very long minute. "You've placed a target on each of our backs, you know that, don't you?" insinuated as he looked at his friend. "If the police questioned the freighter crew, anyone they contact is now a suspect. And that now includes you."

Gregory shook his head. "I don't see it as a problem," he answered. "If anything, I gained an ally in this, Detective Benoit."

Louis stood and paced in front of the window. "You're playing a dangerous game Gregory," he said. "What if the police tailed you? Have you considered the risk you've put us all in?"

Gregory sat at his desk, and listened. He knew the risk and the consequences. What he wouldn't tell his friend was the greater fear for his family, not just the business. "Louis, I won't sit here and try to get you to not worry or have reservations," he said. "I need you to be the voice of reason. You're the one to keep me in check and avoid from going too far."

"So, you don't think you've gone too far with this?" Louis asked.

"Not with what I told the police," Gregory said. "Besides, this policewoman confirmed what we suspected about Ochoa being an informant. Between the British and German authorities detaining him, then he shows up here in Marseille at their headquarters..."

"So, Hector and Pasqual were right when they saw him get taken away?" Louis asked. "Did Claire provide any clue on why Ochoa was detained and then released?"

Before Gregory could answer his friend, the cell phone on his desk rang. A frown gathered on his face as he saw the number. "It's Phillip," before he answered.

On the second ring, Phillip Gaston heard the familiar voice reply to his call. "Monsieur Arsenault, I'm glad you're available," he uttered and took a drag on his cigarette. "I've troubling news to tell you."

The look on Gregory's face told Louis there was something wrong with the Julien LeBlanc's cousin. Phillip was asked to watch over Gregory's niece after she went into hiding in Toulon.

The tone in Phillip's voice caused Gregory to imagine scenarios where his niece might be in trouble. "I'm glad you called when you did Phillip; so, what trouble has Sophia gotten herself into, heh?"

"She's not in trouble," Phillip said as he spied the men sitting outside a restaurant in Toulon. "But for the last three days, I've noticed the same two men come to the pizzeria. And I overheard one server talk with Monsieur Moscone about them. Seems they showed him a picture of Sophia and wanted to know when she would return to work."

"And where is Sophia right now?" Gregory asked.

The young Frenchman coughed slightly as the acrid smoke stung his throat. "She and her friend Celine traveled to Nice for a few days," Phillip answered. "I'm to pick them up later this evening."

While the conversation between Gregory and Phillip continued, the latter offered a detailed description of the two men. The thin one shifted in his chair until his stare caught Phillip. Turning to his companion, the first one sipped his coffee before he spoke. "Who do you think he's talking with?"

"We'll find out soon enough," the second man replied, his smile revealing a crude gold tooth. Under the rumbled coat, the hilt of his knife dug into the second man's burgeoning stomach.

"Phillip, when you pick up Sophia, I want you to bring her back to Marseille, do you understand?" Gregory asked. The men's description gave him the sense Amed Gilles had somehow learned about Claire's daughter and planned to abduct her, if not do something far worse.

"Oui, Monsieur," Phillip replied. "And what about the apartment?"

"I'll see it's looked after," Gregory said. "When you leave Toulon, don't stop for anything. You're to make your way back to my chateau without hesitation, understand?"

This last statement caused Louis to sit up in his chair. Trouble was coming to them and soon. The final part of the conversation Gregory gave Phillip the address to his chateau in the St. Julien quarter of the city. Glancing at his friend, Louis queried him on the call. "How bad is the trouble for Phillip?"

Gregory glanced over at Louis. "It's not Phillip, it's Sophia." He spent the next few minutes to recall what Phillip told him about the men. "Seems Gilles is showing his hand that he knows more about Claire than I gave him credit for," he added. As he paced the room, Gregory stopped and glanced out the window. "Have we heard from Hector? He should have met up with Romain by now."

Louis grinned. "I got a text from Hector. So, I called him. When we spoke, he let me know about a situation they had encountered," he said. "It appears some of Amed's men were followed him and Pasqual, so they stopped at the police station and filed a complaint. It wasn't long after they left the station a patrol car pulled over their tail and was searching the car."

"Clever ploy on their part," Gregory said.

"Anyway, he and Pasqual met Romain and continued to the equestrian center. Elise had everything staged and was ready for them when they arrived," Louis said. "Hector also mentioned they discussed this Benoit woman had arrested one of Amed punks."

Gregory looked over at his friend as he answered. "She's a busy one, isn't she?"

Benoit and Berger returned from the docks and made their way into the station where they found Francine at the front desk. Down the hall, Geneviève spied Claude and Dr. Beringer in conversation.

"What do you think they're talking about?" Benoit asked.

Detective Berger looked in their direction. "I'm not sure. But it's probably safe to say it's not about dinner reservations."

Geneviève made her way past the couple and took the stairs to the detective's office. In a huff, she collapsed in her chair, eyes closed until the vision of Gregory Arsenault came into focus. "What are you trying to tell us?" she muttered. She used her fingers like a comb through her hair, and tugged the band free which held it, then let it fall freely over her shoulders. With the band kept taunt, Geneviève twirled her fingers around, lost in thought.

The clatter of a trash bin dropping startled Geneviève from her thoughts. As she bolted upright, she saw a custodian hunched over, pulling something from their cart. What Geneviève didn't notice was the digital camera the woman took from a box on the bottom shelf. "What are you doing there?"

The temptation of €500 was too much for the woman associated with the Maghrebis gangs. The word had spread amongst other custodians' information on the detectives, especially Geneviève, would result in the generous reward. Seizing the chance between day and evening shifts, the woman only saw the reward, but not the risks. The voice of Geneviève caught the custodian by surprise, causing her to drop the small camera to the floor.

Geneviève pushed herself away from the desk and stood behind the woman. "I asked you a question," she declared. "Why are you in this area?"

The custodian turned and faced the detective. *She's not some giant*, the woman told herself as she took in the Geneviève's appearances. "I'm doing my tasks, that's all," she answered.

Geneviève glanced down and spied a portion of the camera under the cart. "And what are you doing with this then?" She reached past the woman and grabbed the Olympus off the floor. "Give me your identification," Geneviève demanded as she turned to pick up the phone.

In a panic, the custodian saw a chance to leave when Geneviève turned her back. So, without considering where she was, the custodian placed the cart between herself and Geneviève as she stepped into the hallway.

Before she had a chance to call the desk sergeant, Geneviève sensed the custodian move. In moments, she was pursuing the woman out of the detective's office towards the stairwell.

Detective Pierre Juneau had just stepped out of the elevator when he caught sight of Geneviève take down a woman who wore a custodian's uniform. "What the hell's going on here, Benoit?" he shouted.

Geneviève turned to her fellow officer as she snugged the handcuffs closed. "I caught this woman with a camera in our office space," she replied as she brushed back her hair. With a hand on one arm, she drugged the custodian back to the office, and placed her into an empty chair. "This is what she dropped earlier." She picked up the camera and grabbed the phone off her desk to contact the desk sergeant to alert him on the situation.

Detective Juneau looked at the woman and back at Benoit. "Where's her identification badge? She should have it displayed for everyone to see," he asked. "What did you do with your badge?"

Geneviève nudged the woman's shoulder. "Answer the officer."

"Go to hell," the woman uttered quietly in Algerian.

Geneviève shook her head. "Did you understand what she said?" she asked with a glance at her fellow officer.

Pierre Juneau had suspicions on what the woman said, but didn't tell Geneviève. "No, I don't speak Arabic," he answered. Juneau squatted down to face the woman, and spoke in a clear, even tone. "Your replies need to be understood by us, so answer the question either in French or English, please."

"I must have forgotten it at home," the woman answered with her head tilted forward.

The detectives spent the next hour trying to determine the woman's identity and motive for having a camera in a restricted area of the Marseille police station. Meanwhile in Toulon, in the fading light of the September evening, a young Frenchman paced the sidewalk outside the train station.

After his talk with Gregory, Phillip Gaston drove a circuitous route to the station from the pizzeria where he and Sophia Dubois worked. The extra few kilometers he added were just to avoid the men he saw earlier from following him. Now he stood and waited amongst a handful of commuters and travelers for the TGV's arrival.

Sitting in the railcar's comfort, Sophia and her companion Celine didn't realize the dangerous situation awaited them in Toulon. After her uncle's visit, Sophia became extra vigilant, took various routes to and from her apartment, and met Phillip away from the pizzeria only when necessary. Her trip to Nice with Celine was something they'd planned, and she would let nothing deter her from it.

The automated announcement alerted passengers of the rail service of their approach into Toulon. With a sigh, each woman stood and grabbed their bags from the overhead bins and headed toward the exit.

"I wish you could come back to Marseille with me," Celine expressed as she lay her head on Sophia's shoulder.

The train slowed until it stopped with a jolt. "Trust me, I want to come back, but my uncle thought it'd be best to be away for a while," Sophia answered with a kiss on Celine's forehead. "Hopefully, all the dealings my uncle has will settle down and we can get back together. At least we've got tonight and tomorrow for each other," as she wrapped an arm around Celine's waist.

With a whoosh of air, the doors slid open, which allowed harried travelers to disembark. The women joined the throng heading toward the exits. Phillip stood off to the side as patrons pushed their way through the turnstiles. Near the back of a group of commuters, he spied Sophia and her girlfriend and with a shout and a wave, he caught their attention.

"There's Phillip," Sophia declared, guiding Celine toward the exit. Nearing the young man, she continued. "You're never late, are you, Phillip? Such a gentleman," she said with a laugh. "Celine, this is Phillip Gaston."

A slight flush came to Phillip's face at the compliment. "It's nice to meet you," he started with a gentle shake of Celine's hand. "I'm sorry to say, but we've got to get on the road now."

Sophia's brow furrowed, puzzled to hear Phillip's declaration. "And why are we *'hitting the road'* when we just got here?" she asked.

"I'll explain in the car," Phillip said as he took their bags. "Come on, it's over in this area." As Sophia and Celine exchanged glances, they hurried after Phillip who came upon a rather new Volvo.

"Where did you get this car?" Sophia asked.

"I've been saving my wages," Phillip said, closing the trunk before he opened the passenger-side doors for the women. "I wasn't doing anything else with my money, was I?"

As he slipped behind the wheel, Phillip pulled out his phone and prepared a short text to his cousin. After he hit send, he started the car and pulled out of the parking area for the expressway. Every few minutes, he glanced in the mirror, to confirm they weren't being followed.

"So, where are we headed?" Sophia asked.

"To your uncle's in Marseille," Phillip replied. Over the next few minutes, he explained the situation and the men at the pizzeria. He also mentioned the change in the manager's demeanor when he learned Giuseppe Ricci, the pizzeria's owner, was arrested in Marseille.

"And what about my mother?" Sophia asked. "Did my uncle mention anything about her?"

"No, he didn't," Phillip answered as he glanced in the mirror again. "We'll be in Marseille in a few hours and you can ask him those questions yourself. Until then, sit back, relax, and let me concentrate on driving," he said, displaying a renewed confidence in front of the women.

Chapter FIFTEEN

"Now, with a deep cleansing breath, we'll transition from *Marichi* to *Savasana*," the female Yogi's faint whisper emanated through the speaker. The apartment was dark except for a single candle. The flame cast shadows across the wall while a solitary figure drifted from one position to another. It had been the same stress relieving ritual Geneviève followed each night since her early days after the police academy.

As the timer on her phone counted down, Geneviève raised her arms, and took the deep cleansing breath. The scent of musk filled the room as she exhaled just before the chime on her phone sounded. Rolling up from the floor, she walked over to the end table and silenced the alarm before she grabbed her towel.

Geneviève's muted steps echoed in the kitchen. A Styrofoam container of Thai food greeted her as she opened the refrigerator and pulled a liter jug of water from the shelf. "Guess it'll be leftovers again," she muttered.

Back in the front room, she grabbed the stereo remote and selected her meditation playlist. She opened the container, stabbing the noodles, and spun her fork until it couldn't hold any more threads of wheat. After a few bites of bitter vegetables and shrimp, she chased it with a swig of water.

Soon, she was being serenaded by instrumental music as she sat back on her floor mat. As she assumed the *Padmasana* or Lotus Pose, Geneviève closed her eyes and took in another deep breath.

In quiet reflection, her thoughts led her back to the custodian and the photos on the camera she was carrying. Nearly all of them were of her, Nicolas, and Captain Lemieux. The custodial imposter took each one while they were in the station over a three-week period. One image included the moment she and Lemieux stood outside of interrogation while Officer Neuville led his dog in the open door.

The shrill of her timer broke Geneviève's concentration. Releasing her legs, she stretched forward one last time before getting to her feet. As she sat on her sofa, she took a long drink of water, while reflected on the purpose behind the custodian's actions.

While Geneviève pondered the day's events, a car pulled off the expressway near the Saint Julien quarter of Marseille. In the eastern foothills of the city, Phillip Gaston drove to the entrance Gregory Arsenault's chateau. With a light nudge on his passenger's shoulder, he announced their arrival. "Sophia, we're here."

The young woman rubbed her eyes and glanced into the backseat where her companion sat curled up, still asleep. Sophia reached out, giving a gentle tug on Celine's sweater to stir the other woman. "Celine, wake up; we're here."

Phillip looked back in the car as Sophia and Celine grabbed their bags. No sooner did he turn away then a voice came over the intercom. "Who is it?" the man's voice asked.

"Monsieur, it's Phillip," the young man replied into the speaker. The loud clack of a bolt being slid announced the opening of the gate. While the gate swung open, he returned to the car and pulled into the courtyard.

"Where are we?" Sophia asked.

Phillip glanced at her, then Celine, before he answered. "This is your uncle's home." He turned off the engine and got out, walking to the trunk. The women's luggage was pulled out before they walked toward the entry to the house.

Sophia Dubois had never been to her uncle's home before tonight. But to see it now gave her a sense of pride knowing he'd created a normal setting for himself. "Who would have thought he could have something so elegant?" she stated behind Phillip's back.

"How can he afford something like this?" Celine asked as she walked alongside Sophia.

"It's better for you not know," Sophia replied, squeezing her girlfriend's hand.

Just as Phillip approached the entryway, Gregory's current companion opened the door. "You must be Phillip?" Giselle greeted the trio. "And you're Sophia."

Phillip stood in awe of the woman who stood in the doorway. The former track star for the French Olympic squad still kept her figure, though she no longer competed in events. While the segment of Giselle's legs showing from beneath her skirt were lean and muscular, her shoulders were defined but not bulky from continued training.

"And your friend's name?" Giselle asked.

"Oh, I'm sorry. This is Celine," Sophia replied as she motioned towards her lover.

Before an awkward moment could take place, Gregory emerged from the back room and met his guests. "Phillip, it's good to see you again," he started, taking one bag from the young man. "And Sophia," Gregory wrapped his free arm around her and pressed a kiss to her forehead, "it's good to have you back as well." Gregory stepped, and spied Celine standing to Sophia's right. "And you are Celine, aren't you?" Gregory recalled having a talk with Sophia's mother about her daughter's choice for companionship.

Without making eye contact with Gregory, the petite woman nodded.

"It's good to be amongst friends again," Phillip replied, letting the women enter the chateau before he did. "Where can I put these?" he asked as he lifted the bags in his hands.

"In the spare room; Giselle will show you where," Gregory said. "After that, come into the study. There's much for us to discuss." He led Sophia and Celine towards the back of the home.

The women entered the study behind Gregory, who motioned for them to relax. "Please make yourselves comfortable. Would you like some wine?" he offered. "Or maybe something else?"

As she took her place on the sofa, Sophia posed her first question. "What is this all about, Gregory?" she queried while Celine sat at her side.

Before he could answer, Giselle and Phillip entered the room, with the woman taking her seat next to Gregory. "Phillip, something to drink?" Gregory offered again.

"No, thank you. I'm fine."

Sophia stared back at her uncle. "Well? What made you have Phillip bring me back to Marseille?"

Gregory poured himself a glass of wine before he sat next to Giselle. As he took a sip, he looked into the eyes of his niece, wondering where or how to explain her mother was in danger. And with Phillip bringing the two men in Toulon to his attention who asked about Sophia, she was likely now in danger too.

"I'm not going to lie to you, Sophia," Gregory began, "but let me finish what I have to say before you ask questions." Taking another drink, he placed the glass down and began telling his niece and her companion what he knew.

"After you left for Toulon, I had information passed to Nazim Aziz in the hopes the police would arrest him. Somehow, a gang leader here in Marseille became involved and found out about me and is blackmailing me for information," Gregory explained. "And he's using threats against your mother for the information."

As Gregory explained his plight to Sophia, Celine, and Phillip about Amed Gilles and his demands at the chateau, each began to understand his concern. Across the city though, Detective Pierre Juneau had just completed the arrest report on the woman impersonating one of the custodians at the police station.

Pierre sent the report to the printer. While the machine buzzed and hummed, the detective looked through the images from the woman's camera. All but two of the pictures were of his fellow officers: Geneviève Benoit, Nicolas Berger, and their captain, Claude Lemieux.

"What do we have on these?" he muttered, selecting the second from last image. As it appeared on his computer, it displayed a female officer smoking behind the station. "What's your name, Sergeant?"

Detective Juneau tagged the last image. It was the same sergeant exiting a sedan outside the police station. "Who's driving the car?" he asked as he enlarged the picture. Any hope of gaining clarity was lost as the photo blurred with each increase in size.

"Any luck?"

Detective Juneau was caught off guard by the question. Glancing up, he saw Detective Benoit lean against the door frame of the office. "What the hell are you doing here?"

Geneviève pulled out the chair from her desk and sat. "I couldn't sleep," she said. "Between the run in with the custodian and the mystery gentleman from the freighter, my mind wouldn't shut off."

"Well, the custodian was a plant," the detective stated. "Someone paid off someone else to have her roam the halls," Juneau added. "The firm under contract for cleaning the police stations has no information on her. She'll be turned over to immigration services tomorrow where they'll prepare her for deportation back to Tripoli." He handed her the print-out of the report. "Want some coffee?" he asked as he held up the half-full pot.

"No thanks," Geneviève replied without looking up from the report. "And the images? They were all of me, Nic, and the captain, right?"

Juneau sat back in his chair. "All but the last two. Or the first two depending on when the photos were being taken." He swiveled his screen in Geneviève's direction. "They're of a female officer, a sergeant. I think the custodian took them to see if she could use the camera without getting caught."

Geneviève studied the first image. Even though the facial features were not clear, she sensed she'd seen the officer before. "I think I've bumped into this officer before," she declared. "What about the other image?"

Detective Juneau slid his mouse over the file name and opened it. "How's that?"

"Good," Geneviève answered, looking at the policewoman stand next to a Peugeot sedan. "Too bad we can't see the driver or the vehicle plates," she muttered.

"So, who do you think she is?"

Geneviève sat back in her chair and put her hands behind her head, her eyes closed. As she thought, Geneviève twisted and pulled at her hair until it was a tight braid against her scalp. "I'm thinking it might be a sergeant who works in Records," as she answered the question.

"Damn, if I can't figure out how you woman can do that to your hair," Juneau chuckled. Turning his computer screen around, the detective his search of staff records. "So, you think it might be a sergeant from Records, do you?" He scrolled through the department files and came upon the Records staff listing. "There's three sergeants assigned to the department. Aucoin, Dubois, and Vannelli."

"It's Dubois," Geneviève replied without hesitation. "I've bumped into her, oh, at least four separate times. And her profile fits the images."

"Okay, then. What does a woman impersonating a custodian want with pictures of a policewoman working in Records?" Juneau asked.

"Information on a person who's being detained, maybe," Geneviève speculated. Grabbing a rubber band from her drawer, she spun and twisted the end of her braid, capturing the few loose ends.

"What about blackmail?" Detective Juneau asked.

"Maybe… but to what end? Sure, she has access to information, but what sort of information would someone want?" Benoit asked. "Can you access the sergeant's records… her personnel information?"

"What are you thinking?"

Geneviève pulled open her drawer and rifled through the old notebooks stacked inside in a haphazard fashion. "Where is the one from June?" she muttered under her breath. As she piled a handful onto her desk, Geneviève found what she was looking for near the bottom. She flipped through her notes, and stopped halfway through her search.

"What're you looking for?"

Geneviève glanced up from the notebook. "I make notes when something doesn't appear or seem right. This sergeant… I nearly ran her over in the hall one day. She ended up dropping the files she was carrying," Geneviève said as she skimmed through her notes. "But I saw one was sealed, a court file on a suspect Captain Lemieux and I had just arrested. "Can you look for booking information on a Phillip Gaston?"

Detective Juneau searched records of past individuals booked into the station. "Nothing. I've got nothing under that person's name," the officer said as each try came back empty. "Do you think they affiliate your suspect with this woman?"

"No, not Remesy," Geneviève said. "But it could be the person the custodian was working for though. And the sergeant has information or access to it which would be useful to most any felon."

"What about the man you met today?"

The woman drummed her fingers. "Did you get the sergeant's files open? Who's her family, known associates…?"

Detective Juneau looked at his fellow officer. "You know doing this goes against policy, right?" he reminded her as he waited for the computer to finish its search. "Reading into a fellow officer without authorization makes it look like a witch hunt."

"All I'm interested in is if the sergeant has any family members."

The computer screen flashed a warning as Detective Juneau selected the file on Sergeant Claire Dubois from Personnel Records. "Here we go."

Geneviève came around the desk and peered over Juneau's shoulder. "Shows her husband died in a car accident. One dependent, a daughter, Sophia Marie. Too bad we don't have photos to compare with what we got from the custodian," she added.

"So, now what do you want to do?" Juneau asked, looking up at Geneviève.

Glancing up at the clock, Geneviève suppressed a yawn. "I've a few hours before my shift begins, so finding a quiet place to curl up and nap isn't out of the question," she replied. "It'll give me a chance to consider how to explain my suspicions to Captain Duval." She grabbed her phone from the desk, walked over to the small conference room, pulled a few chairs together, and was soon fast asleep.

Chapter SIXTEEN

Light pierced the room as Nicolas cracked open the door, and was greeted with his fellow officer's angelic-like appearance curled up on the floor. "Hey you, it's time to go to work," he declared, nudging Geneviève's shoulder. He reached over and yanked on the cord, pulling the shades up and letting in the morning sunlight. The glare lit the room and his partner who'd contorted herself into a ball in the corner.

Geneviève brushed aside a few loose hairs from her face as she yawned. "What time is it?" she asked while going through a slow stretch.

"It's nearly 7 o'clock," Berger replied. "Detective Juneau said you showed up just after midnight. What made you come in at that hour?"

Geneviève leaned against the wall. "I couldn't sleep," she answered. Pushing herself off the floor, she went about explaining to Nicolas about the custodian and the photos. "When you take the fact that Omar Khalid was willing to have Italian mafia abduct me, but failed, it's obvious he's turned to someone else." After a few more stretches, she continued. "Then there's the mysterious caller from the other day. I'm telling you, Nic, something is not right."

"Maybe Captain Duval can tell us something," Berger said. "He's expecting us in his office right now."

"Guess I don't have time for a cup of tea then, do I?"

Berger shook his head. "Not now," he teased, following the woman out of the conference room.

In a few minutes, the detectives were sitting with Captain Duval, who reviewed their current cases. "It appears in the last week or so, you've become the focus of the city's less desirable again, Detective Benoit," the senior officer stated. "You not only stumbled across the abduction of a fellow officer, but you're someone's center of attention after receiving the anonymous phone call."

"I'm not sure it all has to do with me," Benoit replied.

Berger shifted his gaze from Geneviève to the senior officer. "Captain, what evidence do we have which suggest someone's fixated on Detective Benoit?" he asked. "It's not like she was the one meeting Officer Galant; that was Officer LeBeau."

Captain Duval closed the file and leaned forward onto his desk. "All the cases over the last several months have involved Detective Benoit," he spoke as he nodded in Geneviève's direction.

"From the attempted assault in Algiers, the Italian's surveillance attempts... they're all focused on Benoit," Duval spoke. "And some incidents were rather direct, while others, not so much. But she's still involved." He tapped a finger on the folder. "And now, there's a breach of security in the building, what with the woman filming you two and Claude."

Geneviève placed her hand over her mouth as she suppressed a yawn. "So, where do you want us to go from here, Captain? We've leads on several cases which need to be pursued, and we can't do that from our desks," she said.

"I know, Detective," Duval replied. "It's why Superintendent Chevallier has authorized a uniformed patrol to accompany you on all future investigations until we find the person or persons involved."

"Captain, I'm more than capable of taking care of myself," Geneviève protested "The last thing I need is to place other officers at risk by following me around all day."

"Until we can solve the issue, you'll follow orders," Duval declared. Pulling another folder from his inbox, he flipped it open. "Now, for today," the captain began. "I'd like you to concentrate on investigating the freighters' parent company and their link to the drug trafficking. We need to show the British we're still working the case. Is that understood?"

"Yes, sir," they replied in unison.

"Then let's get to work shall we," Duval said, dismissing the officers.

With the discussion over, Benoit and Berger left Captain Duval and returned to their own office. "Where is Guy at anyway?" Geneviève asked, noting the absence of Detective Masson.

"He forgot to have someone care for his car and it wouldn't start this morning, so he's on the bus," Berger replied. He sat behind his desk, then looked up at Geneviève before speaking. "Since you and Captain Lemieux started the investigation into the freighters, where do we pick up the pieces now?"

Geneviève pulled open the file cabinet and retrieved the case file for the investigation. "You and Guy found the office spaces vacated last month and we've yet to find their new one. So, that's one piece we need to check," she replied as she shifted through other pages. "And according to the harbormaster's office, they're still loading the freighter at Pier 17. What was the name again?"

"The *Joan of Arc*," Berger replied.

"That's it," Benoit continued, snapping her fingers. "It's here for one more day before it leaves. Which means we've only today to see if the crew has any contact with the company owners."

"If you ask me, and by the way, you haven't, I'd say the ownership angle is a dead end," Berger said. "I'm pretty sure the executives from CMA/CMG or Maersk don't traipse the docks every time their freighters pull into port."

"Are you saying the owners at Papillion Transport have no knowledge of the drug trafficking?"

Berger shook his head. "It's not that; I'm just saying I don't think we'll see anyone in a three-piece suit make a public appearance, that's all," he chuckled.

Geneviève gave her partner a woeful scowl. "But here's something we never noted… not once has there been more than one freighter of the four in port at any one time. Why is that, you suppose?"

"They've got a good scheduler, maybe," Berger replied.

Geneviève's expression changed as a once-elusive thought took hold. "Monsieur Arsenault," she muttered.

"Who?"

"Arsenault, the gentleman from yesterday on the docks."

Before Berger could reply, their fellow detective, Guy Masson entered the office. "I don't know how you can stand riding the bus, Geneviève," Guy exclaimed, putting his backpack down. "Those people can be so rude and unappreciative. What did I miss from Duval's lecture?"

For the next ten minutes, Berger and Benoit took turns recalling the conversation with Captain Duval, which included their own interpretations on where to pick up with the investigation.

As the detectives spent the morning conversing with their captain and amongst themselves, Gregory Arsenault entertained his guests with breakfast at his chateau across town.

As she took a sip of coffee, Sophia looked over at her uncle while he cooked. "How long do I need to hide out here?" she asked.

"Just a few days," he replied. "I've made arrangements for an apartment..."

"Why can't I stay with Celine?" she interrupted.

Gregory brought over their food and set it on the table. "Partly because Celine was under surveillance after you were seen at the hospital," he answered. "The police might return unexpectedly and then you'll be in a position I can't control. Besides, I promised your mother I'd take care of you, and I'm not going to let her down." Before Sophia could reply, Celine entered the kitchen, followed by Giselle.

"Good morning, everyone," Celine announced as she leaned in and kissed Sophia.

Sophia held her companion's hand. "Gregory, do you happen to have tea? Celine doesn't care for coffee, do you?"

Celine eyes narrowed as her nose wrinkled, revealing her answer before she spoke. "I find most coffee is too bitter for me," she squeaked.

Giselle reached up into a cupboard over the stove and handed over a tin. "Here you go. I've collected a few flavors over the last few months." She placed the kettle under the water spigot to fill.

Celine took the tin. "Thank you." As she opened it, she turned back to Sophia. "Did you ask?"

The expression on Sophia's face told Celine what she didn't want to hear as her lover shook her head. "We're guests here for the next few days, isn't that right, *Uncle* Gregory?" The look of displeasure on her face spoke louder than her words.

"But I've got work tomorrow," Celine said. "I can't be expected to commute from here across town. I don't have a car; I don't know the bus routes..."

Gregory put his hand in the air, bringing Celine's concerns to a brief halt. "I'll make arrangements to see you're at work on time for the next few days. I just need to make sure both of you can be on your own without being interfered with, that's all," he assured her as he drank some of his coffee. "Until then, consider it an extension of your holiday."

The three women exchanged glances as Gregory got up from the table. Before anyone could add to the conversation, Phillip came into the kitchen with a towel wrapped around his neck and his brow bathed in beads of sweat.

As he looked about, Phillip could tell from the expressions he'd missed out on something. "Was I not supposed to be here right now?" he asked.

Gregory placed a hand on his shoulder. "Nothing of important for you to worry about Phillip. But when you're ready, you and I need to go meet with your cousin and prepare for a meeting… say, twenty minutes?"

"Oui, Gregory, I'll be ready," Phillip answered.

While Celine, Giselle, and Sophia settled into a day of seclusion at the chateau, Phillip drove through traffic as he and Gregory headed to Papillion Transport's former office.

"You've done well for yourself, Phillip," Gregory said as he padded the dashboard of the Volvo.

"Your friend, Monsieur Ricci, was extremely generous with his wages," Phillip replied as he mentioned the Italian pizzeria owner. "But I can't say the same for his manager, though."

"I got the same impression when I met him, too," Gregory said. "There's the garage you can park in," he added as he pointed out the three-story complex to his right. "Your car will be in good hands, I promise." In the distance, he spotted a police car heading towards them. "You can drop me off here. Here's the address to the office; you can meet me there." He handed a slip of paper to Phillip.

"What's wrong, Gregory?"

"We're not alone," he muttered, pointing out the patrol car approaching them. "Better you're not seen with me," Gregory added. Getting out of Phillip's car, he stood on the corner and watched police, but didn't notice the Algerians study him from outside the garage entrance. As he crossed the street, Gregory took the first set of stairs toward the office building.

Behind Gregory, Amed Gilles gang members made their way out of the parking garage and closed the gap behind him. "Your information is unusually good," Yacine said to his underling. As the men climbed the steps behind Gregory, they did so with caution. Reaching the top, Yacine turned to his companion. "I want you to get ahead of him and we'll catch him outside the office."

While the young Algerian crossed the narrow street and quicken his pace, Yacine matched the stride of the Frenchman, and maintained his distance without losing sight of Arsenault.

As he neared the former offices of Papillion Transport, Gregory began to sense something was amiss. With a glance to his right, he saw a few pedestrians make their way on the opposite side of the road. But one stood out amongst the rest.

Riad had tried to keep a few paces behind the Frenchman so he wouldn't be seen. He was unaware that amongst the other pedestrians on the street, he was the only one wearing a *taqiyah*, the short, rounded skullcap his Muslim faith degreed be worn. As he glanced back across the street, he saw Yacine motion him to draw closer to their intended target.

Gregory approached the corner, slowed his pace and stepped aside for a couple who were walking towards him. His forearm scraped along the buildings' plaster facade, tearing at his skin. Gregory pulled his sleeve up and saw it several minor scratches. He returned his attention to the Algerians and saw both men approach more quickly.

A hundred meters from where Gregory stood, Detective Berger pulled the police car to the curb in front of a non-descript building. "It looks so bland and unassuming, doesn't it?" he muttered as he peered out the window.

"I'm think Captain Duval's concerns are more about me being a woman than a detective," Geneviève said, her frustration manifested as she slammed the car door closed.

Nicolas cringed as he heard his partner speak her mind. Stepping up on the sidewalk, he met her stride as he turned toward her. "I'm sure it's more than you just being a woman. He's looking out for the department as well, you know."

Geneviève only heard what she wanted. A familiar face had come into view as a gentleman rounded the corner, heading toward the officers. "Isn't that Monsieur Arsenault?"

At the same time Benoit and Berger stood outside the entrance for ZIM France SA and where Papillion Transport once conducted business, Gregory Arsenault recognized the detectives.

As calmly as he could, Gregory walked up. "Bon jour, detectives," he exclaimed. "This is an interesting place to be seeing both of you. But since you're here, I'd like to voice a complaint against some men," he began with a glance over his shoulder.

The officers exchanged puzzled looks as Geneviève shook her head. "Excuse me? You want to file a complaint? Against whom?" Both she and Berger looked past Gregory at the other pedestrians. "I'm more interested in knowing why you're here, Monsieur Arsenault. I was under the impression you were an independent broker for Papillion Transport and worked from your residence."

"I hate to be rude, but see those men there," Arsenault said, pointing Yacine and Riad out to the officers. "They assaulted me in the Q-park on *Rue Jean Marc Cathala*."

Berger turned and motioned to the uniformed officers. "We'd like to speak to those two men," he told the senior officer. "They might have been involved with an attempted assault and robbery, so be careful."

While Berger directed the uniformed officers, Geneviève continued to question Arsenault. "Why would they want to rob you, Monsieur Arsenault?"

Gregory took a step to this left and leaned against one of the light stanchions which lined the sidewalk. "The other day, after we had spoken at the docks," he began, "I recognized the taller man. He followed me as I left the port." Glancing at the officers questioning the two gang members, he continued. "I think it might have to do with my refusal to negotiate the cargo for Monsieur Remesy."

Geneviève listened to the statement as she wrote in her notebook. *Remesy* she scribbled, underlining it several times. She knew based on Inspector Haddad of the Algiers police that Louis Remesy was in Marseille several weeks ago. "And you've never seen this man or his associate before?"

"No... never."

"And what gives you the impression Monsieur Remesy is behind the assault?"

Gregory observed one of the patrolmen walk past them as he got into the police car and pulled it alongside the curb where Yacine and Riad stood. "As I mentioned the other day, Detective, this gentleman seemed very adamant I broker his cargo on one of the smaller freighters. There are only a few companies which make stops in Algiers, and it's where part of the cargo was to originate."

As Geneviève continued her questioning, Berger returned after interviewing Amed Gilles' Maghrebis gang members. "Monsieur Arsenault, those gentlemen deny they assaulted you as you claimed. Which means either you or they are not telling us the truth," Nicolas stated. "Care to change your story?"

"I assure you, Detective, I was the victim," Gregory declared as he pulled his shirt sleeve up, to reveal fresh lacerations to his forearm. "These are courtesy of being thrown against a concrete column next to my car. And if you have reservations about their statements, why are they being taken away?"

Berger glanced at Geneviève before he answered the question. "The officers mentioned there are inconsistencies in where they declared their residence," the detective answered. "But it doesn't mean they're under arrest, either."

As she flipped to a fresh page in her notebook, Geneviève continued to press Gregory for information. "Back to my original question, Monsieur; why are you here this morning?"

"As a broker, I have to make my own business relationships work to contribute to insure of a comfortable living," Gregory began. "Shipping firms like ZIM and Maersk often sublet their cargo to smaller firms to move goods into harbors too small for their freighters," he lied with ease. "Individuals like myself can do well if they can secure a contract to support movement of this cargo and lease to smaller companies."

"Companies like Papillion?" Berger asked.

"Yes, ones such as Papillion Transport," Gregory replied. "Not all ports within the Mediterranean can accommodate large bulk freighters. A firm with smaller vessels can be an asset, but only when arranged with a suitable supply of cargo and consistent routes," he answered. As he looked over Geneviève's shoulder, he spied Phillip enter the building. "If there's nothing more, I've a meeting to attend to."

"You'll need to appear at the police station within the next 12 hours to sign the complaint on those two men," Berger said, handing the notice to Gregory. "If you fail to appear, they'll be released and you'll be cited for submitting a false report; you understand, Monsieur Arsenault?"

"I'll see to it right after my meeting, I promise," Arsenault answered as he slipped the note into his pocket. "Now, if you'll both excuse me."

Geneviève stepped to one side to let him through and stared as he entered the building. As Gregory disappeared behind the glass entry, she turned to Berger. "Something's not right, Nic," she muttered. "Everything he said was too convenient... too orchestrated."

"I'm going to regret saying this," Berger declared. "Captain Lemieux is right when he said you've not enough experience in the field to rely on 'gut instincts' when it comes to suspects."

Geneviève stepped back to the car, and glanced over her shoulder. "I might not have years on the street, Nic, but I know when to trust my feelings when something isn't right," Geneviève replied as she placed her foot on the bumper.

Geneviève did her best to recall the instances when she followed her instincts resulting in a positive outcome. Opening her notebook, she flipped back a few pages to the information from the earlier interrogation of Claudette Minot in Papillion's offices.

"Are we going to search the office or are we just going to stand here?" Berger asked.

"I want to make sure we've got the right floor and suite number," Geneviève replied. "The earlier entry and search didn't result in anyone from forensics doing a sweep for evidence."

As he entered the building, Gregory acknowledged Phillip standing off to the side by the elevators. "We don't have much time. It's not a coincidence the police are here." He looked anxious as the numbers counted down.

"The woman is the same one from the hospital," Phillip exclaimed as the doors slid open. "I'm sure she'd recognize me if she saw me again."

The older Frenchman stabbed the button for the fourth floor. "Then we need to be quick at obtaining the files, don't we?" Gregory replied as the doors closed and the car began its ascent.

Chapter SEVENTEEN

The isolation of the interrogation room was oppressive to most and a nuisance to others. The former was the case for Riad Zoubir; he'd never been put in a position to be questioned by police. At least not since he arrived from the slums of Oran, Algeria, and joined the Maghrebis gangs. Despite how cool the room was, beads of sweat covered his brow, moistening the band of his *taqiyah*.

Across the hall, Yacine El-Amari sat quiet. The Algerian was more agitated than nervous about his apprehension than his surroundings. As second in command of Gilles's followers, he was more valuable than Riad, but only if the police had information on him and his position. Until then, he'd continue to play the part of immigrant looking for a few euros in exchange for information.

After his police encounter, Gregory, along with Phillip, moved with purpose around the former Papillion Transport offices. While Phillip kept watch for anyone trying to enter, Gregory went into the office he shared with Louis. Behind the desk, he slid the credenza from the wall, and pried off a false panel which caused several bound folders to fall to the floor. He picked them up and entered the outer office and Phillip.

"Time to go," Gregory said, nudging the young man.

Phillip took a deep breath, opened the door and let Gregory lead the way before he pulled it closed for the last time. "Back to my car?" he asked as they entered the stairwell.

"Yes, then to the police station."

"Why go there?"

"I told the police I was being followed by two men, and if I don't sign the complaint, I'll be wanted," Gregory explained as they exited the side of the building, and joined the growing crowd of daily workers.

While the men of Papillion Transport left the building, Detectives Benoit and Berger were waiting for the custodian unlock a third-floor suite to allow them access.

"Doesn't look like they left in a hurry," Berger muttered as he surveyed the office. "Couple of desks, chairs, and a few stray paperclips."

Geneviève stood and took in the emptiness, imagining how the business was conducted. "Not very large for a firm managing a fleet of freighters, is it?" she asked as she stepped to the wall behind what would have been the receptionist's desk. "Nic, how many telephone receptacles would you need for a fax machine and a phone?"

"At least two, why?"

Geneviève grasped the back of the credenza and pulled it away from the wall. "Because there's four here," she said. "And two of them are a different color and size from the other ones."

Nic took his cellphone from his pocket and contacted the forensics lab. After talking for a few minutes, he ended the call. "Two technicians will be here to do a proper dusting." He flipped his cellphone around and leaned in to take several photos of the outlets.

"What are you thinking?"

Berger rested on the credenza's front edge. "One is sure to be the phone line, the second one the fax machine. These others look more like computer terminals, or at least one does."

Geneviève leaned in for a closer look. "Ok, so we've got a phone, fax, and computer," she said. "And the fourth is unknown." She headed to the next office, scanning the walls for a similar arrangement. "Got another," she called out, spying one across the room. "And it has labels too."

Berger entered the room to join Geneviève. "Let's take a look," he said, leaning over to peer at the cover and take another picture of the setup. "Seems we've a T, C, F, and SW," he read off the wires' labels.

Geneviève pulled the desk chair over and sat. "The 'T' would lead everyone to believe it's the telephone," she said. "And 'C' probably stands for the computer, and 'F' for the fax machine. But 'SW' makes little sense?" With a kick of her foot, she began a slow spin of the office. Her eyes crossed the windows facing towards the harbor and she stopped.

"Nic… the freighters. How would they communicate with each other?" as she sat upright.

"I don't know offhand," Berger replied. "With advancements in technology, it could be by cellphones and satellite radios I suppose. Why?"

"And if you needed to talk to a ship at sea, say twenty years ago, what do you think they'd use?"

The question was simple, and Berger lit up as the answer came to him. "A short-wave radio," he replied. "But why have those radios if you're sailing a vessel which has more modern equipment?"

"What if the clients you deal with don't have *'modern'* radios? You have to use something, don't you?" Geneviève asked.

Before Berger could answer, there was a knock on the outer office door. "Municipale Police. Anyone present?" came the announcement from the forensic technician.

"We're in the back office," Berger replied.

While Benoit and Berger had Forensics sweep the bogus office of Papillion, Phillip Gaston maneuvered through traffic while Gregory Arsenault talked to someone on the phone.

As he ended the call, Gregory spoke. "Everything is set," he said. "I shouldn't be in the station over five minutes, then we can go see the others at our new office."

"But what if an officer recognizes me?"

"Don't worry, Phillip. You've been gone for over two months; a great deal has happened since they released you." Gregory stated. "Besides, someone I trust discreetly handled your file. You'll be fine." Before Phillip could respond, Gregory's cell phone rang. With a quick glance down at the number, he shrugged his shoulders at the driver before answering. "Bon jour?" he replied with a sense of trepidation in his voice.

Guillermo Ochoa leaned against the rail of the outdoor café as he spoke with precision and clarity. "Bon jour, Monsieur Richelieu. Don't bother to ask who this is; I wouldn't tell you even if I wanted to," Guillermo began. "There is a woman being held on a yacht at the Pointe Rouge club."

He knows something about me, Gregory thought as he heard the caller use his alias without hesitation, placing him on the defense. "And why is this information of interest to me?" he asked.

"A mutual acquaintance of ours believes it will be a good gesture on your part if the police know of this," Ochoa replied. "It might allow you to gain favor with the authorities and protect your source within the department from retribution."

Gregory held his breath for a moment. *This person knows about Claire*. His mind raced as he tried to consider the former associate, he'd done business with whom might have kept information about their relationship. "And the name of this boat?"

"The *Scirocco*."

Gregory pondered the caller's reason for telling him about an abducted woman. "And what will this information cost me?" he asked, aware information like this always came with a price.

"Safe passage for my friend, at his choosing, when the time comes," Ochoa said.

The former Legionnaire was being blackmailed again, and he didn't know by whom at this point. "And if I'm unable to accommodate your friend's demand, then what?" he asked.

A long moment of silence hung in the air before Ochoa answered. "That discussion will take place at the time of the request. Until then, Au revoir, Monsieur." Picking up his drink, Ochoa nodded to his guest. "That wasn't too hard now, was it?"

Gregory sat in the car, and stared through the windshield, contemplating the position he was just placed in. He felt the uncertain pang of helpless anxiety well up within him. "After the police station, we'll be heading to Pointe Rouge marina," he declared. "Do you have some paper and a pen?"

Back at the office building for ZIM SA and Maersk, Geneviève watched the forensic technician place evidence tape across the inner door of Papillion Transport. "I never paid attention to how patient forensic personnel were," she said to the senior member.

"I can tell you, Detective, it doesn't happen overnight," the technician replied. As he slipped the last of the fingerprint slides into his bag, he glanced around the outer office. "And I'd say we are done." The room had been searched and what little contents existed were dusted for fingerprints and logged. Now, it was time for Geneviève and Berger to file their reports.

"So other than our suspicious electrical outlets, the rooms were almost sterile, wouldn't you say?" Berger inquired while he slid behind the wheel of the police car.

"I'm not sure sterile would be the best description," Geneviève replied, brushing dust from her slacks. "But it was obvious someone took time to remove things of value, though."

Berger started the car and pulled out for the return to the station. "But what would be valuable for a shell company covering for drug smugglers? I'd bet money if any files existed, they'd all be handled by computer."

Geneviève only half-listened to her partner. Staring out the window, her thoughts shifted between the anonymous caller and the revelation the drug smuggler Louis Remesy had been in Marseille last week. More important, she relived Hector's reaction to her confession of being victimized as a teenager.

"Are you ignoring me?" Berger queried.

"Sorry, Nic, I was thinking of the phone call," Geneviève lied. The interruption by Berger broke through her recollection of shame and hurt she confessed to Hector. *And what will happen now?* she asked herself.

"I asked you about Francine mentioning the frequency code she identified from your mystery caller," Berger explained. "It might be a clue to the outlet from the office," he added.

Geneviève shook her head. "But you said so yourself, the office was nearly sterile except for the dust. And if everything was used, we should have seen signs of it on the desktops."

"Okay, I'll give you that one," Berger conceded. "But we can't discount the people running Papillion Transport wouldn't have the equipment and know how to use it." As they neared the station,

Berger spied Gregory Arsenault climb into the passenger seat of a Volvo sedan. "Seems our shipping broker can afford a chauffeur."

"Maybe the driver is a friend helping out," Geneviève whispered. She flipped open her notebook and scribbled the description and plate number. "I'll give this to traffic and let them look up the owner for us."

After Geneviève passed the sedan's description to the traffic division, she and Berger finally made their way to their office, where Detective Masson was focused on a report he just received.

"Finally, he's back to work!" Berger exclaimed.

"And it's a good thing, too," Masson replied.

"You two need to behave yourselves," Geneviève chastised. "What's got you so fixated, Guy?" she asked, slipping her coat over the back of her chair.

"The nice thing about meeting new people is finding out how they can help you," Masson said. "While you and Nic were out, I was catching up on the dead socialite you stumbled across last week. Your reports came up empty on the yacht owner, right? So, I called my new friend, Andre' in Paris who provided some insight."

"Insight on what?" Berger asked.

"Andre' has a friend working with INTERPOL. And that friend checked out the yacht's registration and owner. He found out it's listed under a corporation which originates in Rabat, Morocco," Masson explained.

"Did this friend mention the name of the corporation?" Geneviève queried as she waited for her computer to open its programs. "And why concern ourselves about it being based in Morocco?"

"He's working on those issues as we speak," Masson replied.

"Once we get the company name, you can contact your Algerian friend, Geneviève. Maybe he can offer some answers to the clues, and who's behind it?" Berger asked.

Geneviève sat behind her computer, exchanging glances between the detectives staring at her. "You know, I hadn't considered asking Karim; I guess it couldn't hurt."

Across the city, Phillip and Gregory walked along the promenade at Pointe Rouge marina. Every few steps, Gregory glanced across the water for the vessel the anonymous caller identified, past the empty sailing masts which swayed on the tide.

"What do we do when we find this boat?" Phillip asked as he sidestepped a group of fishermen and their gear. Leaning to his left, he deftly avoided the whip of a fishing rod and its bevy of dangling hooks.

"When we find the boat, we'll start by determining how many people are onboard and if they're being attentive or not," Gregory replied. He already felt his adrenaline begin to surge. It was the sensation soldiers felt only from pursuing the unknown and its potential danger.

"But we're not armed," Phillip pointed out.

"This isn't a contact mission," Gregory replied. "It's a reconnaissance... And there's our goal…" He nodded at the vessel with the name *Scirocco* scripted in red across its stern. Backed into position along the slipway, the small step on the dock was nearly useless, since the transom was a meter in height, allowing anyone to walk onboard.

Phillip took a few more steps and settled himself against a lamp post. Peering toward the yacht, he could see a lone figure on the upper deck, a smoke trail escaping the man's lips. "The one above appears somewhat bored."

Gregory nodded. He watched a smaller boat with two men approach the yacht, and bent down to feign tying his shoe. "We've company on the water, though. Can you see if they've stopped at our target?"

Yawning, Phillip turned somewhat to watch the two men Gregory had identified. "Oui, they're at the front now. It looks like they placed a basket onto the boat. And they just tossed a duffle bag on deck as well."

Hearing Phillip's description, Gregory stood and wandered closer to the fence separating the boats from pedestrians. The men in the boat looked oblivious of his presence and soon turned the smaller motorboat around, heading back from where they came from across the marina. Through the window, Gregory noticed a second man had joined the first and held up a garment.

"Doesn't look like something you'd wear to a dinner party does it?" Gregory asked his companion.

"Looks like a *kaftan* or a *burqa* from here," Phillip said. "I wouldn't be caught dead wearing them though," he added, chuckling as one man put it against his chest as though he was a model.

Gregory heard the comment, but his mind was formulating a plan to see precisely what the men onboard were involved in. "Come on, I've seen what I need for the moment." As they returned to Phillip's car, Gregory pulled out his cell phone and punched in a number. In moments, he heard a familiar voice.

"Central Records, Detainee Processing. How can I help you?"

"Good day, Sergeant. My name is Monsieur Richelieu," Gregory began. "I've information concerning a possible narcotics transaction I'd like passed to Detective Benoit in Drug Intervention."

Claire listened as her brother-in-law described the plight and as calmly as he spoke, she wrote the details given to her. With a glance, she could tell none of her fellow officers were paying too close attention. "Will there be anything else you'd like to add, Monsieur?"

"No, please see Detective Benoit is the one who receives this information, though."

"Oui, Monsieur. I'll see she gets it personally," Claire replied as she hung up. Folding the paper in half, she pushed away from her desk, headed for the door. "I'll be back in a moment, Justine."

Within minutes, Sergeant Dubois entered the detectives' office space where many were busy with paperwork. As she walked to the inner office, Claire could sense her pulse quicken. *Okay, Claire, you told Greg you'd be an agent provocateur; time to prove it*. Putting her head in the doorway, she saw Masson and Berger discussing something in one corner. "Excuse me, Detective Benoit?"

Geneviève picked her head up from behind the computer. "Oui, what is it?" she answered before she noticed who it was. "Oh... Sergeant Dubois, isn't it? How can I help you?"

Claire stepped to Geneviève's desk and handed over the note. "An anonymous call came in and they asked this information be passed to you," she said, mustering all of her courage to stay calm in front of Geneviève.

"Why pass it to me?"

"The caller just mentioned it should be passed to you," the sergeant repeated.

Geneviève unfolded the paper and read the note. "This is all they said? The name of a boat at the Pointe Rouge marina..." she expressed loud enough to get Berger and Masson's attention.

"What's the problem?" Berger asked.

"The sergeant received an *'anonymous'* tip which mentioned a drug transaction," Geneviève said. "It is or was taking place onboard," she looked down at the note again, "the *Scirocco*."

"Drugs on boats at another marina," Berger said. "It's beginning to be a popular theme this week."

Claire took in the banter between the detectives with mild disinterest. Standing near Geneviève made her uncomfortable. With a slight cough, she got Geneviève's attention. "Ahh, if there's nothing else, I need to get back to my desk," the sergeant muttered.

"Fine," Geneviève replied. "But I'll expect a copy of the call report from you in the next two hours. By the way, was the caller a man or a woman?"

"It was a man," Claire answered before leaving the room.

Berger looked at his partner across the room. "What are you thinking?"

Geneviève sat in quiet reflection for the moment. She speculated about potential suspects, but wasn't ready to concede her thoughts to Nicolas just yet. "I'm just wondering if there's a connection between our actress, the banker, and Papillion Transport," she lied.

Chapter EIGHTEEN

Bare masts reached skyward along the horizon as the detectives' car neared the marina. "Did I tell you the custodian we arrested had pictures of Sergeant Dubois?" Geneviève asked her partner. "There were at least eight to ten images of her alone."

"As a matter of fact, you did," Berger answered. "As did Pierre when he caught me in the hall." Slowing down for cars entering the roundabout, Berger glanced over his shoulder as a group of youngsters on their Vespa-like scooters thread their way past them.

"Why do you think the sergeant got called in the first place?" Geneviève asked.

Watching the scooters zip pass a bus, the last one narrowly missing the front bumper, Berger looked at his partner. "I don't know. Someone just happened to dial her number? I don't think it matters at this point," he answered, easing past the bus which stopped to discharge passengers.

Near the marina, Geneviève's cell phone rang. Digging it out of her pocket, she saw the number on the screen. "It's Guy," she announced. "Hello Guy."

"Geneviève, I've got dreadful news for you," the detective began. "The corporation your yacht is registered to is on INTERPOL's human trafficking watch list," Guy said, reading from his notes. "One person under surveillance is a Moroccan named Youssef Raif."

Geneviève listened to her fellow officer as she struggled to balance the notepad in her lap as Berger searched for a parking spot. "Do they have anything they can share about this Moroccan?" she asked as she heard papers being shuffled in the background.

"From what Andre' learned, this guy Raif, he's well connected, but in a dangerous way," Guy said. "The locals have never caught him doing anything illegal, at least not enough to arrest him. And when they have evidence to implicate him for a crime, prosecution efforts were done more as courtesy to appease locals rather than incarcerate him."

Nicolas found a spot and parked their car a few meters from the marina entrance. "We're at the marina. Was there anything more?" she asked as she slid out of the car. Several seagulls flew overhead, swooping towards the water in search of fish scraps floating on the surface.

Guy flipped through the few pages he'd gotten from his friend. "I'm still going through the information. I'll have more in an hour or so."

The heavy odor of the open sea greeted Geneviève. "All right, we'll see you when we're done here," she replied, trying to catch up to Nicolas who'd made his way to the marina's office. Stuffing her phone into her jacket, Geneviève did her best not to run after Berger, who stood waiting.

"Anything I should know or care about?"

"We'll know more when we get back to the station," she said, somewhat out of breath. "But it appears that Guy's friend found information on a person of interest for us to investigate centered on the yacht."

Berger held the door open as Geneviève slid past him and walked up to the counter. Though not cavernous, the marina's office was unoccupied at the moment, and she tapped her finger on the bell positioned in the center.

Berger leaned against the counter. "Is no one home?"

"Doesn't look like it," Geneviève replied tapping the bell twice, only harder this time.

"In a minute," came a woman's voice from behind a door swinging open. "I heard you the first time."

The detectives exchanged glances as Berger took the lead. "It's the police, madame. We need to talk to whoever is in charge here."

True to her statement, the woman entered the office space. Her lean and wiry figure partially veiled under a fisherman's shirt and baggy shorts still showed off weathered limbs. Sliding on glasses that hung from her neck with a tarnished silver chain, she looked over the detectives. "Now, how can I help you officers today?" she asked, peering at their credentials.

Geneviève opened her notebook. "We're here to look into a possible report of drug activity on one of the boats. It was supposed to have been on or around the vessel *Scirocco*."

"I see," the clerk answered, pulling a ledger from under the counter. Flipping open the stained fabric cover, the woman hummed to herself as she fingered through several pages of hand-written entries before stopping. "The boat is at slip number 7, space 13."

"That's it?" Berger asked. "Isn't the access to the boats secured by fencing or behind locked gates?"

The clerk chuckled at Berger's question. "Of course, they are, Detective. We've got many of Marseille's wealthiest putting their boats in our care. Lots of money is spent on them and the owners expect us to watch over them," she declared. "I'll contact the security guard to let you in."

Geneviève fought hard to hide the smirk from her lips. "We'll meet your security guard at the slip then. Shall we go, Nic?" She looked at her partner while holding the door open.

With sunshine sparkled off the waves sending bright chips of light against white boat exteriors, Geneviève couldn't help but squint as she looked for slip number 7. "Remind me to keep sunglasses in the car," she declared as she shielded her eyes. Off in the distance, a uniformed guard stood at the open gate, waving towards them.

Just as Benoit and Berger approached the guard, a marked police car pulled up from the opposite direction. The driver got out and walked up to the detectives while adjusting his ball cap. "Detective Berger is it? I'm Corporal Huet." He held out his hand. "I was directed to provide you and your partner any support... if necessary."

Berger looked over at Geneviève. "Captain Duval seems serious about our safety," he declared. Turning his attention back to the corporal, he continued. "Very well, Corporal Huet. Are you and your partner armed?" Not every patrolman had the luxury to carry a firearm.

"*Oui*, Detective. We're prepared for any possibility," Huet replied as he gave his partner a thumbs-up signal. At the patrol car, the other officer opened the trunk and pulled out two Heckler & Koch submachine guns, and their non-lethal Taser.

"Let's hope you don't need to use them," Geneviève said, pushing past Berger. "Shall we get on with this?" She motioned to the security guard to open the gate for Slip 7 and the docks beyond.

Geneviève reached under her coat, to pull her Sig Sauer pistol free. "You can wait here," she told the guard. After a fifty-meter walk, she approached the stern of the *Scirocco*. With the yacht backed in against the dock, she could look into the main salon, its dark mahogany wood a stark contrast to an intricate rug under the table. She looked back and noticed the patrolmen move cautiously a few meters behind Berger.

"It doesn't appear to be occupied," Berger said, standing next to Geneviève.

"Shall we?"

"You take the bridge. I'll go below," Berger answered as he waved Corporal Huet and his partner forward. "One of you is with me, the other with Detective Benoit," he ordered. With directions given, he nudged Geneviève in the back. "Let's go."

In moments, the officers were on board the yacht, with Geneviève and Huet making their way up the steps to the bridge. Meanwhile, Berger and the other officer slid open the doors to the salon and began their search.

Geneviève took deliberate steps toward the closed hatch which led upward, while Corporal Huet scanned the exterior for trouble. Leaning to her right, she could look into the space, and realized no one was inside. "It's clear," she uttered, twisting the handle to open the doorway.

Meanwhile, Berger and the other officer had made their way along the stairway towards the stately berthing suites. In the first, they found evidence of someone being onboard earlier, as the bed was unkept and men's clothes were piled in the corner.

In the other stateroom, the scene was the same. The notable exception was three to four pieces of what looked like women's clothes hung in the closet space. On the bridge, Geneviève had made her own discovery of the occupant's intentions.

"What do you make of this?" Geneviève asked, pointing out a handful of nautical charts to Huet. The maps showed France's southern coastline, which included Marseille, Toulon, and Nice. "Does *X* really mark the spot?" she muttered, as she pointed out the crimson designation in the middle of the Mediterranean Sea.

"It means something to someone," Huet replied.

Geneviève pulled a pair of gloves out of her jacket and slipped them on before she slid several charts aside. Underneath, she found a hand-written note and picked up the slip of paper by its corner. "You wouldn't happen to read Arabic by chance?"

Huet shook his head. "It wasn't part of the academy curricula, I'm afraid," as he looked over the writing. "But those are something we can read." He pointed to numbers scribbled across the back.

Geneviève flipped the chart over to look for herself. A series of numbers was scrawled in pencil which read 43.19/5.23. "Does they mean something to you?"

"What did you find?" came the question from Berger from behind Geneviève as he climbed the inner stairs from the lower deck to the bridge. Behind him, the second patrolman stayed a few steps below, his head the only part visible to the others.

"A chart with an *X* on it, and this note in Arabic. But there's also these numbers," Geneviève replied, showing Berger the paper while nodding to the chart. "What did you find in the lower decks?"

Berger recounted what he and the other officer found in the staterooms, but also what wasn't found. "For receiving a call about possible drug activity, there's no sign of drugs," he finished. "We need to bring a dog onboard to see if there were traces of any narcotics before dismissing that, though."

"You know, those numbers look like coordinates on a map," the second officer said aloud as he looked over Geneviève's shoulder. "Did you look to see if they were part of the chart on the table?"

Geneviève stared at the officer for a moment. "You know what those mean?"

The patrolman shrugged his shoulders. "My parents pushed me into scouting when I was young and one lesson they taught us was map reading." Reaching across the table, he grabbed a ruler and pencil. "Excuse me, Detective," he said as he squeezed next to Geneviève. The first series of numbers he found listed on the left margin. Next, he found the second, and placed the ruler along the lines, finding where they intersected. "*Planier Light*," he announced, tapping the pencil where the lines met.

Geneviève exchanged looks with Berger before speaking. "Why is that spot so important?"

"We'll find out when we get that note translated. Until then, we wait for Forensics to arrive," he stated, pulling out his cell phone to make the call. "Corporal Huet, if you could, set up the police tape to keep the public away."

While the detectives contemplated the reasons behind the off-shore location, Nazim Aziz watched the outskirts of Marseilles grow larger from his seat on the TGV. While his mentor Omar Khalid was in Morocco to talk about Officer Galant's abduction with Youssef Raif, Nazim struck out on his own. Driven by knowledge of who killed his cousin, Nazim decided to meet the Maghrebi gang leader, Amed Gilles, to learn about the abduction mix-up on his own.

Nazim took a calculated risk traveling as Monsieur Jacques Vignes, tempting the devil by using his new alias the Italians provided again. The brief experience with the passport agent in Toulouse was not unexpected once he learned the clerk was only working his third week at the international terminal. After a twenty-minute taxi ride, Nazim was soon relaxed on the TGV as it left the station for the 4-hour trip to Marseille.

A jolt under his seat woke him. "We'll be arriving in Marseille in twenty minutes," came the announcement over the speakers. Nazim leaned over to retrieved his leather satchel and placed it on his lap. Flipping it open, he pulled out a notebook and looked over the directions he had taken on who he was meeting and where.

Just outside the train station entrance, Amed exercised patience while sitting alone at a small table shaded from the sun by an umbrella. Close by, three of his followers stood, scanning the crowds in the event someone tried to harm their superior. It wasn't long before an announcement signaled the TGV's arrival from Toulouse.

Nazim made his way from the platform, strolled outside the station until he neared the café. He dodged a family of five trying to climb the steps into the station and caught sight of Amed. *At least his description was correct.*

"Monsieur Gilles?" Nazim asked with a slight bow.

"Yes. And you are Monsieur... Vignes, aren't you?"

Nazim held his expression as neutral as he could. The manner the gang leader addressed him caused him to begin second guessing their encounter. It gave him concern Gilles might know more about him than he cared to consider. "Oui, I'm Monsieur Vignes," he answered. "Thank you for agreeing to meet me on such short notice."

He pulled out the chair on the opposite side of the table to sit, and the gang leader stared, his gaze fixated on Nazim, but not seeing him. He was more concerned about those who might try to harm him. "Your mentor Khalid said you wanted to ask a few questions about an event I might be aware of; is this correct?"

Nazim looked across the table. He wasn't in the mood to be toyed with, but he needed to know what the gang leader's plan was for the policewoman his men were guarding.

"Yes, it's true; I need some clarification on a matter you're possibly aware of," Nazim answered, waving a waiter to the table. "A Perrier with a glass please," he ordered. "Something for you?"

"I'll have the same, please," Gilles replied.

Nazim returned his attention to Gilles as the server left. "I understand there was a kidnapping which took place several weeks ago," he began. "But those involved might have abducted the wrong person," Nazim added, his last statement setting Gilles back in his chair somewhat.

Before Gilles could answer, a waitress returned, and placed drinks on their table. Amed took one bottle and poured some into his glass and drank. Wiping his lips with the napkin, he leaned onto the table. "I've been told that information on this particular victim is worth €250,000," Gilles answered. The sum of money he spoke of was more than Khalid offered, and now he was telling the French-Algerian it would cost more for the policewoman.

"I'd be surprised if those offering the reward would pay for having the wrong individual handed over," Nazim replied as he poured his own water into the glass. "And I'm quite certain I'm right when I say the party in question have the wrong woman."

The revelation his men might have abducted the wrong woman caused Amed to grow visibly pale, even under the afternoon sunshine. "How can you be so sure of your information?" he asked.

A wry smile came to Nazim's face as he looked across the table. "Because, last week I saw the officer you were paid to abduct at a crime scene. She was at the marina where the socialite was murdered."

Gilles was not used to hear he was wrong, and the public café was no place to show his disdain. He took another drink before answering. "Really? The news or television hasn't mentioned how the mademoiselle was found. How do you know it was a murder?" he asked, curious how Nazim had gotten information about Yvonne Segal. "Besides, what does it matter which woman your mentor has at his disposal?"

"The woman you were told to abduct was to be held accountable for..." Nazim began to declare before catching himself. *He doesn't need to know about Hakim's death or who killed him*, he told himself. "She's responsible for the death of a member of Khalid's household."

As the two men sat discussing the issue of Officer Galant's abduction, the waitress who brought out their drinks was on her phone. "Hello? Tell Monsieur Carbone his guest is outside the Saint Charles train station," the woman stated in a hushed tone. "He's with another gentleman at Caffe San Carlos facing the fountain," she added. As she ended the call, the server took several snapshots of the men, and sent them to the call's recipient.

Across town, a Carbone mafia member wrote down notes to hand over to the crime syndicate leader when images arrived from the waitress. This information would be exchanged because of an arrangement between the mafia Don and a former Foreign Legion member now controlling the former shipping assets of the Carbone family.

Chapter NINETEEN

Hector Dupont's phone rang just as the roar of an *easyJet* A319 Airbus filled the office. Undeterred by the noise, he glanced at the blinking light, and quickly stabbed his finger on the button to answer. "Yes, what is it?" he responded while he reviewed the detention and incident report. The month had been busy for the airport security director and his personnel as tourists from Northern Europe made one last trip before winter settle in their homeland.

Across the airport, the communications office was a hive of activity as each technician scanned their respective video screen and computer. Each member had a list of potential threats and received direction by Dupont on which key groups or individuals needed closer scrutiny.

"Sir, we've just received an alert from Saint Charles train station about one of our suspects," the technician answered.

"Which one?" Dupont asked, circling a date and time on the report to investigate further.

"They have a possible match to the suspect, Jacques Vignes."

Hector Dupont put down his pen and selected a file on his computer screen. In moments the grainy images from the airport in Algiers filed the screen. "Can you contact the security officer and have them scan their video feed for any possible images?"

"Oui, Director," came the reply before the line went dead.

As the light went out on his phone, Hector selected his outside line and punched in another number, one he knew from memory. The phone began ringing as he tagged another image on his computer of the suspect *Jacques Vignes aka Louis Remesy*. As the picture came into focus, a familiar voice answered his call.

"Hello, Hector," Geneviève said.

"Are you busy?"

"I'm at the office... of course I'm busy," the detective replied before she stepped into the hallway. "Why? You're not wanting to discuss what happened after dinner the other day, are you?" She kept her voice low as another officer passed her in the hall. She knew their brief conversation about her sexual assault would just be the first of many.

Hector cleared his throat before beginning. "What you and I discussed is too personal to talk about over the phone. If I wanted to continue our discussion," she paused, "I would have come by the station and done so face to face."

Geneviève let out a sigh as she felt the initial tension fade away. "Thank you. I appreciate hearing that, Hector," she replied faintly as a tear formed in the corner of her eye.

The security director drank some coffee before he continued. "I'm calling because I was just contacted by our communications staff," he said. "They were alerted by security at the Saint Charles station of a possible sighting of your suspected drug smuggler, Vignes."

"He's here? In Marseille?" Geneviève exclaimed loud enough to startle officers walking passed. She rushed back into the detectives' office, and grabbed her notebook and jacket and waved for Berger. "Where did you say he was seen?"

"At the Saint Charles station," Hector repeated. "I'm trying to get security footage from their cameras now."

The sudden outburst by their colleague startled Berger and Masson as they both worked on their respective reports. Berger was the first to recognize Geneviève's animated look as she grabbed her jacket from the desk chair.

"What is it?" Berger asked.

Geneviève pulled the phone away from her ear. "Hector was just informed the drug smuggler Vignes... I mean Remesy, was spotted at Saint Charles station. Hello... Hector you're still there, aren't you?"

Overhearing the talk in the background, Hector sat and waited for a chance to speak again. Picking up the question from Geneviève, he answered, "Yes, I'm still here," before finishing the coffee from earlier.

"When did you receive the warning?" Geneviève asked.

"Oh... maybe five, ten minutes ago," Hector replied with a glance at his wristwatch.

Finally, another chance to close this case, popped into Geneviève's head as her thought of confronting Louise Remesy came into focus. Blinking hard, she pushed aside the distractions, focusing only on what needed to be done.

A few paces behind her, Detective Berger ordered the watch officer to arrange for patrolmen to be dispatched as backup and to meet near the train station. Meanwhile, Detective Masson had printed photos of Louis Remesy and began to pass them to the patrolmen.

As policemen began mobilizing on the information concerning the drug smuggler Remesy, a phone call was taking place between Claudio Carbone and a reluctant partner.

"You asked for my help and I'm now delivering on your request," the mafia don said. "The gentleman you wish to meet is at the Saint Charles station," Claudio continued. "And it appears he is meeting with your former associate."

Gregory Arsenault listened intently. Wanting to confront the leader of the Maghrebis gang was his first concern, the Legionnaire knew. But, to hear his former partner was nearby would allow him to tie off one more loose end from his past. "Merci Claudio," the former soldier replied, ending the call.

Across the city, Detective Berger led two police cars toward the central train station in hopes they'd be successful in apprehending Louis Remesy. With a quick glance, he noticed Geneviève staring intently through the windshield, her focus on the possible confrontation etched on her face. "You okay?"

"Yes, I'm fine," she replied, seeing the glass and concrete facade of the station grow larger as they approached. She knew the drive from the police station would give the suspect time to disappear. *But a chance to get my hands on Remesy is worth the attempt*. Without thinking, Geneviève rubbed her hands along her slacks, a vain attempt to rid them of perspiration.

As he neared the station, Berger radioed to Detective Masson, who followed behind with one of the other patrolmen. "Guy, you head to the lower exit," he said. "Benoit and I will start at the main entrance and work our way towards you, okay?"

Detective Masson pointed the driver to veer right at the traffic circle as he listened to his friend. "I'll meet you inside, then."

Nazim sat at the café, and glanced at his timepiece. *Thirty-five minutes before the return train to Toulouse*, he told himself. "The way I see it, Monsieur Gilles, you have two choices before you," Nazim said, resting against the table.

"And what are those?"

Nazim finished off his Perrier before he explained. "You get the correct person in your possession, or you don't get paid," he said in a matter-of-fact tone. "Rest assured, I'll see you never get the reward offered if you try to pass off the wrong woman," he added before getting to his feet. "You have one week to correct your mistake, Monsieur."

Before Amed could reply, one of his men came to the table and whispered in his ear. Amed picked his head up and glanced to his left while still listening. With a nod, he rose to his feet as the other guards came into view.

Nazim noted the sudden concern by Gilles's followers. "Remember, you've one week; Au revoir, Monsieur Gilles," he declared with a wave before he walked away. Searching the train station entrances, he caught sight of a marked police car entering the parking structure.

Off to Nazim's left, Benoit and Berger directed six uniformed officers on their role in finding the drug smuggler. "Remember, we don't believe the suspect is armed, but you're to protect yourselves and the citizens at all costs," Geneviève said.

"Here's the latest photo we have on the suspect," Berger added, passing out copies of the surveillance photo. "Concentrate on the TGV platforms; our information shows him traveling here on them." Each officer nodded.

"Remember, he's a suspect wanted for assaulting a police officer, drug smuggling, and... kidnapping," she hesitated on the last word, "which means we want to talk to him. So, if you apprehend him, keep him alive," Geneviève said.

"We don't know if he's involved with Patrice's disappearance," Berger said.

"Nic... I'm confident he knows something," Benoit said. "Let's go." She spun on her heels and trotted up the stairs to the station's entrance. Taking steps two at a time, Geneviève soon crested the top and paused as she scanned the crowd exiting the station.

Berger soon joined her as he directed the other officers toward their respective areas to search. "What are you thinking?"

"My hope is that we're not too late."

In the lower concourse of the train station, Detective Masson made his way toward the exits when a patrol officer encountered one of Gilles's men. In moments, the police officer was shouting for the man to get on his knees, and Masson discovered three others move in his direction.

Hurrying around a delivery truck, Masson positioned himself to confront the others. Stepping around the vehicle, the detective put his hand out. But before he could warn Gilles and his two followers to halt, the closest member to him plunged a knife into Masson.

Though the spring-loaded blade was a mere five inches, its sharpened edge drove deep as the men collided. Masson felt the sting as the blade penetrated and felt the slow trickle of blood ooze from the wound.

The gang member wasn't as fortunate in the confrontation. Masson had drawn his weapon and while stumbling into the detective, the gang member caused Masson to fire at close range. The bullet tore through the man's thigh, and nicked the femoral artery before exiting out the back. The pain and shock of the injury caused Amed's follower to drop his knife as he fell away from the detective.

The sound of the gunshot reverberated through the underground parking area, causing Amed and his other follower to stop duck for cover. Glancing around, the two men caught police officers rushing to help their fallen colleague, which gave them a chance to make their own escape.

"What about Najm?" the follower asked.

Amed shook his head. "Nothing. He's on his way to meet Allah," he replied. "Get on your feet. We must leave.... now." He pushed the man towards the stairs. To his right, he caught his other follower gesture in their direction before pointing at the train station gates.

With emergency sirens growing louder, Amed and his followers made their way to the entrance, soon mingling with onlookers trying to understand what happened inside the complex.

On the main platform, Benoit and Berger heard the call of an officer being injured, but didn't know it was their partner Masson.

Officer Abel looked at Geneviève. "What should we do?"

"We've a suspect to look for," she replied. "Nic, you and the other officer go figure out if they need any help."

"And what are you going to do?" Berger asked.

Geneviève scanned the crowds as they scurried toward their respective trains. "I'm going to find Remesy," she said, her voice exhibiting a level of confidence he'd not heard before today. Gesturing to the patrolman, she nodded towards the TGV platform. "Let's go."

Nazim Aziz had made his way into the terminal when police encountered Amed Gilles's gang member. He didn't hear the gunshot, though he could hear the wail of emergency vehicles sirens as they approached the station. As he strode toward the departure track, he stopped and glanced at the digital display of arrival and departure times.

Wind swirled under the atrium covering the tracks as the scent of cooking wafted from the nearby food court. Nazim strolled further down the platform horn blared, announcing another trains' arrival. Walking toward the track, he tapped his pocket to reassure himself the key to the storage bin at the Toulouse station holding his clothes, and other documents, was safe.

Geneviève and Officer Abel stood 50 meters from Nazim, looking in the opposite direction. A crowd of tourists from Ireland was gathered around their guide as they prepared to board their train to Lyon.

"The train headed back to Toulouse is on Track A," Abel declared, pointing to the departure display.

"You walk along the trackside; I'll stay back along the wall," Geneviève replied as they both began the deliberate search for the drug smuggler. "Don't forget, I want him alive," she added before reaching under her jacket to feel the Sig Sauer on her hip.

Nazim paused across from the empty track and sat on the bench. His mind swirled, attempting to understand how Gilles could mistake one policewoman for the detective he so desperately wanted to see pay for his cousin's death. Seeing Geneviève at the marina was luck, but he believed it was Allah's will which placed him there.

Geneviève neared the halfway point along the track when she noticed the profile of a gentleman sitting by himself, waiting for a train's arrival. She could look just past him; as Abel closed in from the opposite side. As she waited for a couple tugging their luggage along the platform to pass, she began to maneuver through the growing crowds toward her suspect.

The chime of the intercom echoed through the station, and announced another train approaching. In the distance, lights twinkled and could be seen as the commuter service crept closer to the station. Geneviève's suspect, heard the announcement, and moved closer to the platform's edge.

A rush of wind accompanied the train's entrance to the station with the high-pitched squeals emanating from the first several railcars in the string. As the train halted, doors slid open, allowing passengers to disembark, while those departing Marseille pushed to gain their seats.

Geneviève saw her suspect make his way toward the open doors. Not wanting to lose the chance of arresting Remesy, she pushed her way closer until she stood behind the man.

Drawing out her police credentials, she reached out to the traveler. "Excuse me, sir, but I need to talk with you," Geneviève declared, grabbing the man's arm and spun him around.

"What do you think you're doing?" the businessman demanded, pulling his arm away.

Looking at the man's face for the first time gave Geneviève the sudden realization she'd identified the wrong person. Looking at the surveillance photo and the businessman, she could understand her mistake glaring back at her.

"I'm sorry, Monsieur; you have the same characteristics as a suspect we're looking for," she stammered. "Again, my apologies. You're free to go." The look of embarrassment on her face was in full display as many travelers were now focused on her.

"Wrong person, detective?" Abel asked, stepping next to her.

"Yes," Geneviève replied as she stared into the windows of the train cars. She walked the length of the platform, examining each face of gentlemen sitting at each railcar window in hopes of spotting Remesy.

Nazim had settled into his seat and was jotting down his thoughts when he detected someone staring at him from the platform. A wry smile came to his face. *What must you be thinking?* He could see the realization Geneviève was close to her prey, yet still unable to capture it. In moments, a chime sounded to alert those onboard the doors were closing before the train began rolling away.

Geneviève scanned most windows until the last car. There, she recognized the familiar expression she'd seen in the past. *It's him. That's Remesy.* Pulling the surveillance photo from her jacket, she looked at it before returning her gaze back to the passenger. She rushed towards the railcar and was about to climb onboard when the doors closed and the car lurched away from the platform.

Rushing to her side, Abel stared as the train moved out of the station. "Did you see the suspect?"

"Yes, I saw the suspect," she uttered while watching the train pull away. Glaring at the red tail lights of the last railcar, Geneviève's frustration grew inside. She caught the smile form on Nazim's face and knew she'd missed her chance at capturing him.

Chapter TWENTY

"Yes... in the last railcar," Detective Benoit stated for the third time. As soon as the train which carried Nazim left the station, Geneviève was calling Captain Duval. "He was wearing a beige sport coat from what I could see," she added. "We've only a few hours before the train arrives in Toulouse though..."

While Geneviève discussed her failed attempt at apprehending Nazim Aziz, Detective Berger strolled up behind her. Leaning against the police car, he only half listened to the conversation, his thoughts concentrated on Guy Masson.

"Yes, sir... Officer Berger is here now. We'll be back in the office in a few minutes," Geneviève said before hanging up.

"What did the Captain say?"

Geneviève looked down, scuffing her shoe along the pavement before answering. "Let's just say he's not happy at the moment," she answered. "How's Guy?"

"The medic treating him was concerned there wasn't more blood loss from the wound. He thinks there's internal bleeding," Berger replied. "They took Guy to Timone' on *Boulevard Jean Moulin*." Berger ran his hand across his face before he spoke again. "So, we missed out on grabbing this guy Remesy, heh?"

Geneviève glanced at Berger. She could tell he was questioning why they rushed into action without considering the consequences. "He was here, Nic. We just missed him by a few minutes," she answered, her spirit defeated.

"Come on," Berger said. "You told Captain Duval we'd be in the station in a few minutes. We better go." He climbed into the car, waiting for Geneviève to join him.

Geneviève scanned the streets surrounding the train station. *Why were you here? More important, were you meeting someone, and who were they to you?*

As the detectives left the station, a car followed a delivery van along the A47 motorway, northwest and away from the center of the city. In the van, Julien LeBlanc and his cousin, Phillip Gaston, kept their distance while watching the afternoon traffic, not wanting to draw attention to themselves.

Phillip maintained the cars' his distance from a tour bus in front of them. He shifted with nervous anticipation in the driver's seat. "You think Monsieur Arsenault is right to confront this man?"

Julien smiled. "Gregory is a man who does what is necessary to either level the terms of an encounter, or gain an advantage," the former Legionnaire replied. "Besides, all Gregory wants to do is talk with this gentleman," he chuckled. Julien was well aware Gregory would do the talking, expecting Amed Gilles to listen. Or else...

"Then why are we armed like we're going on patrol then?"

"Because you can't be too safe... can you?" Julien replied.

Just behind them, Pasqual Sequin and Hector Pichon sat behind their quarry, each in quiet concentration as the destination their employer chose for Gilles internment neared. Gilles was unaware Pasqual was fluent in Arabic and understood the gang leader's instructions to his men. The Frenchman now knew who the Maghrebis gang would look towards as second-in-command.

Behind the van, Louis Clement manipulated his sedan around a slower car, keeping the delivery van in sight. "Where do you want to release Gilles when we're done with him?" This wasn't the first time for Sequin or Pichon to abduct someone, having tracked poachers and mercenaries in the Congo as part of their Legionnaire platoon.

Gregory tapped his fingers on the car door as he thought of a response. "How about the *Joan of Arc?* We can have Marcel and Anton set him adrift in a dingy just passed the breakwater. A few hours might make him realize we're not to be taken lightly, heh?"

The driver glanced at his friend. "That's not a good idea, you know," Louis answered. "Do you want to expose our operations, not to mention Marcel and his crew to these thugs just to prove a point?"

Shaking his head somewhat, Gregory knew Louis was right. *Why expose more men when it wasn't needed?* "I'll have Julien give him a sedative," Gregory replied. "Then we can have Elise discover him and call the authorities."

Watching the van approach an abandon warehouse, Louis slowed down as he pulled up to the gates. "Simple as that?" he asked.

"Yeah, simple as that," Gregory replied.

Back at the police station, Benoit and Berger waited for Captain Duval to return. Each were lost in thought, recalling the events that surrounded the afternoon.

"Why do you think Remesy risked coming back to Marseille?" Geneviève asked.

"What?"

"I said, what would compel Remesy to return to the city? He must know we'd be looking for him after the shootout at Il d'If, right?"

Berger leaned forward in his chair, wringing his hands before answering. "I don't know, Geneviève. Maybe he had to finish some transaction? Maybe it was to pay off those who helped him?" He threw his hands up in defeat. "I don't know. You and Captain Lemieux started the case, you tell me...." Before Geneviève could answer, Captain Duval came through the door.

"Both of you, in my office." He strode past the detectives without looking at either of them. As Duval entered, he circled behind his desk and sat heavily in his chair. Frustration mixed with hopeless worry etched on his face.

Benoit and Berger each took a seat across from Duval, both looking across the desk, unsure if they should address him. It was Geneviève who spoke first.

"How's Guy?"

The captain looked at her as he drew in a deep breath before answering. "Detective Masson is undergoing surgery," he said. "The wound nicked his liver and the doctors were attempting to control the bleeding."

"But he's going to be okay?" Berger asked.

Duval leaned back, his hand gliding through thinning hair which looked to grey as the minutes passed. "I'm not going to admit to his chances because I don't know them, Nicolas," he answered before leaning forward in his chair. "Now, let's discuss why you took the actions you did."

Geneviève slid forward in her chair, glancing down at her shoes. *It was my fault.* Peering up at the captain, she drew in a breath before speaking. "It's my fault Guy got hurt, Captain."

"Detective Masson could have gotten injured strolling the promenade on a Sunday afternoon," Captain Duval replied. "I want to know why three officers ran off to arrest a suspect without proper authority? Do you have any documentation? Any arrest warrants?" he asked.

Awkward silence filled the office for a few moments as Benoit and Berger exchanged glances. Each knew their actions went against department policy. It was Geneviève who broke the silence again.

"It was my fault, Captain," she sighed in defeat.

"Actually, Captain..." Berger began to say but was quieted by the senior officer's upheld hand.

Duval nodded towards Geneviève, who'd dropped her head to accept her fate. "Go ahead, Detective Benoit," he said.

For the moment, Geneviève just stared off, looking towards a row of framed citations on the wall. With a long, exhaled breath, she looked at the captain before closing her eyes to prepare what she wanted to say.

"Earlier this morning, I received a call from Monsieur Dupont at the airport," she began.

"And who is he?" Duval asked.

"Hector... I mean Monsieur Dupont, is the director of airport security," Geneviève replied. "He was contacting me about a suspect from the raid on Chateau Il d'If."

"Ahh, yes. I remember Captain Lemieux mention the director when we took possession of the Algerian," Duval stated. "Go on, Benoit."

"Well, sir, it appears our suspect Louis Remesy was able to obtain a new identity and re-enter the country several weeks ago," the detective continued. "That's what I was trying to tell dispatch when I saw the him on the TGV."

Berger listened to Geneviève as she described learning of Remesy's new identity. It was just four years prior Nic encountered a similar case as a new detective, but his altercation didn't result in the injury to another officer. Geneviève's eagerness to rid herself of this suspect had, though.

"So, you responded to this call based on a series of grainy airport images from an Algerian police inspector, mobilizing a half-dozen officers to arrest one man?"

Tension in the room felt like a weighted blanket draped around the detective. As she sat, Geneviève wrapped her arms around her chest, feeling numb. Her thoughts switched between *How could I let this happen?* and *What will happen to me now?* as Captain Duval kept his focus on her.

"Captain, I'm sure the information supplied by Inspector Haddad was genuine and can be validated by Monsieur Dupont's records at the airport," Geneviève replied. "And we shouldn't forget we had evidence from Scotland Yard on the suspect, too."

Duval ran his hands across his face. The superintendent had pushed him on being kept up to date on the drug smuggling efforts. He even pressed him for information they could share with their British counterparts in London. The buzz of the phone jolted him from his thoughts. "Yes, Clarise, what is it?"

"My apologies, Captain," the woman replied. "We've just learned Detective Masson is out of surgery and in recovery. The doctor's mentioned you can see him in a couple of hours if you'd like..."

A look of relief came over the three officers' faces hearing the news. "Thank you, Clarise," Duval answered before ending the conversation.

"Thank God for that," Berger uttered, forcing a smile to his face.

"Well now," the Captain began. "Since we know Masson has left surgery, we can get back to the plight at hand." Staring directly at Geneviève, he waved his pen at her. "Detective Benoit, I want you to gather every piece of evidence, every report, dispatch or citizen's tip on your suspect, is that understood?"

With a curt nod, Benoit responded with a firm, "Yes, sir."

Duval turned to Berger. “And I want you to put together a file on the tip you received on the drug movement at the marina from earlier,” he directed.

“How did you know...?” Berger queried, exchanging a quick glance with Geneviève. “We haven’t even completed our write-ups on what we learned from the marina.”

“After Captain Soucy received his tip on Officer Galant’s abduction and the sighting near the marina in the Les Riaux quarter, I’ve asked for all reports,” Duval answered. “You’re not the only officer who’s concerned about her, Detective. I expect your reports on my desk by 2100 hours tonight.”

Benoit and Berger left Duval’s office, and kept to themselves as they made their way to their own section of the police station. Passing one of the debriefing rooms, the detectives glanced in as they picked up the excited voices of colleagues arguing about the superintendents’ new policy on uniform regulations.

“I’ve forgotten all about that,” Geneviève muttered as they passed the open door.

Berger tilted his head to the side. “Afraid your patrol uniform won’t fit anymore?” he replied. Nicolas had no worries about his uniform fitting, since he’d always prided himself in maintaining his weight after training.

Geneviève heard her partner’s comment, but put little concern towards it. She knew because of the continued unrest following the yellow vest demonstrations, Superintendent Chevallier had mandated all officers be prepared to wear service uniforms when directed. “It’s not that the trousers and shirt won’t fit,” she replied as they entered their office space. “I can’t stand wearing those damn boots they issued.”

“At least you won’t have to worry about busting a heel when chasing after a suspect.” It had led Geneviève to try to send a voucher to replace her fashionable footwear, leading to a series of snide remarks by her fellow detectives.

“Those shoes cost me over €300 to replace,” Geneviève answered.

"I noticed you don't wear them very much anymore, though," Berger chided as he rifled through the files for copies of earlier reports.

Geneviève flashed a smirk towards her colleague before powering up her computer. The display flashed as she starred into the monochromatic void. Remesy was in Marseille for a reason, but what was it? He knows we'll be looking for him, so what's so damn important? These questions were just the first of many which clouded her thoughts. A nudge on her shoulder nearly caused her to fall out of her chair.

Berger stood over her. "Are you going to work on what the Captain wanted or just look into space?"

Geneviève glanced up at Nicolas and blinked. "What did you say?"

Berger shook his head. "You've been sitting there like a gargoyle statue on Notre Dame for the last ten minutes," he said. "I wasn't sure if you were awake or sleeping. Oh, and I was wondering if you had any notes about the boat at the marina, too?"

With a tug on the handle, Geneviève opened the bottom drawer of her desk where she kept her notebooks. Grasping the top one, she flung it towards Nicolas. "Here you go. The notes are on the last page with writing on it," she explained before turning her attention back to her computer.

Moving her mouse across the desktop, Geneviève began the task of collecting the reports Captain Duval ordered her to compile. As she waited for the files to shift from one folder to another, she grabbed the phone and dialed the office number to Hector Dupont. After the third ring, her call was answered.

"Aeroport Marseille Provence, Monsieur Dupont's office," the woman answered.

Geneviève sat upright in her chair. This was the first instance someone other than Hector answered his private line at the security office. And for it to be a woman whose voice sounded young and seductive led her to consider something more than just another hired clerk. Was this a sign her feelings for Hector were deeper than she wanted to admit?

"This is Detective Benoit with Marseille DJSE; is Monsieur Dupont available?"

"I'm sorry, Detective, he's stepped out. Is there a message you wish to leave?" the clerk asked.

Geneviève could only imagine the worst case hearing the young woman speak. It wasn't jealousy, or was it? Gathering herself, she turned her attention back to the reason for the call. "Can you please have him contact me the minute he returns?" Geneviève queried. "He can contact me at the following number," she began before reciting the station's central number. "And if that's busy, he can call me at my personal number."

In the airport office, the clerk dutifully transcribed the numbers as Geneviève recited them. "Oui, Detective, I'll see he gets your message," the woman said. "Will there be anything else?"

"No, that'll be all," Geneviève said, ending the call with a simple, "Merci."

Berger watched the whole exchange. He noticed Geneviève's demeanor change as the conversation progressed from first greeting to ending and surmised something wasn't right. "Trouble with your gentleman friend Hector?"

Geneviève jerked her head up at the comment. "What? No... there's nothing wrong," she defended. "Why are you asking, anyway?"

Berger chuckled. "It sounded like you weren't talking with someone didn't you expected to, that's all," he replied. "At least it wasn't Hector... am I right?"

Geneviève's face grew red. Her coworker asked about something trivial which she made personal without realizing it. "Hector wasn't there, and a clerk answered his phone, that's all," she blurted, trying to deflect the query. "It wasn't anything more, Nic."

"Then why did you feel the need to bend your pen in half?"

Throughout the brief conversation with the clerk, Geneviève's subconscious had led her to act in a way she'd never done before in public. *At least Nic doesn't know about Hideki-san*, she thought. When she was younger, the self-defense master from Sasebo, Japan instructed Geneviève to concentrate and trust her skills. He did this by having her prove it on a slab of wood one day in his dojo in Cherbourg. Though her hand ached for hours afterward, the pride displayed by her smile lasted for weeks.

As Berger pointed out, she looked down at her hand which clutched the remains of her ball-point pen bent over in an obscene angle. In feigned disgust, she flung it into the corner, where it landed amongst the empty cans of sports drink.

"And that's why I do my best not to piss you off," Berger said with a chuckle, watching the pen come to rest. "Still, you say nothing was bugging you about the call?"

With a scornful look, the detective reclined for a moment in her chair. As she tilted her head back, Geneviève grabbed her ponytail and pulled the fabric tie from it. She flung her head forward, covering her face with waves of burnt-auburn tresses. Seconds later, she pulled it tight and spun a black band around it to set it back in place. "I'm fine," she replied with a huff. "Now can we get on with our work?"

Before Berger could answer, the office phone began ringing. With a shrug towards Geneviève, he picked up the receiver. "Drug Interdiction, Detective Berger."

While Nicolas was on the phone, Geneviève moved a series of files on her computer, queuing them up for print. The printer buzzed and chirped into life as the papers slid onto the tray.

After a minute of conversation, Berger hung up the phone. "Good thing you're sitting down," he told her, "'cause you're not going to believe what I've just learned."

"What's that?"

"A patrol near the equestrian center has reported finding a suspected member of an Algerian gang hanging around the stables," Berger chuckled.

"And you find it funny?"

Berger gathered himself, doing his best to fight of the inclination to laugh at the victim's predicament. "Sorry. It's just the patrol found this individual hanging..., as in strung up by the ankles, in the stables."

Geneviève blinked at the last statement. "Strung up? As in tied up… like a cow?" she asked.

"As if he was being prepared to be drawn and quartered by a butcher," the detective replied. As he took a deep breath, Berger became more serious. "And when they cut him down and took off the gag he wore, he demanded police protection. Seems this gang member professed to know the identity of those responsible for his dilemma, but feared retaliation if he talked."

"Did he mention any names?" Geneviève asked.

"No, he didn't." Berger said. "He just mentioned knowing who the leader was." He picked the phone back up to dial Captain Duval. "After the earlier event, this call is something the captain needs to handle, don't you think?"

"Better him than us," Geneviève replied, watching the image of Louis Remesy fill the computer screen as her file printed.

Chapter TWENTY-ONE

Echoing soft clicks of high heels on the tiled floor announced the arrival of a familiar guest to the detectives' office. "Hey you. I thought we were grabbing dinner tonight?" a voice asked from the doorway. Francine LeBeau stood in the doorway; her lab coat slung over her arm.

"As a matter of fact," Berger replied, "I just finished my report."

"How about you Geneviève? You up for some dinner?" Francine asked.

Geneviève was deep in thought piecing together her report. From the Customs account of drug smuggling on cruise ships, she traced the known and alleged movements of Louis Remesy. Francine asking about dinner gave her a reason to pause her work. "Ahh, thanks, but I've got a few more reports to review and get together for Captain Duval," she replied, glancing up at the clock.

"You haven't finished yet?" Berger asked.

"There's more to these reports, Captain Lemieux, and I worked than yours, Nic," Geneviève answered, tapping her pencil on the monitor. "You two enjoy yourselves."

Berger shrugged his shoulders as he pushed a handful of papers into the folder on his desk. "Suit yourself," he said. Flipping the cover closed, he checked off several boxes on the cover sheet before signing his name to the bottom.

Francine stood off to the side, watching Geneviève stare at the computer screen. The lab technician observed the woman shift the mouse side to side, then up and down. Every few seconds, she'd notice Geneviève blink and her head sway left to right as she read through notes.

"I'm ready," Berger announced, shouldering his backpack while clutching the folder.

"Okay," Francine said. As they walked out of the office, she turned back to her friend. "Au revoir, Geneviève," she said with a wave.

"Au revoir," the detective replied without looking up.

Francine gazed back at Geneviève as she and Nicolas left. "Is she going to be okay?"

The detective looked over his shoulder. "She's taking it on the chin on this one," Berger replied. "Captain Duval didn't say she was directly at fault for today's altercation, but she took it that way. I just hope she can push past the negatives and learn from it. She should be okay."

Officers for the evening shift already began making their way into the briefing room as Geneviève placed the last few comments in her report before printing it.

"Another late night?" came a voice from the doorway.

As she craned her head to look over her computer, Geneviève saw the familiar smile of fellow detective Pierre Juneau, his distinctive clean-shaven scalp aglow with the shade of a newborn piglet. He was the senior officer on shift and caught her working after hours on several occasions the past few months.

"Hi Pierre," she said. "Yeah, Captain Duval wants an update on our cases by 9 o'clock tonight. And with Captain Lemieux still out, I'm left doing the clerks job," she added with a slight smirk.

Detective Juneau shook his head. "Every officer has been there at some time," he said. Dragging out a chair, he sat across from Geneviève before saying anything. He tilted his head to the side to look past the computer screen, and with a feigned cough, asked his next question with caution. "So, how are you doing?"

Geneviève leaned around the computer as she heard the question, keeping her eyes locked on Juneau. "I'm fine..." She saw the expression on his face. It was the look concerned fathers gave their child. She'd seen it on her own father, and recently on Hector's face as well. "Why are you asking me this, anyway?"

"I just finished reading the daily dispatches," Juneau said. "Seems Masson had a run in with a few thugs. Based on the notes, you and Berger were acting on a tip about a possible suspect; am I right?"

Her head spun hearing the tone Juneau used. Geneviève felt he was questioning their judgement, attacking the actions, and was preparing to chastise her personally. "What are you trying to say, Pierre?"

The detective held his hands up in defense. "Whoa, there, I wasn't saying anything but what I read, okay?"

"You make it sound as if we shouldn't have done anything. We should have just routed the tip through channels," Geneviève said. "This drug smuggler Remesy needs to be caught. If we don't do something, we're never going to rid the city of this plaque he's brought on." Her voice cracked as it grew louder. "He's potentially the one responsible for the deaths of at least two tourists."

Juneau saw the passion Geneviève placed on arresting the suspect, but he also knew there was more than just a single individual responsible for Marseille's drug problems. Before he could speak, the phone rang. "Detective Juneau," he answered after the second ring.

Geneviève only half listened to the call. She was still agitated because of the detective's insinuation toward herself and her fellow officer.

Juneau finished talking and hung up the phone as he got out of the chair. "Let's take a walk, shall we?"

"Why?"

"You heard about the fellow found at the equestrian center, haven't you?" Juneau asked. "He and his lawyer wish to discuss something... with you," he explained as they headed toward the elevators.

"After seeing the Captain, I've been here all afternoon," she replied. "I haven't heard of any specific arrests involving me. I've been here with Nicolas working on our reports."

Juneau stopped at the elevator behind Geneviève "Guess we'll find out in a moment, won't we," he said as the doors slid open. Juneau pressed the button for the lower level and the doors glided closed. "I heard Masson's going to be okay too."

"Yes, I know," Geneviève replied. "Nic and I were in with Captain Duval when he received the message on Guy's surgery results. I'm sure he didn't think this is the manner he'd finish his time with the department." As both officers exited the elevator, they made a quick turn to the right, proceeding straight to interrogation.

"Here we go," Juneau said as he swung open the door. "After you, Detective."

The clanging of keys against the door alerted Zaman and his lawyer they were being joined by police interrogators. Beads of sweat rolled down the back of the gang enforcer's neck, the moisture darkening his shirt collar. Looking up, he saw the female officer enter first. The sight of Geneviève entering the room caused Ilyas to recoil in his seat somewhat. Dark auburn hair drawn back contrasted with the fairness of her skin against the brown leather jacket, caused the memories to creep back from his youth.

As the detectives entered, Ilyas Zaman's lawyer lifted the gang enforcer's arm, displaying the handcuffs secured to his wrists. "Why is my client being held like this...? I want to know what he's being charged with."

Zaman studied Geneviève's features as she stood three meters from him. They were refined, more so than those of a teenager walking past the graving yard where he struggled to learn a new language and earn a meager living.

Geneviève saw the expression on Zaman's face, but dismissed it as another chauvinist. Just another man who looked upon women as a trophy and not a person. *It was the culture of his country.*

Detective Juneau closed the door behind him and took a seat next to Geneviève. "Monsieur Zaman, my name is Detective Juneau. This is Detective Benoit."

An emotionless smile crossed Detective Juneau's face as he gestured for Geneviève to a seat and waved for the lawyer to sit down. As he took the chair next to Geneviève, Juneau placed a folder on the table. "I believe your client was detained for trespassing, Monsieur."

Geneviève fixed her gaze upon the enforcer for the Maghrebis gang. She could see Zaman's shoulders sag briefly while he let out a sigh that conveyed his annoyance at the whole affair. As Geneviève kept her focus on Zaman, Detective Juneau had opened the folder and read off the charges of being on private property after hours.

The lawyer turned his back to the officers and spoke in a hushed voice with Zaman. "It's a simple infraction, minor one at best; you should be out in an hour, no more."

While the two conversed, each detective sat stoic without interrupting the conversation. The detectives knew being quiet allowed the technician recording the session with the best acoustics. "My sergeant also mentioned your client wishes to convey information in exchange for a more lenient charge; is this correct?" Juneau asked, closing the folder as his attention turned to Zaman.

The lawyer leaned closer to Zaman and whispered something neither officer heard. With a raised eyebrow, Zaman contemplated how much he should confess. He nodded and sat up in his chair. His restraints rattled against the metal surfaces as he placed his hands on the table.

"The citizens of this city have many voices," Zaman began. "And some have made it apparent they are afraid there is a component of the police force which can't be trusted." He quickly glanced between the two officers. "One of your own is helping advance the work of a criminal element."

"And you know who the individual is?" Juneau asked.

"Of course, I do, Officer," Zaman feigned. "More important is to ask yourself; why don't you know?"

"And who's saying you're not part of those criminals who want to further their own cause?" Geneviève asked as she shifted herself in the chair to lean on the table. "It's known there are various ethnic factions attempting to control their own quarters of the city. Some have even gone so far as to assault police and emergency personnel trying to help."

The Maghrebis enforcer snorted at the remark. "And where is your proof, woman? Just because I'm a foreigner trying to better myself, you assume I'm a criminal."

Detective Juneau held his hand up. "Enough arguing, Monsieur," he interrupted, trying to calm both Zaman and Geneviève. "Do you have information to substantiate your claim as your lawyer mentioned earlier? If not, you're being charged as noted and will have the opportunity to pay the fines and be released."

Zaman could see disclosing the name of Gregory Arsenault and his contact would gain him no leverage at the moment, so he sat back in silence. His lawyer twisted in his seat, once again leaning near his client to confer with him. After a few moments, both men looked to be in agreement as to their next course of action.

"Monsieur Zaman will pay the fine on the trespassing charges," the lawyer said. "And has nothing further to say on the matter of police members and their activities."

Detective Juneau slid a sheet of paper from the folder in front of the lawyer. "You and your client will sign attesting to the admission," he declared, pointing to the lower section of the form. "I'll see this is processed in a punctual manner." Detective Juneau was not fond of suspects like Zaman wasting his time with false accusations.

As the lawyer and Zaman went through the motion of signing the complaint, Geneviève turned back to Detective Juneau. "If there's nothing else, Pierre, I need to finish the other reports."

"No, I think we're done for the moment," Juneau said. "I'll be up in a few minutes once they're done."

Leaving the interview room, Geneviève made her way back to the detectives' office. She couldn't help but think Zaman was part of some criminal component. "If he was, who could get close enough to abduct him and place him in a position where we'd catch him?" she muttered aloud as her computer came back to life.

Though no more than twenty minutes had passed on the clock, to Geneviève, it felt like two hours. She continued to piece together reports she and Lemieux compiled on the drug trafficking when a chorus of voices outside caught her attention.

"Well, that was certainly the strangest half hour, wouldn't you say?" Detective Juneau said as he entered the office.

"Time in my life I'll never get back," Geneviève replied. "And for him wanting to say something on our supposed 'mole' turned out to be nothing," she added. "I know Captain Duval said he's already working with the other senior members to conduct an internal review on everyone's activities."

Juneau shrugged his shoulders. "And if they go through all that work and find nothing, then what? We're back to having someone saying something to the wrong person and lose their job and never find the true source or reason behind the scheme," he added.

The throbbing in Geneviève's head had yet to subside. Gawking at the screen had taken its toll on her concentration. Flexing her hand, she selected what she hoped would be the last files to compile. "There, done at last," she declared as the reports printed on the copier.

"Is this late evening putting a dent in your social life?" Juneau asked while reviewing additional police reports.

Geneviève sighed. Her look told the officer across from her the answer. She and Hector had not committed to a routine of seeing each other yet. Though she'd felt a sense of relief by telling Hector of her past, it didn't provide the closure to allow their relationship to move forward or grow. At least, it didn't for her.

Juneau glanced at the clock. "You know, if you hustle getting those file upstairs, you can make the next bus for your ride home." He was one officer of a handful who knew Geneviève moved throughout the city by bus.

"Thanks for the reminder," Geneviève answered, as she placed the last report in the folder. She grabbed her holster and slipped it on her waist before pulling her jacket over it. With a wave of the folder, she was soon dashing out of the office. "Au revoir, Pierre," she said over her shoulder.

Ten minutes earlier, Sergeant Dubois had left the station and strolled toward the bus stop, heading home for the evening. In the shadows of a shop entrance, two men sat in a sedan and watched her stand near the covered bench with several other citizens.

"Too many people tonight, but we can follow her and see where she exits," Yacine El Amari said to his follower. "By then we'll have a better idea what Amed wishes to have done with her." His companion's only reply was a simple grunt in agreement. The handful of citizens boarded the bus, the sergeant being the last to enter and take a seat. Belching exhaust, it pulled away from its stop with the sedan carrying Amed Gilles men following close behind.

Chapter TWENTY-TWO

Across from the police station, the bus stop had but a few patrons waiting under a single dim light while darkness engulfed the sidewalk. As she crossed the street, Geneviève noticed finding a seat wouldn't be a problem. She stepped onto the sidewalk as the next metro service rounded the corner. There were just a handful of people onboard, with plenty of empty spaces to choose.

With the seat behind the driver empty, Geneviève sat, sliding all the way against the window. She leaned against the glass and allowed the cool surface to ease the throbbing of her temple. Shifting in the seat, she peered out as the bus departed. Her thoughts still revolved around Louis Remesy's appearance in the city. During the gun battle at Chateau Il d'If, Geneviève saw the look on his face as he leapt onto the launch as bullets peppered the hull: the look of someone who would seek revenge.

Lights from various shops and cafes danced across the glass as the sun's faded glow of orange and yellow painted the western horizon. The bus slowed as it approached a roundabout near Geneviève's apartment complex, and the jerking motion announced the arrival at her stop.

After checking her postal bin, Geneviève trudged up the stairs, keys in hand. She unlocked the door and swung it open, the light from the hallway casting her shadow across the narrow entrance. With a nudge from her elbow, she closed the door behind her. As she bent over to untie her shoes, she froze.

The faint aroma of men's cologne lingered, and it wasn't what Hector usually wore. Geneviève finished pulling her shoes off with her left hand while her right snaked upward, grasping the pistol off her hip. She tried for the light switch while the right held the Sig-Sauer in front of her.

Touching the switch with a fingertip, Geneviève flicked on the hall light. A gasp escaped her lips as the familiar figure of Gregory Arsenault appeared across the room. A tingling sensation coursed through her limbs, and her eyes narrowed as she focused on the shipping broker, if that's what he did do for work. Her pulse raced; the physical thumping of her heart suggested it might burst through her chest.

Leveling the pistol on the intruder, the detective in her reacted. "How did you get into my apartment?" Geneviève demanded. Her eyes darted about the room, trying to gain a sense whether she was alone with Arsenault or if there were others lurking nearby.

"How I got in is not important," Gregory replied, palms held open for her to see. "But if you must know, I'm friends with a very competent locksmith, he let me in," Arsenault answered with a mild chuckle. "Plus, it was important that I have a conversation with you in person, Detective, but in private."

Geneviève's eyes narrowed. "And why should I believe that? What's the real reason for you to be here?"

"As I mentioned, I wanted to talk with you," Arsenault replied. "And hopefully, in the end, we'll both get what we want out of it." He kept his hands in the open for her to see. "Now, if I may suggest, how about you place the gun on the table and have a seat," he began, motioning to the sofa across from him. He could see the detective still felt unsure as the hand holding the pistol twitched.

Slow and deliberate, Geneviève moved out of the entryway, letting light from the overhead lamp illuminate the intruder. Swiveling her head left and right, she tried to determine if anyone was lying in wait for her. "Who else is here with you?" she asked.

"No one, I assure you," Arsenault replied. "Please, sit down; I'm only here to talk. I promise."

Geneviève kept herself facing Arsenault as she sat on the edge of the settee. With her eyes locked on her intruder, she deftly switched the pistol from her right to left hand. Then she leaned across the end table and turned on the small lamp which cast its light towards the kitchen, allowing her to see he told the truth. No one else was in the apartment with them.

Gregory shifted his weight to the front of the chair, and locked eyes on Geneviève before he spoke. "Earlier this afternoon, I was able to have a conversation with a gentleman who should be in police custody by now," he began.

"Who?"

Gregory clasped his hands together on his lap. "His name is Ilyas Zaman," he said, "an illegal immigrant from Algiers who currently is part of the largest Maghrebis gang in Marseille. And while we talked, I learned he may have been involved in your officer's abduction."

The detective grunted her disbelief at the comment. "Why should I believe you?" Geneviève asked. "Besides, I've already met him. He was arrested for trespassing. But he didn't profess to being a member of any gang, though," the detective added, her eyes locked squarely on Arsenault.

Gregory sighed. "I understand your reluctance to trust me, but I assure you it's the truth." He blinked several times before continuing. "Did your police records disclose anything about this man? I would guess they had nothing on him, right?" Gregory asked. "Like I said, I believe the information I'm about to share will be a help for both of us. You get a chance to exorcise one of Marseille's criminal leaders, and I…"

"And what? What do you gain from this?" Geneviève interrupted.

"And… I'll also help you locate Monsieur Remesy," Gregory added, sweetening the deal.

Geneviève's head began to spin as she soaked up the information "How is that possible? You said you only met him once. Now you say you can locate him? My instincts tell me to arrest you for obstructing an ongoing investigation," she added in a polite but forceful tone.

"Without my help, you'll never get another chance to arrest Remesy after today," Gregory said. "I have a few friends I can call on to help ascertain his location, at which point you and your colleagues can make your arrest."

Geneviève contemplated the offer. *To get a chance to arrest Remesy would be a fine achievement,* she thought. Claude would be proud if she could see the drug smuggler apprehended, locked in a cell behind the walls of Fresnes Prison. "How did you learn about today?

Besides putting away another drug peddler, what other help am I going to reap for helping you?"

"As I mentioned, I can help you locate Remesy," Gregory said. The former Legionnaire took a deep breath before answering the woman. "It's only fair you learn why I'm asking for your help. So, since you asked, all I'm wanting you to do is disregard rumors of an officer in your station as an informant," Gregory said. "And I can promise by doing that, your position on the police force and in the station will be secured."

"And what is this individual to you? Are they keeping you abreast of police activities so you can do something illegal?" Genevieve asked, tired of the verbal exchange. "As a police officer, I've a duty to report this person's name to my superiors. You understand, don't you?"

Gregory felt the cell phone in his pocket vibrate as the detective posed her questions. Peeking at his watch, he was reminded of how long he'd been in the apartment, and knew it was his friend Louis calling to assure all was well.

Geneviève heard the slight hum of the cellphone. "If you're going to answer that, do so very carefully," she warned, motioning the pistol at Gregory.

Gregory dug out the phone and answered. "Bon jour, mon ami. Oui, all is well. I'll be through in a few minutes." He ended the call and slid the phone back in his pocket. Glancing across at Geneviève, her pistol still held steady, Gregory offered Geneviève one last chance to accept his offer. "Well, Detective Benoit, are we in agreement?"

"I want the name of your contact in the station. Now... tonight," Geneviève demanded.

Gregory sighed. He knew disclosing his sister-in-law would place her in a position she'd be unable to escape. "First, I'll help you find Remesy so you can arrest him. Then afterwards, I'll provide you with my contacts identity, agreed?" he asked as he calmly got to his feet.

The detective followed suit, getting to her feet but kept her pistol pointed at Arsenault. Geneviève didn't know what to do. Her instincts and training told her to arrest Gregory under the guise of attempting to bribe an officer. But he also offered the chance to get her hands on

Remesy, and this was becoming too great a temptation for her to resist.

"One last thing," Gregory said as he reached into his jacket to produce a small envelope. "This might be of interest to you. Call it a 'good faith' gesture of my intentions."

She accepted the envelope and shook it open. A folded slip of paper hung in the slit, which Geneviève pulled out. *Southern Warrior*, 43.19/5.23 were written out, along with a date. "Where did you get this information… these numbers?" she asked.

"Monsieur Zaman was quite happy to furnish me with information after, shall we say, gentle persuasion," Gregory answered. "Based on the time, I'd say we both should call it a day, don't you?" He nodded to the small desk clock perched on the hutch. "The number on the bottom is my cellphone. Call me with your decision by 6 o'clock tomorrow night," he said as he exited the apartment.

Geneviève stood frozen in place. Arsenault mentioned things she wanted in the worst way. First, was the arrest of Louis Remesy. Then, produced information she and Berger learned earlier in the day; the coordinates to the outer lighthouse on Isle Planier. But what about the name, *Southern Warrior*? And what was the significance of the date?

Shuffling out of the apartment, Arsenault strolled up the street where his friend had parked. He climbed into the sedan and let out a brief sigh as he glanced at the driver. "And now, mon ami, we wait."

"And if she decides she doesn't want to call you, what then?" Louis asked.

Gregory didn't enjoy thinking of the negative prospect to his case with the detective. He realized if Genevieve didn't cooperate, he'd have to arrange for his sister-in-law to accept his plan for her premature retirement from the police force. "She'll call," Arsenault said with a degree of confidence. "This woman wants Nazim just as bad as we do."

Louis maneuvered the car through the late-night traffic. "And how do we fulfill our end of your bargain when we don't know where Nazim is at the moment?" he asked. "It's not like you've kept in touch with him, you know."

Gregory heard his friend's comment and realized he would need to make another deal with Claudio Carbone to learn of Nazim Aziz's whereabouts. Doing so would only deepen his debt to the mafia don in a way he tried to avoid. "I do know one person we can contact."

"And who would that be?"

"Omar Khalid."

Louis glared at his friend sitting in the car next to him. "You're not serious, are you? He's the one Nazim answers to; he's not going to give you any information on him."

Gregory's mind began working on a plan as quickly as he could consider the idea. The whole case would come down to the deceitful practice of each individual. "We'll give him a reason to grant us one last opportunity to meet."

Louis had spent many days and nights working with his friend on plans to capture or kill mercenaries during their time in the French Foreign Legion. He recognized, with a simple glance at Gregory's face, he was already putting pieces in place to make sure his plan succeeded.

The streetlights marked their space as the night passed, pushing back the shadows from the buildings. Louis exited the expressway leading towards Gregory's chateau when his phone rang. "You want to answer that?" he asked, looking at his friend.

Gregory saw the caller ID flash. "Bon jour, Phillip."

In the chateau not far from where Gregory and Louis were driving, Phillip hesitated. "I'm sorry, Gregory, but they're gone," he stammered.

Puzzled at the statement, Gregory could only reply, "What are you talking about?"

Phillip looked over at Gregory's mistress Giselle sitting at the table. With a gesture, persuaded him to continue. "Your niece and her companion are gone, Monsieur."

"How?"

"I had gone out to clean my car, and they were sitting on the veranda," Phillip began. "When I went in to the house to put things away, they were gone... with my car."

Louis only heard half of the conversation, but could see the look on his friend's face and noticed something was not right. “Trouble?” he asked, turning towards the chateau.

“We’re almost to the chateau; you can finish when I get there,” Gregory spoke before ending the call. As he tossed the phone on the dash, he turned to Louis. “It would appear when I told Sophia she needed to stay at the chateau, she took it as a suggestion,” Gregory said. “She and Celine are gone, and they took Phillip’s car.”

Chapter TWENTY-THREE

Sleep came as an unwilling companion to Geneviève. And while the clock showed she'd slept four or so hours, lying in bed she felt as if it were one after a restless night's slumber. The alarm on her cellphone grew in volume. Geneviève's hand slid across the nightstand, until she found her phone and tapped the screen twice to silence the noise.

After the visit by Gregory Arsenault earlier that evening, Geneviève sat alone, her apartment lit by the table lamp. She stared at the note, contemplating her next course of action. All he offered was information in exchange for more information. It wasn't long after Arsenault left that she'd forced herself to bed and much-needed sleep.

Settling under the comforter, Geneviève again allowed her thoughts to race towards an elusive goal. Before she could contemplate where those thoughts led to, her phone chimed again.

As she grunted in protest, Geneviève rolled on to her side, and propped herself up on one elbow. She slid her finger across the phone until the alarm function illuminated and she silenced it for good. She got her herself off the bed and was greeted by the chilly surface of her bedroom floor.

With the grace of a small dog's exuberance, Geneviève plodded off to the bathroom and a quick shower. Soon, she was awash in hot water, cleansing the previous day's trouble from her thoughts and preparing for the day ahead.

Within an hour of the alarm's chime, Geneviève was dressed and headed out of her apartment. In stark contrast to last night's bus ride, the morning jaunt on the metro vehicle was more like a fishing trawler at the end of its run. Stepping on the bus, she was greeted by standing room only patrons, each grasping the rail for support.

With her left hand clutching the pole behind the driver, Geneviève kept her right hovering near the Sig-Sauer holstered on her belt. Each sway of the bus around a corner or swerve to miss a parked car caused her to jostle about. After an eventful route through the city, she soon saw the police station loom closer.

With a loud and meaningful sigh, Detective Benoit stepped off the bus to join the pedestrians' stream across the boulevard. In the station, some of the officers were already in their navy-blue uniforms, while others wore street clothes.

She walked to the security post where she flashed her credentials at the officer, who checked her weapon and swept a metal-detecting wand across her torso before she headed upstairs to the detectives' office.

It wasn't long before Nicolas appeared in the doorway holding a bagel and a sports drink. "Hey, you," he greeted her as he placed his food and drink down. "When did you get in?"

"About a half hour ago or so," Geneviève answered as she looked over the computer screen at Nicolas. Her nose twitched as she smelled the sourdough bagel sitting across from her. "Is that fresh?"

"Yeah, they were just putting them out on the trays, why?"

The grumble in her stomach reminded Geneviève she'd left her apartment without breakfast. "It smells really good, that's all." She pushed her chair away from the desk and grabbed her wallet. "I'll be back," as she rushed out.

In minutes, Geneviève stood in the cafeteria behind other officers waiting her turn to select one of the bakery items. As she stepped forward to retrieve her bagel, Geneviève felt a nudge. She glanced over her shoulder to the now familiar face of Sergeant Dubois.

"I'm sorry, Detective," Claire announced as she stepped back. "Seems everyone found out there's fresh baked goods and they all want one," she explained, nodding to the crowd behind the pair.

"Yes, so I noticed."

Claire glanced down at the floor before looking back at Geneviève. "I'm sorry to hear about Detective Masson. I understand he's going to be okay though, am I right?"

Geneviève forced a polite smile. "Yes, I got the same news too," she replied, stepping to the cashier to pay and pulled out €20. "I'll cover the sergeant's as well."

"Thank you," the sergeant replied, picking up her items.

Geneviève watched as Claire made her way towards the Police Records office. "Merci," she said as the clerk handed back her change. After she picked up her herbal tea and bagel, the detective scampered back to the office and the search for information on the city's drug dealers.

Just as Geneviève stepped onto the landing from the stairs, she was caught by Detective Berger, who came out of the detective's office space, holding her jacket. "You can eat that on the go," he said, tugging her elbow to turn her away from the door.

"Where are we going?" Geneviève asked. Inserting the bag containing her bagel between her teeth, she slipped her jacket on and followed Berger down the stairs she'd just climbed.

"The harbor," Berger explained. Both officers made their way through the exit next to security and towards the secure parking structure.

"And what's happening there?" Geneviève asked as she tore off a chunk of bagel and bit into it.

The detective spun around in his tracks. "Really?" Berger asked once they reached their assigned police car. "Did we not find a clue onboard the yacht *Scirocco* and its possible movements yesterday?"

"Sure, we did," Geneviève replied, sliding into the passenger seat.

"They mean something to someone," he replied. As he pulled out of the station complex, Berger spend the next few minutes explaining his theory about the yacht and the coordinates.

"Let me get this straight," Geneviève said through another bite. "You think the people who own the *Scirocco* are the same ones who might be responsible for the yacht *Le Femme Fatale* and the socialite?"

"I admit it's just one possibility," Berger said. "But we need to know more about why the location on the charts is so significant, don't we? Besides, it wasn't really my idea about heading to the harbor; it was Francine's."

Geneviève smirked. "Your bedroom talks center around work issues, do they?"

"What? No, what are you... we weren't in bed discussing the case," Berger stammered as he defended himself. "Besides, our time together is not open for discussion, okay?"

"I'm sorry, I couldn't help myself, Nic," Geneviève said. Taking another bite from her bagel, she began wondering if the visit from Gregory Arsenault last night could also be tied to the dead socialite and the yachts.

As she swallowed some tea to wash away the last of her bagel, Geneviève shifted her weight around the passenger seat. "So, what are we going to ask the staff at the Harbormaster's office besides what the numbers represent? I mean, we already know they relate to coordinates off the coast according to what the patrol officer told us."

"Well, I'm glad you asked," Berger said, pulling the police car into the parking space near the Harbormaster's office. "I thought we could also try and learn who maintains the *Ile du Planier* lighthouse. If it's only cared for on a part-time basis, someone could be using it as their temporary base."

Geneviève tilted her head to the side, letting Berger's idea take hold, if just for the moment, as she got out of the car. "You think the smugglers are paying off yacht owners to help bring the drugs ashore from the larger freighters to avoid Customs?"

Berger got out and closed his door. "It's just one theory, but with the evidence we've been handed, it would seem plausible, don't you think?" He tipped his head forward in her direction, his eyebrows raised.

Geneviève nodded in agreement, and contemplated how the information her evening guest would come into play. *Monsieur Arsenault had the same coordinates as the ones from the Scirocco*, she told herself. But did he actually get them from Gilles? She shook her head as she followed Nicolas up the steps and into the office.

Across town, Phillip Gaston was busy fixing coffee for those in the chateau. He'd been up all night reliving the events from earlier where Sophia and her companion drove off in his car and hadn't been heard from since. A noise behind him caught his attention. It was his cousin Julien. "*Bonjour,* Jules."

Julien clasped the young man on the shoulder. "Did you ever get some sleep?" he asked while grabbing a cup off the shelf.

"No, I never slept; I've been up all night."

Julien shook his head. "Don't take Sophia's actions personally; it wasn't your fault," he assured him while adding cream to his coffee. "Uh... this is pretty good," he added after taking his first sip and sat down. "Trust me, Gregory won't place the blame on you."

"What am I not doing?" came the voice of Gregory as he entered the kitchen.

Julien sat up in the chair. "I was just telling Phillip you wouldn't blame him for your niece's disappearance. She's acting like any normal adult woman would."

Gregory grabbed his own cup and poured some coffee into it. "Speaking of Sophia, who's watching her apartment right now?" he asked as he took a seat at the table.

"Pasqual relieved me just after one o'clock," Julien replied. "And Louis will be switching out with him in about thirty minutes."

"Are you hungry?" Phillip asked, feeling left out of the conversation.

Gregory nodded his head. "Breakfast sounds good, Phillip; you'll find everything in the refrigerator and pantry. Julien, do we know where Hector is this morning?" he asked with a glance across the table. "He and Romain shouldn't have taken too long to dispose of the vehicles from the stables last night."

"Oui, he's picking up some documents from Monsieur Dumont this morning," Julien replied. "But he hasn't checked in yet."

As the three men discussed the past night's task, they each turned their heads as the sound of a closing door filled the house. With the softness of a ballet dancer, Gregory's live-in partner Giselle entered the room to the surprise of the men in attendance.

The former Olympian was clad in running tights and vest, the latter being the shade of a ripened piece of Valencia citrus. Giselle pulled out her cell phone and plugged in a set of headphones. Leaning over Gregory, she placed a kiss to his cheek. "I'll be back in an hour," she said before setting the earpieces in place.

Gregory nodded. "Be careful, and remember your keys," he said as she walked away. The svelte yet muscular gait caught each man's attention as Giselle closed the door behind her. "Now, where were we?"

"I believe Phillip was going to cook us some breakfast," Julien declared, lifting his coffee in his cousin's direction.

Meanwhile, Detectives Benoit and Berger were engaged in conversation with the senior harbormaster, Enzo Tasse. Standing in the open office, the detectives could pick up the chatter between the clerks and the various merchantmen being guided to and from their respective berths. On occasion, the blast of a ship's horn would reverberate across the harbor, to announce a freighter's maneuver.

"Detective Berger, most navigation components and fixtures in use today are autonomous," Tasse said. "The work of this lighthouse is no different."

The harbormaster's explanation began to settle in the detective's psyche. "Meaning no one lives there, right?" Geneviève asked.

"Correct, Detective," Tasse replied. "We do, however, send out a maintenance crew on a quarterly basis. You know, check on the solar panels, batteries, and the visual markers. We do this because we can't control the actions of divers or weekend fishermen who set foot on the island."

Detective Berger glanced at Geneviève before he posed his next question. "People can dock their boats there?"

The harbormaster shook his head. "Not an actual dock in the true sense of the structure," Tasse answered. "The island doesn't have a purpose-built pier, just a small alcove our crew used to access the isle by inflatable boat."

Geneviève flipped open her notebook and scribbled down what the harbormaster described. Learning there were signs of activity meant someone else knew it would be a possible rendezvous point. One without outside interference, for the most part. "When the crews conducted their maintenance, have they encountered anyone on the island?" she asked.

"Of course," the harbormaster answered. "On most occasions, like I said, our people will have the run-ins with recreational boaters.

But we've never been made aware of any wrong-doing if that's what you're alluding to, Detective."

"I'm not going to be so foolish to ask how we could hitch a ride to the island," Berger quipped. "But what type of boats do crews use to make their way out to the lighthouse? And when are they headed out again?"

Benoit cocker her head to the side while glancing at her partner. "What are you thinking, Nic?" Geneviève asked.

Berger held his hand up, gesturing to the woman he wasn't finished. "And what can you tell us about these numbers?" he asked, handing over a slip of paper to the harbormaster.

Tasse took the paper as he put on his reading glasses. "Hmm, they're coordinates just off the coast," he explained. As he stepped away from the counter, Tasse gestured for the detectives to follow him to a table where a nautical chart depicting the southern coast of France was spread.

With his fingers, Tasse traced the latitude and longitude lines until they met. "These are coordinates near the lighthouse," he said, handing back the slip to Berger.

Geneviève studied the map. "What about those?" she asked, pointing to a series of dashes emanating from the Marseille harbor.

"Those are the designated shipping routes freighters and coastal ferry boats use when entering or leaving the territory," Tasse explained. "It provides the Navy with a sense of control over the merchant ships, and a starting point if there are any problems."

Geneviève studied the lines. She noticed the one closest to the isle tracked straight to the chart's edge and oblivion. "Can you tell me where this route ends?"

Tasse slid next to the detective, then, tracing the line, saw the small script written just above the margin. Taking a magnifying glass, he slid it over the text and read it aloud for them to understand. "It's the common route used to transit between Marseille and Algiers," he said.

Geneviève's head lifted; her eyes wide yet focused. "You said most common. Is there another route a ship would use?"

Tasse chuckled at the question. "Once in open water, a ship could sail in any direction its captain chooses; it doesn't need to follow a line on the map."

Berger turned to Geneviève. "Okay, now it's my turn to ask. What are you thinking?" he asked. "You've got that look on your face, Benoit."

"The proximity of this route to the lighthouse. Quite convenient, don't you think?"

"I'm sure you would share your information if you could," Tasse said. "But I'm not following why the proposed shipping lanes are important."

"Monsieur Tasse, we can't divulge sensitive information, but I can assure you, the significance is important," Geneviève said. "By the way, can I see a list of vessel movements for the next, say… two weeks?"

As the harbormaster walked to an adjacent desk to retrieve a folder, Berger tugged on Geneviève's elbow. "Mind sharing what you're searching for there, Detective?"

"Claude and I were initially looking into the freighters being used by Papillion Transport for the drug smuggling," she began. "And now we have at least two instances where pleasure craft are involved. So, who's to say smugglers aren't coordinating a rendezvous at the lighthouse to drop off the drugs?" With a quick glance over her shoulder, Geneviève continued. "And let's not forget about Monsieur Remesy's connection in Algeria either. It's all beginning to make sense, don't you think?"

The harbormaster held the folder towards Geneviève. "Here you are, Detective," he said. "You'll find the departing freighters listed on page six and the arrivals on page ten."

Geneviève accepted the folder and turned to the latter pages to begin combing the list. The record of freighters was sorted by date and time, not by name or parent company. "Damn it," she muttered.

The explicative from the policewoman surprised Berger. "What's the problem?"

In a huff, Geneviève glared back at her fellow detective. "I can't remember the names of the other freighters for Papillion. They're in my other notebook," she lied. She was actually looking for the name given to her by Gregory Arsenault last night, the vessel named *Southern Warrior*.

The squat figure of the harbormaster leaned against a clerk's desk, listening the exchange between Benoit and Berger. After a few moments, Tasse offered his help. "Excuse me, but I can get those for you."

Berger turned in his direction. "Thank you, that'll be a great help." Setting his gaze back on Geneviève, he prodded her for more information. "So, you think the freighters drop the drugs off with a smaller craft near the lighthouse, right?"

Geneviève leaned against the chart table, staring at the lines. "I can't think of another means of a freighter getting drugs past Customs, can you? I know it's not a monumental sum, but what other means can you use to explain what we've found out so far?"

Berger scratched his chin, contemplating what Geneviève just said. Before he could voice his concerns, the harbormaster returned with a hand-written list of three freighters sailing for Papillion Transport.

"Here you are."

Once again, the detective opened the folder, feigning a search for the ships, but didn't find anything resembling the vessel named *Southern Warrior*. She closed the folder and handed it back to the harbormaster. "Merci, Monsieur Tasse."

"Is there anything else I can do for you?" Tasse asked.

Berger glanced over his shoulder at the nautical chart one last time before speaking. "No, I believe you've told us what we needed for the moment," he answered. Handing over his business card to Tasse, he added. "Do give us a call if your staff learns of any suspicious activity at the lighthouse, though."

While the detectives made their way outside, Berger paused at the police car. Looking across the harbor, he stared at the outbound freighter gliding passed the breakwater. "I think you and I need to go on a fishing excursion, Benoit. What do you say? Feel like 'catching' something to eat?"

Geneviève understood the question, but recoiled in surprise. "What are you talking about? How is a fishing excursion going to help our investigation into the drug smuggling, and Louis Remesy?"

As Berger climbed in the car, he turned to Geneviève before answering. "Just work with me on this; I've a feeling it will be worth the effort," the detective said. "Be ready to back me when I tell Captain Duval about our plan though, okay?" he finished, pulling into traffic and headed back to the office.

Chapter TWENTY-FOUR

"The answer's no, Detective Berger," Captain Duval said emphatically. "What you propose doesn't even fall under our jurisdiction," he added glancing between the detectives. "Not to mention we've no means to undertake such an effort." With a tilt to his head, the captain continued. "Tell me, Detective, where were you going to get a boat from, or a crew to sail it, heh?"

Berger dipped his head while the captain spoke. The idea sounded simple enough and easy to manage. He and Benoit would pose as vacationers on a chartered fishing boat with a handful of SWAT members along with their captain to act as deckhands. Once they arrived at the lighthouse, they would conduct a search for evidence. And if they encountered anyone, the team would take whatever action was necessary.

Geneviève sat next to Nicolas, doing her best to demonstrate a supportive front. She'd listened to his idea in the car on their return from the harbor, and it sounded simple to execute. But it was almost as worse an attempt to gather evidence than their foray to the train station to arrest Louis Remesy. *At least I saw Remesy.*

When Duval paused, Geneviève spoke up in her partner's defense. "Captain, it may be out of our normal jurisdiction, as you say, but we've retrieved evidence which points to the lighthouse from searching the *Scirocco*," she said. "Plus, the K-9 unit hit on the possibility drugs were present onboard. Which fits mine and Detective Berger's theory of small vessels being used to transport drugs ashore."

Captain Duval sat listening. It had been weeks since the detectives had a tangible lead they could follow. And Benoit was right; the yachts could be the latest method to smuggle the harder drugs like cocaine and heroin ashore. Moving across his desk, he opened a phone line to the receptionist. "Clarise, could you see if Captain Picard or Georges can come to my office, please?"

The demeanor of both detectives changed as they heard Duval mention the two SWAT officers. It was Berger who was first to comment. Judging his words with care, the detective straightened up before addressing his captain. “Are you considering our proposal, sir?”

Duval pulled a folder from his inbox. “In a word, Detective, no. At least not for the moment,” he replied. “But I will discuss your theory with Picard and Georges to garner their view on its plausibility.” Flipping the folder open, he slid several sheets of paper in front of the detectives. “Now, let’s discuss these, shall we?”

Geneviève grabbed the top sheet and scanned it. It was a letter of reprimand. “Why are we getting these?” she asked as Berger continued to read over his copy. “We’ve done nothing to necessitate being disciplined in writing.”

“Read the fine print, Benoit,” Berger uttered. While Geneviève voiced her disdain for the censure, Berger took the time to digest the content. They were being disciplined for their hasty actions the other day at the train station. “Where do I sign?” he asked, looking at the captain.

Geneviève looked over at Berger. Beads of sweat began forming on her brow as her emotional state rose. “Nic, we did nothing to deserve this,” she declared. “We acted on a credible tip about a suspect, there was nothing wrong in what we did. Captain, this doesn’t sound fair at all,” her voice cracking as she directed her frustration across the desk.

Captain Duval took in a deep breath before speaking, to keep his voice even and emotionless. “Detective Benoit, this action is the lesser evil from the one Superintendent Chevallier demanded. He wanted both of you brought before the police tribunal for a formal hearing,” he added. “I convinced him to leave it with just the letter, and not the weeks-long suspension the tribunal would issue.”

Geneviève eased back in her chair when she heard the term “suspension.” She’d already endured one instance of being suspended after her involvement at Chateau Il d’If. *But it came without a formal letter*, she reminded herself. This would be placed in her file and follow her throughout her police career.

Before the conversation could continue, the desk intercom buzzed. "Yes, Clarise, what is it?" Duval asked.

"Captain Georges is here as you requested, sir."

"Send him in," he replied. "And what about Captain Picard?" Duval asked.

"He's assisting a disturbance in the Verduron quarter," the woman replied. As she spoke, the office door swung open and Captain Georges entered. "Very well, I'll speak with him later," the senior officer replied before hanging up. "Have a seat, Captain Georges," he started, gesturing to the only empty chair. As the SWAT team leader took his seat, Duval swept the two letters up and placed them back in the folder.

Then, over the next thirty minutes, Captain Duval relayed the idea devised by the detectives about investigating the Planier lighthouse. Georges let the captain speak and then listened to Berger fill in the few details Captain Duval hadn't mentioned.

"Why don't we just have a helicopter drop the detectives on the isle and let them conduct their investigation?" Georges asked. "It's perhaps a twenty-minute flight as opposed to a two-or three-hour boat crossing, and that's just going one way."

Captain Duval sat back in his chair as his head swayed back and forth. "Your recommendation has merit, Captain," Duval said before he pulled himself forward, "but in the interest of safety, can you spare four of your members to back up Benoit and Berger?"

Both detectives exchanged looks. It was Benoit who spoke first. "You're letting us go out to survey the lighthouse after all?" Geneviève asked. "Why the change of heart, Captain?"

Duval let out a slight chuckle. "You said it yourself: the evidence from the yacht. I'll give the three of you 24 hours to prepare your plan and we'll contact the *Gendarmerie* detachment at the airport for helicopter support."

***

While the four officers discussed the logistics for the excursion to Planier lighthouse, a member of Gregory Arsenault's crew fought the boredom from sitting hours with nothing to do.

Louis had arrived outside the apartment shared by his partner's niece and her companion. Being outside the building and looking into the morning sun, Clement was at a disadvantage. He knew he could recognize Sophia having seen her up close while in the hospital. But Celine was another story. Except for Phillip, no one really knew anything about the young woman.

On the opposite side of the street, two other men had the same interest in the location, but for a different reason. Amed Gilles had directed his henchmen to find where Arsenault's sister-in-law, Police Sergeant Claire Dubois, lived. The previous evening, they'd followed the officer to this apartment, unaware the sergeant was also Sophia's mother, and lived on the same floor.

With his focus centered on the building's entrance, Louis let his guard down. Wandering down the sidewalk, Hector Pichon strolled past two older women waiting for a market to open before he ended up behind his friend's sedan. He bumped his leg against the fender and laughed at the former Legionnaire's reaction.

The sudden sway of the car caused Louis to draw his weapon out as he twisted to see what caused the motion. "Damn you, Hector," he cried out. The action, though comical to Hector, also alerted the Algerians looking to abduct the police sergeant they might not be able to execute their plan.

Tugging open the passenger door, Hector slid in beside Louis. "Good morning to you, too," he said. "You're getting soft in your old age if I can sneak up on you in broad daylight."

"It's only because I'm sitting on my ass, you know," Clement replied, sliding the pistol back under his jacket. The swinging of a door caught his attention at the apartment building. In a moment, he saw Claire step through and onto the sidewalk. Her police uniform made it easy to spot her. Seconds later, a slim petite woman in her 20s stepped into the morning light. "There's Claire, but who's that?" Clement asked.

"I don't know, but she's quite cute," Pichon replied as they watched Celine walk away in the opposite direction from Claire. "Do you think she knows anything about Sophia's whereabouts?"

Clement glanced at his friend. "Which one, Claire or the other woman?"

As the men exchanged their views on who knew whom, the Algerians watched the sergeant across the street and approach the bus stop with their van parked nearby. The position of the vehicle hid the passenger side from the Legionnaires across the street. "Get in back and be ready," the driver told his companion.

Doing as he was told; the second gang member climbed into the back and grasped the door handle. It was a simple action they planned and had practiced on numerous occasions to abduct individuals who were at odds with Amed Gilles.

Sergeant Dubois was busy looking at the reflection of herself in the small compact she pulled from her purse to notice the van or its occupants. As she neared the bus stop, the door slid back and a man grabbed her arm. Well-rehearsed in kidnapping, the Algerian slid the plastic restraint around her one wrist before pulling Claire inside the vehicle.

In mere seconds and without warning, the sergeant was soon pushed against the seat of the driver in the van. Though a clerk with the police, her reflexes allowed Claire to strike out at the Algerian who'd grabbed her, landing a kick against his arm. With her free hand, she struggled to plunge her thumb into the eyes of the driver. Her assault failed in striking his face, but in recoiling from the woman's attempt, the driver leaned back, causing the horn to blare.

Across the thoroughfare, Louis and Pichon were talking and keeping the vigilance on the apartment where Celine had left. The sound of the horn caught their attention though, as they caught a glimpse of the driver's movement inside the cab.

"Have you seen Claire?" Louis asked, craning his neck closer to the windshield to see the bus stop.

"No," Hector replied sliding out of the sedan. His focus was the van as it swayed back and forth. Through the glare of the sun on the window, he noticed the police uniform worn by the sergeant. Turning to his partner, he motioned towards the vehicle.

Before getting out of the car, Louis reached into the center console and pulled out a silencer for his pistol. In moments, he had the cylinder secured to the muzzle. He stepped out of the car and trotted across the boulevard until he was just a few meters from the van.

Hector had already reached the sidewalk. Stepping between two cars parked in front of the van, he drew out his knife. The Karambit-style weapon fit neatly in his right hand; its curved blade poised like a tiger's claw as it prepared to take a swipe at its prey. Reaching the van, he saw the door was ajar, and heard the sergeants' struggle. He glimpsed through the passenger door and noticed the driver hold a pistol in the direction of the rear seat. With a simple gesture, he let Louis know the driver was armed.

Inside the van, Claire continued to thrash about, doing her best to avoid having her right arm restrained like the left. In the tight confines of the vehicle, it took all her strength to keep kicking at the gang member.

"Get her tied down, you fool," the driver exclaimed. Out of the corner of his eye, he saw a passerby, but dismissed it. It wasn't until he heard the door sliding open, did he realize the passerby intended to help the police woman.

Hector was greeted by the abductors' back as he opened the door, allowing him to grasp the man's arm and pull him off Claire. The driver saw what had happened and leveled his pistol at the Frenchman when the sound of a window breaking resonate inside. The unbroken glass fragments were sprayed with blood and tissue and the driver's head suddenly slumped to the side.

Louis had just made his way to the driver's door when he saw the pistol being leveled at his companion and took action to eliminate the threat. Stepping around to the other side, he saw Hector subdue the second kidnapper with a vicious blow to the temple, rendering him unconscious.

Claire stared at the men with the shock of the driver's demise fresh in her mind. "Who are you?" she muttered.

Louis and Hector shoved the Algerian past the back seat as a few onlookers gathered behind them. With his knife still in his hand, Hector reached toward Claire and freed her from the zip-tie holding her left arm to the seat. "Time to go, Mademoiselle," he spoke with a gentle politeness as if they were at a dinner party. In the distance, the wail of sirens resonated.

Louis had already made his way across the street and had the back door of his car open and waiting. As Claire and Hector got in, he trotted around to the driver's side. In less than five minutes of her being assaulted, the two men and the sergeant were driving away from the scene.

"Give me your phone," Hector said, tapping Louis on the shoulder.

Louis kept his eyes and focus on the road ahead, and passed his cell phone over his shoulder to his companion. They came to a roundabout and Louis slowed to maneuver around the growing traffic just as two police cars emerged from the street to his right.

Claire sat quiet in the backseat. The shock of the kidnap attempt was ebbing away, replaced with a new emotion: fear. *Who are these men, and why did they do what they did?* she asked herself. Claire glanced down and noticed trace remnants of the driver spotted across her uniform. The thought of the man's head being pierced by a bullet caused her to gasp as bile rose from her stomach.

Hector noticed Claire's reaction and leaned across her to roll down the window. "A little fresh air might help," he said, dialing a number each man knew by memory.

Across town, Gregory had just finished his breakfast. "Well done, Phillip," he said, getting to his feet. With the plate in hand he walked to the sink and laid the dish amongst several others. He tilted his cup and emptied the contents in a single gulp before adding it to the sink. The ring of Gregory's phone caught the men by surprise.

"I'll bet that's Hector," Julien said as he leaned back in his chair.

As he grabbed the phone, Gregory shook his head. "You're wrong; it's Louis. Oui, mon ami, how are things?" he asked.

In the car, Hector looked over at their passenger before speaking. "Oui, Captain, there's been an altercation."

Gregory's demeanor changed in an instant. They all had agreed to use prior military status to announce any encounters so the recipient understood the significance of the call. This was one case he'd not expected to be appraised of this morning. “Where are you now?” he asked.

Hector looked out the window as Louis navigated the morning traffic. “Where are we now?” he asked.

“Two kilometers out,” Louis answered.

Hector relayed this to Gregory. “And you should realize, Captain, we are one heavy. There will be information on the end result, and they won’t be positive.”

Communiqués about the assault and attempted kidnapping of Sergeant Dubois spread throughout the police stations. The first officers who responded to the incident cordoned off the street and unceremoniously draped a cover over the van’s windshield. Other officers interviewed witnesses who remained at the scene. Several of those interviewed provided rough descriptions of Louis and Hector and their car, which was now the focal point for every patrol in the city.

Gregory turned to Julien and Phillip. “Get your weapons; Hector and Louis are on their way and they have a guest,” he said in a calm yet commanding voice.

“Anyone hurt?” Julien asked.

Gregory shook his head. “Hector didn’t mention it, so for the moment, you can keep your medical kit closed.” Following the two men towards the bedrooms, Gregory ducked into his study and retrieved his HK45 from the desk along with two extra magazines. As he walked back to the front of the house, he heard the chime of the sensor indicating someone was at the front gate.

“Phillip, you stay by the house entrance; Julien you’re on the left.” He stepped up to the gate, sliding a small panel aside to see Louis, who was in the front. To his surprise, Hector was in the back, and next to him, Claire.

The sight of her brother-in-law emerge as the gate swung open surprised Claire. For all the time living and working in Marseille, she’d never known or had reason to learn where Gregory lived.

As soon as Louis pulled the car in and killed the engine, Claire was stepping out of the backseat. “These men work for you?” she queried Gregory who was now standing next to her. "This one... he shot a man in cold blood, right on the street."

Holding her by the arm, Gregory motioned towards the house. "Good thing he did or you wouldn't be here," he replied with a distant, nonchalant tone. "I'll explain everything once we're all inside."

Chapter TWENTY-FIVE

The azure waters of the Mediterranean glided below the AS 365 Dauphin helicopter as it flew southeast from its base at Marseille airport. Inside the aircraft, six Marseille police officers took in the scenery. Off to their left, they could make out a small boat power through the water, headed in the same general direction they were going. But cruising at 135 kilometers per hour, the helicopter soon passed the boat and left it well behind. To their right, all they saw was the vast expanse of water and several specks on the horizon.

Situated behind the pilots, Detective Benoit, Berger, and four members of Captain Georges' SWAT team did their best to focus under the drone of the helicopter's twin engines. Geneviève peered out the side window and took note of the vessel. From this height, it was next to impossible to discern any features, and so she dismissed it as just another group of fishermen.

As they drew closer to the lighthouse, the pilot slowed the craft down to judge the wind direction and survey the spit of land he had to set his helicopter on. "We're about three minutes out, Detective," the co-pilot warned.

"Got it," Berger replied as he keyed the headset's microphone. He then held up three fingers so the SWAT team who sat across from him knew what was communicated. The team loosened their belts and began checking their gear and weapons.

With the lighthouse growing closer, the helicopter slowed as it descended toward the exposed rocks on the southern edge of the atoll. In a spray of seawater, the pilot deftly touched down. Benoit and Berger followed the SWAT team and ducked their heads as they stepped under the spinning rotors.

"Corporal Lavigne, you and Corporal Cormier are with Detective Benoit," Berger ordered as they approached the steps leading to the lighthouse. "You two are with me," he finished, singling out the other members. "Benoit, you begin sweeping the building to the left."

Before Geneviève could offer a reply, the co-pilot of the helicopter trotted up next to Detective Berger. "We just received a call about a sailboat with a medical emergency; you're on your own until we return," he said. "We'll leave our survival kit in the event you need to spend the night." He motioned to a large orange duffle bag just in front of the helicopter.

Berger just nodded in acceptance. The rest of the team looked at each other and shrugged it off as part of the procedure. Geneviève was more concerned than they were, though.

"How long are they going to be gone?" she asked over the growing whine of the helicopter's engines.

Berger shielded his eyes as the helicopter lifted off before he answered his partner. "They didn't say," he replied. "But they left the survival bag just in case we have to camp out here. Let's get back to what we came here to do, shall we?"

With SWAT members at her side, Geneviève stepped deliberately up the stairs to the level surface of the small courtyard-like clearing. The two buildings and lighthouse tower, all constructed of stone, showed the weathered effects of exposure to the harshness of the sea. The once smooth surfaces of the structures along the water's edge were now pockmarked from the years of assault by wind and tide.

As Cormier led the trio, Geneviève peered over his shoulder at the first entrance. She could see rusted remains of a steel doorway in the shadows. The entry, once suitable for securing its contents, was now guarded behind a web of chain-link fence, which had been put in place in recent years.

Berger and his team surveyed the exterior of the lighthouse, its spire of stone looming eighty-five meters above the water. Reaching the only entrance, he noted the lock was still intact as was the security seal from the maintenance crew. Though not the greatest deterrent, it still showed if there had been any intruders.

Geneviève's team completed their sweep of the lower building when they met up with Berger at the main building. Shielding her eyes, she watched her partner walk the last few meters toward her. "Did you find anything interesting?"

Berger shook his head. "Nothing. What about you?"

"The chain-link fencing seems secure with no disturbance," Geneviève replied. "And all the original entrances appear rusted in place. Which leaves the main structure here." She nodded at the three-story facade looming over them.

One of the SWAT team came walking up to the group. "Detective Berger, someone's been here," he announced, pointing to the ground behind him. "The fence has been pulled aside, and more than once, if I had to guess."

The group walked over to the main building's north end and saw what the SWAT member discovered. A furrow of dirt indicated where a post of the fence section had been pulled open. Geneviève stepped over to where two sections of fence were joined. "This lock is almost brand new," she noted, pointing out the shining metallic combination lock hung on an equally new chain.

"Anyone good at picking locks?" Berger asked as he pulled on some gloves.

"I've got a special set of picks," Cormier replied, pulling out a pair of bolt-cutters from his backpack.

Lavigne chuckled while he shook his head. "Always the Boy Scout, aren't you, Pierre?"

In minutes, the team's demolition expert had cut through the fence, creating a gap large enough for everyone to step through without getting snagged. "Nice work, Pierre," Geneviève said with a smile as she slipped under fence frame.

Another rusted and weathered entrance greeted the officers. "Who else needs gloves?" Berger asked, swaying his hands in front of the others. It was a foolish question. The SWAT team had donned their Nomex gloves during the flight, and Geneviève had slipped on a pair of gloves just outside the building.

Stepping through the entry, they paused so their eyes could adjust to the darkness inside. The SWAT members flicked on small lights slung under their weapons. Beams of light danced across the foyer as they took stock of their surroundings. The enclosed space gave off a musty odor like a home long abandoned.

"Nic, you take your team to the second floor and we'll begin with this one," Geneviève said, gesturing to Cormier and Lavigne. "And then we can search the basement as a group."

"Let's get this done then," Berger replied. "Remember, we're treating this as a potential crime scene; don't touch anything if you think it could be considered evidence," he instructed, looking at each of the SWAT members directly.

As Benoit and Berger led their respective team on their search, a twelve-meter sport boat approached the island. A three-person group led by Yacine El-Amari swayed back and forth on their feet as they rode through the waves. On the boat's stern, a crude litter had been fabricated with lengths of rope for securing their victim wrapped to the bamboo poles.

Yacine tapped one man on the shoulder. "Are you sure you brought enough sedative?" Before the man could answer, the small radio mounted to the ceiling crackled to life.

Onboard a west-bound freighter, the first officer did his best to ask for a clarification from the smaller boat. His disadvantage was trying to speak the handful of Arabic phrases written down for him, though he had no ear for the language.

Yacine grinned as he heard the officer struggle over the radio. He grabbed the handset and acknowledged the transmission. The Algerian gave his reply in French, knowing the mariner was more fluent in it than the Berbice version of Arabic he was struggling to speak.

Back in the main building, Geneviève, Cormier, and Lavigne were finishing their search of the last room along the hall. They found a locked set of doors leading outside the building and Geneviève stepped up to the doorway. Her feet pressed against the already broken shards of glass from the door's windows. As she looked out, the only thing visible was the faint trail of smoke from a freighter drawing closer to the coast. "Not much of a view is it?"

Upstairs, Berger and the others had better luck when they encountered several rooms that showed signs of recent use. One room the SWAT team entered appeared to have had the floor swept and several crude blankets hastily folded and piled in the corner. An adjoining room had the remains of a desk pushed against the wall; its metal surface charred from repeated uses as a makeshift cooktop. A turned over box sat under the lone window in the room with the sun acting as a spotlight for whoever sat on it.

At the end of the hall, Berger found a room someone had been using to relieve themselves. The stench of urine was overpowering, and his flashlight exposed what appeared to be a pile feces in the far corner. "Well, someone has been staying overnight. Let's get downstairs."

In the foyer, Benoit, Cormier, and Lavigne milled about, with the later taking the occasional glance outside. The patter of footsteps on stone alerted them of the others coming down the stairwell.

Berger trotted down the stairs until he met up with Geneviève. "There are signs someone has been here. And it looked like they had provisions for staying more than one day too"

"That just leaves the basement," Geneviève replied. Nodding at Cormier, she led him aside along with Berger. "We'll need you and the others to lead us down and sweep the area."

"Do you want to leave one of us here to keep the tourists away?" Cormier asked with a feigned chuckle.

"No one's here to disturb us, are they?"

Cormier gave his head a shake. "No, Detective, there isn't," he answered. "At least not at the moment."

As he switched his flashlight on, Berger motioned toward the steps. "I suggest we get on with our search," he muttered as he felt the damp air rise through the stairwell. "Corporal, you've the lead."

As the group descended towards the bowels of the facility's main building, the atmosphere in the space changed. The once musty and stale air above ground had turned cool and damp, with an odor none of them recognized.

"Pierre, what is that smell?" one of the SWAT members asked of his leader.

Cormier shook his head. "If I had to guess, burnt wiring or something else electrical." The light from the group's flashlights pierced the darkness in swaths of brightness as they crisscrossed the hall. Each sweep brought new objects into view on the way, and in moments, the light reached the end of the dark hallway.

Corporal Lavigne used his flashlight to illuminate one of the open rooms. "I think I found the source of the smell, Pierre," he said as he found a small generator and a coil of wiring. Along the string of wire, light bulb sockets were attached in a haphazard manner, with several scorch marks evident at their connection.

Before Benoit and Berger could comment, the sound of a chain pulled across metal echoed through the dark behind them. The once obscure blackness of the hallway was now awash with light as a side door swung open and the police were joined by three other men.

Corporal Cormier seized the moment, using hand signals to direct the SWAT team into action as they prepare to confront the visitors. "You two stay back," he whispered to Benoit and Berger, motioning to the corner in the room.

Yacine El-Amari walked a few paces behind the others as they entered the hallway of the building. "We don't need to use the lights," he spoke in Arabic as he watched the smallest man struggle with the makeshift litter. "And I told you these poles were too long for this," he added, chastising the man as he helped lift one end.

What felt like two minutes for Benoit and Berger were mere seconds as Cormier and his men stepped into the hall behind El-Amari and the other men. "Halt, gentlemen," the corporal commanded as he leveled his weapon on El-Amari. "Raise your hands slowly if you please." His men took positions to surround the group.

As Detective Berger and Corporal Cormier conducted a crude interrogation, Geneviève made her way to the room where the Algerians emerged. She found the doorway lead outside the structure. Nudging the door open, Geneviève spied the motor launch which brought them men to the lighthouse. On the boat, the lone operator heard the door open and when he saw the officer, knew something wasn't right and began pulling away. Before Geneviève could make it to the landing, the boat was twenty-five meters away and increasing its speed.

The crunch of boots on the gravel caught her attention. Twirling around, she saw one of the SWAT team coming towards her. "Detective Berger needs you inside," the young man said.

Geneviève nodded as she glanced back, wishing she'd seen what the boat's moniker was before it sped away from the shore. Re-entering the hall, she heard voices echo from the end of the hallway. "What is it, Nic?"

Detective Berger stood outside one of the last rooms. "Inside," he gestured over his shoulder.

Geneviève stepped past him and saw one of the SWAT team members leaning over the room's occupant. As she stepped to his side, she saw the frail figure of a woman. The garments she wore were filthy and stained with sweat, her hair, stringy mop of brunette was matted. "Patrice?"

The woman, whom the SWAT medic had propped up in a sitting position, slowly lifted her eyes to the detective. Tears emerged. "Thank you for not giving up," she uttered, her voice a rasp whisper from dehydration.

Encountering her fellow officer in such condition began to fuel Geneviève's rage against the Algerians who sat in the hallway. As she stepped through the doorway, Berger caught her arm and pulled her aside.

"They'll get what they deserve," Berger said. "We can't drop to their level or we'll be no better; you know this."

An hour after discovering Officer Patrice Galant, the sound of an approaching helicopter echoed across the spit of land. As the helicopter made landfall, a team of medical personnel properly equipped to handle the woman entered the building and soon carried her to the waiting aircraft.

With news of Officer Galant's discovery, the commander of the *Gendarmerie* force dispatched a high-speed patrol craft to help the officers. Upon its arrival, it was placed into service to transport the three Algerians back to Marseille along with the other members of the SWAT team. Several lab technicians had disembarked the patrol craft and were met by Detective Berger. After a brief discussion, he led them into the building so they could begin processing what evidence they could from the kidnapping site.

Two hundred and fifty meters off the islet, a freighter steamed through the channel. As she stood on the patrol craft, Geneviève watched it plow through the azure water and spied two men standing outside the freighter's bridge, apparently watching her and the activity on the island. One of them raised a set of binoculars to his face and swept them back and forth. As he dropped them from his eyes, Geneviève could see the man turn and say something to the other.

"What did you see?" she muttered under her breath.

As the freighter drew closer to the lighthouse, Captain Coetzee had seen the arrival of the large helicopter and knew something wasn't right. He and his first officer observed members of crew unload what appeared to be a stretcher and several bags bearing a red cross.

"It seems we won't be getting our fee, Mister Walls," Coetzee said to his companion. "Have the watch set course for Barcelona and increase speed to 15 knots. We need to make up our lost time."

"Yes, Captain," Walls replied. Orders were passed inside the freighter's bridge, and soon, a plume of black smoke curled from the exhaust as water behind the vessel began to churn.

Geneviève set the eye pieces of binoculars to her face. As the freighter picked up speed, she scanned the superstructure for any identifying marks. As her scan reached the fantail, where she made out the vessel's name. *Southern Warrior.*

Chapter TWENTY-SIX

Three days passed since Officer Patrice Galant's rescue. The interrogation control room had turned into the backstage of a theatre as senior officers wanted to learn how three Algerians managed to abduct one of their own. Front and center stood Captain Duval, Captain Soucy, and Superintendent Chevallier. The men were fixated on the monitors displaying the three occupants, each in a separate room. Geneviève leaned her shoulder against the wall, but struggled to hear each of the separate whispered conversations and the interrogators.

A faint buzz accompanied the vibration of her cell phone for an incoming call. "Excuse me," she said to the others while she pulled the phone up to see the number. As she entered the hallway, she answered. "Bonjour?"

In his chateau nestled in the foothills of Marseille, Gregory Arsenault had just learned about the policewoman's rescue through his contact. After visiting with Geneviève earlier in the week, he was sure now was the time to cement his position with this call.

"Hello? Who is this...?" Geneviève demanded as she paced the halls.

"Bonjour, Detective. This is Monsieur Arsenault," Gregory replied, an odd calmness in his voice. "I wanted to congratulate you and your fellow officers on acting so quick with the information I provided."

Geneviève froze in her steps. She could sense her pulse quicken recalling how Arsenault had made his way into her apartment just the other day. "How did you hear about this? Nothing was released to the news outlets yet," she stammered as she glanced down the corridor.

Gregory sipped his coffee. "So quick with the rebuke; no sign of gratitude for helping you find your fellow officer? I thought you'd be pleased to see my information was genuine, Detective Benoit. I'd still hope you'd understand I want nothing more than to be your ally, and not an adversary."

Geneviève noticed a technician motion for her to return to the room. "As you might imagine, I'm very busy, Monsieur Arsenault. Since you have this number, why don't you send me a message. Just let me know where we can meet." She hesitated outside the control room. "That is, so I can thank you in person. Until then, Au revoir, Monsieur."

Back in the control room, Detective Benoit stood next to Captain Duval as they watched the proceedings between Detective Berger, Yacine El-Amari, and the Algerian's lawyer.

"Something of importance, Detective?" Duval asked.

Geneviève shook her head. "Just a call to confirm an appointment for later, that's all, Captain," she replied, turning to the screen. Nicolas was in the middle of questioning the gang member.

"It would appear you've been busy, Monsieur El-Amari," Berger said.

The attorney for the Algerian leaned on the table, his focus on Berger. "Officer, why do you insist on addressing my client by that name?"

Berger smiled, restraining himself from reaching out and striking the smug look from the lawyer's face. "Monsieur, your client was apprehended by police for trespassing on federal property," he began. "And our investigation provided us with some latitude with other nations the last few days."

"I appreciate you contacting your friend in Algiers," Captain Soucy said as he turned to Geneviève. "Seeing them identify the suspect so quickly was a windfall for us."

"I'll pass your gratitude to Inspector Haddad," Geneviève replied.

Over the next several hours, Detective Berger and a member of Captain Soucy's task force described the charges Yacine would face for abducting their fellow officer.

In the middle of Berger's description of the findings at the lighthouse, Yacine stood up and walked to the corner of the room, his back to the officers. Surprised, the lawyer joined him. "What are you doing?"

Yacine glanced at the attorney. "Tell them I want to discuss a lesser charge for information," he whispered. "I assure you, it will be something they'll find acceptable," he added, as he faced the concrete wall.

The lawyer nodded before sitting back at the table. "My client wishes to discuss a reduced charge for information on what he knows of those who were responsible for your officer being placed on Isle Planier."

In the control room, Captain Soucy and the others exchanged looks of disbelief. "Why would he want to negotiate so soon?" Geneviève queried. "What does he hope to gain by doing it?"

"His freedom," Captain Soucy answered. "Or more important… his life." Turning to one technician, the senior officer asked to have Detective Berger end the interrogation. In the hall, a police officer unlocked the door and whispered the instructions to Nicolas.

Berger listened and nodded. "If you'll excuse us," he said. "This officer will see to your client's comfort. Wait here for the moment, please."

Berger entered the control room. "Why was I directed to stop?"

"Something doesn't appear right about this suspect," Captain Soucy answered. "We need to make sure our information from the Algerian authorities is solid before we agree to anything. Besides, he's not going anywhere soon. So, we've time on our side," he added with a glance at Superintendent Chevallier. "Am I right, sir?"

"Yes, you are, Captain," the senior official replied.

Confused. That's how Geneviève felt as she listened to what was discussed. She and Berger had the three Algerians involved in the abduction of their fellow officer. They were arrested and found to have a sedative and stretcher ready to move Patrice off the island. What more did they need to charge El-Amari?

"Detective Berger, have the lawyer provide a written request based on this suspect's declaration; it will buy us additional time," Captain Duval said. "Detective Benoit, I want you to go over all the information provided by your acquaintance from Algiers. Verify everything is correct and prepare a communique for Lyon," he added.

"With your permission, Superintendent, I'd like to see if the people at INTERPOL can help."

"I have no objection, Captain," Chevallier said.

With the discussion over, the detectives left the control room, Berger to the interrogation room, and Geneviève back toward their office. A few minutes later, Nicolas caught Geneviève at the stairwell. It was Geneviève who broke the awkward silence between them.

"What information do you think the Algerian has to offer?"

Berger hesitated as he climbed the stairs. "I don't know... and I honestly don't care," he replied. "All I know is we caught the bastard and his friends on *Planier*. They had drugs to sedate Patrice and looked as if they were prepared to move her. That's enough in my books to have them sent off to prison for a long time," he said, flinging the door open for Geneviève.

The buzz from Geneviève's jacket announced an incoming message. "I'll be a minute," she said, digging her phone from her pocket. Swiping the face, she saw the brief text: an address and a time.

Several hours passed as Benoit and Berger went about their respective tasks assigned by Captain Duval. The buzz in the police station was electric as most officers had been briefed on Officer Galant's rescue. Every so often, one would stick their head in to congratulate the detectives.

Geneviève looked across her desk at Berger. "Is Francine still spending time at the hospital with Patrice?" she asked, knowing how close his companion was to the other officer.

Berger glanced over the computer. "She was until they moved her," he answered. Unsure of the motive behind the abduction, Superintendent Chevallier arranged for Officer Galant to recuperate at a facility away from Marseille. "But she wants me to see if there's any way she could visit, you know, in an 'official' capacity," he added before returning to his work.

Geneviève returned to her own work. As she flipped through the folder of information Inspector Haddad in Algiers had provided, a phrase on a police report caught her attention. "Maritime Repairs of Oran." "That's interesting," she muttered under her breath.

"What's so interesting now?" Berger asked.

Geneviève flipped over the report and began reading. "Our suspect El-Amari was once a foreman at a shipyard in Oran," she said. "Says he was reassigned shortly after an incident involving the death of a co-worker," her voice trailing off as she read. "It mentioned he was cleared of any wrongdoing, but he'd then left the country."

"This guy is involved in a suspicious death, is cleared, but still leaves his homeland," Berger surmised. "That does sound somewhat odd. But it gives us a clue he might understand freighters, doesn't it?"

Geneviève was only half listened as she typed the shipyard name into her computer. Seconds later the screen flashed as information from her search filled the blank space. The Algerian facility was a subsidiary of PSG, the same group who owned Construction Mechanical Normandy (CMN) shipyard in Cherbourg. Seeing the company name again from her hometown caused Geneviève to shiver briefly.

As quick as she opened the search, Geneviève deleted it. It was if the very notion of her past reemerging would cause it all to happen again. Moving away from her desk, she headed for the door. "I'll be back."

In a few moments, Geneviève had made her way outside. Drawing in a deep breath, she worked to calm herself from the demons haunting her from her youth. As she leaned against the wall, Geneviève wrapped her arms around her chest, hoping the sensation would help settle her nerves. But it didn't. The clouded vision of the assailant filled her thoughts as the sensation of being held down returned. This time, unlike so many others, the mist shrouding her memories cleared, and the face of Yacine El-Amari appeared.

The sense of someone approaching brought Geneviève back to reality. It was Sergeant Dubois, standing off to one side with a cigarette dangling from her hand. "Are you okay, Detective?"

A puff of wind sent the smoke from the sergeant's cigarette toward Geneviève. In doing so, she felt her nose twitch while her face tingled as the breeze contacted the damp remains of tears on her cheeks. Nodding her head while swiping the back of her hand across her face, she acknowledged the other woman. "I'm fine. Thank you, sergeant."

Geneviève composed herself before continuing. "How are you doing?" It was known by the station Claire was herself a target of an attempted abduction. Most everyone concluded the act as a growing concern between the African immigrants and the French authorities, not her brother-in-law's feud with the gangs.

"I'm doing better," Claire replied. "I just wish I could thank the men who stopped the others attempt. They even took me to the clinic."

"Sounds like you and Officer Galant were lucky in the same week," Geneviève said.

Claire nodded. "It does look that way, I guess. How is she doing? Has anyone visited her lately?"

"I've not heard anything recently, but I'm sure the department will furnish everyone with news when they can," Geneviève said, looking off in the distance. Along the fence, she could see several transients make their way along the boulevard.

A shrill chime broke the silence between the woman, and Claire quickly reached into her pocket to quiet the alarm. "Break time's up," she chuckled, holding her phone. As she turned from Geneviève, she paused. "If you can, Detective, let Officer Galant know I'm glad she's okay, will you?"

Geneviève nodded. "I'll do what I can." After glancing around at the parking space and the Annex trailers, she returned to the unfinished work still on her desk, settling in behind her computer and typing in a new search.

"Glad you decided to come back," Detective Berger said as he returned to his own desk, a fresh sports drink in his hand. "While you were out, your phone chimed twice and there's a message from Hector Dupont."

"What did he want? Did he say anything?"

Berger shook his head. "I didn't ask. I figured it was personal and he could tell you himself when you called back. Oh, and Captain Duval stuck his head in to say Internal Affairs would be calling both of us in the coming week as part of their investigation."

Geneviève's head snapped up hearing the term investigation. "Investigation? Why are we being looked into? Who's singling us out to be questioned, and for what?" the woman demanded.

"I think it's part of their search for the suspected mole," Berger answered. "But relax, it's probably just a formality since you and Juneau caught the custodian with the camera."

Why are you so worried? she asked herself. *You have nothing to worry about, right?* Geneviève's head swirled with uncertainty on how to deal with another inquiry where too many questions would be asked.

Outside the station, the faint ringing of church bells echoed through the city. Both officers had been so engrossed in their respective work, neither one had taken notice of the time.

"Damn, five o'clock already," Berger said with a moan.

Geneviève let out a suppressed laugh. "Are you late for something with Francine?"

"No... I'm not," Berger shot back. "I'm still waiting for the lawyer's statement so I can add it to the report going up to the superintendent," he sighed, leaning on his desk. "At this rate, I'll miss my date with her though."

"Thankfully, I can return to my task in the morning," Geneviève answered as she logged off her computer. Closing the file from Inspector Haddad, she stepped over to the file cabinet and locked it away. "And now, I'm going home," she said with a flourish while grabbing her jacket.

"Fine. You go and relax," Berger said. "I'll just sit here and rot."

As Geneviève strolled through the main entrance, she glanced down at her phone. The text message appeared, displaying the address where she was to meet Arsenault. Walking to the curb, she hailed a taxi and slid in the back. "The Irish Pub on *Avenue de Mazargues*."

"Oui, Mademoiselle," the man responded.

After fifteen minutes negotiating the evening traffic, the taxi pulled alongside the curb just short of the restaurant. "That will be €27.35, miss," the driver said, turning to Geneviève.

"Merci," she said while she handed over €30. "Keep the rest." She stayed on the curb, but glanced up and down the street. It was getting busy as the working class returned home and the tourists, evident by their conversations, searched for somewhere to eat they might find familiar.

Sauntering a few meters to the entrance, Geneviève caught the host's attention as he returned to his station. "I'm meeting an associate," she said. "His name is Monsieur Arsenault."

The host peered at his listing. "He's here already. If you'll follow me," he replied while he grabbed a spare menu from the podium. The restaurant was filled with fans of the Irish football club, the Shamrock Rovers, who were in town for their match against Marseille. Cheers and singing were the order for most of them along with half-filled glasses of beer.

"Here we are," the host announced, gesturing to the back table and Arsenault. The man rose briefly as he greeted his guest. "Can I get you a drink?" the host asked, noting Gregory already had a glass before him.

"Just a glass of ice water, please," Geneviève replied, and the host nodded before leaving.

"Thank you for agreeing to meet," Gregory said as he watched the young man walk away.

Geneviève studied the man across from her. As before, she saw confident mannerisms. And he wasn't cocky. The Frenchman was dressed casually for the evening and had no jewelry to flaunt, she noticed. "It would seem I should thank you for providing the department with the information," she said.

Before Gregory could say anything, a young woman appeared and placed a glass before Geneviève, then poured it full of ice water from a pitcher. "Another cocktail?" she asked Gregory.

"I'm fine for now, thank you," he replied before turning back to Geneviève. "To your fellow officer's speedy recovery," Gregory said, lifting his glass towards the detective.

Geneviève took the glass of water, acknowledging his well wishes. "Asante," she replied as she took a sip. "Now then," she placed her glass down, "you mentioned providing me with means of apprehending Louis Remesy." Geneviève paused as another server brought bowl of chips to the table. "After that, you would likewise name the person you wish to be looked after within the station, isn't that correct?"

A loud cheer echoed throughout the restaurant as the big screen TVs displayed the players entering the stadium, and their respective national anthems being played. The Irish fans were soon in full voice reciting the "The Soldier's Song" with most singing the English version while a handful sang in their native Gaelic.

Gregory Arsenault hesitated for a moment, letting the patrons finish the anthem before he spoke. "This Remesy fellow you wish to arrest so badly," he began, "has agreed to meet me here in Marseille on Thursday. He believes I'll have a list of merchants who wish to begin a business venture," he lied.

Geneviève kept her focus on Arsenault as she listened to his explanation. "And are these merchants involved in some form of illegal act?" she asked. "You once said that Remesy gave you an impression he wanted something or someone willing to engage in a dishonest endeavor."

"Yes, it's true I had my concerns," Gregory replied. "But a former business associate passed along this information on how to contact him. And since I'm in the business of brokering shipping consignments, I thought the ruse was simple enough to persuade Remesy to return."

Geneviève listened to Arsenault, doing her best to weigh the risk of accepting his explanation on how she could confront Remesy. "And what are you going to do after I've made the arrest?" she asked. Geneviève sensed Arsenault wanted the drug dealer out of the way for something bigger, but what? And how could she go along and not exceed her position as a police officer?

Cheers from the crowded bar area soon turned to groans of disappointment as the television screen showed the visiting team give up a score to Marseille's club. Arsenault could see the policewoman begin to doubt the reason he was offering to hand over Remesy. He knew now was the time to tread carefully.

"What do you say, Monsieur Arsenault? What benefit are you deriving from this man's arrest?" Geneviève asked again, this time with a sharper delivery.

The cellphone on the table flashed as a message popped up, and Gregory tilted the screen so he could read it. *We found her; she is safe*, was all it read. But he knew the importance of the text and let out a sigh as his shoulders dipped.

"Something significant, I take it."

"Yes, my niece ran away from home," Gregory replied. "But she's been found and is safe now." He took his glass and emptied the contents.

"Well?"

Gregory looked across at Geneviève and cleared his throat. "My hope is having your drug dealer arrested will send a message for others to think twice before they attempt to engage in such enterprise."

"Is that your message being delivered to others or the police?"

"Both, I suppose," Gregory said. Once again, his cellphone flashed as another message popped up. "It would appear your chance to make the arrest will happen. Remesy just confirmed to meet."

Geneviève pulled a small notebook from her jacket. Moving the water to the side, she used the back of her hand to wipe away the puddle of condensation. "Where and when?" she asked, poised to copy down the information.

Gregory reached in his jacket and pulled out a slip of paper and slid it across the table. "Here, this is where I agreed to meet him." It was the location of an office building near the warehouse frequented by Gilles.

Geneviève took the paper and read off the location in her head. She wasn't familiar with the neighborhood, but would check it out in the morning. "Nothing more?"

"The only thing left is for you to trust me," Gregory said.

Chapter TWENTY-SEVEN

The mood of the police station was still upbeat with Officer Galant's rescue. There was an air of politeness amongst the patrols and the investigative departments. But it didn't take long for the continuing yellow vest protests to dampen everyone's spirits. Weeks of unrest by the labor unions in Paris saw metro system drivers refuse to work.

As the church bells chimed eight o'clock, Detective Benoit hurriedly paid the taxi driver and bolted from the vehicle. Pushing through the crowded entry, she bounded up the stairway two steps at a time, stumbling into the briefing room just as Captain Duval prepared to review the earlier days' reports. "Nice of you to be on time, Detective."

"Sorry, sir," she muttered.

Captain Duval spent the next ten minutes going over the highlights of the preceding evening's police activity. "The last two items I wish to pass along is that Officer Galant has been released from care and is doing well," he said. "She's been granted two weeks convalescent leave, and when ready, she'll assume her post in Nice." He paused as several officers gave a smattering of applause at the news.

"And I'm happy to mention Detective Masson has been released from the hospital as well and will transfer to his new post in Paris," he said.

"Captain?" Geneviève said raising her hand. "Is there any news on Captain Lemieux, and when he'll return?"

Duval took a deep breath before answering. "There isn't any news to be shared at this moment, Detective Benoit. When there is, I'll make sure those who have a need to know are informed. That'll be all, so let's get to work," he finished before strolling out of the briefing room.

As the officers began filing out, Berger nudged Geneviève. "Why were you late?"

"Those damn bus drivers are calling out and it's played havoc with the route schedules," she replied as they headed to their office. "I was lucky to hail a taxi when I did." She sat down at her desk and turned the computer on. While she waited, she noticed the slip about the call from Hector. "Damn it, I forgot about this."

"You didn't call him?" Berger asked.

Geneviève shook her head. "No. And he didn't call me either," she muttered. Glancing across her desk for a distraction, she added, "Francine must be happy to learn about Patrice, isn't she?"

Berger took a sip of his drink before answering. "She will be," he answered. "The captain's remarks are the first anyone has been told about Patrice's condition since she was moved from hospital here in Marseille."

While the screen came to life, Geneviève pulled out her notebook and typed in the address Gregory Arsenault supplied her last night. The view of the city moved onto the screen as a single red dot pinpointed the location.

"Nic, how would you handle information concerning a potential suspect?"

Berger's head came up from his report. "Is this a trick question?"

Geneviève shook her head. "No, it's not. Last night, I met with the shipping broker, Monsieur Arsenault," she began. "He mentioned having the chance to contact our suspect, Remesy, and was willing to help make it possible for us to arrest him."

"Just like that? Someone we have suspicions about now wants to play the dutiful citizen," Berger remarked. "It sounds sketchy if you ask me. Oh, wait... you just did."

"I'm not saying I trust him, Nic," Geneviève declared. "But is his information any different from what Captain Soucy's people obtain off the street? And might I remind you, we've acted on information ourselves just two weeks ago."

Getting to her feet, she pressed her theory on her partner. "Besides… where would we be if we didn't get the tip about the

Scirocco? We found the coordinates to Ilse de Planier, didn't we? And that led us to finding Patrice."

Berger leaned back in his chair. "Whoa, now," he began, putting his hand in the air. "You're starting to act like Francine when we can't decide where to eat."

"Whose Francine?" came a voice from the doorway.

Both detectives looked at the entry. Standing in the door was a short-statured man, who couldn't be more than five-and-a-half feet tall. The stretched fabric of his dress shirt failed to hide his physique.

"Who are you?" Geneviève asked before turning to Berger. "Do you know who this is?"

Before the visitor could speak, Captain Duval stepped up from behind and showed the man inside the detectives' office. "I do know who this young man is," the senior officer said. "I'd like you to meet Detective Aidan Vidal. He's the department's replacement for Detective Masson."

"Bonjour, Aidan," Geneviève said, extending her hand. "I'm Geneviève Benoit."

"And this is Detective Berger," Captain Duval said, motioning to Nic, who was still eyeing the man from his seat.

"Nicolas," he introduced as he held his hand out to the new officer.

"I expect both of you to fill Detective Vidal in on your latest cases," Duval stated. "And make sure he's introduced to the others you're dealing with as well. And Benoit, no betting, you understand?"

Geneviève could feel herself blush at the remark. "Yes, sir," she replied as Duval left.

Detective Vidal stood glancing between each of the officers. "Was I not supposed to know about your gambling problem?" he asked, looking at Geneviève.

"You'll learn soon enough," Berger replied with a chuckle, motioning to Guy's desk. "Take a seat; it's going to be yours anyway."

Geneviève took her own seat while keeping her eyes on the newest member to their office. "So, Aidan, where are you transferring in from?" she asked.

"DDGI in Brest," Aidan replied, adjusting the chair height so his feet touched the floor. "Started out in maritime enforcement before moving to Customs."

"Well, you'll find things here pretty similar, then," Berger said before downing the remains of his sports drink. "Being on the water, that is. Besides that, we're neck deep into most drug dealers and types. From marijuana to heroin and everything in between!"

"I've kept up on the reports from the last month," Vidal answered. "Is there anything new I can help with since I'm here now?"

Geneviève moved to the file cabinet and pulled out the folder containing notes on their case for Yvette Segal and the drugs found on the *Le Femme Fatale*. "There was nearly a million euros worth of Fentanyl found on this yacht, along with a victim who'd been shot," she said, putting the folder before Aidan. "Give us your opinion on who might be the shooter and how the drugs ended up onboard."

Vidal's eyes grew large as he noted the size of the folder, its contents spilling out from the side. "Don't you guys keep things on the computer?"

Berger let out a slight chuckle. "Eventually, the notes and reports end up getting transcribed, but this… it's a fresh case, not more than three weeks old," he explained. "We're still trying to decide the 'how' behind the drugs getting on the boat and the 'who' when it came to killing the woman."

Aidan flipped open the folder. "Before I came in, you two were talking about acting on tips from citizens, weren't you?"

Geneviève's jaw dropped. "You overheard us talking about that?" she queried. "But you weren't even in the doorway then, were you?"

Aidan looked up from the report. "Ah, no I wasn't in the doorway, but I still heard you talking," he said. "I've been told my hearing is like a bat, just without the ears," he joked as he tugged on his own.

Berger looked at the young man. "I'm not sure if that's an asset or a liability worth having," he said. "You must find it awfully hard to relax if you keep hearing the littlest of noises."

Aidan flipped another page without looking up. "Not really. It just comes down to being able to decipher what's important or not. Who is Officer Favre?"

"He's the undercover officer we encountered the day our victim was found aboard the yacht," Berger answered as he tossed his empty drink in the trash. "Why do you ask?"

"According to this, he was in the vicinity of the yacht, right?" Aidan read. "Don't you think he would have heard the gunshot? Or someone coming off the yacht afterwards?"

Geneviève shook her head. "It's not possible. The medical examiner determined time of death was roughly six hours before we arrived on scene. Besides, the marina office confirms the berth for the yacht wasn't available until 7 o'clock that morning."

"Still, I wouldn't clear this Officer Favre so fast," Aidan said. "And I wouldn't take a citizen's tip at face value either, unless you trust them and can figure out if they're being honest to some degree."

Geneviève looked over at Nicolas before speaking. "If what you're saying is correct, Aidan, Nicolas and I can accept the tip from the citizen since we have had earlier indicators what they told us were true?"

"What are you saying?" Berger asked.

Geneviève began twirling her finger through her hair. "Let's just say the tip we received about the *Scirocco* came from the same citizen? The clues we found onboard led us to Officer Galant, right?" she said. "And now we have another offer of information about Remesy, so we could consider it as genuine based on what Officer Vidal described, right?"

Berger shook his head. "You're making an assumption the tips are all coming from the same individual," he said. "Just because we scored one for the good guys doesn't mean we won't be penalized the next time we act on something this source tells us."

With her pencil stuck in her ponytail, Geneviève leaned forward in her chair. "And if we don't take the tip serious, then what? What if we find out this drug dealer has been given another avenue to peddle his filth amongst the innocent? And there're more deaths because we didn't act? Are we then complacent in our duties?"

"She makes a compelling argument," Aidan said. "I would add caution by attempting to collaborate the tip if possible."

Berger looked at Vidal first, then over to Geneviève. "Okay, then. This might be an instance where you contact your associate at the airport for help, Benoit."

"You've an informant at the airport?" Vidal asked, glancing at Geneviève.

"No... I don't," she replied. "Hector's not an informant. It's just as the security director, he has helped identify several suspects in the past," she added before turning to Berger. "And I'm not sure if Hector would have anything to contribute on our latest tip anyway. By the way, where's my pencil?"

Detective Vidal stifled a laugh as Geneviève pushed the papers aside looking for her pencil before he tapped the side of his head.

Geneviève noticed the gesture and reached her hand to her head, finding the pencil where she left it during the conversation. "Merci. Nic, did the Toulouse office ever send their report from last week?"

"Did you check the online files?"

With a shake of her head, Geneviève let out a sigh. "No, I didn't." She moved her mouse to the drive section of her computer. Soon the national operation came up listing the major municipalities with DJSE offices. In moments, Geneviève was looking at patrol logs from the station in Toulouse.

"Nic, do you recall if we encountered Remesy on Wednesday or Thursday?" Geneviève asked while rifling through her stack of notebooks. "There doesn't appear to be any mention of officers increasing their patrols of the training station."

Berger slid his folder aside and looked at his desk calendar. "It was Wednesday."

As she scrolled through the reports, Geneviève's thoughts traveled back to the train station. As she stood on the platform, she could see the face of Remesy, his smirk taunting her from behind the train window. *I was so close*, she thought watching the date/time stamps roll top to bottom. "There's no mention they ever passed to the station, Nic," she uttered.

"What does that mean then? Is your suspect still in Toulouse?" The question came from Vidal.

"There is one way to find out," Geneviève said, grabbing the phone and dialing. In a few moments, she was connected to the main switchboard at the airport. "Bonjour, is Monsieur Dupont in this morning?" she asked in her most polite voice.

Berger glanced over at Vidal. "I knew she'd end up calling Hector."

"She deals with him that much?"

Berger gave his head a slight tilt. "You might say that," he muttered. "Geneviève and this gentleman have been seeing each other on and off socially for the last few months."

"This guy is a police officer with the airport?" Vidal asked.

Berger let out a chuckle. "No, he's much more important than mere security patrol. You see, Hector Dupont is the head of security."

"Are you two done with the gossip?" Geneviève declared, her stern expression harkening that of a teacher or mother. Before either of the men could answer, she heard the familiar voice in the earpiece.

"Bonjour Geneviève," Hector replied. "Are you just now returning my call from last night?"

Embarrassed, Geneviève dropped her head towards the desk. "No, I'm sorry... it's just..." she muttered as she struggled to explain.

Berger motioned Vidal towards the door. "Let's give her a moment."

Hector could pick up in her voice that she was conflicted. "It's okay. I just wanted to let you know I have a meeting in Paris next week and need to change our plans," he said. "You did get my message, though didn't you?"

"Yes, Nic gave me the note. I was just in the middle of something else," Geneviève replied. "But the reason I'm calling now though, Hector…" she hesitated, not wanting to divulge her discussion with Arsenault. "It's about the gentleman you helped identify, Monsieur Jacques Vignes."

The head of Marseille's airport security leaned back in his chair. "What about him?"

"Is there any way you can contact your associate in Toulouse to see if there's a chance he slipped past them and left the country?" Geneviève asked.

"Why Toulouse?" Hector asked.

"When he was last seen, it was on the TGV service from here in Marseille," Geneviève explained. "I'm just trying to determine if there's a notification he left the country."

Hector slid closer to the desk and selected a file on his computer. In seconds, a series of names scrolled across the screen. "There have been no further hits on passport control with his name," he read as he studied the listing. "But if he changed it before, it means he could do it again, you know?"

Geneviève sunk lower into her seat. The revelation Hector just made felt like a mule's kick. She didn't consider how resourceful the suspect might be when he evaded her at the train station.

"Is there something I need to be made aware of?" Hector asked, breaking the silence.

Frustrated, Geneviève let out a sigh before answering. "No..." she muttered. "I'm just trying to establish a pattern of behavior. We've a possible tip he might have been seen recently," she lied. "I'm just looking into the possibility of it being true or not, nothing more."

The roar of an airliner taking off echoed through Hector's office as he contemplated the real reason for Geneviève's call. "You know if there's anything on the suspect, I would contact you first."

Before Geneviève could respond, Berger and Vidal had returned. Berger had his sport drink in one hand and two bagels in the other, while Vidal held two cups, one he set in front of the policewoman.

"I know you would, Hector," she responded before mouthing a *thank you* to Vidal. "I'll let you go for now and give you call this afternoon, okay?"

"I'll do my best to be in the office," Hector said. "Au revoir."

"Au revoir," Geneviève replied and hung up.

Berger set a bagel in front of Geneviève. "It's fresh baked today, before you go asking," he said. "Did Dupont offer anything more on our suspect?"

Geneviève could smell the lavender and jasmine waft upward from the cup Vidal had placed in front of her. "Nic told you what flavor of tea, didn't he? Just remember, I don't always succumb to politeness with tea and pastries." She tore off a piece of the bagel. "Mm, it's still warm."

"I'll make a note of your preferences," Vidal said taking a seat.

"No, Hector mentioned that he's not received any alerts to the name of Jacques Vignes," Geneviève said, sipping her tea. "But he also pointed out the fact we don't know if the suspect is using another alias now, either."

"And there's nothing from your friend in Algiers?" Berger asked.

"Not since the last email I received."

Detective Vidal half listened to the others as he flipped through the file on the socialite Yvette Segal and the drugs found on the yacht, *Le Femme Fatale*. Overturning the next page, he froze. "This is interesting," he quipped while flipping back three sheets of paper.

"What is?" Berger asked.

Vidal held up the last page he read. "The yacht owner. I had a case in Brest involving the same group. It was a coastal fishing boat, though, not a yacht. An investigator stumbled onto it when looking into the influx of refugees."

"Smuggling them on the fishing boat?" Berger asked.

"Yeah, they found a false compartment under containers where the refugees were kept."

"And this relates to our case in what manner?" Geneviève asked.

"The trawler was owned by the same group who own your socialite's yacht. They're from Morocco, in Rabat."

"What became of the case?" Berger asked.

"It's still being tried in the courts," Vidal answered. "The trawler's captain must have had friends on speed dial though," he chuckled. "They were good, too, since he was on the street less than 36 hours after his arrest."

"How about we get back to our current issue," Geneviève interjected, "which is whether to trust the information from the person who provided the info or not?"

"Based on our current standing with Captain Duval, I'd let him make those decisions," Berger said as he finished his bagel.

"I don't have much understanding of things yet, so I'm going to go along with him," Vidal replied, pointing a thumb towards Nicolas.

Geneviève pushed herself back from the desk. "If that's how you both feel; then I'll go and have a talk with the captain right now." She tossed her empty cup in the trash and grabbed her notebook. "I'll be back in five minutes with an answer."

"Does she have a chance of convincing the captain to let you both act on the information your tipster provided?" Vidal asked once she was out of the room.

"Not a chance in hell," Berger replied.

Chapter TWENTY-EIGHT

"I don't care if you have a chance to avenge your honor," Omar Khalid spoke into the phone. Getting to his feet, the elder man paced the veranda overlooking the city, his robe swayed as he walked. "Nazim, this action you've undertaken will jeopardize everything I've established with Gilles," Khalid said. With his return to Algiers, Khalid had been informed by Aisha that his nephew had returned to Marseille. What she didn't know was the reason behind the departure.

As Nazim sat in his room near the Marseille airport, he could see the inbound flights, their lights twinkling through early morning mist as they approached. "I understand you're concerned about this, but I can't pass up this chance to teach Arsenault a lesson."

"It's not safe," Khalid replied. "Since you left, I've not had a chance to contact Gilles to arrange protection. If something were to happen, you'd have no one to turn to for help. You understand what I'm telling you?"

Nazim closed his eyes, attempting to place himself in Omar's position and trying to understand his mentor's apprehension. But his only concern now was getting his share of profits from the drugs sold. It was money the ship captain, the one selected by Gregory, lost when he allowed the Irishman to steal their cargo three months ago.

"What about your friend, the Italian; can he offer any help?" Nazim asked. The loud sigh in his ear told him the answer before Khalid even spoke.

"Senor Scuderi is reluctant to engage in anything outside of Naples, I'm afraid," Khalid answered. "He's worried about the exposure his two men held in Marseille are going to bring about if, or when, they talk."

While Khalid discussed how to arrange protection for Nazim Aziz, Gregory Arsenault was making the final plans for meeting with the French-Algerian the next day.

Gregory looked at Hector Pichon. "You're sure the building is empty?" he asked.

The slender figure of the former Legionnaire came upright hearing the question. "Oui Gregory, I went through each room personally last night. One large conference room on the first floor along with five smaller offices and the bathrooms." He ran his finger down the list. "And eight equal size offices on the second floor and the bathrooms."

Louis Clement looked at his friend and former squad leader. "Do you think the policewoman will come alone or with her partner?"

Gregory wrung his hands over the table. "No, I don't think so," he replied. "Claire mentioned they used a four-man team when they flew out to *Planier*. So, I'm willing to bet she'll have something similar tomorrow morning as well."

"And how do we assure Gilles' man is there as well?" It was Julien asking from across the room, stuffing the last of the bandages into his medic's kit. "After we left him in the stables, no one has seen or heard from him."

Gregory shrugged his shoulders before answering. "We don't know. Tomorrow is all about letting this policewoman have her small victory first though. First, we exclude Aziz, then we can concentrate on ridding ourselves of Gilles' gang."

This was not the first time the six men gathered to prepare for an altercation, though the last time was over five years ago in the Congo jungle when they hunted down a band of Soviet-backed mercenaries. Tomorrow's action would be different only in location, not results, as each knew the importance of eliminating Nazim Aziz.

Across town, Geneviève sat waiting to meet with Captain Duval so she could explain her reason to trust Gregory Arsenault and his tip for arresting Remesy.

A rustle of papers outside the door announced the senior officer's arrival. "Detective Benoit, what brings you to see me so early?" Duval asked, strolling past her.

"I need your guidance..." she began, "about how to proceed with information I've been given about the drug smuggler Remesy."

"You and Berger are investigating this person," Duval said, setting down his folders. "So, go. Investigate, then. Unless you're concerned about the legitimacy of this information."

She leaned on the empty chair between her and the desk and took a deep breath. "I believe the information to be genuine, but Detective Berger has reservations as to the motive behind it," she explained. "This person, was the same one who gave us corroborating evidence on Officer Galant's location."

"And we now know it was correct information, don't we?" Duval stated as he dipped honey into his tea. "Is there concern this someone might be assisting the drug dealer?"

Geneviève stood a little straighter behind the chair. "There's always the possibility. It was something Captain Lemieux taught me to always consider."

"Yes, Claude was always more cautious than most. But he had a good reason to be," Duval replied. His friend and colleague learned a hard lesson after being shot in the chest once. The captain took his cup and leaned back in his chair as he considered how to instruct the detective. "The order from the superintendent is still in effect for you and Berger, so any action you take about this tip better include adequate backup, do you understand?"

"Yes, sir," Geneviève replied. "Does this mean you would act on the tip if you were in my position, Captain?" She fought the temptation to reach for her hair as she waited for an answer.

Duval reached forward and put down his tea. "You're a detective; you investigate and look for evidence to solve crimes. Go investigate on this tip as if it were a clue to this drug smuggler. Just understand, at the first sign of trouble you and Detective Berger are in over your heads, you end things and call for backup. Am I clear?"

Geneviève had to force herself not to smile. "Yes, sir. Thank you, Captain," she replied, turning away to leave.

"Benoit, I mean it; the first sign of trouble, you stop," Duval repeated.

"Understood, Captain," she answered as she closed the door. As she headed for the stairway, Sergeant Dubois hailed her from the elevators.

"Detective Benoit!" the sergeant exclaimed, holding a folder above her head.

Geneviève stopped short of the stairs as the sergeant approached her. "Here is the file you requested on Monsieur Arsenault," Claire stated as she held out the folder. "It isn't much based on what we gathered from the computers, but I hope it helps."

"Merci, Sergeant," Geneviève replied.

Berger was in the middle of telling Vidal about the case against Remesy when the door opened. The grin on Geneviève's face told Berger what he previously suspected. "He bought it?"

Setting the folder with Arsenault's information down, Geneviève pulled out her chair and sat. "In the words of Captain Duval, 'you're a detective, go and investigate,'" she replied. "But we need to arrange for backup."

"Who's patrolling the neighborhood?" Vidal asked.

"We can't have any added uniformed officers seen in the field," Berger replied.

"You're right," Geneviève added. "I considered contacting Captain Soucy. Maybe some of his people are nearby and they could act as our backup."

"Who's Captain Soucy?" Vidal asked.

"He heads up the Gang Infiltration Unit," Geneviève replied.

"I don't think he'd want to risk exposing them to others in the neighborhood, either," Berger explained as he drummed his fingers on the desk. "You've heard him talk about the difficulties they have infiltrating certain quarters of the city."

"Who does that leave then?"

"Georges or Picard?" Berger suggested, glancing at Geneviève. "They're used to being out of sight, but more than capable to react if we have trouble."

"Can't the department responsible for the sector just increase the number of vehicle patrols?" Vidal asked.

"There are areas were even the patrols and medical responders are attacked by gang members," Geneviève said. "And there are the neighborhoods where subdivision commanders just won't let their people enter for fear of being hurt. Didn't your department have issues like that in Brest?"

"Sure, we did," Vidal replied. "But we still attempted to keep things in check. How else do you remind the law breakers that there're consequences to their actions? Just look at the *jaune gilet* movement, we're not backing down from those protests."

The discussion, as invigorating and thought provoking as it was, still wasn't getting them to a solution. With an outstretched arm, Geneviève reached for the phone and dialed the extension number she'd scribbled on her desk plotter.

"Who you calling?" Berger asked.

"Captain Georges."

"And you're expecting what from him?"

Geneviève looked across her desk at Nic. "A 'yes' to my request for assistance tomorrow," she said. "I'd rather have an excessive response than a feeble one."

Chapter TWENTY-NINE

The sight of a stray dog tremble in the rain near the entrance where Geneviève was to meet Gregory Arsenault made her feel sad. Trudging along the narrow sidewalk, she drew closer to the doorway and the animal disappeared. Geneviève stayed alongside the building; its walls strewn with colorful depictions from local graffiti artists. Here the immigrant community left messages for others, and it only reinforced Geneviève's sense of dread at what was to happen next. As she glanced behind her, she ducked behind the barrier meant to keep others out from the ruined building, a declaration of destruction stapled to the plywood.

Phillip Gaston looked on from the building on the opposite side of the street. The earlier sound of raindrops striking the glass intensified as a gust of wind blew through the street. "Do you think it's safe for Gregory to be alone in the building?" he asked, glancing at his cousin.

Julien didn't have to consider his response. "Gregory knows what he's doing," he answered as he peered through the rivulet of water streaming across the glass.

Across the street, Arsenault sat in the abandoned conference room, waiting. On the table, a small tent lamp better suited for camping than the expansive conference room glowed next to a scrunched-up bag, each sitting within arm's reach. He could only imagine how his former partner reacted when told about getting his share of €100,000 drug money from the Frenchman. "Let's hope it was enough to lure him," he muttered as checked his watch.

Ten minutes later, the screech of metal on metal alerted him to someone entering the building, but not from the main doorway. The crunch of footsteps on the garbage- and glass-strewn tile floor told him there was movement, and it was getting closer. "Bonjour," he said at the silhouetted figure which came into view past the double doors.

Remaining in the shadows, Geneviève could see the person in the doorway, but even with the miniscule glow of the tent light, their features escaped her for the moment. She brought her hand to her ear, and touched the button to signal the others.

"Bonjour, Gregory," Aziz replied. His sense of caution near its peak as he glanced about the room. Turning his gaze to the Frenchman, Aziz caught sight of the bag resting on the table. "Is that my money?"

Gregory reached out and patted the sack. "It's the reason you're here, isn't it?"

"Good. Now do us both a favor: get on your feet and lift your coat," Aziz demanded. "I don't want any surprises." He watched Gregory display he had nothing hidden.

"And you?" Gregory asked while he sat back down.

Aziz slid the Glock pistol from under his jacket. "You can never be sure, can you?"

Gregory smirked. "So much for being a trusted soul."

The drug smuggler just shook his head. With a wave of the pistol toward the table, he continued. "I'm glad you and your associates with the freighters realized the error in the way you handled this particular transaction," Aziz remarked as he took another step closer. "Your actions set me and my friends in Algiers back nearly eight months. Do you know how much those efforts cost me?" he exalted. Aziz tilted his head to the side. "Where is your other friend?"

Gregory shifted himself in the broken chair he'd found. "He decided not to accept any more risks, so he left," he lied. "It turned out to be profitable for me; less money to split after completing my affairs."

Aziz shuffled his feet. "Did it now? You're plying your skills to the highest bidder by yourself, now?"

Gregory sat and kept quiet, he wanted Aziz focused on him while the police, who he suspected were outside, surrounded the building. "Let's just say the less I have to explain to others, the easier I sleep at night," he spoke with an air of confidence. "But you… you're still using others to gain an edge, aren't you?"

"You mean Gilles? He's a puppet for Khalid, but a useful one if you pull the right strings." Aziz chuckled at the question. "It's just another way of keeping myself from being associated with the likes of idiots such as Laurent."

A triple tapping in her earpiece signaled Geneviève the men from Captain Georges' team were in position outside the building. All she needed to do was convey her signal and they would storm the entrance.

"Tell me, Gregory, have you figured out why the Italians never came to your aid?" Aziz asked. "I'll tell you why." He paused as he sensed something nearby. "The young man in Toulon… Ricci, wasn't it? You see, he was always working for me and my mentor, Khalid. And yet you never figured it out, did you?"

Geneviève had heard enough from the men. As she prepared to step out from office where she hid, an arm wrapped around her neck. Before she could react, Geneviève felt the knife's tip sink into her cheek.

The tussle behind Gregory caused him to face the noise.

"You didn't think I'd come alone, did you?" Aziz declared as one of Gilles's men drug the policewoman into view. "Not only am I going to collect my share from the drug deal," he declared with a grin. "But I'm also going to show Khalid how I handle being disrespected by a woman."

Gregory swore under his breath. He'd underestimated Aziz. The French-Algerian somehow arranged for someone to help him from the Maghrebis. Now he was alone and at a distinct dis-advantage.

Nazim noticed the bewildered look on the face of the former Legionnaire. "Come now, Gregory," he said. "You didn't think I would be here alone, did you? I mean, Khalid... he thought it was foolish to come back. But he didn't know I'd made separate arrangements with one of Gilles's men months ago. You're not the only one with a confidential source, you know."

As Aziz continued to speak, Geneviève listened to Berger pass along instructions to the SWAT team through her earpiece. It was a matter of minutes before they would try to make their entry and capture the drug dealer. "It sounds as if you don't trust anyone, Remesy," she said trying to buy herself and Gregory time.

Aziz glared at Geneviève. "Shut up, woman! You will not speak unless I allow it," he added. As he turned to Gregory, Aziz could sense the hatred swell within him as he looked at the Frenchman stare back at him. "Wait a minute, you said Remesy...?" Aziz exclaimed. "She doesn't know my real name, does she?" he asked, glaring at Gregory. "Not unless you've told her beforehand, am I right? Did he tell you?"

Geneviève recognized her presence had made the drug smuggler angry, and now was confused. "Monsieur Arsenault didn't need to tell me anything," she said, tilting her head towards Gregory. "Once the inspector from Scotland Yard identified you two months ago, we had everything we needed to piece together your identity."

The Algerian grew angry as he leveled his pistol towards Geneviève. "I said shut up, woman," Aziz declared again. He gestured to the gang member and ordered, "Gag her with something!" in Arabic.

Without speaking, the gang member tugged Geneviève toward another empty chair near the table. But in doing so, the knife inched away from her face, enough for her to feel capable of putting up a defense. As she felt her captor twist and reach for the chair, Geneviève stepped back, bringing the full weight of her body down on the man's foot. This action, known as an axe kick in martial arts, caused the gang member to drop his knife as he crumbled to the floor. The action allowed Geneviève to spin around and place a chokehold on the would-be captor.

The sudden response by Geneviève startled Aziz, who fired his weapon. In a panic, he turned away and ran toward the stairs. Moments later, he stumbled through the dark as he descended the steps. He pushed through the doorway and hesitated. *Which way?* he thought, glancing left and right. Taking a chance, Aziz went right, and in moments was rewarded with the wall section he and the gang member had come through just ninety minutes earlier.

Before checking on the policewoman, Gregory stuffed the money back in his coat. As he looked back at Geneviève, he knew she'd subdued the gang member. "Are you all right?"

"I'm fine," she answered, tightening her handcuffs around the man's wrist. "Which way did Remesy go?"

"I'm not sure," Gregory replied just as a series of flashlights shone in his face.

"Freeze," shouted Corporal Cormier, holding his submachine gun at Gregory's chest. Berger and Vidal were next to appear behind the officer.

Geneviève held up her hand. "It's okay. The suspect is getting away though; search the building," she said directing the others. "Vidal, escort Monsieur Arsenault outside for his safety."

The team broke up into pairs with Geneviève pulling a familiar face towards her. "You're with me," she said. As Cormier and Geneviève approached the open door to the stairwell, the officer turned to look at her. "Which way, up or down?"

"Down."

Illuminated by the flashlight secured to his weapon, Cormier took the lead as he began the descent toward the basement. With a slow, sweeping motion, the light showed enough for Geneviève to avoid the garbage squatters left behind.

Meanwhile, Phillip and Julien had watched as police members stormed through the entryway where their leader had put himself two hours earlier. Now, all they could do was sit and wait for something positive to happen.

Pulling out his cell phone, Julien dialed the number for their second-in-charge, Louis. On the second ring, his call was answered. "Louis? It's Julien. Something's happening with Gregory."

Situated behind the building where Gregory was to meet Aziz, Louis and Hector sat in one of the vehicles they stole from a delivery service. The van allowed them to stay unseen as they waited for their leader to emerge when he was done. The call from Julien changed all that, though, as Louis listened to the scene on the other side of the building.

"Wait a moment, I see him," Julien declared as Gregory was escorted away by Detective Vidal.

Clement closed his eyes for a brief instance. "Is he okay?"

"Oui, for the moment. I can't see anything wrong from here," Julien replied. "But he's being put into a police car. I don't think he's being arrested though because they didn't handcuff him."

"Keep your eyes on him," Clement replied. "If they take him away, I want you and Phillip to follow. Hector and I will stay behind," he added before ending the call.

In the basement, Geneviève and Cormier found the crude tunnel Aziz had escaped through. "I recommend we call for a K9 unit," Cormier stated, offering a more cautious approach.

Geneviève knew the corporal was right, but she didn't want to miss another opportunity to capture the drug smuggler. "Call for the dog; I'll keep guard here," she replied as she grabbed his spare flashlight. "Send Detective Berger down here when you see him."

"Oui, Detective," Cormier answered as he scurried back upstairs.

Geneviève watched the officer disappear up the stairwell. After counting to ten, she turned and entered the tunnel. "He's not getting away," she muttered as she stepped through the rock-strewn cavern.

Detective Berger had gathered with the other team members in the conference room, watching Corporal Lavigne pick the lock on the suspect's handcuffs. "Leave it to Geneviève to forget we need her key," Berger muttered.

As Lavigne freed the suspect from the chair, Cormier walked up to Detective Berger. "Detective Benoit and I found a tunnel in the basement," he said. "She wants you to come down while I call for the K9 unit to help with the search."

Berger pointed to another of the team. "Make the call," he directed. "Corporal, you're with me." Aided by flashlights, Berger and Cormier found the entry point.

"She's gone," Cormier said.

"Yes, of course she is," Berger sighed as he pounded his fist on the wall.

Chapter THIRTY

Nazim stumbled through the tunnel as he fled from Gregory and the police. What had taken him and the Maghrebis gang member five minutes to navigate now took him twice as long. The rough-hewn passage took him toward the city's sewers. As he sloshed through the filth pushed by run-off from the rain, he could make out the noise of cars above him. After thirty or so meters, Nazim rounded a corner, and could hear the voices of women. He felt his way forward and came across the crude metal ladder that would free him from the obscure passageway.

Geneviève, aided by Cormier's flashlight, maneuvered through the tunnel with a sense of ease compared to Nazim. But twice she stopped and listened while approaching a section where the drug smuggler could have hidden himself.

As she neared the tunnel's end, Geneviève found herself stepping through water which flowed in from the sewer. The flashlight beam played off filth-encrusted walls, the tide line showing where rainwater had once climbed. Claws ticked against metal, and she flinched when the flashlight beam caught the tail end of something scurry along a rusty pipe ahead of her. The growing dampness made Geneviève shudder.

Though the water rushed past ahead of her, Geneviève heard a faint noise come from the tunnel she'd just traversed. She swung the light around just in time to see the glowing eyes of an animal as it stood in the shadows.

A low growl emanated from the canine as Geneviève's grip on the pistol and flashlight grew tighter. In the close confines, she knew outrunning the animal was not an option. She could sense her fingers growing icy as the blood fought to make its way through her body. The few tense moments came to an end as a voice in the dark spoke a command, causing the dog to sit.

"Detective Benoit?" the man's voice declared as he came into view. "I'm Sergeant Emile," he introduced himself, stepping forward, petting the German Shepard between the ears.

"Who else is with you, Sergeant?"

"Who do you think?" came the familiar voice of Detective Berger. "I should have expected you'd run off if you had a chance," he added, stepping alongside the dog towards Geneviève. "Did you happen to see which direction our suspect went when he ducked through that hole?"

"No, he'd slipped through before I got here," Geneviève replied. The increasing flow of water from the rain was making its way into the tunnel where they stood. "But I think it's time to have another talk with Monsieur Arsenault, though," she continued as she stepped further away from the rising water.

While Benoit and Berger searched underneath the streets for Nazim, Arsenault was busy sending a text to his men. It was an outline of a plan they would commence later in the day. After he sent it, he leaned back in the seat, feeling the bundle of single euro bills press against his ribs.

Before he could lean forward and ask the officer watching over him if he could stretch his legs, Detectives Benoit and Berger emerged from the building. The determined expression on the woman's face told Gregory their next discussion would not be cordial.

Geneviève's stride outpaced her partner's as she reached the patrol car. With a tug on the door handle, she swung it open and stuck her head inside. "You and I are going to have a talk, monsieur."

With a nod, Gregory replied. "As you wish, Detective," he muttered as he slid towards the door.

"Back at the station, though," Geneviève answered, slamming the door on him. She looked over her shoulder and spied Detective Vidal talking with one of the SWAT team. "Detective Vidal, see to Monsieur Arsenault's comfort back at the station," she directed the young man.

"Where? In the detectives' briefing room?"

"No..." she answered. "Place him in interrogation until I return," she directed before she turned her attention to Corporal Cormier.

Across the street, Phillip and Julien watched the scene unfold from the third-story window.

"What do you think they'll do with Gregory?" Phillip asked.

Julien didn't answer right away. He was too busy observing the gestures and movements of the officers next to the car. He'd seen the woman burst through the boarded-up doorway and walk straight to the passenger side where Gregory sat.

Julien tilted his head towards his young cousin. "I do believe Gregory is going to be asked some tough questions," he inferred as he turned back to the scene below them. "I'm curious though… how do you think Aziz could have eluded the police so easily?" he muttered under his breath.

Phillip stole a glance at Julien. "Someone helped him."

Julien nodded in agreement. "Yes, someone apparently helped him. And it wasn't just the poor soul the police escorted out of the building earlier," he continued. "No, mon ami, I think someone else is working with Aziz right now."

Similar conversations took place between the other men who worked with Gregory. As soon as the text message appeared on Louis's cell phone, he directed his companion to drive off and away from the scene.

"How far do you think Aziz got from the building?" the driver asked Louis.

Louis shook his head. "I don't know. A lot depends on how prepared he was to assure his own safety," he said. "Hector, when you checked out the premises, did anything look out of place?"

The driver took in a deep breath as he ran through his steps from the other day. He saw himself slip through the boarded-up entrance and walk into each room. "Nothing I can remember, Louis," he answered.

"Did you check the basement?"

"Of course. You know I did," Hector replied. "There were two storerooms and a mechanical room for the boiler."

Louis shook his head. "Then how in hell did that camel's ass make it past us on the outside?"

"He couldn't," the driver answered. "We would have seen him. Which means he was waiting there ahead of us, right?"

"I wouldn't bet one of your Cubans on that happening," Louis replied. "You saw how he was when we handled the drugs. Did he ever lift a finger before this? He'd never helped with the transfers or anything were he'd dirty himself. I doubt Aziz would spend more than five minutes in an abandoned building."

Hector slowed the car for a bus pulling away from the curb. "So, what do we do now?"

While Arsenault's men contemplated the next step in getting Aziz arrested, the former Legionnaire was escorted into the police interrogation room. As he took a seat, Gregory noted the four cameras, one in each corner. *Mind what you say and do, mon ami,* he told himself.

Upstairs, Geneviève stopped at the woman's restroom. As she stood in front of the mirror, she noticed the small crimson line left by the gang members knife. "An inch lower and I'd have an excuse to wear a turtle-neck," she muttered. With a wet towel, she swiped the trickle of blood away, and then with a new sheet, cleaned the rest of the tunnel's grime from her face.

In the ready room, Detective Vidal waited for the others to return. Though briefed on what was to take place with the meeting, Adrian was still confused as to why Detective Benoit could have so much trust in the citizen Arsenault. And why Berger appeared to go along with her.

Geneviève made her way into the office and set her weapon in the drawer before laying her coat across the back of her chair. "Where's Detective Berger?" she asked while pacing around the detective's ready room, sorting out her own thoughts.

"He didn't tell me where he was going." Vidal answered. "Can I ask you a question, Detective?"

Geneviève stopped. "What is it?"

"This morning, you seemed to put a great deal of trust in this gentleman. Why?"

Geneviève knew the real reason she listened to Arsenault, but the young detective wouldn't understand why. "He's been instrumental with providing information in the past," she said, her lies coming easier to recall. "But today was an example of what happens when we don't take in all the possibilities when encountering a criminal."

Before Detective Vidal could reply, the door swung open as Detective Berger stepped through. As he looked at Geneviève, he hesitated before grabbing his chair. "Were you waiting for me?"

"Waiting... what for?" she asked.

"You had Aidan put Monsieur Arsenault into one of the interrogation rooms."

"Damn... I forgot about him," Geneviève replied as she reached for her notebook. Before she could reach the door, Berger grabbed her by the arm.

"Before you head downstairs," Nic said. "I want to hear what you're going to ask him. A few minutes more of waiting won't hurt him."

Geneviève took a few steps back before she fell into her chair. "I want him to explain why our suspect, who we know as 'Remesy,' became so angry when I mentioned his name. His reaction was more shock from hearing it." She slid her pencil into her hair. "It looks like you might have been right about being more cautious."

"So, you think this person Arsenault has an ulterior motive?" Vidal asked.

Berger got to his feet. "We'll know in a few minutes. Come on, let's see if he changes his tune."

The woman sat motionless. Geneviève knew she'd placed too much on the possibility of arresting Remesy or Aziz, whichever name was the suspect's true identity. And for what? To clear her name, get promoted, or revenge for a fellow officer? She was becoming confused with what was right and wrong.

Berger tapped her arm. "Geneviève, let's go."

As she tossed the pencil from her hair onto her desk, Geneviève pushed herself to her feet. Before following Berger through the door, she reached across the desk and grabbed her notebook. She couldn't help but tug on the creases of her slacks as she noticed traces of slimy moss on her shoe.

"There goes another pair of shoes," she uttered as Vidal stepped next to her.

"Do you go through that many?"

Geneviève glanced to her right at the detective while avoiding another officer in the hall. "No, I don't," she said. "But in the last three months, I've ruined two pairs. Yet when I walked a beat in Cherbourg, they lasted practically a year."

Vidal shrugged. "It all depends on how they're made, you know," he replied with a touch of sarcasm.

Geneviève held her comment, knowing it wouldn't matter. As she pushed through the door, she descended the stairs towards the basement. At the bottom, Berger stood holding the door open, waiting.

"Glad you two decided to join us," he said as he watched the detectives walk towards interrogation where Captain Duval stood. Berger came up behind Benoit and Vidal and nodded towards the senior officer.

"Detective Benoit, I'm sure you won't mind if I sit in on your discussion with Monsieur Arsenault?" Duval queried. It was more a statement rather than asking for her permission.

"I've no issues with your attendance, Captain."

"Good." the captain said. "Oh, Detective Vidal, I'd like you to return to my office. You'll find Clarise has a task I want you to undertake."

"Oui, Captain," Vidal replied, the look of bewilderment visible on his face.

Duval turned his attention to Geneviève. "Shall we?" he replied, motioning her towards the doorway where an officer stood waiting. "Oh, and Detective, no introductions."

Geneviève took in a deep breath and nodded while she waited for the guard to open the door. As it swung open, she spied the back of Arsenault, his hands folded on the table in front of him.

Gregory glanced up for just a moment and saw the policewoman enter, and she wasn't alone. Behind her, he saw what he guessed as a senior officer following her. "I'm glad you're here," he said. "I was starting to think you'd forgotten about me," he smiled.

Geneviève took one of the seats while Captain Duval pulled the other away from the table. She saw this and glanced back at him with a questioning look.

"I'm here to listen, nothing else," Duval exclaimed as he kept his eyes on Arsenault.

Gregory gave a brief nod. He knew the session was being recorded, which would be used to decide if he was to be treated as a criminal or an innocent civilian. "Then I'll do my best to be polite."

As she flipped open her notebook, Geneviève looked across the table. *Are you a friend?* she wondered looking at the man in front of her. *Or are you someone to be suspicious of?*

"Monsieur Arsenault, two weeks ago you provided information to myself and Detective Berger about a wanted suspect, a gentleman who identified himself as Monsieur Louis Remesy, is that correct?" she asked before putting a check next to a notation.

Gregory glanced at Captain Duval. The senior officer sat quiet, looking back at him with no expression to interpret. As he returned his focus to Geneviève, he cleared his throat. "Yes, I did."

Geneviève focused her gaze on Arsenault. "And Monday, you contacted me with information this suspect would be in Marseille and offered to facilitate a meeting, didn't you?"

"Yes."

With a brief stroke, Geneviève marked the page. "The location you identified; did you consider if it was safe to use as a place to conduct this meeting? Or if the suspect would have a means of entering and leaving without being seen by others?"

Gregory leaned forward. "The choice for the meeting was meant to assure no innocent civilians would be injured if the man in question became violent," he declared. "But I'm a shipping broker, not an architect so I had no knowledge if there were alternate means to enter the building."

Captain Duval sat; his eyes fixated on Gregory as he spoke. He could see the slight pause before he answered each of Geneviève's questions, as if to measure his responses to keep from saying something incriminating.

"And when the meeting took place this morning, the suspect reacted oddly when I addressed him," Geneviève continued. "It was like he didn't expect someone like myself, much less a woman, to know that particular name. Can you explain his reaction, Monsieur Arsenault?"

"No more than you can, Detective," Gregory answered with a shake of his head. "It was the name on his business card which I gave you and the other officer. If he is known by another name, I wasn't aware of it after just one meeting with him."

As she tilted the notebook upward, Geneviève shifted herself in the chair, moving away from the table. The notes on the page had nothing to do with what Arsenault provided at the docks three weeks ago, or the other day. Why was she being singled out? And what did he want in the end? *Questions,* she told herself. *Too many damn questions and not enough information or answers.*

"Detective Benoit?" It was Captain Duval's voice interrupting her thoughts.

Geneviève glanced to her right. "I'm sorry, sir." She turned to Arsenault and flipped to a blank page. "When the suspect revealed himself, he mentioned being paid off for a transaction. But earlier you mentioned not having any dealings with him, so did you lie to Detective Berger and me at the dock, or are you lying now?"

Gregory felt like he was headed toward an ambush with no means of escape. "When I told you and your partner I had just the one experience with your suspect, I was telling you the truth," he lied.

"The suspect mentioned you looking for help from the Italians, as he put it," Geneviève queried. "What help were you seeking and what are the names of those individuals?"

Gregory slowed his breathing. *She's fishing for information*, he told himself. So far, he was being asked what he knew, and his ability to conjure lies was the only thing keeping him from being locked up in a cell.

"My business ventures are not solely kept to French entities, Detective" Gregory said. "I have, in the past, looked to other avenues where I could secure work. And it included contacting various firms in Italy, Spain, and Greece."

"And what about North African countries? Algeria, Morocco, Libya… any transactions in those countries?" Geneviève asked as she recalled the criminal Khalid's name mentioned by Remesy.

"I do my best to avoid those areas where the government is, shall we say, less stable," Gregory answered. "As mentioned before, Detective, I'm in the business to secure contracts to ship goods throughout the Med, and I'll do so to make the most money. But those contracts originate with shipping from here in France, not from other countries to here."

Before Geneviève could ask another question, a light above the door flashed, signaling a needed break by the control room. With her focus centered on her notebook, Geneviève missed it, but Captain Duval did and got to his feet surprising both Gregory and Geneviève. "This session is over."

"Why?"

Duval pointed to the door as the light flashed again.

"And what about Monsieur Arsenault?"

"Has he been placed under arrest?" Duval asked.

Geneviève shook her head. "No, sir, he hasn't. Not at this time," she added with a glance at Arsenault.

"Is that all? I'm now free to leave?" Gregory asked, exchanging looks between the officers.

Geneviève looked at Gregory as she stood and stepped to the now open door. "I'll see you're escorted to the lobby."

Gregory could see on Geneviève's face they would meet again, and soon. Getting to his feet, he followed the instructions from the officer who stood guard at the door and walked away from the detective and her captain.

Geneviève glanced over her shoulder and watched Arsenault walk away. The interrogation didn't go as she planned. Planned? She did have a plan to question the Frenchman. But what was she actually looking for from him? Forgiveness. Redemption, or maybe closure for her ill-timed actions.

Captain Duval stepped into the control room and found Berger waiting. "What ended the session?" he asked.

Berger paused before answering as he watched Geneviève step into the room. "We just took a call from airport security five minutes ago. Remesy was spotted on one of the cameras along the airport's perimeter fence," he said.

"From Hector?"

"Yes. He mentioned they have him as their top priority for surveillance now," Berger replied. "He stated they'll do their best to detain him while we make our way there," he added, this time looking toward the captain. "I've already alerted Captain Georges and his team."

Arsenault was ready to leave when he heard the announcement over the station PA for members of the reaction force to report to their department. Several officers spun on their heels and headed away from him, leaving the lobby in a flourish. One officer looked unphased by the alert as she walked toward him.

The officer, a sergeant, paused. "Is there something I can help you with, Monsieur?"

"No... but thank you anyhow, Officer," he replied.

Claire turned to face her brother-in-law. "They have word on your friend, Remesy," the woman said in a calm and controlled voice. "He's been seen near the airport."

"Merci." Gregory pulled out his cell phone as he pushed open the lobby door. In moments, a familiar voice answered. "The police found Aziz. Alert the others; we're headed to the airport," he said before ending the call.

Chapter THIRTY-ONE

The floor's trap door concealing the tunnel entrance swung upward as Nazim Aziz appeared from below. Several women looked in his direction, but continued with the chore of mending stacks of clothes. One woman, Asiya Fatah, got to her feet and held the makeshift wooden floor, allowing the man to finish extracting himself. After all, the drug smuggler paid her a €1000 to see to his safe passage.

"Merci," Aziz said. Rising amongst the women, he could sense the remnants of his escape through the sewer drip down his torso, visible from the puddle on the stone floor.

Before motioning to Aziz, Asiya slid a small rug over the tunnel entrance. "This way, Monsieur," she motioned to a back room. As she stepped through the doorway, two young men, teenagers actually, got to their feet. "These two will see you safely to your destination."

While Aziz was being readied by members of the Maghrebis gang, Gregory waited outside the police station for Louis to arrive. After spending time in interrogation with Detective Benoit and being questioned about Aziz, he began to regret his plan to use her to protect his sister-in-law, Claire.

Standing near the street, Gregory noticed the parade of police vehicles leave the station. As they disappeared around the corner, the brief blare of a horn caught his attention. He spun around and saw the familiar face of Louis and Hector in a car pull up next to him.

Gregory slipped into the backseat and directed Hector on the route he needed to take to follow the police. "Where are Julien and Phillip?" he asked.

Louis glanced over his shoulder. "They're still across from the building," he said. "Did the woman ask you questions we need to be worried about?"

Gregory looked at his friend. "It depends. Inside the building, Aziz said quite a few things, so it depends on what the detective wants to concentrate on: her hatred for him or implicating us."

"Nothing specific, though?" Louis asked.

"Aziz brought up our relationship with Giuseppe," Gregory answered as he watched the traffic ahead of them. "And he farther mentioned our dealings with 'associates' and the freighters. But if the police had a means to record what was said, then he did more to incriminate himself than us."

"Which way, Gregory?" the driver asked as they neared the motorway entrance.

"West... toward the airport," Gregory said.

"You have a plan, mon ami?" Louis asked.

"Maybe... just maybe."

Louis could see the expression on Gregory's face. It was the same one he'd seen when Gregory played to the odds, which rarely went against him. "Did Aziz say anything else?"

"He mentioned the deals with Franco," the former Legionnaire said. "That's the only thing I'm honestly worried about. If the police link him to me, they'll have reason to suspect I'm involved in his drug dealing."

"Not to mention me," Louis replied. "I was the one who was with him when the detective confronted him on the street. And it's not like I want to go around with this disguise the rest of my life, you know," he added, tugging on the beard he'd grown.

"But you look so handsome," Hector declared as he maneuvered through the traffic.

Before Louis could reply, his cell phone rang. With a glance at the display he saw the call was from Julian. "Oui, Jules, what is it?"

"We haven't seen any more movement from the police since Gregory was taken away," Julien said. "How much longer do Phillip and I need to keep watch on the building?"

Louis shifted himself in the front seat. "Julien wants to know how long he and Phillip are to wait."

"Tell him to head for the equestrian center," Gregory said. "Make sure Elise doesn't have any troubles with Gilles. We might need to add him to the mix if we want the police off our backs," he declared. "But tell them to be careful," he added, knowing he needed to protect the Algerian as a pawn in his plan.

As Louis relayed the instructions from Gregory, the traffic on the motorway began to slow while Hector tried to maneuver around the other cars. "Now's not a good time for an accident," the driver declared, slowing down until they stopped.

Ahead of the three men, the police had established a checkpoint at Captain Duval's direction. Though they had reason to believe the suspect was already at the airport, police checked all vehicles to minimize others coming to aid Aziz's aid.

Benoit and Berger made their way through the airport terminal and straight to Hector's office. Before they could enter, a member of security intercepted them. "Detectives? Monsieur Dupont is in the control room," he said. "This way, please."

In moments, the detectives were in the nerve center for Marseille's airport security services. As Berger looked at the expansive display of video monitors, he froze, attempting to comprehend the complex activity. "Wow."

Meanwhile, Geneviève walked up to Hector. "Thank you for the call," she said with a smile.

Dupont glanced over his shoulder at the detective. "You're welcome, I guess," he replied. "Pull up the image," he directed the technician sitting in front of him. In a second, a grainy surveillance photo appeared on the screen. "It's a 68% match to our earlier images."

"Those don't seem to be very compelling numbers," Berger replied as he joined Geneviève and Dupont.

"What type of vehicle is he in?" Geneviève asked.

"One of the local delivery trucks," Dupont answered. "There are two men with him. But they didn't register in the database. But we'll add them for future reference."

"They appear pretty young," Berger pointed out.

As she studied the image, Geneviève turned to her partner. "I'm not worried about them, just our suspect," she stated. The detective looked to Dupont, posing her next question. “Is there a live feed to show where the truck might be right now?”

Dupont tapped the technician’s shoulder. “Pull up the cameras at P-7,” he said. “Put the feed on screen 4.” The display filled with images of vehicles traveling along the roundabout at the airport entrance.

Geneviève squinted at the image. “Can’t you improve the picture?”

The technician overheard the question and typed in another command. The image grew larger, but the quality was no better than the first. “Best we can get,” the technician said.

Berger watched as the camera image swung on its axis across the sector, displaying numerous vehicles which traveled the motorway outside the airport. While the camera stopped, the image showed the far edge of the parking section. “There, isn’t that the vehicle?” he declared, pointing at the rear of a van.

All eyes focused on the delivery van as it grew smaller. “It’s moving away from the airport. Can’t you zoom in?” Geneviève asked.

The technician selected a few commands and the trio watched, waiting for the image to change. “The camera is at its greatest distance. I’m sorry, sir.”

“Wait? Now there’s a second van,” Berger exclaimed as another, with similar colors as the first, appeared. This one turned, entering the airport. “Can you have your security stop them?” Berger asked looking at Dupont.

“Oui,” Hector replied, pulling his radio off his belt. In moments, security had pulled the delivery van to the side. Dupont tilted his head as he placed a hand over his earpiece. “My supervisor said there’s just one person in the vehicle, and his papers are correct.”

“Then Remesy must have been in the first truck,” Geneviève said. “Nic, let’s go; we can still catch up with the other one. Hector, keep us informed if anything changes,” she added before leaving the control room.

The detectives and their backup officers drove away from the airport in the delivery van’s direction. As they pulled out of the airport, the driver looked over at Detective Berger. "Do we know where we're going or what to look for?" he asked.

Berger gave him a description of the delivery van. "It headed north," he said, "away from the airport."

"That model van is used by a lot of delivery services," the driver replied. "There could be a dozen or more on the road at any one time."

Berger turned his head and peered at Geneviève. "He's got a point."

"We only need to find the one with Remesy in it," she replied, staring through windshield.

While the police left the airport, Nazim and the two Maghrebis gang members pulled behind a restaurant a few kilometers away. Nazim looked at the tallest one. "How do I know these people can be trusted?"

"He is my aunt's brother," the young man replied. "She told him what was needed and how much he would receive for helping you. We'll see the police follow us once you are inside."

Nazim slid out of the van and before reaching the entrance, the door swung open and a slightly build man, his apron stained with tomato sauce, ushered him inside. "Merci," Nazim uttered as the door closed.

The restaurant owner held out clean clothes to Nazim. "Put these on, then we'll see you safe to your next stop."

Nazim grabbed the clothing and before he stepped to the men's room, noticed the two men drive off in the van. His only hope was they succeeded in luring the police away, and he could return to his hotel. Surprisingly, he found the cloths fit him well.

Remaining in the restaurant's kitchen, Nazim summoned the owner to his side. "Can your people get me to this place?" he asked, giving the hotel's address to the elder.

"Oui, we have a car waiting."

In a few minutes, the owner slid behind the wheel while Nazim sat beside him. As they pulled away from the restaurant, the car turned south towards the hotel. After a few kilometers of silence, they arrived without incident, and the owner wished Nazim well.

"Bienvenu, Monsieur," the hotel clerk exclaimed as Nazim entered.

"Bon chance," he answered. Strolling passed the clerk, Nazim went straight to the elevator and to his room. Once there, he grabbed the few items he had, shoved them unceremoniously into his bag. As he returned to the lobby, Nazim approached the counter.

"How can I help you, Monsieur?"

Nazim placed his key on the counter. "I'm checking out," he declared.

The clerk nodded, processed his account and slid the single sheet of paper before Nazim to sign.

"Do you have the means of getting me to the train station?" Nazim asked.

"Oui, monsieur," the clerk replied. "We can arrange for the shuttle to take you." Past the doorway, the driver struggled to unload the luggage trolley. A husband and wife stood next to the open van door, ushering in their two children.

"Merci," Nazim said.

Chapter THIRTY-TWO

Benoit and Berger stood outside the small market. Across the parking lot, two uniformed officers questioned the young Algerians. The taller of the two was identified driving the van which had been used to transport Aziz. The senior officer strolled up to the detectives and shook his head.

"As luck would have it," the officer began, "these two have legitimate work papers. The tall one is licensed to drive the van." As he glanced over his shoulder, he continued. "They each profess not having your suspect with them or giving him a ride, either."

"But we've got them on video," Geneviève declared. "It's obvious they're lying to you, Sergeant," she said as she took a step towards the men, but Berger grabbed her arm.

"Whoa, there..." Nicolas said. "The video shows a van like this. And the images aren't that spectacular to start with, are they?"

Geneviève sulked at Berger. She knew Nic was right, but didn't want to admit it. If they arrested the two men, they would have a hard time proving any connection with the drug smuggler. "What do you suggest we do now?"

Frustrated at hitting a dead-end with the Algerians, Berger looked at Geneviève "Back to the airport, I guess. We can see if your friend can help piece together a timeline from when Remesy was first reported."

"I'll let the sergeant know, then," Geneviève replied, trudging toward the others.

Meanwhile, as the detectives returned to the airport, Nazim sat nervously in the hotel shuttle's front seat. The driver was busy talking with the couple about which departure terminal they needed for their flight.

He looked out the window and spotted a security patrol walk along the curb twenty meters from the van, scanning each vehicle entering the airport. As they approached the car in front of him, Nazim saw an officer produce a flyer with a photo. His thoughts conjured the worst-case scenario they were searching for him. "How long will you need to off-load these passengers?" he asked the driver.

"Only a few minutes, monsieur," he replied.

Space opened ahead of the shuttle, allowing the driver to pull up and park. Before the driver could get out, Nazim grabbed his bag and slid out of the passenger seat. "Monsieur, I thought you wish to be taken to the train station?"

"I changed my mind," Nazim exclaimed, walking away. Entering the main terminal, he recognized other security walk through the crowds. He turned to his left and saw the snake-like queues filled with passengers carting luggage in front of the Air France counter. Glancing up, Nazim stared at the digital monitors display flight departure and arrival times, and the associated airlines.

Nazim noted a smaller crowd near the Iberian Airlines counter, and headed towards the line. As he shuffled along with other passengers waiting to purchase tickets, check bags, and be scanned by security, it was evident why airlines wanted patrons to arrive hours before flights departed.

"Excuse me, sir," a woman's voice asked from behind Nazim.

Turning, he saw a uniformed clerk with a clipboard in her hand. "I'm sorry, did you say something?"

"I noticed you have no luggage to check; you can move over to that line," the woman declared, gesturing to the express counter for check in. There were just three passengers waiting with their itineraries.

"Thank you, I wasn't sure about which line to choose." Ducking under the stretchy fabric designating queue lines, Nazim strolled up to the near empty counter. As he reached the front, he saw the digital monitor display flights with information. *Barcelona, Madrid, or Valencia?* he wondered. Two flights left at the same time.

"Next, please?" the ticket agent requested.

Her blouse reminded him of ripe cranberries, while her skirt had him recalling sunflowers. As he stepped forward, Nazim pulled out his passport and wallet from his coat. "Are there any available seats on the flight to Madrid?"

The clerk reviewed his passport. "You don't have ticketed travel, Monsieur Vignes?"

Nazim smiled. "No, I'm afraid not. My meeting scheduled for today was cancelled rather abruptly."

"I'll see if we can accommodate you," she replied, entering his name and passport number into her computer.

Three hundred meters away in airport security, a warning flashed across screens inside the data center. Within the recording room, the myriad of computers and screens recorded audio and video from the dozens of security cameras and devices through the airport. One specific computer scanned and logged each suspicious traveler in the database and was only activated when names and other information were entered.

The technician typed in a command, sending an automated announcement throughout the terminals. In less than a minute, his phone rang next to his computer.

Standing near a security checkpoint, the airport's senior security manager viewed the repair to a body scanner when he overheard the PA announcement. "This is the Director, what have you got?" Hector Dupont asked.

"We've received an alert on a passport used by Monsieur Jacques Vignes," the technician replied. "It came from Iberian Airlines."

"I'll take it from here," Dupont replied. Getting the two-way radio off his belt, he selected a separate channel. "Captain, we have a suspect sighted in the main terminal at the Iberian Airlines counter. Have four men stand by for an arrest, but do not approach until I tell you to."

As Dupont gave his directions, he pulled his cell phone out, thumbed a single digit to speed dial Geneviève. After two rings, he heard the detective answer.

Sliding out of the police car, Geneviève pulled the vibrating phone from her jacket. "Yes, Hector?" the woman replied.

Dupont strolled through the crowds gathering outside the checkpoint as he headed towards the ticket counters. "Your suspect has returned to the airport. Where are you right now?"

Geneviève froze. Pausing outside the entrance to security, she glanced over her shoulder at the terminal building. "We just came back from checking out the delivery van. We're outside your building."

Berger walked up to Geneviève and stood beside her, his head tilted to the side while he raised one eyebrow and gave her a *what now?* expression.

Geneviève covered the phone for the moment. "Remesy, he's here," she muttered before returning her attention back to Hector. "Which airline did you say?"

As the conversation between Geneviève and Hector went back and forth, Nazim stood at the counter while the clerk processed his credit card. Over the hum of conversations, he could hear names of unfortunate passengers announced over the intercom as the Air France attendants declared the cancellation of the Paris flight.

"My apologies for the delay, sir," the Iberian clerk said. "The computers have been unusually slow the last few days."

"It's not your fault," Nazim replied with a nervous smile. To his left, he could hear raucous arguments break out amongst irate passengers. Just past the crowd, though, he spied two uniformed officers' pace between the exit and the doorway leading to the departure gates.

"Here you are, Monsieur Vignes; if you could just sign at the red check mark," the clerk declared, sliding the payment slip and a pen in Nazim's direction.

The clerk's request caught Nazim off-guard for the moment. "I'm sorry," he replied, taking the pen to sign for his ticket. In his distracted state, he didn't use his alias and hastily wrote his given name.

"Here's your passport along with your ticket," the clerk said. "You'll pass through security screening," she instructed, gesturing to her right. "From there, your flight is scheduled to leave from Gate 3 in Hall Two."

"Merci," Nazim replied, accepting his passport and ticket. As he turned, he caught sight of the security detail again. This time, they'd moved closer to the screening entrance.

Outside the terminal, Hector saw the French-Algerian at the counter. It didn't take long for Benoit and Berger to join him. "Where are your other officers?" Hector asked.

Berger nodded to his right. "We told them to stay outside the entrance unless we called for them," the detective replied. "No sense causing a scene with all these people."

Geneviève stared through the glass. "Which one is he?"

Hector looked down at the woman. "You can't tell who he is?"

Geneviève glared back. "Hector, this morning I caught a glimpse of him in a darkened room of an abandoned building," she exclaimed. "I didn't actually get a chance to see what he was wearing."

"He's the gentleman headed toward the security screeners," Dupont replied. "He's wearing the off-white *taqiyah* and wheat-colored blazer."

Geneviève looked over to Berger. "Are you ready?" she asked as she pulled her jacket aside, reaching for her pistol.

"That's not necessary," Hector declared.

"Hector, he was armed earlier," Geneviève replied. "I won't take another chance of being surprised."

Berger placed his hand against her arm. "Let's not create a situation we can't control," he said. "If he's still armed, we don't want him taking a passenger hostage or do something worse."

"Geneviève, I've men just beyond the checkpoint," Hector said. "Once he goes through, we'll have your suspect in a situation where he can't escape."

Overhearing his senior officer describe the situation, Dupont replied with more instructions. "We'll need to head over to the baggage screeners to enter the terminal unseen. I've already had the passage cleared of unnecessary staff."

Nazim entered the security area and stood, staring past the kiosk of agents checking paperwork. Beyond them, queued lines of passengers waited their turn to enter. At this juncture, uniformed security agents wearing latex gloves scanned personal items while others used handheld metal detectors to sweep over each person.

As passengers cleared the screening area, glass doors parted, to show departure gates beyond security. The floor-to-ceiling windows provided travelers a chance to view the planes waiting to be loaded. On the tarmac, luggage trains and ground crew scurried to load multi-colored bags into each cargo hold.

It wasn't long before Nazim stood before the Customs officer. As he handed over his boarding pass and passport, he smiled politely at the agent, waiting for the standard questions.

"What is your business in Madrid, Monsieur Vignes?" the officer asked, reciting Nazim's alias.

"I'm an agricultural products broker, citrus fruits, mainly," Nazim lied. "I'm work with a consortium to increase the import of a new varietal of oranges," he continued. "Ever since the Americans introduced a beer garnished with Valencia orange slices, there's been a higher demand for the fruit."

The officer chuckled as he initialed the boarding pass. "I'll never understand why someone would want to do something to their beer like that." After several more questions, the agent made a note on the back of the boarding pass before handing it and his passport back. "Have a pleasant trip."

Nazim took his passport back. "Merci," he replied, stepping toward the queue of people waiting for their bags to be checked and scanned. He could feel the sweat on his shirt collar expand as watched the officer go through the woman's handbag in front of him.

"Next person, please," the officer announced, waving him forward.

Nazim placed his bag down. Here the officer pulled it closer and unzipped the compartments, starting with the top. With a brief glance inside each space, the clerk swept her hand through the contents. "Is that everything you have, Monsieur?" she asked.

Nazim nodded. "Oui."

The clerk pushed the bag aside. "You're free to go," she declared as she waved the next person forward.

Nazim grabbed the backpack, and pushed past a family of seven who struggled to gather their parcels and make their way out of the area. The glass doors parted with a hiss as he approached the sensors, allowing him to escape the throng.

Clear of security, Nazim glanced at the display for departing flights. His flight to Madrid was leaving from the section to his left, which he proceeded towards in a slow and leisurely fashion. In turning away, he failed to recognize the security staff headed in the same direction.

The crackle of Hector's radio echoed in the corridor used by terminal staff as he led Geneviève and Berger through the building. Taking the handset, Dupont relayed another set of instructions to the officers already in the terminal.

Geneviève grabbed the security director's arm. "What is it, Hector?"

Hector stopped behind the corridor's exit leading into the terminal. "Your suspect has cleared security and is headed toward the departure gates," he replied. "I've four officers in the area, and you just heard me tell them to continue their normal patrol."

"Aren't we placing the travelers in danger?" Berger asked.

The look from Dupont told the detective what he needed to know. "Since your suspect has cleared security without raising an alarm, it's to our benefit. Plus, he isn't carrying any weapons, which is also to our advantage," he said. "But he can still be a danger to them by other means."

Chapter THIRTY-THREE

Pockets of sunlight appeared as the early morning storm passed through the city, creating streaks of light through gray clouds meandering across the sky. As he picked his way through the crowd, Nazim squinted at each splash of sunlight piercing through plate-glass windows. As he approached his departure gate, the drug smuggler picked through a slew of young travelers, each passing time texting or talking on phones, while others read books.

The beeping of an approaching cart caused Nazim to glance over his shoulder, where patrons parted like the Red Sea for Moses. Just beyond the cart, he noticed a pair of security officers stroll towards him.

To his left, Nazim saw janitorial staff push cleaning trolleys towards a restroom. In moments, they set placards up to close it, much to the dismay of a mother and her newborn child.

Stopping across from the departure gate, Nazim watched the security officers as they continued to make their way closer. Nazim leaned against the wall as his nervousness grew amongst the crowd, shuffling his feet and trying to wish the clock to reach his departure time. The arrival of flight attendants, comparing their experiences in a rapid exchange of Spanish, took his attention from officers for the moment.

"Excusez-moi, monsieur?" a youthful woman asked, holding up her electrical device charger.

Confused, Nazim glanced at the university student. "Pardon?"

"I need to charge my tablet; you're blocking the outlet," she said, motioning behind Nazim.

He glanced down to his left. "Of course," he said, stepping aside.

Within moments, the girl settled on the floor next to him, her tablet displaying a video while it charged. "Thank you," she replied, glancing upward before turning her attention to the screen.

The few minutes it took with the woman was enough distraction for Nazim to miss the announcement over the PA system. The gate attendants just advised everyone their aircraft had landed and would be at the gate in a few minutes, but he did hear their appeal to clear the aisles and allow the passengers deplaning to pass.

Nazim watched as a handful of travelers were asked to move by gate attendants. One, however, had become a nuisance. A middle-aged man, who showed he'd spent his morning drinking, was passed out against a trash bin.

Seeing the attendants' effort to wake the gentleman caused the onlookers to chuckle and smile, including Nazim. But in doing so, he lost track of security, who were now between him and the departure gate.

At the opposite end of the terminal, Geneviève and Berger stood behind Hector as he spoke to the supervisor at the screening station. When he finished his discussion, Hector turned to the two detectives.

With a heavy sigh, Geneviève smiled, a forced display for those around her. "Well, did he come through here?" she asked.

"Yes, he passed through here," Hector replied. Before he could say anything else, his radio crackled with the call for aid at one of the departure gates. Picking up the handset, he acknowledged the announcement. "And on top of that, there's a passenger who's too drunk to fly."

Berger chuckled to himself. "If it's not a few stiff drinks, it would be a handful of pills, wouldn't it?"

He shrugged his shoulders. "Some people just don't like the thought of not being in control or being stuffed in a plane with others they don't know," Hector answered. "Getting back to your suspect, though… seems his gate is in the vicinity where the call for service came from. So, we'll need to use a more cautious approach."

"Why? If there's a response with security and medical personnel, we could easily approach him without being noticed, couldn't we?" Geneviève asked.

"It could also put him on edge just as easy," Berger said.

"Either way, we still have to be careful because of the others in the terminal," Hector reminded them as he motioned for the others to follow him. He pushed his way through travelers strolling through the concourse, scanning back and forth for their suspect.

The flash of a red strobe on a cart caught their attention as they rounded the corner towards the terminal's end. Pausing, Hector scanned the crowd, straining to spot the suspected drug smuggler.

"What's wrong?" Geneviève asked, standing next to her companion.

"Your suspect was wearing a *taqiyah*," Hector replied. "But it doesn't appear any gentlemen are wearing one now."

"Wait? You're saying he's not here?" Berger asked.

"Could he have passed us?"

"No, I don't think so," Hector answered while slowly making his way towards the departure gate.

The whine of jet engines filled the concourse as the flight from Madrid pulled closer to the jetway. The approaching aircraft filled the window, much to the joy of the children waiting behind the glass.

Nazim edged closer to the departure gate. He noticed the medical staff had placed the inebriated passenger on a gurney to the man's dismay. A slew of profanities could be heard from the gentleman as the cart maneuvered away.

"You're being taken to the infirmary, Monsieur," an attendant declared, trying to calm the drunk.

"I've a meeting in Valencia today I can't miss," the traveler slurred.

One of the uniformed police officers stepped next to the gurney. "If you refuse to cooperate, we'll have you spend an extra week here in Marseille." His authoritative delivery caused the drunk's face to lose color.

Nazim took in the exchange. He'd almost forgotten how close security had gotten to him. While the medical cart left the area, it was soon replaced with three others. These carts, along with porters pushing them, were an obvious sign there were passengers who might be disabled or of limited-mobility onboard the arriving jet.

An airport clerk propped the jetway door open, and a blast of cool damp air mixed with jet exhaust entered the concourse. In moments, Nazim and the other travelers watched a line of passengers' exit.

While some looked to gain their bearings and decide where to gather their suitcases, others now jostled for a position in the queue for boarding.

The flight crew and airline support staff were gathering at the jetway entrance to board the plane, the movement taxed Nazim's concentration as he noticed an attendant argue with a couple for not following proper carry-on guidance. The woman, whose satchel was stuffed to the bursting point, complained it was no larger than carry-ons handled by others. She even pointed out the diaper bag a young mother used to carry her child's toiletries. As she tried to force her bag to fit in the example bin used to verify acceptable pieces, her companion stood in obvious embarrassment.

All this commotion stressed Nazim. As he glanced amongst the crowd, he caught sight of a familiar face coming closer. With a darting gaze, he attempted to take in everything and determine his options to avoid the woman. Nazim's mind raced as he realized his choice to flee on the Spanish airline placed him at the end of the terminal building.

As Hector neared the departure gate where Nazim was denoted to be at, Benoit and Berger slowed their pace and began scanning the patrons. Most of those walking towards them had come off the flight.

"I believe I have our suspect," Hector said over his shoulder.

"Where is he?" Geneviève asked.

"The one in the beige sport coat. He's got his back to the wall near the jetway," Hector replied as he turned away and looked at Benoit and Berger. "He's cornered for the time being. So, let my people move in and handle this, if you don't mind."

"He's awfully close to the jetway," Berger pointed out.

"He won't get far if he takes that route," Geneviève said. "The plane is full of cleaning personnel, not to mention the flight crew."

Nazim's mind fixated on worst-case scenarios as he watched airport security members continue to mill about the area. Transferring his weight from one leg to the other, Nazim twisted himself against the wall, doing his best to avoid eye contact with the officers.

To his relief, Nazim overheard an announcement from the gate attendant; they'd be boarding in minutes. This caused some travelers to shift in their seats, and for those standing to begin shuffling toward roped-off lanes designating the order for boarding.

"I've lost him," Hector declared as he glanced back towards the wall where Nazim had stood.

As travelers continued to ready themselves, Nazim found the discarded jacket where the drunk patron had been. Without making a fuss, he reached over and picked it off the chair. As he slipped the jacket on, he was surprised to discover it almost fit him. The discarded item provided Nazim a false sense of security as it camouflaged his previous attire.

Geneviève had positioned herself near the restroom. She slowly scanned faces of all the men waiting their turn to board the airplane. Some conversed with other travelers, while some kept to themselves.

Nazim had made his way into the line next to the young woman traveling with her two children. As he glanced at the child in the woman's arms, he couldn't help but engage in small talk with her. "Your child has a cute smile," he said, setting his backpack against the window.

"Thank you," the mother replied, brushing a curl from the child's forehead. "She takes after my mother." Looking down, she saw her other child, a boy, make his way toward the open door. "Emile, come over here," she said, motioning to her side. The child giggled but pointed to the jet on the other side of the glass.

In an odd twist of fate, Nazim spotted an opportunity to facilitate his escape. "Allow me to help," he said, looking at the young mother. Proceeding forward in the line, he pursued the young boy who was now stood feet from the open jetway, peering down the hallway.

Geneviève noticed the man's movement. As Nazim continued toward the door, she saw him glance at another traveler, and that's when their eyes met. It was if she replayed the image in her mind: his face, eyes, the close-cropped haircut. "It's him... it's Remesy," she muttered, moving toward the doorway.

Berger discovered the woman moving, her stride purposeful and direct. "Geneviève?" he called out, trying to push past several businessmen.

Hector followed her out of the corner of his eye. Looking to his left, he heard the commotion made by the man as he reached after the young boy. He grabbed his radio and signaled an alert to the rest of the airport security.

"Excusez-moi, Monsieur," Nazim said offering his apologies to those in line. When he looked up, he noticed the detective from the train station. Her look was unmistakable. And now, he noticed the determination etched on her face expending every effort to reach him. Looking to his left, the boy Emile had made it to the doorway, so Nazim stepped forward and gathered him in his arms.

"Your mother is worried about you, young man," Nazim said looking at the boy's cherub face. "Let's go look at the big plane."

The young mother had observed the drug smuggler follow her son, feeling grateful for the stranger's help. But her joy soon turned to fear when she watched Nazim pick up her son and disappear down the jetway. "Emile!" she screamed. "Where are you taking my son?" she exclaimed, going after the man while clutching her daughter against her hip.

Geneviève caught the movement and ran toward the departure gate. "Remesy, put the child down," she declared, pulling her pistol from its holster. The sight of the weapon caused most of the travelers in the area to shy away, giving Geneviève a clearer path to her suspect.

Nazim heard the detective's command as she screamed his alias, but ignored her, pushing past those who waited to board the jet. He reached the bottom of the jetway and spied a baggage handler in the open doorway tossing luggage to his partner.

Before Berger could reach Geneviève, she was already inside the jetway in pursuit of their suspect. With a glance to his right, he saw Hector bark orders at three officers, motioning back towards the checkpoint entrance before returning his attention back to the detective.

"Where did Geneviève go?" the security director asked.

Berger nodded towards the jetway. "She's gone after Remesy," he replied. "And he took a small child with him when he entered the passage."

Hector swore under his breath. He didn't need a hostage situation on top of pursuing the drug smuggler. Taking his radio, he again rattled off orders through dispatch to prepare his forces for the possibility of the child's involvement.

Nazim reached the doorway and placed the child in the unwilling arms of a businesswoman as he pushed the baggage handler aside. Taking the steps two at a time toward the tarmac, Nazim landed in a puddle left from the earlier showers. He soon spotted an open doorway under the building, and in moments, Nazim found himself amongst a myriad of conveyer belts, half-full baggage carts, and luggage being handled by a group of men.

"Hey, you're not allowed in this area," one shouted as Nazim skirted past the first cart.

Behind him, Geneviève had made it to the bottom of the jetway. A sense of relief swept through her when she noticed the young child being held by the woman. "Where did the man go who had this child?" she asked.

"Out the doorway," came the response from the baggage handler.

Outside, the wail of sirens could be heard over the whine of the jet's auxiliary motor. Walking through the door, Geneviève trotted down the steps until she stood on the tarmac, stepping into the same pool of water as Nazim. She turned on her heels and scanned the area, for any sign of the drug smuggler.

By this time, Berger and Hector had made their own way to the bottom of the jetway and out onto the stairway. Hector saw the policewoman first. "Geneviève, wait," he cried out over the noise as security vehicles arrived on scene.

Geneviève looked over her shoulder. "We're going to lose him," she shouted. As she paced in a circle, armed security members exited the vehicles, and with weapons drawn, approached the detective.

"Put your weapon down," the lead officer commanded.

Before she could comply with the order, Hector Dupont had made his way to diffuse the situation. "Stand down, Carlos; she's with us."

The commotion made by security's arrival had drawn the baggage crew outside from the terminal. The lead handler walked toward the police and security gathering under the nose of the jet. As he drew closer, he recognized Hector and approached him. "We had an unauthorized entry a few minutes ago," he declared while pointing towards the open doorway.

Hector turned to his officer. "Carlos, take your squad and secure the eastern end of the terminal." Hector switched channels on his radio and spoke hastily to the recipient in the control room, advising them to begin scanning all interior camera feeds. Impatient, Geneviève headed towards the group of handlers who stood near the open doorway.

"Where are you going?" Berger asked as he followed his partner.

Without turning around, Geneviève answered. "Remesy is here somewhere and I'm not going to lose him like I did at the train station," she declared. Nearing the handlers, she pointed to the only woman. "Did you notice which way the man fled who ran through here?"

"He ran past the conveyers, but I didn't get a chance to figure out what direction after that," the woman replied.

Geneviève spun around and looked at Hector. "Are there exits beyond the conveyors Remesy can use for his escape?"

Hector held up his badge. "They're all electronically coded for access cards similar to this type. He won't get far without one."

After encountering the handlers, Nazim made his way through the bowels of the terminal, passed several doorways, each with an electric keypad which controlled the locks. As he turned a corner, he came across a break room used by ground crew, and glanced through the window before entering. He sidestepped along the near wall and began rummaging through any open locker in hopes of finding something less conspicuous to wear.

His search lasted three minutes, when Nazim came across an open locker. Here he found some clean coveralls and a ball cap. "It's a little large, but they'll do," he muttered, pulling the azure blue garment from the hanger. In minutes he'd shed the business suit for coveralls and made his way out of the room.

While Nazim changed clothes, Geneviève, along with Berger and Hector, continued to search the building. The clash of a cart against another had Geneviève spinning back and forth, anticipating an encounter with their suspect.

For the better part of thirty minutes, Geneviève and Berger, along with Hector's security detail, searched the baggage handling operation below the terminal. Each airport employee encountered led to the same questions being asked.

Hector could see Geneviève's frustration grow. From her constant deep breaths and exhales to trying to roll the tension from the shoulders while rubbing the back of her neck.

The group stopped outside the break room Nazim had been in earlier. Geneviève turned and faced her colleagues throwing her hands up in defeat. "He's gone... again," she declared. "This bastard is going to be the death of me, Nic."

Before Geneviève could say another word or Berger could respond, the radio on Hector's hip crackled to life. Keeping his hand to his ear, the security director listened to the message from the control room. He held up his free hand. "He's been spotted," he muttered. "Surveillance located him near parking area 5." With an executive secretary's deft touch, Hector's fingers glided across the touch pad of the cypher lock. With a *PING*, the locks released, and he swung the door open. "This way."

Chapter THIRTY-FOUR

Louis Clement glanced into the backseat at Gregory. "Do you really think this idea of yours is any good?" he asked. "You know we're putting ourselves at a helluva risk." Each of them had assumed greater risks as Legionnaires, but they still could fight their way out of trouble. That wouldn't be the case if they encountered the police. The sedan the men sat in was making its third circuit of the airport's parking areas since they arrived. "What if the police stop us and start to ask questions?"

"Claire mentioned Nazim was seen here. So, for the moment, I'm willing to accept the risk," Gregory replied. As he glanced passed rows of cars, a security vehicle rushed along the front of the airport, its lights ablaze, though no siren was heard.

It was five minutes after the three men cleared the checkpoint on the motorway that Sergeant Dubois called her brother-in-law. She'd heard the dispatcher at the station call for Captain Duval, and with some gentle prodding, learned of Nazim Aziz's location.

Now, Gregory and Louis, along with Hector Pichon, were searching for their former partner in the drug smuggling effort. It looked like a futile effort, but Hector and Louis knew Gregory's tenacity to follow his instincts, which paid off more than once in their favor.

A second security vehicle snaked its way through traffic, headed in the same direction as the last. "Looks like security have something going on up ahead," Gregory spoke. "Hector, be mindful on how close we get."

"Oui, Gregory."

Clement cocked his head to the side, his eyes squinting as sunlight burst through the clouds. "Do you think it's Aziz?" he asked without looking back at Arsenault.

Gregory shrugged his shoulders. "Maybe. It certainly looks like they're making a big deal of something, though." He watched a third vehicle speed towards them as Pichon navigated the roundabout.

After changing into the handler's work clothes, Nazim made his way towards the opposite side of the terminal and bluffed his way past a security officer. Now, outside, he saw the sign for rental car returns and began walking towards the holding area. With a feigned ignorance to the movement behind him, Nazim continued to make his way through the parking lot near the terminal, failing to notice CCTV cameras positioned at each corner of the fenced in space.

Allowing the security vehicle to pass, Hector pulled the car to the side. Now, he glanced into the mirror and made eye contact with Gregory. "Do we go around again?" he asked.

Gregory closed his eyes and exhaled gently. He knew acting on the tip from his sister-in-law was, at best, a long shot. But he wanted to rid himself of Nazim and the constant fear of being betrayed. Looking back at Hector, he nodded. "Let's head out after circling this lot and we'll make one more pass on the western end of the airport."

"Then what?" It was Louis asking as he ran his hand across his face and his lengthening whiskers.

"Then we'll pay a visit to Amed Gilles," Gregory replied. Gilles had been the unwilling guest of Gregory's men for the day, and it would soon be time to rid themselves of the nuisance.

As he walked further away from the airport, Nazim did his best to keep his stride as calm and stress-free as possible. Every few steps, he'd glance over his shoulder, anticipating the arrival of security. With each stride, fears of being found lessened, but only until he heard something from behind, or he caught sight of something unfamiliar.

As he rounded the corner near the Air France cargo office, Nazim paused for a car exiting the lot. The driver, a middle-aged woman, lowered her window. "Do you need a ride, Monsieur?" she asked.

Nazim smiled at the gesture. "No, but thank you for the offer," he replied. "I'm okay for now."

"Just thought I'd ask," the woman answered, raising her window as she pulled away.

Nazim watched as the car drove off. It soon dawned on him he'd lost an opportunity to place some distance between himself and the authorities. In moments, he continued his trek towards the rental agencies, hoping his plan to secure a car would pan out in his favor.

Meanwhile, Gregory and his companions had made their way to the end of the airport grounds and prepared to make their last pass. Each of them scanned the vicinity for any sign of Aziz in the hope of ending their search with something to show for the effort.

As Hector pulled away from the stop sign next to the parking area, it was Louis who spied the lone figure walking along the road. "Hector, wait a minute, will you?" he said, patting the driver's arm.

"What is it?"

Clement gestured at the person. "Doesn't it seem odd, a worker heading away from the airport in that direction," he said with a glance back at Gregory. "Especially since most employees have their own area on the other side."

Arsenault stared at the figure, watching each stride the person took. In his mind, he tried to fashion an image of Nazim and the manner in which he walked, putting the images side-by-side. "It could be..." he muttered. "Let's see if we can help this lost soul," he said with a tap on the driver's shoulder. "We treat this like we're back on patrol, gentlemen..." he added, so both men knew to use their military status when speaking.

Hector backed up enough to maneuver the car down the side road and toward the lone walker. Keeping his eyes moving, he scanned each of the mirrors for any security vehicles making their rounds. "How close do I get?" he asked.

As the lone figure in the azure coveralls strolled further away, Gregory answered the driver. "Don't run him over, but get close enough for Louis and I to keep him from running." He slid to the other side of the sedan. "Louis, are you ready?"

"Yes." He pulled his pistol from under the seat.

The sounds of another aircraft approach the terminals soon faded as another rolled down the runway. This caught Nazim's attention as he turned to his right and away from the roadway. The noise was enough of a distraction. He failed to notice the sedan pull up to his side until it was too late. Caught off-guard, the French-Algerian drug smuggler spun around to find two men and found his former partner staring at him.

"Out for a walk, Nazim?"

Nazim saw the other man standing beside Gregory, a Glock pistol held in his right hand. "I'm not sure the beard suits you, Clement," he stated. Turning his attention back to Arsenault, he stared at his former partner. "I assume you have something in store? You never did anything on the spur of the moment."

Gregory shook his head. "Nothing too elaborate," he said. "You helped make my next step very easy after you tried abducting the detective," Gregory stated as Hector slipped a set of zip-tie handcuffs on Nazim.

Nazim winced as Hector snugged the plastic strips tight against his flesh. "What's the woman to you anyway?"

Gregory scanned the area. He knew if they stood long enough, security would arrive and begin asking questions. "She means nothing to me in the terms of value," he answered. "But as they say, *'Keep your friends close, but keep your enemies closer.'*"

"Captain, we've been here long enough," Louis said.

With a nod to Hector, he stepped to the rear door and pulled it open. "We'll see how cooperative you are when we discuss what your future entails."

Going to the other side, Louis climbed in and leveled the pistol against Nazim's side while Hector fastened the seatbelt. "Don't want you getting hurt in an accident," Louis muttered as the door closed.

Frustrated with himself, Nazim turned away from the gunman and stared off into the distance. *Why didn't I see this happening?* he asked himself. He knew the answer to the question: it was the person who sat in front of him. He'd always relied on Gregory's abilities as a former Legionnaire to plan contingencies. And now, it was clear his lack of foresight would be his demise.

Hector slid behind the wheel, glancing over at Gregory. "To the others?" he asked.

"Yes, without fanfare, though," Gregory replied.

Back at the airport terminal, Geneviève paced amongst the passengers being questioned. Dupont's security detail was being as thorough as possible with the interviews. After each traveler completed the discussion, they were allowed to make their way onboard the waiting aircraft.

"Thank heavens this wasn't a full flight," Berger muttered, scanning the travelers. "Just a few more to go. And they all have the same story - nothing more than our suspect appeared to be another passenger."

Geneviève spun around at the comment, wagging her finger in her partner's direction. "How do we know someone wasn't here helping him though, Nic?" she declared.

"Because surveillance shows him enter the airport alone," Hector's voice came from behind her.

Geneviève took a few steps back as Hector walked up to her. Drawing in a deep breath and releasing, she replied to her companion. "I'm well aware of that. Let's not forget the need to question the hotel staff when we're done here as well."

"It just shows our suspect planned on coming and going in a hurry," Berger said, glancing in Geneviève's direction. "We can't discount the young men who helped him, though. This Remesy had to make arrangements for help at some point," he stated. "It might just explain the sighting at the train station, don't you think?"

Geneviève took another deep breath, her eyes narrowed. "If that's true, we need to get our hands on the men he met at the train station from last week." She looked up at the two men who stood over her, more confused than ever.

Chapter THIRTY-FIVE

"How much longer do we have to keep guarding this scum?" Phillip asked his cousin Julien. His disdain for Amed Gilles was not lost on how he addressed the man. Phillip had learned this was the man who stalked Gregory's niece, who Phillip had grown fond of while in Toulon. As the wind shifted, the stench from the earlier stable occupants overwhelmed him. It wasn't like Phillip hated animals; it was the fact he'd never been this close to farm animals. Getting to his feet, he leaned against the stall near an opening, and inhaled the fresh air. *And this was just their first day.*

"As long as necessary," Julien replied. As he got to his feet, the former Legionnaire medic strolled to the open stall where Gilles was tied up and gagged. With a tilt of his head, the Algerian stared back at him. A grin formed on Julien's face. *You're just another pest.*

The sound of horses neighing brought Amed's head off his chest. He could pick up the faint sound of handlers interact with the animals as they cleaned out enclosures. *I'm at the racetrack.* A slight sense of satisfaction caused his mouth to curl upward on the edges of his gag.

"What so funny?" Julien asked.

Amed shook his head, though his grin remained. In his mind, the Algerian was already working on a means of escape. From there it would be retribution against the men holding him captive.

Julien saw the gang leader in the same light as Boko Haram gangs he and his fellow Legionnaire squad hunted in the African bush. The ruthlessness of those gangs was strewn across villages of northeast Nigeria and Cameroon. Here, the Frenchmen witnessed first-hand the results of those who crossed paths with militant gunmen. Village elders were tortured while most women raped, and left children to fend for themselves.

The gang leader watched Julien pace near the stall's entrance. If not for being chained against the far end of the enclosure, Amed would have considered rushing his captor. But the handcuffs he wore were secured to the rail normally meant for the horses.

Outside, sudden sounds of snorting and grunting from several horses signaled the approach of someone to the area. He could hear the handlers talking or clucking their tongue at the animals attempting to soothe their fears of the strangers. Phillip and Julien both turned as they heard the latch of the stable door being set into place.

As the door slid open, the men inside could pick up the huffing breaths of the horses outside as they settled down. Casting a stark brilliance of light behind them, the shadowy figures of four men emerged, followed by a lone woman.

"You've brought another guest," Julien joked as he watched his fellow Legionnaires drag the former drug smuggler inside.

With a firm grip on either side, Hector and Louis pulled Nazim into the stables. "We thought your guest could use a companion," Hector replied.

A balled-up rag and a length of rope was tossed at Hector's feet. "Sergeant, see he keeps his thoughts to himself," Gregory directed. "We can't have our guests exchanging pleasantries."

"Oui, Captain."

Both Julien and his Phillip overheard the exchange and understood how to address those in attendance. Phillip straightened up and his demeanor changed, while Julien stepped over to help Pichon secure the gag in Nazim's mouth.

As all this took place, the woman stood a few feet away, watching the men. Her face was obscured by a surgeon's mask to keep from breathing dust kicked up by the horses. As the men secured Nazim in the stall opposite Gilles, she stepped alongside Gregory.

"Captain, you need to know this building must be vacant by six o'clock tomorrow morning," Elise said.

Gregory tilted his head towards Elise as he listened to her comment. He was well aware of her relationship with his former platoon scout, Romain Neuville. The woman wasn't going to stop traffic with her looks, though her attire did little to hide the fact how well she cared for her voluptuous physique.

"We'll have them both out of here before sunrise," he replied.

As Gregory and his men made their way to the ranch northeast of the airport, Benoit and Berger returned to the hotel where Nazim stayed. With uniformed officers searching his room, the detectives questioned the desk clerk.

"And you say the man had only been here two nights?" Detective Berger asked as he repeated the clerk's answer.

The man shook his head. "Oui, officer. He checked in on Monday evening and left this morning."

Outside, Geneviève questioned the driver who dropped Nazim at the airport. "Did the man say anything about which airline he wished to be let out at?" She held the surveillance photo from the airport security for him to study.

"No, he didn't," the driver replied. "At first wanted to be taken to the train station. But I was taking a family to catch their flight, so this man agreed to come along."

"Did he say anything about which train he would catch?"

"No... just that he wished to be driven there," the driver replied.

"Merci, Monsieur," Geneviève replied as she turned away to enter the lobby. As she strolled to the counter where her partner continued questioning the desk clerk, Geneviève replayed the scene from the train station where she encountered Remesy.

"Hey... you okay?" Berger asked with a nudge to Geneviève's arm.

"What?"

Berger shook his head. "I asked if you're okay." He nodded to the clerk. "He's going to let us look over the security tapes if you're interested," the detective added. With an eye on Geneviève, he walked around the end of the check-in counter as he waited for her to follow.

Geneviève took a deep breath and ran one hand over her hair, smoothing the few loose strands away from her face. The close calls on the case were adding to her frustration, and it began to show. As she noticed her partner and the clerk standing at the counter, she swiped her hand across her face. "I'm coming," she replied, shuffling her feet.

In a few minutes, the clerk showed Benoit and Berger replays of the security feed from the hotel entrance. Frame by frame, images from the morning showed a handful of patrons walk out and huddle near a bench, each of them lighting their cigarettes.

"What a waste," Geneviève muttered as she watched the smokers get their nicotine fix for the morning. Soon, an image showed a sedan pull up to the entrance. Nazim Aziz stepped out and turned toward the hotel's entrance and the camera.

"There's our guy," Berger stated as he pointed to the screen.

"Go back to the car pulling up," Geneviève demanded.

The clerk reversed the image until the car could be seen.

"What are you looking for?" Berger asked.

Geneviève shook her head. "I was hoping we'd get the license number for the car," she replied. "But the people on the bench are in the way." As she turned away from the screen, she leaned against the wall, her arms folded across her chest. "Remesy is not that elusive," she uttered. "There's got to be some way we can get catch him."

"He's going to be found," Berger said just as the chirp of his cell phone announced an incoming text. With a slide of his finger, he unlocked the screen. "Seems Francine wants to go to lunch," he chuckled as he typed in a reply.

Geneviève chuckled to herself. "Did you forget to check out with her?"

Berger gave the woman a stern look before speaking. "I don't need to let her know where I'm going every minute." As he looked back at the image of their suspect on the screen, he continued. "But we have a more pressing issue besides my lunch date." With a glance back towards the clerk, he returned to the task at hand. "Thank you, Monsieur."

Benoit and Berger walked out of the hotel to find the sergeant and his partner next to the patrol car. "We found nothing significant in the room," the officer said as the detectives approached.

"But you found something?"

The sergeant held up the evidence bag in his hands. "Just a change of clothes. One set looks like they came from a second-hand store," he replied. "While this set came from a men's boutique in Paris." He reached in the car and pulled out another transparent bag with a business suit.

"Nic, that's the same color suit Remesy wore when I saw him at the train station," Geneviève declared as she took the bag from the sergeant. Holding the clothes in front of her, Geneviève's memory took her back to the train platform where she'd come the closest to Nazim. "Was there anything else found?"

The officer shook his head. "Nothing, not even a razor or comb."

Berger chuckled out loud.

"Something funny, Detective?"

"I'm sorry, Sergeant," Berger replied. "It's just the suspect has close-cropped hair; he'd have little use for a comb."

Geneviève only half listened to the exchange. She stared at the clothes, realizing someone else had helped the drug smuggler with his escape. "Can I look at those?" she asked as she pointed to the other evidence bag of clothing.

The sergeant reached into the car where the clothes were and handed them to her.

"Now what?" Berger asked.

Geneviève didn't reply. She stared at the second-hand clothes, a desperate attempt to see beyond the fabric and identify who might have helped their suspect. As she flipped the bag over, she noticed the crude stitches holding the pocket to the shirt. It was similar to one she'd seen before today.

Chapter THIRTY-SIX

The stack of papers looked to be bottomless to Detective Vidal as he flipped another page. The reports Captain Duval asked him to review came from the department's file on unsolved crimes. This one had all the makings of an accountant whom the Mafia had turned into their personal banker.

Each observation focused on one suspect, Pierre Segal. The senior account executive of Banque Palatine was regarded as the middle-man for money laundering activities for several illegitimate groups. If a criminal member looked for someone with a weakness to exploit, it appeared to be Segal.

"How did you get your start?" Vidal asked himself. With a finger on his current page, the detective flipped a dozen or so sheets back where his pencil stuck out. Leafing through the report, he soon found the interviewing officer's remarks. *Suspect was concerned he learned too much about someone and being viewed as a threat to be eliminated.*

"Sounds like a gangster movie from the '30s," Vidal muttered, returning to the last page. As he flipped the paper, he heard a scuffing of shoes across the floor outside the office. Shoving himself away from the desk, Vidal stuck his head out the door.

Down the hall from the detectives' office, Asiya Fatah swept the floor with a damp mop. After each stroke left then right, the woman shuffled back from the section she'd just finished.

"Excuse me, are you supposed to be in here?" the detective asked as he tapped the woman's shoulder.

The intrusion caused Asiya to spin around where she came close to striking Vidal with her mop. "What?" she exclaimed, pulling out one of her ear buds.

Although new to the Marseille office, Aiden knew protocols existed to access specific areas of a police station. And in this case, he wanted to learn if they allowed custodial staff in the detective's area unescorted.

"I asked if you have permission to be here," Vidal said.

Asiya grasped her badge hanging from her neck. "I've been cleared for all areas except the lab," she stammered in broken French to the detective.

He bowed his head a fraction. "My apologies," Vidal said, glancing at the woman's badge. "I didn't expect you in this space, that's all." As he sat behind his desk, Vidal reviewed another set of notes. He learned the bank's manager, Monsieur Ulysse Reno, had provided several years of performance records on Segal.

"A fine, upstanding member of the banking community until three years ago," the detective muttered aloud. The evaluation on Segal had notes from several employees who caught the accountant making notations on records outside his specialty. This would have cost each shareholder €100 a month, they noted.

Vidal leaned back as he placed his feet up on the lowest desk drawer. He placed his hands together, formed a peak with his index fingers, and tapped them against his chin. "Were you getting in so deep with other criminals that you couldn't get out, Monsieur Segal?" he mused. He closed his eyes for a moment as he tried to piece together potential scenarios involving the accountant.

"Aren't you going to say something, or just stare at me?" Vidal queried the officer standing in the doorway.

The night shift's senior detective felt his jaw drop. "I guess I should ask if you're comfortable?" he asked. "But how did you realize I was standing here?"

The detective dropped his feet and spun towards the door. "Just so you know, first, yes… I was comfortable," he replied. "And second, I'm known to have exceptional hearing. And you are...?"

"Detective Sergeant Juneau," the officer answered. "Pierre. And you?"

Aidan got to his feet and extended his hand. "Detective Aidan Vidal; I just reported here from Brest the other day." Anyone he encountered never intimidated a half-head shorter Aidan, even when it was a fellow officer who outranked him.

"Where's Benoit and Berger?" Juneau asked as he set his things on the floor.

"They had a tip on a suspect named Remesy and are at the airport," Vidal answered as he turned his attention back to the files from Captain Duval.

Juneau's forehead furrowed as he heard the response. "Why didn't you go along with them then?"

Vidal tapped a finger on the files stacked on the desk. "Captain Duval wanted me to review these. I'm assuming he thinks this case is tied to the one involving this Remesy fellow."

The senior detective scrutinized the file Aidan handed over. "I remember hearing about this," he said. "Man showed up at the station, professed to have information on several syndicates. But he demanded full immunity from the magistrate before he would hand over any evidence. Next thing you know, he's disappeared."

"Yeah, I read that much, too," Vidal said. "But nothing so far in the files point to involvement in Benoit and Berger's case on drug smuggling operations or their suspect."

Detective Juneau reached down and grabbed another summary sheet off the desk. "Did you consider their current evidence?"

Vidal shook his head. "Why? Based on the information provided by the banks, he managed accounts for corporations, businesses, stuff like that," he explained, thumbing through the papers. "It all points to money laundering and skimming profits from shareholders."

"You can see the water, but still not watch the waves, can you?"

"I don't get what you're trying to say."

Juneau slid the summary page in front of Detective Vidal and placed his finger just above the suspect's name. "Segal. It's the same surname as their dead socialite, Yvette Segal," the senior detective stated. "Is it possible they're related?"

Vidal didn't respond to the detective. Instead, he got to his feet and stepped out of the office where he found the custodian, her back to the door jotting down something in a notebook. "Why aren't you still mopping the floor?" he asked, tugging on the woman's arm.

As the detective took hold of her, Asiya's feet shuffled under her as she let out a sharp scream. Grasping the cleaning cart, the woman dropped the pen into the bucket, landing on filthy strands.

Detective Juneau heard Vidal confront the custodian and stepped around the detective. "Is there a problem, officer?" he asked with his gaze fixed on the woman.

"It would seem our conversation wasn't as private as it could have been," Vidal answered, passing the notebook to Juneau.

Juneau looked over the script. His command of the Arabic language was crude at best. It was even more suspect as he noted what he surmised to be Berber verses mixed in with the rest. The detective grinned as he read. "I'm glad to know some words don't translate well," he said, observing "Segal" and "Remesy" spelled out in crude letters.

Detective Vidal glanced at Juneau. "She'd written enough to describe what we discussed about the money and drugs," Aidan stated with a nod to the notebook. "Not to mention your thought of the socialite being linked to the case."

"You can read Arabic?"

Vidal shook his head. "Enough to keep from ordering the wrong dish at a restaurant," he replied. "It came in handy on previous cases I worked."

Juneau shook his head. "Let me contact the lobby and get a female officer up here. This is becoming an all too often occurrence around here."

While Detectives Juneau and Vidal dealt with the custodian, Benoit and Berger returned to the airport to review security footage with Hector and the senior officer of immigration control.

The tension in the control room was felt by the officers as they stood next to the airport's security director. They watched the screen display each frame which captured the images of their suspect.

"Here he is getting out of the hotel's shuttle," Hector pointed out, "and right past two of my officers," he sighed under his breath. "I'd guess when he looked at them patrolling, he panicked."

Geneviève only half listened to Hector as she watched Remesy leave the van and walk into the terminal. Her focus was on apprehending him, and once again, she'd missed the chance at the departure gate.

"Why do you think he paused here?" It was Detective Berger who asked while pointing at the display. "He doesn't look confused, but he's not showing signs of having a plan either." The display showed Remesy glance to his right, then left before looking upward.

Geneviève looked at Hector. "What section of the terminal is the suspect in again?"

"It's the one used for most domestic travel," the security director replied. "But you could walk fifty meters and be at a counter serving an international carrier."

Geneviève spun around and stared at the back wall of the control room. Taking a few steps, she stood in front of a floor plan of the terminal buildings. The detective slid her finger across the illustration. "Hector, which camera are you showing?" Both Berger and Hector looked back at Geneviève, wondering to themselves what the woman was thinking.

"It's number five," Hector replied.

"What's on your mind, Benoit?" Berger asked as he stepped beside her.

"He wanted to leave quickly," Geneviève began. "To his right would have been the Air France counters, right? But they were too crowded, so he went to the one with the least number of people."

"We learned this already," Hector said, adding to the detective's discussion. "We were alerted when the staff scanned his passport, remember?"

"He was making his escape; I don't think he cared which airline he flew on," Berger declared, turning back to the security video.

Geneviève shook her head. "No, he needed one he could get on that would connect him to North Africa," she stated. "Nic, he needed to return to Algiers because that's where he feels safest."

Hector nodded his head. "That's a plausible reason for his choice," he said. Turning to one technician, he added, "Have the Iberian Air manager meet me in my office right away."

"And our next step is...?"

"Hector, can you show the images from the departure gate? Not inside, but the ones where the baggage handlers work?" Geneviève asked. She could detect on her partner's face he would not let her pursue the suspect alone.

In moments, the display showed the landing gear of an airplane with several members of the ground crew milling about the stairs leading to the cabin. Every few minutes, a bag could be seen tossed down to a waiting handler.

"There he is," Geneviève exclaimed as Remesy's image came into view at the bottom of the stairs.

"Follow him," Hector directed the technician.

Each instance where Remesy disappeared from view, the technician used a deft touch as he punched in commands to change the camera view. It was on the fourth display the detectives looked at their suspect enter the break room and minutes later exit, only to be dressed as a baggage handler.

With her focus on the display, Geneviève spoke to her companion. "Can you tell where he's headed?"

"Not yet," Hector replied just as the technician switched camera views. The next one showed Remesy open a doorway and disappear.

"Where is he going now?" Berger asked.

"Switch to the exterior cameras at P-5," Hector directed the technician. As the display cycled between cameras, the image of a person in a handler's jumpsuit could be seen exiting the terminal near the back entrance to the coffee shop.

"Can you follow him?" Geneviève asked as the person walked out of the picture.

"This is a video feed, it's not live," Hector answered. "We can only examine what the camera recorded at the moment we selected during the taping."

"And the chances of seeing our suspect or anyone who might have helped him are now zero," Berger declared.

Hector's shoulders drooped as he realized his security detail didn't help Geneviève and her partner. "I'll review the footage. There's something here on how we can avoid this from happening again."

"Like what?" Geneviève demanded.

Berger reached out to Benoit. "Hey..."

"It's okay, Detective," Hector replied. "Geneviève, for every mistake we come across, there's a means of improving ourselves so it doesn't happen again. Nothing is ever perfect with security. Someone will always exploit it, or in this case," he nodded to the frozen image, "find a gap we didn't realize existed."

As she placed her hand on his, Geneviève looked into Hector's eyes. "I'm not placing blame on you or your staff, Hector," she said. "You gave us a chance, and we appreciate it, don't we, Nic?"

The detective closed his notebook and slid his pen into his jacket. "Yeah, we can't do our jobs without help from you and the others trying to keep the city safe, can we?"

Looking past the security director, Geneviève focused on the grainy image of Remesy as he walked towards the parking section, and his freedom once again.

Chapter THIRTY-SEVEN

Benoit and Berger each avoided eye contact with the senior officer sitting across from them. Both their heads were dipped, looking down at the floor while being lectured. "Your suspect has proved more elusive than most criminals, wouldn't you say?" Captain Duval declared.

Geneviève's head came upward for a moment. As she sat before Duval, she and Nicolas had spent the better part of ten minutes waiting, to feel their flaws to be displayed. With another tug on her jacket, she continued to cross and uncross her legs, parading her nervousness.

"I'd say he's kept a step ahead..." Berger stated.

"Because someone obviously helps him," Duval replied, finishing Nicolas's statement. "Wouldn't you agree, Detective Benoit?"

Geneviève sat straighter in her chair. "Of course, he's being helped," she answered. "We've a suspect from the building, two adolescents in the truck..."

The captain raised his hand, stopping Geneviève in her tracks. "And your *'concerned citizen'* as well," Duval added. "What about Monsieur Arsenault? Shouldn't we suspect him of putting you and Berger onto this man for his own benefit?"

Geneviève slid forward in the chair as her tongue circled the edge of her lips. "Monsieur Arsenault didn't approach us until after Remesy's attempt at Chateau Il d'If," she stated, diverting attention from the shipping broker. "And we wouldn't have had the success finding Officer Galant without his help, either."

Captain Duval took a moment to gather his thoughts. He knew Geneviève told the truth, but he wasn't sold on the idea Arsenault was innocent. Nor that he just happened to have information on their suspect.

“I want to learn more about Monsieur Arsenault,” the captain said. “If he’s been cited for being drunk in public, a parking ticket, whatever it might be… I want to know about it.”

Berger rolled his shoulders to straighten them from their earlier slouch. “We’ll get right on it,” he replied, displaying his normal willingness to take the lead. “If there’s something on him, we’ll find it, won’t we?”

Geneviève nodded her head in agreement. “Just like he said; we’ll get started right away,” she answered. Forcing a smile to her face, she made eye contact with Captain Duval, raising her eyebrows as she spoke. “Are we to suspend our search for Remesy and let the patrols take over?”

Duval leaned back in his chair. “It’s still your case to work. But I want both of you to exclude Arsenault, or at least ensure he’s not trying to use this department to further his own interests,” he replied. “Is that clear?”

“Of course,” they answered.

The captain slid his drawer open and removed a folder, sliding it across the desk. “Here’s the transcript from the medical examiner on the man Detective Masson shot at the train station.”

Geneviève picked up the folder. Scrawled across the top was a name, *Mohamed Najm*. Inside, the detailed report spelled out how the former gang member died, which was no secret to anyone. “And what’s important about this person?” she asked while looking at the captain.

“Captain Soucy had him linked to the Maghrebis gangs,” the senior officer replied. “Since there’s concern your suspect is being helped, the personal information gathered by the coroner might prove useful.”

Berger tugged at Geneviève’s jacket. “Let’s get to work.”

As she rose from her chair, Geneviève paused. “Is there any word on how Captain Lemieux is doing?”

Julien Duval’s demeanor softened at the question. He and Lemieux had come through police training and assignments during the same time. “I’ve not heard anything from Doctor Beringer,” Duval said. "But I'll make a note to call her later to see if she's heard anything. And if I can, I'll share what the doctor has to say."

"Thank you," Geneviève replied as she followed Berger out the door.

Berger paused at the stairs. Facing Geneviève, he stood in the doorway with his arms crossed. "What's on your mind?"

"Nothing."

"Don't give me that. You're holding something back, I can tell," Berger declared.

Geneviève stepped aside before leaning against the wall. "Nic, I've already had the records for Arsenault pulled. There's nothing in them to suggest he's anything but what he claims to be... a concerned citizen."

Berger tilted his head to the side. "Wait, you've already looked to see if he had any citations? When did you do this?" he asked while running his hand through his hair. Taking a step away, he paced a tight circle before stepping in front of Geneviève. "Are you sure of this?"

As she pushed off the wall, Geneviève straightened her jacket. "Nic, like I said, I've read the file, there's nothing in it to suggest any criminal acts or intentions. I had Arsenault's information searched and merged when we were given the information on Patrice Galant."

Before either of the detectives could respond, each of their cell phones began chirping, the ringtones battling for attention.

"We're suddenly popular," Berger said, pulling his from his jacket. Sliding his finger across the screen, he saw the text from his current companion. "Seems Francine is getting hungry. Want to join us for a late lunch?"

Geneviève didn't respond. She was looking over her phone and the message she'd just received. The message was from Arsenault, and once again, he was providing her with information.

"Geneviève, I asked if you want to go eat?"

"Ahh, no thanks, Nic, I'll grab something on the way home," she answered as she turned away and headed up the stairs.

Across town, Gregory thumbed his cell phone off just as Louis walked up to him. "What's on your mind?" he asked, turning his attention to his lieutenant. Behind them, Elise paced at the stable entrance.

Louis scratched his chin as he continued to get accustomed to the bristly scruff of his beard. "I know we talked about turning Nazim over to the detective, but what are your plans for Gilles?"

Gregory leaned against an idle tractor. "You mentioned handing him over to Claudio. So, now Claudio's interested in having a conversation with him. He thinks there might be someone on the fringes of his family playing both sides."

"When can we hand him over, then?"

Gregory kicked a stone away from his foot before answering. "It won't happen until we get the detective to deal with Nazim. After that, we'll arrange with Claudio to take him off our hands."

Louis lifted his foot onto the tractor's tire, leaning over to look at Gregory. "We still won't have any guarantee for our safety by letting Claudio deal with Gilles. He's seen all of our faces except for Elise's."

"I know," Gregory replied without looking up. Before Louis could ask another question of his friend, his cell phone began ringing. Pulling it from his pocket, Gregory looked at the number and shrugged his shoulders. "I don't recognize this number, do you?"

"I don't have a clue," Louis replied, shaking his head.

After the sixth ring, the phone went silent as the caller left their message. Gregory studied the display, and waited for the voicemail icon to appear. In less than a minute, the symbol displayed to let him know a message was left. "I guess the person had something to say."

"I'm concerned who might have your number though," Louis said.

"Let's find out," Gregory replied, as he played the message.

As both men huddled together to listen to the message, Elise made her way to where they stood. "Something interesting?"

"We'll know in a moment," Gregory answered as he turned up the volume.

"Monsieur Richelieu, I'm aware one of your men killed a follower of mine last week. This inexperienced man was a devoted Muslim who only wanted to make a decent life," the caller began.

"You'll regret having them take such action. There is nowhere you can hide," he warned. "And your family will not survive either."

"Who was that?" Elise asked.

Louis and Gregory exchanged glances before the latter spoke. "I've an idea who will know," He looked past his friend at the stables. "But the most important question is how they tied the action you and Hector took saving Claire to me?"

Louis straightened up and took a few steps away from his friend and the woman. As he paced, he froze mid-step. "The one in the back, the one Hector subdued, could have seen us leave..."

"Are you sure he saw you?"

Louis shook his head. "No, but we were in my car, just like when you met with Gilles..."

"And if Hector's victim was at the restaurant during our meet with Gilles, he'd have an idea who to consider," Gregory added, finishing his friend's statement. The former Legionnaire and his men had several instances where they'd been compromised, but it was always in a plight they could control.

"Do you think this person took over for Gilles and control of the Maghrebis gang?" Louis asked.

Gregory nodded. "More than likely, yes, I believe they are," he declared. "And I'm thinking now is the time we took matters into our own hands; wouldn't you say so?"

While Gregory laid out his plan to deal with the Maghrebis gang, Detective Benoit was engaged in a serious discussion with Berger.

"I've looked over every page of the report and there's nothing pointing to Arsenault's involvement in illegal schemes," Geneviève declared as she waved a pencil in the air.

Berger peered over the folder. "Hey, I'm not arguing with you," he replied. "But doesn't it look odd how *CLEAN* this report is? I mean… to read this, you'd think the guy could run for parliament."

Geneviève opened her mouth to say something, but stopped. *Was Nic right?* she thought. As she tugged open the desk drawer, she piled notebooks on the desktop, glancing at the dates as she pulled each one out.

"Was it something I said?"

Geneviève paused. "Not what you said, but something I overheard during a prior conversation." She he reached for the last notebook at the bottom of the drawer. "Ah ha," she muttered. With her index finger, she flipped it open. A few pages in, she soon found notes taken while interrogating Franco Laurent and Hakim Talib in Algiers.

Berger closed the folder on his desk and watched the woman across from him flip through pages. "Mind sharing what you're reading?"

"After Inspector Haddad released the suspect Hakim Talib to us, he mentioned the information concerning his past activities came from our records department," she stated. "And it was quite detailed..."

"Detailed in what way?" Berger asked.

Geneviève lifted her head and peered at Nicolas. "As if someone wanted to make sure his earlier crimes matched the current crime." She pushed herself away from the desk, and made for the door. "I'll be back."

Geneviève marched through the entrance to Central Records. Her arrival caused several clerks to raise their heads to watch who came through the door. In the back, she spied the familiar face of Sergeant Dubois, who was talking with another officer.

Geneviève walked right up to the sergeant, and didn't wait for an acknowledgement before spoke. "I need to have a word with you, Sergeant Dubois... now."

Claire was surprised by the sudden presence of the detective, and more so by how she was addressed. "I'll be back in a minute, Julia," she said with a nod to the other woman before headed towards the doorway with Geneviève close behind.

Once outside her department, Claire turned down the hallway a few paces before stopping. As she stood there in the passageway, she stared into Geneviève's eyes. "Is there something you want to ask me, Detective?"

Without a moment of hesitation, Geneviève confronted the sergeant. "How do you know Monsieur Arsenault?"

Claire blinked hard as she heard her brother-in-law's name. "Excuse me?"

Geneviève pushed her question on the sergeant again. "I want to know everything between you and Gregory Arsenault," she demanded, glancing up and down the hall. "You gave me a record on him the other day," the detective said. "It's all very rosy; no entry out of place, no citations..."

Claire leaned against the wall. "It's the information we had on file, Detective," she replied. "And I'm not sure what you mean by need to know if there's something between myself and the gentleman you mentioned."

Geneviève stood her ground. "I want to know what he is to you, or better yet, what influence he has over you. And just to remind you, Sergeant Dubois, aiding a person involved in ongoing investigations carries serious consequences."

A bead of sweat formed at Claire's hairline before meandering down her forehead. She felt she couldn't admit to Geneviève her relation to Gregory. But she likewise understood if something happened, she'd be culpable as an accessory in whatever crimes Gregory was investigated for by the detective.

"Well, Sergeant, what's it going to be...?" Geneviève asked.

"He's..." Claire began just as Geneviève's cell phone rang.

Geneviève looked at the screen. A cruel smile formed on her face as she swiped her finger across the screen. "Bon jour, Monsieur Arsenault," she answered her gaze fixed on Claire.

The color drained from the sergeant's face. Claire kept her focus on the detective, as she waited to hear what might come next.

Chapter THIRTY-EIGHT

The reply from the Records Department clerk at the police station wasn't what Gregory Arsenault wanted to hear at that moment. His call to her was meant to confirm Claire's move to a vacant apartment in the same complex as Papillion's secretary, Claudette Minot.

"Damn it," he muttered under his breath. As if dealing with his former partner Aziz and the gang-leader Gilles weren't enough, now he had to decide how to steer Detective Benoit away from Claire.

As he took a deep breath, Gregory dialed the detective's number and waited. In a moment, his call was answered. "Good afternoon, Detective Benoit," he said. "I hate to intrude on your conversation, but may I speak with Sergeant Dubois?"

A brief pause followed before the officer spoke. "Oui, Monsieur, can I help you?" Claire asked, her voice uneasy in its response.

"Claire, I'm sorry for getting you involved with this," he said. "I'll handle Detective Benoit," Gregory replied with a sigh. "I was calling to see if you're ready to move your things tomorrow? Claudette said the apartment would be ready for you and she'd have the keys."

As she stood in the hall under the gaze of Detective Benoit, Claire took a deep breath before replying. "Oui, Monsieur, all is ready," she stammered her nervousness now on display.

Gregory could only imagine what his sister-in-law was dealing with as she stood with Geneviève. The risk of Claire being arrested for her involvement with him had come to a head as he tried to manipulate the detective to create his legitimate business persona.

"Everything will be all right, I promise. Can you give Detective Benoit her phone?" he said.

Sergeant Dubois gave Geneviève back her cell phone. "The gentleman wishes to talk with you," she stated.

Geneviève took the phone. "What do you wish to say before I place the sergeant under arrest for her role in your criminal activities?" Geneviève asked.

Though he rarely felt conflicted in his decision making, Gregory took a moment to consider what he wanted to tell Geneviève while struggling to find the right words. Taking another deep breath, he sensed the heaviness of the circumstances weigh on him now. "I had hoped this conversation would take place after you arrested Remesy," he said.

Geneviève stared at Claire as Gregory spoke. "Why wait until then? You've got my attention now," she replied. "Why don't you start with telling me who the sergeant is to you."

"Sergeant Dubois is my sister-in-law," Gregory answered, exhaling after he spoke.

Geneviève blinked hard in surprise.

The awkward silence on the cell phone gave way to a chirp on Gregory's end as another caller attempted to contact him. Looking at the screen, he realized it was Claudio, head of the Carbone mafia. "We can finish this later; I've got another call," he declared and switched lines.

"Wait..." Geneviève exclaimed before the line went dead. Peering at Claire, she nodded in a mix of understanding and disbelief. With a quick glance up and down the hall, she tried to decide how to deal with the sergeant. "Arsenault is your brother-in-law?"

Claire let out a sigh. "Yes... he is, Detective," she answered. Straightening up her blouse, she did her best to gather herself. "Now, what are you going to do with this information?"

Good question, Geneviève thought. "I'm not sure since he's done nothing which resembles a crime, yet..." the detective admitted. "But I want to know what you both have discussed in the last several months."

Claire's chin rose as she stared Geneviève in the eyes. "I'll be happy to tell you what has transpired between Gregory and I," she replied. "But only when we're all in the same room."

"I don't think you're in any position to dictate terms, Sergeant," Geneviève said. "Remember, if you aided anyone in a crime... and I mean *anyone*, you're as guilty as them. Just like if you were at the scene where it happened."

Back at the equestrian center, Gregory answered the incoming call. "Ciao, Claudio," he greeted the mafia don. "I assume you got my invitation to meet later today?"

"Bonjour, Gregory," the Italian replied. "And yes... I'm calling about your desire to meet. Can you be at the café near Stade Weygand Pupilles, say... in thirty minutes?"

Gregory glanced at his watch before answering. "It's the one on *Avenue Corrot*, isn't it? I shouldn't have a problem," he replied. "I'll have one of my men with me, just so you can let your people know who to expect."

"Bene! Then I'll see you in thirty minutes," Claudio replied as he ended the call.

Gregory strolled into the stable and motioned to Phillip, who was still leaning near the open window behind Amed Gilles. As the young man made his way to the door, Louis stepped up next to Gregory.

"Something you want to tell me?" Louis asked.

"Yes, Captain?" Phillip asked as he came to Louis's side.

"I need you to drive me to a meeting," he said. "Go get your car, I'll be there in a minute."

Louis turned his back to the men held in the stables. "Is this your meeting with Claudio?" he asked.

"Yes."

Louis glanced at his watch, then back at Aziz and Gilles before looking back at Gregory. "How long do you expect to be gone? We still need to prepare to move those two after sunset. And you know it won't be easy."

With a pat on Louis's shoulder, Gregory gave his friend a smile. "That's why I've got you as my second-in-command, my friend," as he chuckled. "Don't worry, Phillip and I'll be back in time to have those two delivered, I promise."

"And what about the detective?" Louis asked. "What if she doesn't show, heh? Or worse, she shows up with a squad of policemen, then what?"

Gregory shook his head. "You always look for the silver linings, don't you?"

Louis grinned. "It's kept you alive most of the time, hasn't it?"

As Gregory turned away, he paused. "I'll be back before six o'clock," he said before trotting towards the space where Phillip parked.

After a short drive across town, Phillip pulled up to the small pizzeria where Gregory and Claudio agreed to meet. "Seems awfully empty, don't you think?" Phillip asked.

"It doesn't have to be busy to have a quiet talk," Gregory replied. He gestured to the small grocer next door. "See what you can pick up for tonight's meal. And don't forget, we're feeding the squad."

"I'll cook as long as you get Pasqual to clean afterwards," the young man replied.

Gregory chuckled. "I'll make sure he does," he said as one of Claudio's men exited the pizzeria. The man was as thick in the waist as he was tall, which didn't mean he couldn't move swiftly when he needed. Gregory stepped forward toward him, palms raised.

"That's close enough," the guard replied. With a deft touch, he frisked Gregory for weapons before he let him enter the eatery.

Pausing beside a cart of fresh vegetables, Phillip watched the scene play out and instinctively slid his hand behind his back for his pistol. While he watched Gregory and the guard, he sensed someone behind him and spun around to see the shop owner.

"Relax, young man, they're only going to talk," the shopkeeper declared.

Phillip noticed the barrel of a gun protrude from under the man's apron. With slow and deliberate moves, he pulled his hand away from the small of his back. "He's my mentor. I'd hate to have any harm come to him."

"You'll find the cabbage and peppers are the freshest today," the man answered, pointing to the produce.

Inside the pizzeria, Claudio Carbone sat with his back to the kitchen, a single empty chair facing him. As Gregory entered, he paused long enough to let his eyes adjust to the darkened interior.

"Thank you for coming," Claudio said and motioned to the chair.

Gregory pulled the chair away from the table. "I'm grateful you agreed to meet," he replied. "I won't waste our time with idle chatter, I've come with a proposal."

The waiter brought out two bottles of mineral water, and Claudio waited for the server to finish pouring the drinks. As the young man left, he returned his focus to Gregory. "Another? What is it you wish to offer this time, my friend?"

"Amed Gilles."

Claudio looked up from taking a drink, staring back at the former Legionnaire. "What about him? He's a pig."

Gregory took a long sip of the water before continuing. "He's currently my guest," he said after dabbing his lips with a napkin, "And I thought you might want to meet with him... to discuss your competing business interests."

Claudio tugged on his ear, and contemplated the Frenchman's offer. The Maghrebis gangs had begun to make their way across his part of the city, block by block. The opportunity to put pressure on their leader would be beneficial. "And after I've had my chance to talk with the Algerian then what? Am I to return him to you?"

A smile came to Gregory's face. "After you your meeting, you're free to do what you like," he answered. Leaning toward Claudio, Gregory continued. "But if he's as much a nuisance as I suspect, I'd never let him see daylight again," he stated. "And I'm only asking for one favor."

Claudio chuckled to himself. "I'm a businessman, you know, Gregory. I don't eliminate my competition for the sake of profits or territory, I let others do it for me, like you," he said. Inside, he already considered what control of the docks would do for his standing among the other criminal entities in the city.

"If you don't take advantage of this, there'll be someone else to negotiate with," Gregory said.

"And what is the favor?"

"After I complete the transaction in Turkey for you, we cut ties when it comes to moving your product."

"You've made a generous offer, handing the Algerian over to me," Claudio replied. "Yet you place a condition difficult to accept."

He counted on Gregory's freighters to move his heroin from Istanbul to Marseille. "Are you concerned about the risks?"

Gregory shook his head. "No, I'm not worried about the risks to myself, but I am thinking of the men onboard the freighters. After the issue with the British, I've made a decision along with my senior members to work with a less volatile product."

"I'm not sure I see the benefit in agreeing to grant you this favor."

"With Gilles eliminated, you'll have the means to control most of the waterfront," Gregory answered. "Which allows you to control what comes and goes onboard the vessels making port. That's a significant and lucrative position to be in, Claudio."

The Mafia don sat silent. The flood of possibilities engulfed his thoughts. He had Gregory committed to move his drugs at least once, and knew he'd need his help some other time, creating another negotiated transaction. Claudio took a long sip of his drink. "When can you introduce me to Monsieur Gilles?"

Outside the eatery, Phillip leaned against his car, watching Gregory shake hands with a dark-haired man. Gregory strolled over and joined him without looking back. "Did it go as you wished?" he asked.

Gregory nodded. "For the time being, it has, Phillip," he replied. "So, what's on this evening's menu?"

Chapter THIRTY-NINE

The crush of people on the bus heading home earlier didn't give Geneviève anytime to reflect on the discussion she had with Nicolas. They each argued valid points on why Arsenault should or should not be considered an associate along with Remesy. Geneviève couldn't convince Nic he could be trusted, but she didn't accept his argument on why the former Legionnaire should be arrested.

Now, sitting in the taxi, she stared at the message on her phone. "Another night alone," she muttered, rereading the text from Hector. This was the third time she'd cancelled plans with him since she'd confessed being victimized as a teenager. As the taxi slowed down, she looked out the window.

"Are you sure this is where you wish to get out?" the driver asked, nodding to the side entrance to the city's largest cemetery.

"How much do I owe?" she asked, ignoring the driver's question.

"It's €22.80 madame."

While Geneviève fished through her purse for change, she didn't notice the Volvo sedan park at the end of the street. Inside, Phillip sat, watching the taxi door open and the woman get out, and head straight for the cemetery entrance. Lifting his radio, he made his observation known to the rest of the team.

As the quarter-moon rose, the graveyard transformed. Pale, translucent light breathed life into worn, faceless statues rising from the mist. In the faint glow, crooked headstones appeared while Geneviève tread with care towards the agreed upon space. Tangled weeds grew from cracks in the pavement, as she neared the cemetery section that hadn't been maintained in months.

Each step Geneviève took led her along the winding, narrow path. All around, there were signs she had entered the cemetery's older section, its crumbling and cracked headstones etched with dates from the past century. Geneviève instinctively touched the small cross around her neck as a fluttery feeling crept into her stomach.

The shroud of fog left droplets on the woman's eyelashes. "Nothing here to worry about," Geneviève muttered, though the scenarios created in her mind told her otherwise. Geneviève pulled a slip of paper from her jacket, held it up so the moonlight could illuminate the writing.

Several hundred meters away, Nazim Aziz felt the dampness from the mist seep through his trousers, while tingling in his feet reminded him the blood flow had slowed. His arms ached as his fingertips became icy from being trussed up against the marble marker for the last hour. Flexing them gave little relief.

Earlier in the day, Nazim and Amed had been taken from the equestrian center by van, still bound and gagged, and their faces covered in hoods. As Nazim sat in the mist, he pondered Gregory's fate, but didn't dwell on the outcome.

It wasn't until several hours past did Nazim comprehend where he'd been taken. As he struggled to search through the mist clinging to the ground, each unfamiliar noise brought a greater sense of dread. The creak of metal on metal caused Nazim to twist his head to his right.

Flexing her fingers, Geneviève curled her hand around the wrought-iron gate protecting the dead and pushed it open. She followed the path to her left, towards the section where foreign soldiers were laid to rest.

In the shadows, a lone figure hunched down, and watched the detective approach. "I've got her now," Pasqual Sequin whispered into his radio. Acknowledgement came in a series of clicks in his earpiece.

On the opposite side of the cemetery, Gregory and Louis stood behind the mausoleum of a prominent family in Marseille, listening to their scout's observation on their own radios.

"I'm still not sure if this was an excellent idea," Louis whispered. "What if Aziz puts up a fight; then what do we do?"

Gregory glanced at his friend and smiled. "From what Claire told me, this detective is more than capable of handling herself in a fight," he uttered. “And you’ve learned the hard way about her skills with a pistol.”

Louis rubbed his thigh out of habit. “Thanks for the reminder,” he whispered.

“Besides, we’ve got her back in the event something happens,” Gregory added.

“What if she has backup we didn’t see?”

Gregory clapped his hand on Louis’s shoulder. “Phillip followed her; we know she’s alone,” he whispered before he turned his attention back towards the soldiers’ gravesites.

The gate groaned in protest against Geneviève’s touch. To her left and right, the marble headstones stood as testament to the fallen from battles fought a century ago.

The sudden vibration against her breast caused Geneviève to stumble as she fought to pull her phone from her jacket. “Ah, shit,” she cursed under breath. The screen illuminated her face as she swiped her finger across the screen.

The subdued surroundings did little to mask the outburst of the detective. Sitting fifty meters away, Nazim saw the sudden glow from the device and the silhouetted figure of the woman. In moments, he could see her step closer, until she stood over him.

Geneviève looked down at the drug smuggler. He was bound hand and foot against the marble cross of a grave marker. “I’ve waited a long time to finally be face to face with you,” she declared.

All Nazim could do is offer a stifled mumble.

Geneviève pulled her phone out and slid her finger across the screen, illuminating the suspect. She studied the crude towel and rope used to gag Nazim. Drawing a knife from her jacket, she exposed the blade with a flick of her thumb. “Promise not to shout and I’ll free the gag,” Geneviève stated, holding it near Nazim’s face.

With a slow dip of his head, the drug smuggler nodded in agreement.

As she slipped the sharpened edge under the rope by Nazim’s ear, Geneviève gave a sharp tug, allowing the knife to slice the rope.

Nazim did his best not to flinch while the icy steel blade slid across his skin. Free of the rope, he shook his head while spitting out the towel. Flexing his jaw, he glanced up at the policewoman. “I had a feeling you’d be the one to show up, Detective,” Nazim said. “Are you here to arrest me... or kill me?”

“If I wanted you dead, I’d have done it at Chateau Il d’If,” Geneviève replied. “Now then, where is your companion, Hakim Talib? Is he the one here in Marseille helping you?” she asked, glancing around the stone markers. “Or are there others as well?”

Nazim stared at Geneviève. “You should know Hakim was my cousin. And because of you, he’s dead,” he uttered. “And for that, I will see you pay for his demise. You’ll suffer twice as long as he did, and in a far worse manner than just a bullet.”

Geneviève shook her head. “You’re not in a position to make threats. Once I get you to the police station, I’ll want to know everything about your smuggling operations. And I’ll likewise expect you to tell me where the drugs come from and how they’re brought ashore and distributed.”

Nazim gave a brief chuckle to the statement. “You certainly want to know more than you can comprehend,” he uttered. “But if you wanted to learn how the drugs are moved, you should talk to Gregory,” he replied. “He’s the one who knows the people controlling the freighters.”

The woman let out a sarcastic laugh. “Of course, Monsieur Arsenault knows people who own freighters; it’s his business,” she said. “Besides, he’s confirmed his usefulness by arranging this meeting.”

Nazim shook his head. “And you haven’t figured out he wants something from you in return for his ‘good behavior,’ have you? Gregory doesn’t give anything away unless there’s something in it for him and his men in return.”

Geneviève took a step towards Nazim and hesitated.

The evening mist which shrouded the cemetery earlier had faded, allowing Nazim to look at the woman before him. The drug smuggler caught a glimpse of Geneviève’s face in the moonlight and noticed her uncertainty. “Something wrong, Detective?”

In the distance, Pasqual peered through his night-vision goggles. He looked at the same uneasy expression on the woman's face Nazim did. "Gregory, we've a problem."

"What is it?"

Pasqual got to his feet and leaned against the crypt he hid behind. "I think we did too good a job securing Aziz to the grave marker," he replied. "The woman doesn't know how to release him without putting herself at risk."

"Shit," Gregory cursed under his breath. Turning to his partner, he handed over his radio. "Keep tabs on everything, Louis."

"What are you doing?"

"She knows I'm the one who set this up, so I'm the only one she'd expect to come across here," Gregory said. As he reached behind his back, he pulled his Glock, and gave it to Louis. "It wouldn't look good if I showed up armed, would it?" Turning away, Gregory began a slow trot toward Nazim and Geneviève.

Geneviève kept her eyes on Nazim as she circled behind the stone cross he was tied to. "Someone is talented with knots," she declared while shining her phone at the rope.

"And you're trying to decide how to release me," Nazim replied. "But still keep your advantage, am I right?"

Geneviève kept silent. Being armed gave her the advantage against the drug smuggler, but getting him secured with her handcuffs would be a challenge. "When I cut lose your arm, I want you to roll onto your side. Do you understand?" her knifed pressed against his cheek.

Nazim snickered. "I could sue you for assault of a restrained captive for that."

Just as Geneviève slid her knife along the gravestone, Gregory emerged from the shadow of a nearby tree. The sound of him kicking a bouquet of dead flowers startled the detective and her captive, alerting them to his presence.

With the disturbance, Geneviève drew her pistol and leaned against the headstone. "Stop where you are or I'll shoot," she announced. The hint of moonlight didn't offer enough light for her to see, but it was enough to notice the shadowy figure step away from the tree. "Who are you and what do you want?" she demanded.

The Frenchman stopped in his tracks. "Detective Benoit, it's me, Gregory Arsenault."

While Geneviève got to her feet, she kept her pistol leveled on the figure. "Go ahead and take four steps out of the shadows," she commanded. "But keep in mind I'll shoot you if there's any sudden movement."

Nazim sat listening to the exchange between the policewoman and his former partner. "How nice of you to join us, Gregory. It's rather convenient you being in the neighborhood, isn't it? Have you come to make sure your conscience is clear?"

Geneviève glanced back and forth between the two men. "Do you have something to confess, Monsieur Arsenault?" she asked. "This man claims you were partners. He also said you arranged for freighters to move his drugs. And now, you look to have something in return from me for making this arrest."

Gregory measured his response with care. He knew he had to make Nazim out as the culprit in this or there would be too many questions by the police. "Like I said before, Detective Benoit, he approached me to secure a freighter to move his product. He even offered €100,000 to make sure no questions were asked. How would you interpret such an offer?"

As Gregory spoke, Geneviève had made her way around so she stood before Nazim and kept the Frenchman in view. *Do I continue to trust Arsenault? And is Aziz trying to cut a bargain to save himself?* she asked herself as silence fell between the three of them.

"One thing you forget about your predicament, Monsieur Aziz," Geneviève said.

"What's that?"

The policewoman looked down at the restrained figure. "You've been associated with a known criminal element in Algiers," Geneviève said. "Later today, the Algerian police will arrest your mentor, Omar Khalid, for his role in the drug smuggling you've engaged in," she added.

"You're lying."

"Am I now?" Geneviève replied. "How do think we tracked you? It was the cooperation of the Algerians who identified your false passport."

Straining to glance over at his former partner, Nazim Aziz glared at the Frenchman. "You told her, didn't you, Gregory? There's no way she could have learned about the alias I used without your help."

"Monsieur Arsenault had nothing to do with having you identified," Geneviève replied. "It was simple police work and your foolish vanity which allowed us to track where you had been and your destinations. Once your trial in Marseille is complete, I'm sure my superiors will discuss the next step with the Algerians and British. Then they can decide who prosecutes you next."

The realization of prison didn't sit well with the smuggler. "So, Detective, you're willing to forego your principles as an officer, and for what? Just so you can make a name for yourself?" Nazim said. "You're being used and you don't even realize it's happening, do you? Well done, Gregory."

The former Legionnaire shook his head. "Like Detective Benoit said, you did it to yourself," he replied. "I had nothing to do with helping the police track you down."

Geneviève stepped closer to Gregory; her hand extended. "I'll need your help in cutting the rope," she said as she held the knife in one hand and her pistol in the other.

Taking the blade, Gregory knelt behind Nazim. "I'd behave if I were you. She's an excellent shot with the pistol."

Nazim grunted as one arm, now free from the restraint, fell to his side. Rolling his shoulder, he did his best to force the blood flow back into his hand. "Tell Pasqual his knot skills are still excellent," he uttered.

As Gregory cut through the last restraint, Geneviève reached behind her, producing a set of handcuffs. As Gregory sliced through the rope securing Nazim's legs, Geneviève stopped him. "Wait," she ordered. With a kick to Nazim's feet, she gave her next command. "Roll over and place your hands behind your back," she said while tossing the cuffs at Gregory.

Even with the glow of the quarter-moon, Gregory still had trouble seeing the chrome-plated restraints tossed from the detective. It wasn't until they nearly hit him in the face, did he reach out for them. Doing so caused him to drop the knife in the grass surrounding the grave.

The slight miscue by Arsenault took Geneviève's eyes off Nazim, who took a chance and got to his feet. With the moment's hesitation, Nazim was able to knock Gregory down as he scurried past him and sprinted between the headstones.

The abrupt move by Nazim caught Geneviève by surprise. "Stop or I'll shoot," she screamed. But the sudden sight of Gregory getting to his feet as she brought her weapon to bear caused her to hesitate. Her command was loud enough to alert Gregory's men who were positioned throughout the cemetery to the trouble.

Chapter FORTY

The outburst by the woman caught Louis and the others by surprise. From the moment Gregory left his side, Louis had directed Pasqual to keep his sights on the trio, and give a running dialogue on their actions. Aziz's sudden escape from the detective and Gregory was not what any of them expected.

Near one of the exits, Romain Neuville and his canine partner Hunter understood the shout from Detective Benoit. The sudden commotion caused the Belgian Malinois to perk its ears up, and his tail sway in anticipation. Romain grabbed his radio, and called out to Louis. "Can someone tell me what happened?"

"Nazim is on the loose," Louis answered the K9 officer. Next, he called his scout, who was the only member with night vision goggles. "Pasqual, can you figure out which way he went?"

When Aziz made his escape, Pasqual jumped to his feet so he could track the man's movement easier. "He headed towards the southern end of the cemetery."

"Julien, did you catch Pasqual's last transmission?" Louis queried as he moved away from his hiding place.

"Oui, I'm near the gates leading to *Armee d'Afrique*," he replied as he positioned himself for the potential conflict headed his way. "And Phillip is here with me as well." To his right was a wall of rough-hewn stone, a 3-meter tall obstacle he hoped he wouldn't have to scale.

After he fled from Geneviève and Gregory, Nazim, still clutching the knife, paused behind a granite crypt. He leaned against the stone to catch his breath, and tried to gain a sense of where he was within the cemetery. To his right, was a stand of trees, while his left would lead him into the newer section and open ground.

With measured steps, Aziz tread slowly away from the crypt, through the grave markers, taking care to avoid announcing his location. He made it to an enormous oak tree, crouched down and moved with purpose into the shadows.

The sudden action by Aziz forced Geneviève to instinctively rush after her suspect. In doing so, she left Gregory to fend for himself. Cursing at her foolish behavior, she did her best to follow Aziz as he ran towards the perimeter wall protecting the grounds, but soon lost track of him as she ducked in and out of the shadows.

Watching the detective pursue Aziz, Gregory gradually made his way back towards Louis. As he neared the mausoleum, he noticed Louis standing away from the complex, straining to look through the darkness.

"Well, this turned into a shit sandwich rather fast," Louis declared as his friend drew close. "Pasqual saw Aziz head toward the south wall. What the hell happened, anyhow?"

Gregory told Louis what had transpired leading to Nazim's escape. "You were right, I should have considered what he might try being as desperate as he is."

It was Louis's turn to pat his friend on the shoulder. "What's done is done, *mon ami*," he replied. "Let's not compound it by acting foolishly from this point forward, heh?" He handed back Gregory's Glock before the radio. "What do you have in mind?"

Gregory took the handgun and slid it behind his back, then the radio before he paused and thought of his next action. "Pasqual, do you have a visual on Aziz?"

"I lost him near some trees," the scout replied. "But the woman is getting very close to where he might be," he added, sweeping the night-vision sights to his right to notice Geneviève lurk amongst the gravestones.

Gregory tugged on Louis's elbow as he moved toward the section Aziz was last seen. "We'll try to flush him out for the detective," he muttered. "But don't let her catch you, okay?" He got a nod of understanding from his partner as they meandered along the path.

While Gregory and Louis made their way towards Aziz, Geneviève tread amongst the gravesites near the drug smuggler. With each step, she gave the appearance of a leopard on the hunt for its prey. Her police training instructors continually stressed the eyes catch changing colors, lights, and movement far quicker than the mind can handle was coming in handy. With each step, Geneviève kept her eye movements slow and focused.

Hunched low near some bushes, Aziz noticed Geneviève lurking nearby as she drew closer to where he hid. *I've got to make my way to the gate somehow*. Examining the space behind him, he made out the perimeter wall forty meters away. The sound of footsteps along the gravel path alerted him to movement from his left.

Aziz strained to watch through the shadows as he lost sight of Geneviève. Clutching the knife in his right hand, he steadied himself against a broken headstone. The footsteps stopped, but rustling leaves drew his attention. Aziz glanced to his left, and noticed two squirrels scamper out of the shadows, their tails swaying back and forth as they darted into the moonlight for just a moment. The sight caused a brief smile to cross his lips.

Julien and Phillip had made their way along the perimeter wall from the exit near *Armee d'Afrique*, with Pasqual giving directions to approach Aziz from behind him. Skills learned while tracking mercenaries in the Congo gave them the advantage on how to stalk the drug smuggler.

With a series of hand signals, Julien directed his cousin to wait and guard the escape route which they had just traversed. Phillip gave a single nod acknowledging the order, remaining in position.

As Julien prepared to confront Aziz, Geneviève spied the crouching drug smuggler and moved to confront him. "Stay where you are," she shouted, her pistol at the ready as she approached.

The sudden confrontation startled Aziz, who leapt to his feet and ran for the perimeter wall. In doing so, he stumbled into the waiting arms of the Legionnaire. Julien wasn't aware Aziz was armed with the detective's knife, and the confrontation resulted in him being stabbed.

As she rushed toward the two men, Geneviève leveled her weapon as they grappled for control of the knife. Soon, a narrow beam of light penetrated the darkness from behind a tree, and Geneviève stepped sideways as she tried to focus on the men fighting and the approaching intruder.

"Stop right there," she commanded, the pitch of her voice a few octaves higher than usual.

Gregory froze in place, knowing the woman was armed and nervous. "It's Gregory, Detective Benoit," he replied.

To her left, Julien and Aziz continued to fight. The drug smuggler still held the knife and used his bulk and momentum to control the smaller man. In an abrupt show of strength, Aziz forced Julien to tumble backwards. The Legionnaire struck his head against one of the many granite markers, which allowed Aziz to continue towards the perimeter.

While he watched the men struggle, Gregory closed the distance between himself and Geneviève. The ugly sound of Julien's skull impacting the headstone caused him to wince, knowing a potential concussion, or worse would be the result.

As Aziz sprinted towards the perimeter, Geneviève dropped to a knee and took aim, letting loose two rounds from her Sig Sauer, the gunfire echoing across the cemetery.

Aziz ducked when he noticed Geneviève take aim. As he fled, he did his best to dodge between the graves, hoping to avoid the next round fired by the detective. Just ahead, he saw the single light hang above the gates leading to the city street.

As Geneviève pursued Aziz, Gregory signaled Louis to join him. Kneeling down next to the fallen member of his crew, he gently cradled his head while easing his torso flat on the ground. "Look after Julien," he commanded. "And give me my gun." Out of the shadows, Pasqual appeared and was soon joined by Romain and his canine partner.

"Pasqual, get Hector to have the car ready, both of you get Julien to the chateau," Gregory directed. "Louis, call Marcel on the *Joan of Arc* and have Dr. Singh meet them to look after Julien. And tell him the doctor needs to treat a knife wound as well."

"What are you going to do?" Romain asked.

"Something I should have done when I had the chance," Gregory replied. "You and Hunter need to keep Aziz from getting out of the cemetery." In the distance, a siren's wail grew louder.

As Gregory saw to his friend, Geneviève walked between the crypts, sweeping her pistol from left to right, expecting an encounter with the drug smuggler. "Aziz, you can't escape, you know. I'll have you pay for what you've caused," she declared, her voice steadier and more confident.

Aziz knelt down in the shadow of the Virgin Mary statue atop a crypt, listening. Peering around the corner, he saw the silhouette of the woman approach, the glint of moonlight reflected off her pistol. *If I run, she'll see me,* he told himself. The sound of quick stepping on the gravel alerted him to someone else advancing on his position. Unable to see ahead past the maze of crypts, Aziz didn't notice Romain and Hunter trotting behind him towards the wrought-iron gates.

As he turned his attention back to Geneviève, Aziz saw the detective only a few meters from him. The shifting passage of the moon kept him in the shadows, which proved to be his best ally.

Geneviève picked up the movement off to her right unaware it was Romain heading towards the gate a hundred meters ahead. She swept her weapon to the left, and something behind her caught her attention.

It was too late. Aziz timed his assault on Geneviève with near perfection. The only thing he couldn't control was the gun fire as he surprised her. Wrapping his left arm around her neck, his right hand brought the knife up to her neck. "Drop your gun," he uttered, the blade held just below her jaw, drew a trickle of blood. "You're my way out of here now."

Geneviève held her arm out to her side and released her grip on the pistol, letting it hit the gravel path. As Aziz pushed against her back, Geneviève shuffled her feet, slowing both of them. She felt the knife's tip against her skin, and knew any sudden move would be lethal. "You'll never get out of here," she uttered. "The exits will all be manned with police." She knew the approaching police cars were alerted to the cemetery after she fired her gun.

"We'll just have to see, won't we?" Aziz replied, using his weight to force the woman to keep moving. As he looked over Geneviève's shoulder, he spied the familiar silhouette of a dog sitting, its tail swaying back and forth. The sight caused Aziz to halt their progress.

Geneviève had spied the animal as well. She hadn't encountered the dog when she arrived and now was hopeful it belonged to a sentry roaming the grounds. "You're not afraid of dogs, are you?"

To their left, Gregory had made his way toward them and saw Aziz force the police woman to discard her weapon. Any hasty movement on his part and she'd fall victim to a lethal knife wound. Clutching his radio, he related what he saw to the others. *If she can just give me two minutes, this will all be over,* he told himself while he treaded along the path.

Aziz continued to push against Geneviève as they inched closer to the cemetery's exit. A noise from behind him caused him to stop. "Is that you, Gregory?" he asked, spinning the woman around to act as a shield against those behind him.

Phillip stepped away from the crypt's shadow, his Glock pistol held against his side. "I don't know who you are, Monsieur, but I can tell you that escape is not an option," he declared.

"You must be one of Gregory's men," Aziz replied. "That's too bad. But I've got the upper hand though."

Phillip's sudden appearance was enough for Gregory to make his move. Stepping away from behind the crypt, he stood in the middle of the path leading to the gate. "That's as far as you're going, Aziz," the Legionnaire declared.

Aziz glanced over his shoulder and spied his former partner. "Is the policewoman's life that valuable to you, Gregory?" he asked, his grip tight around her neck. A quick look back allowed him to notice Phillip had ventured no closer. Still, he was now caught between the two men.

Geneviève felt Aziz shift his weight with each turn, and on one shift, she lifted her foot and brought the full weight of her body down on his right foot. Using her martial arts skill again, she caused Aziz to loosen his grip enough for her to spin out of his grasp. This put her on the offensive where she pressed her attack against the drug smuggler.

Aziz swung the knife wildly at the woman as he tried to defend himself. Each attempt to thwart the woman's advance took him another step closer to Gregory. It had turned into a no-win situation for him. In desperation, Aziz grabbed the woman's arm and pulled her closer to him.

The knife caught the sleeve of Geneviève's jacket. The cut made it through the leather, but snagged on the satin liner. She cursed to herself, realizing she'd gotten too close. However, the force of Aziz pulling on her gave her the advantage to twist her arm and out of his grasp. Now, she was between Aziz and Gregory, who'd remained at a distance.

The flashing blue lights of a police car on the other side of the perimeter wall provided a brief distraction that Aziz used to attempt his escape. Rushing between the crypts, the drug smuggler stumbled and fell in the darkness. Looking back, he could see two silhouetted figures in pursuit.

Geneviève trotted to where she dropped her gun before taking up the chase of Aziz. Gregory saw her grab the weapon before heading after the drug smuggler. He had the advantage of a flashlight he'd taken from Louis earlier. The halogen beam cut through the darkness as he swung it in the direction Aziz had run.

Geneviève saw the light swing towards her. "He's headed to the right," she shouted, trotting after Aziz. In moments, the drug smuggler was illuminated in the shaft of light as he pushed himself off the ground. Time stopped as the echo of gunfire erupted.

Aziz struggled to gain his footing again as he tripped over yet another fallen gravestone. It was enough time to allow for his former partner to direct the flashlight on him. Clutching a stone cross, he pulled himself to his feet. The bullets had found their target, causing him to stumble against the memorial.

Gregory froze in place, hearing the shots being fired. As he looked to his right, he spied Geneviève make her way towards Aziz, pistol held in a two-fisted grip, ready to fire again. Behind him, he could hear the crunch of feet on the gravel path. He turned around to see Phillip move toward him. As he held his hand in the air, the junior man froze. In the background, Gregory took in the reflection of the police strobes bouncing off the surrounding buildings.

Geneviève walked up on Aziz and saw the damage her bullets caused to her suspect. A pair of growing circles of crimson stained the azure coverall where each round struck. The drug smuggler gazed upward, looking at the policewoman.

"Is taking my life worth it?"

"You won't die, Aziz; that I can promise you," the detective stated, holstering a pistol. "Unless it's by your own hand or those you offend in whatever prison you're put in."

"And now... you are going to have to explain to your superiors why you shot an unarmed man," Aziz uttered as the pain ebbed from the wounds. "And how you were manipulated by a criminal element."

"I don't think that'll be the case," Geneviève answered. "Monsieur Arsenault was just a concerned citizen who aided a police officer. Weren't you?"

"How will you explain being here, in this cemetery, then?" Arsenault asked.

Geneviève pointed to the granite headstone Aziz sat against. "I was paying my respects." It read *BENOIT*.

Chapter FORTY-ONE

Once again, Detective Benoit had become the police department's center of attention. When word passed through the rank and file of officers, it seemed everyone wanted to hear the story of her escape from the would-be attacker. Even Sergeant Dubois made it a point to be seen with her as Geneviève discussed the tale.

But just a day removed from her encounter, Geneviève also found herself in Annex #3 where she was being interviewed by Internal Affairs. Along with her was the police union's representative, a harried and disheveled woman who had recently held a position in Central Directorate of Public Security (DCSP). And although the conference room was equal in size to her office which she shared with Detectives Berger and Vidal; Geneviève still had a sense of dread sitting at the table.

As the door opened, two male detectives strolled in and took seats opposite Geneviève. "Sorry to keep you both waiting," the older one spoke. "Officer Savard and I will do our best not to keep you any longer than needed."

Geneviève glanced at both men with uncertainty. Officers on most police forces were never fond of colleagues assigned to Internal Affairs, and she already had two earlier encounters with its members. "I appreciate your thoughtfulness," she replied with a smile. The union representative just nodded.

The older detective opened his notebook and slid on a pair of horned rim glasses. "Shall we begin with your activities over the last 24 hours, Detective?" he asked. "Was there anything unique about your day?"

Geneviève tugged on her jacket sleeves before leaning onto the table. "Everything about my day is unique," she replied. "However, Detective Berger and I were alerted to a possible suspect at the airport," she said. This began a forty-five-minute monologue where she related everything about her day leading up to her encounter with Nazim Aziz.

Everything except her confrontation with Sergeant Dubois and the phone calls with her brother-in-law, Gregory Arsenault. They didn't need to learn any of those details. "And when I got to my apartment, I realized the other day was the anniversary of my uncle's death," Geneviève answered before reclining in her chair.

The older detective jotted down a note as Geneviève replied. "I see," the older detective said in acknowledgement. "So, when you were accosted by the suspect, did you announce yourself as a police officer?" he asked, checking off another line on his notepad.

The grin on Geneviève's face didn't disclose what she thought. "Before I could, I felt the knife to my throat," she explained, pulling her collar aside. The thin red line was still visible. "Because the suspect came from behind," she added, "I didn't get a chance to see a weapon until he held it against me."

"And since you were there at night, it's safe to say there wasn't enough light for you to see anyone there with you?" Savard chimed in on the conversation.

"That's correct, Detective Savard," she declared.

"And because you were off-duty, you didn't have the benefit of a backup, did you? Even though Captain Duval mandated you and Detective Berger have patrol members work with you?" the older detective asked, reading from his notes.

"Like you say, I was off-duty."

Geneviève spend the next several minutes answering additional questions. Some of her answers were obvious lies which only Arsenault could dispute. She knew she couldn't explain Arsenault's presence without being questioned about his involvement.

Savard flipped another page over from the opened folder he'd placed on the table. "Tell me, Detective Benoit, what led you to be at the cemetery so late at night?"

Even as Savard asked his question, Geneviève could sense tightness in her chest. She'd endured questioning before from IA members, but that was when she was clearly justified in her actions. But this was different.

"With the case load I've been working, I haven't slept much," Geneviève replied. "I needed some fresh air, and as I said before, since the anniversary of a family member's death was this past week, I decided to pay my respects." She glanced at the union rep and continued. "I must have fell asleep while I was praying."

"And while doing so, this drug smuggling suspect," he continued, glancing down at the report, "Nazim Aziz... he attacked you?"

Geneviève shook her head. "Yes. It's well documented there's been several instances where I've been singled out by various criminal elements," she answered rather easily. "I can't let someone like this man Aziz dictate how I live my life, can I, Detective?"

"And wasn't this the same person of interest from the assault at Chateau Il d'If?" the officer pressed.

"Yes, Aziz was one of a dozen individuals who raided the facility," Geneviève answered. "It's all documented in the report Captain Lemieux and I submitted."

Detective Savard wrote down his observations as Geneviève answered the questions. "Did you at any time consider your actions as provocative, Detective Benoit?" he asked.

The question caused the union representative to put her hand in the air. "Detective Savard, what are you insinuating about Detective Benoit?" she asked.

"Nothing. You're well aware these are just standard questions," Savard answered.

Geneviève looked confused at the exchange. "I'm not sure what you mean, either."

Savard flipped through several pages. "In the last six months Detective Benoit, you've been involved in two altercations and one shooting," he read. "At least... those are the ones you and your colleagues have reported."

"You forgot about me being assaulted in Algiers and having to defend myself," Geneviève replied, pulling the band from her hair. Turning to the side, she swung her head forward letting her hair cover her face. "You can keep asking questions, I can listen to you just fine," she stated. Clutching her hair with both hands, she pulled it tight from her forehead and back together as she twisted the band back around her fingers.

Savard and the other detective just sat and watched as Detective Benoit primped herself like she prepared to go for a jog in the park. "Detective Benoit, I'm not sure you understand the seriousness of this inquiry."

Geneviève finished fixing her hair and dropped both hands onto the table. "I'm very aware of the importance behind these proceedings, Detective," she said. "But I shouldn't be grilled like this. At least not for defending myself, or am I missing something in the translation?"

The older detective leaned back in his chair. "This inquiry is to ascertain if you blatantly discharged your weapon without concern for injuries to others," he stated. "Other than that, there's nothing else we're looking into."

"Well then, seeing how I had to defend myself from an attack..." Geneviève said. "And since the only person injured was the attacker and not an innocent bystander, I'd say we're done, don't you?"

Detective Savard made a notation in the file. "You'll receive results from the Disciplinary Council by the end of next week, Detective Benoit," he said. "Until then, you're free to return to your department."

As she pushed herself away from the table, Geneviève stepped to the door and swung it open. "Have a good day, gentleman," she declared, leaving the conference room. As she strolled across the parking lot, she listened to faint applause echoing from the open entry behind the station.

While Geneviève was interviewed by Internal Affairs, Detective Vidal sat in Captain Duval's office. The senior officer was reviewing the notes Vidal had prepared from the case he'd been assigned.

"Interesting hypothesis, Detective," Duval declared.

"Thank you, sir," Vidal replied. In reviewing the murder of Yvette Segal, Vidal had learned of a family member and their involvement in a case of embezzlement from the local bank.

Duval flipped over the page. “Tell me, Detective what led you to make the connection between the socialite and our missing bank employee?”

“Besides the occurrence of their last names, you mean?”

“Yes,” Duval replied, folding his hands on the desk.

“It was Detective Benoit and Berger’s file on the drug smuggling,” Vidal answered. “I believe Benoit interviewed the executive of Banque Palatine, Ulysse Reno. And he mentioned discussing the matter with Pierre Segal, his senior accounts manager. As it turns out, Monsieur Reno already began an internal investigation into Segal about his embezzlement scheme.”

The captain shook his head in wonder. “And from those notes you made the connection he was related to our socialite?”

“I just looked at normal information to confirm his identity,” Duval answered. “That’s when I saw his birthplace and parents,” he added. “Then I backtracked Ms. Segal’s identity and she had the same birthplace, parents, and an older brother.”

Captain Duval flipped over the next page of the write-up from Vidal. “So, based on your review; you consider this the only suspect with means and opportunity to commit the murders.”

Vidal brought his arms across his chest. “I’m confident my findings will lead to the arrest of the person who murdered both Pierre and Yvette Segal.”

The senior officer closed the folder and opened his center drawer. “Then you’ll need this,” he said, pulling a search and arrest warrant out, its gold emblem glistened under the desk lamp. “Don’t forget to brief Berger in on this before you head out.”

“What about Benoit; shouldn’t she know as well?”

Captain Duval looked at his watch. “She’s in the middle of something right now,” he said. “I wouldn’t expect her to be available for the rest of the day.”

“Yes, sir,” Vidal replied, taking the offered folder and warrant. Leaving the office, it took him five minutes to find Nicolas. The detective was amongst a handful of officers congratulating Sergeant Claire Dubois on her promotion to Supervisor in Criminal Records.

Berger felt the tap on his shoulder. Turning around, he glanced down at Vidal. "What's up, Aidan?"

"We've work to do," Vidal replied, waving the warrant in his hand. "You, me and four uniformed officers are going to make an arrest," he continued as the two men walked away from the festivities.

"Is this about the case Captain Duval gave you the other day?" Berger asked.

Vidal shook his head. "It's time to catch another criminal. And you and Benoit helped with some of the pieces, too."

Ten minutes later, Vidal and Berger entered Banque Palatine. Wandering up to the receptionist, Vidal spoke first. "I'd like to see Monsieur Reno," he explained as he showed his credentials.

"I'm sorry, Detective. But he's gone for the afternoon," the woman replied.

"Do you know if he returned home or went somewhere else?" Berger asked, leaning on the counter.

The receptionist smiled at Nicolas. "He mentioned to several of the staff he'd just been granted his license for Bluefin this week," she answered. "It sounded like he would be headed out to try his luck right away."

Berger turned to his colleague. "Now what?"

Vidal already anticipated the banker not being available. "Now we head to the marina in the L'Estaque district," he explained, giving the receptionist a polite wave as he walked away. "It's where Monsieur Reno rents a slip for his yacht."

"Whoa... how do you know he's there right now though?" Berger asked, hesitating at the door.

Vidal ignored the query from Berger as he trotted toward the police car. Before climbing in, he briefed the uniformed officers of their next stop, just as Berger joined him.

"You didn't answer me; why the marina in L'Estaque?"

"Benoit and Captain Lemieux had an encounter there with him when they shadowed a drug dealer," he replied. "It was in their report. But when I checked on the yacht the socialite was killed on, Reno's yacht was listed as moored at the Old Marina slipway. Besides, you heard the receptionist: he's anxious to go fishing."

"That means nothing," Berger argued. "I'm sure people move their boats back and forth all the time."

"Maybe... but I've got Captain Duval convinced the banker is a person of interest in the disappearance of his account manager," the detective said. "And that's all I need for the moment. Besides, I was getting tired of being left in the office while you and Benoit chased your suspect."

The drive from bank to marina took an awkward twenty minutes where Berger and Vidal kept to themselves. As the police car pulled into the parking at the marina's office, Berger broke the silence.

"What's the name of Reno's boat?"

Vidal pulled out his cell phone and scrolled to his notes. "The vessel's name is *'C'est la vie'* and being 25 meters long, it'll be easy to find," he said. After a few minutes, the detectives came upon the yacht.

The crimson hull and white superstructure were stark contrast to the azure waters of the marina. "You weren't kidding," Berger exclaimed as he let out a low whistle. Walking up to the transom, Vidal stepped aboard as Berger directed the four uniformed officers to take up positions at either end of the vessel.

Striding onto the aft deck, Vidal noticed a man in the main cabin. "Excuse me," he said getting the man's attention. "I'm looking for Monsieur Reno."

Vidal held his credentials up for the man, and Ulysse Reno hesitated before walking out. He was expecting one more of Yacine El Amari's gang members, not the police. Ducking as he passed through the door, the statuesque figure of the executive approached Detective Vidal. "How can I help you, Officer?"

Vidal craned his neck upward at the vessel's owner. "Are you Monsieur Reno?"

"I am."

Detective Berger had made his way on deck from the dock and leaned against the rail, keeping his distance. Though the yacht was tied to the dock, the outgoing tide allowed for gentle rocking.

"I've a warrant to search this vessel," Vidal declared, producing the document. "Is there anything you'd like to tell us before we begin?"

Reno held out his hand. "May I see the warrant?"

"No, you may not at this time," Vidal replied. "I'll ask you one more time; is there anything illegal that we might find onboard?"

Ulysse Reno was not known to cower from any man; it made for poor business. But with the police, it was a different matter. He had a reputation in the district, and if he let the detectives search his boat, it would be ruined. Reno surrendered to the shorter detective and stepped aside. "I'd be happy to give you a tour."

"We'll be fine on our own," Berger answered as he pushed off the rail. "And for your safety and ours, we'll have you wait here on deck." He waved one of the uniformed officers toward him. "Go ahead and make yourself comfortable, Monsieur." As the detectives entered the salon, Reno sat under the watchful eye of the patrolman.

"You're in charge here, Aidan," Berger said, scanning the opulent surroundings of the space. "What are we looking for again?"

"The actress was shot, but there was no exit wound from the bullet," Vidal said. "And the coroner's report classified the wound inflicted at under a meter, which means she let the shooter up close."

"Geneviève came to the same conclusion when she found the victim," Berger said. "Which means we're looking for a weapon," he determined as he leaned over and opened a cabinet. "Do we know the caliber of the bullet?"

Vidal lifted the cushions from the bench behind the captain's position on the bridge. "It was a 9mm, according to your lady-friend."

"My lady-friend? You mean Officer LeBeau, right?" Berger asked slightly miffed. "Did she say anything else? I mean as far as the forensics on the bullet." Shoving aside some linen, Berger came across a box of ammunition. "Jackpot," he exclaimed.

The detectives' voices echoed through the salon and outside where Ulysse understood the discovery. *Having a means of protection isn't a crime,* he told himself as he maintained a neutral appearance for the patrolman.

Berger joined Vidal in the main stateroom. "Anything jump out at you?"

Vidal side-stepped along the bed toward the nightstand. "Nothing," he replied, opening the drawer. Shuffling his feet, he returned to end of the bed and opened one of the doors only to push aside several hangars of shirts and slacks. "Notice anything?"

"All his, and no hers," Berger replied, closing the drawers.

"This is his boat, and everyone else are just guests," Vidal replied. "Which means his activities are done away from his family; smart."

As both detectives left the room, Vidal stepped to the door leading to the aft section, but found it locked. "Why would you lock any door?" he asked, looking over his shoulder at Berger.

"It's where he keeps his cigars and wine," Berger snickered.

Vidal pointed over Berger's shoulder. "Let's find the other entry. I'm sure there's more than one to this room."

Berger led Vidal to the upper level and the pilothouse. Looking around, he spied a hatch in the floor. "I'm feeling lucky this might be your other entry." He unlatched the cover and pulled it open, exposing a narrow ladder leading below deck. "After you."

Vidal climbed down the steps. Looking toward the back of the yacht, he could see the lights glow from the compartment. It was a short trip through the passageway before he entered the engine room, which for the moment was quiet.

"Find something interesting?" Berger asked, coming up behind Vidal.

Vidal shook his head. "Nothing yet. Here's the easy way in," he said, pointing to the hatch they'd previously found. "And that must be the way to the sauna," he joked, indicating a doorway on the opposite side.

Berger approached the door with his hand held up and a finger across his lips. He could pick up muffled noises from the other compartment, but not enough to tell if someone was in distress.

"Uninvited guests?" Vidal asked.

"Or the house boy who cooks," Berger replied, his pistol now unholstered. Clutching one of the dogged latches, he began freeing the hatch. With the first open, he grasped the second and nodded to Vidal. "You ready?"

"Let's do this," Vidal replied as he steeled himself for what would happen next.

With second latch free, Berger yanked open the hatch, to reveal the crew's quarters and two men. The detective's appearance was not what one man expected, but for the other, it would prove to be lifesaving.

"Police," Vidal declared as he stepped forward.

The Maghrebis gang member had little time to react since he didn't consider anyone would approach from the engine room. Surprised by their appearance, he froze as he felt Vidal's Glock pointed at him.

"Hands on your head," Vidal ordered as he watched Berger tend to the other man.

Bound hand and foot, Pierre Segal lay on the crew bunk, his eyes glazed over and his skin a cool clamminess. "He's been drugged," Berger stated, feeling for a pulse. "But he's alive."

With handcuffs on the gang member, Vidal pushed him towards the hatch that led to transom deck. "Monsieur Reno will have some explaining to do after this," he said.

The sudden appearance by Vidal caught the attention of the uniformed officers on the dock. "Call for a medical team," he shouted to the closest policeman. As one officer ran to his car to call for aid, Vidal handed the Algerian to the other officer.

Vidal climbed to the deck where Ulysse Reno sat. Void of any emotion, he stared out across the water. It was obvious he knew whatever scheme he attempted to complete; it was now undone.

As he stood in front of the executive, Vidal felt nothing for the man. "You'll have the opportunity to speak with your attorney when we get back to the station," he explained as he read Reno his rights to representation before turning to the officer holding Reno. "Take the suspect into custody."

Berger appeared on the deck as Reno was being led off the yacht. "I found this in the drawer next to the bunk," he said, holding a MAB Brevete PA-15 M1 pistol. "And it's loaded with 9mm cartridges."

Vidal took the loaded magazine from Berger and pushed out one of the shells. “It’s a rim-fired cartridge. Let’s see if it matches the ammunition you found and the ballistics report from our murdered victim.”

Chapter FORTY-TWO

The defense team for Nazim Aziz met in the corridor as patrons and prosecuting attorneys filed out of the courtroom. Amongst them were Detectives Benoit and Berger. A handful of reporters pressed forward with attempts to catch the detectives or attorney's attention. The questions they shouted fell on deaf ears as the officers walked toward the elevator.

Before Geneviève reached the elevator, she turned instead for the stairwell. Between the trial and the Internal Affairs inquiry, she felt like an animal in a test lab. The constant questions endured from both made it hard for her to keep a clear head. She needed time to herself.

Berger saw her turn away. "Hey, where you headed?"

Pulling off her bonnet, she hesitated at the door. "I just need to burn off some energy," Geneviève replied, pushing through the door and down the stairs. As she paused between floors, she took a deep breath before grasping the handrail and descended toward the ground floor.

After her encounter with Aziz in the cemetery, Geneviève had not spoken with Gregory about the ramifications of their meeting. She wasn't aware of his effort with his sister-in-law to alter the arrest records. It wasn't until the prosecution presented its case against Aziz would she realize what happened.

Once she reached the ground floor, Geneviève took another deep breath in anticipation of more reporters, but as she opened the door, she was caught off guard by Captain Lemieux.

With disregard for the crowd, she threw her arms around him, letting her joy of seeing him overcome the burden of the trial. "Claude, what are you doing here?" she asked, stepping back from the embrace.

"I decided to take a few days' vacation after I left the hospital," he replied. "After I was discharged, Captain Duval called me to bring me up to speed on you and Berger. He was happy with most of the work you both put in on the case against Aziz."

Geneviève took a step back. "Most? He wasn't pleased with our arrest of a drug smuggler and his network of dealers?"

The senior officer placed his arm around Geneviève's shoulder, guiding her to the exit and outside. "Julien is more concerned about the actions you took to make those arrests," he said. "You've begun to show a reckless side in your conduct. This is the second incident where you shot the suspect."

"He attacked me," Geneviève exclaimed, pulling away from Claude. "He's lucky to only lose the use of his arm. And according to the IA report, I was justified in my actions."

"Next time, you might not be so lucky in persuading the investigators of your actions over the results," Lemieux declared. "I can guarantee your next session with IA won't be as easy."

Geneviève shook her head in disbelief. "You don't know how IA will conduct themselves if I'm ever questioned again," she said. "You assume I'll do something where they'll have cause to investigate my actions again."

Claude leaned against the wall and took a deep breath before he answered. He hadn't told anyone of his decision to transfer, except for Captain Duval and Superintendent Chevalier. "I've put in my papers for reassignment," he declared with a glance toward Geneviève.

"Why?"

Claude shrugged his shoulders. "There's a few reasons, but none of them involve our time together," he said. "During my rehab, I had time to consider how I wanted... actually, how I *needed* to move on from Nadine," he explained, wiping a tear from his eye.

The shock of her colleague's admission caught Geneviève off-guard. "Are you moving away? I mean... does the transfer mean you're leaving Marseille?"

A brief, foolish grin appeared on Claude's face. He knew the next thing he said would be a shock to the woman. "No... I'm not leaving. The transfer will take me out of the Drug Interdiction Unit though."

"Then where?"

"Superintendent Chevalier asked me to head up Internal Affairs," Lemieux replied. "So, in a way, I do know your next run in will be more difficult than the two past instances."

The shock of hearing Claude transferring was hard enough, but learning his move would be to Internal Affairs made accepting it even more difficult for Geneviève. His move would allow him to be investigate everything she was involved in, both past and future.

"Come on. You can buy me a coffee," he declared. "Don't forget to wear your bonnet; you're supposed to be an exemplary example of a detective for the citizens."

Geneviève made a face at Claude, her nose wrinkled as she squinted her eyes. With a flair for the dramatic, she placed the police cover on her head, hiding the auburn tresses except for her ever-present ponytail. "This might be the last time I'll ever buy you coffee," she replied with a chuckle. "You know how we rank and file officers look upon IA investigators?"

"We'll see," Lemieux replied, walking alongside the detective.

Across from the courthouse, Omar Khalid watched Geneviève and Lemieux from the second story office building. He'd been notified about Nazim Aziz's arrest by one of Amed Gilles's followers. It had taken three weeks before his nephew was well enough to be present in court. With help from his connections within the Algiers police force, he made his way to France so he could follow the trial.

Just last night he'd learned Nazim would be found guilty and remanded to Baumettes Penitentiary on the outskirts of Marseille. "Are you sure of this information?" Khalid asked, handing the attorney back his paper.

"Yes, Monsieur Khalid," the lawyer replied. "The courthouse clerk confirmed they're preparing for your client to be placed in isolation. There's concern a rival faction will take retribution against him."

"I thought you could guarantee my nephew's safety?" Khalid asked, this time to a gentleman sitting away from the window.

Guillermo Ochoa looked up from his beverage. "I could still guarantee it," the American DEA operative replied. "But his current situation presents a greater risk. And for that, there's a higher price to be paid."

"And what about his safe return to Algiers?"

Ochoa took a long drag from the cigar in his left hand, letting the smoke roll lazily from his lips as he stared at Khalid. "I've got assurances he'd have safe passage as well."

"And what about the woman?"

Ochoa leaned back in his chair. "My counsel to you would be to forget about her, Khalid," he declared. "And I'd recommend you pass those same cautions to your associate, Youssef Raif, as well."

"I can't control what manner of action he undertakes," Khalid answered as he returned to the window, his thoughts centered on his nephew. "Learning the results of the trial though, it's possible he'll do something drastic just to prove a point."

"Then I recommend you return to Algiers," Ochoa replied. "And do so with haste less you are found here," he warned as he stood. "I'll contact you when I've completed my task."

Khalid looked at the lawyer who'd kept to himself during the exchange with American. "Can you have someone escort me to my hotel, then to the airport?"

"Of course, Monsieur," he replied as he watched Ochoa leave.

Outside the office building, Hector and Julien enjoyed a drink from the juice bar stand on the street. Both men were aware of the threat to Detective Benoit, and had prepared themselves to neutralize it at any cost.

"He's on his way down," a voice said in the earpiece each man wore.

Julien tapped the piece to acknowledge the other person.

"You ready?" Hector asked.

Julien tossed his cup into the trash bin. "Let's get this over with," he sighed, sliding his hand across the pistol in his jacket.

Hector turned just in time to see Guillermo Ochoa emerge from the building, the cigar hanging loose from his lips. The American paused long enough to put on a pair of sunglasses.

Hector had already began moving once he spotted Ochoa, and Julien followed close behind. As Hector rounded a parked car, he placed Ochoa between himself and Julien. Walking along the path, he soon came face to face with the American.

"Good to see you again," Hector declared as he encountered Ochoa.

Recognizing the former Legionnaire caught the DEA operative off-guard. In a panic, he turned away to avoid getting within arms-reach of Hector. It would be a fatal move on his part.

While Hector confronted Ochoa, Julien had walked up behind him with the silenced pistol at the ready. As Ochoa turned, Julien shoved the barrel into the stomach of his target and pulled the trigger. The low-velocity bullets tore through the soft skin and internal organs. With a twist, Julien shot twice more in an upward angle, and sent bullets into Ochoa's major organs.

Guillermo Ochoa didn't consider himself a target, so his defenses were down. The fact his attacker was once a colleague made it harder for him to comprehend. As the blood gathered internally, his vision clouded as felt the life ebbing, drop-by-drop, from his body.

As Ochoa fell away from the gunfire, Hector guided him onto a nearby bench. "*Au revoir mon ami,*" the Frenchman said as he walked away. In less than two minutes, Arsenault's men had eliminated one threat to the policewoman. Slipping into the passenger side of Julien's car, he pulled out his cell phone to make a call.

News of the murder soon overshadowed the transfer of Nazim Aziz to prison the following day, and along with it, Omar Khalid's desire to protect his nephew from harm. With Ochoa's death, though, the Algerian crime leader was able to recoup the American's €100,000 fee his service demanded.

***

Geneviève swung her legs back and forth as she sat in the conference room, anxious to hear what Captain Duval had to say. In a few minutes, the door opened, and her fellow detective's Berger and Vidal entered. "What are you doing here?" she asked.

"Captain Duval's secretary called," Berger replied. "She said we're to be here for a briefing."

"Don't ask me; I'm just following along," Vidal chimed.

Sitting in silence, each detective was left with their own thoughts on the matter. After five more minutes, a noise from behind the door caused each of them to sit up in their chairs as the door opened and Guy entered.

Geneviève bolted out of the chair to embrace her friend as he entered the room. "It's so good to see you again," she exclaimed, kissing his cheek. "How are you feeling?"

"I'm fine," Masson replied, shaking Berger's hand as Geneviève stepped aside.

Aidan Vidal stood and waited for the others. "Hi, I'm Aidan," he introduced, offering his hand to the detective.

Masson shook it before he stepped back. "I just wanted to say my goodbyes in person," he began. "I head off to Paris tomorrow to begin my orientation."

"They still want you?" Berger asked with a playful smile.

"Guess so," Guy answered with a shrug.

Before any more words could be exchanged, Captain Duval entered the room followed by Claude and Superintendent Chevalier, who held a folder under his arm.

"Detective Masson, I didn't think you'd still be here," Captain Duval said. "You can stay if you'd like."

"All right," Guy replied, and sat next to Aidan.

Superintendent Chevalier opened the folder. "Detective Benoit, if you'd please join us."

Geneviève glanced at Berger, who just shrugged his shoulders. Getting to her feet, she stepped forward and took her place between the two senior officers.

"I thought it would be relevant to acknowledge all of you for your effort in bringing Nazim Aziz to justice," Chevalier said. "But likewise, to be present as witnesses to the promotion of Detective Benoit to her new rank of Senior Detective."

The men gathered in the room broke out in applause as Superintendent Chevalier held out the citation for Geneviève. Her reaction to the promotion was genuine, especially after her recent bout with Internal Affairs.

Before she could say anything, Geneviève was surprised by the appearance of Hector. Looking at each of her colleagues, she could sense her face redden. "I'm not sure what to say," she uttered, looking at Chevalier, then Captain Duval.

It was the next action which brought her to tears. Claude Lemieux stepped alongside her. "In keeping with tradition of the *Surente'*, I'd be honored if you'd accept this," he declared, and held out his Senior Detective's badge.

As she accepted the golden shield, Geneviève smiled while brushing away her tears. "I'll do my best to make you proud," she said. "And I'll try not bring any dishonor to the force while wearing it."

As each detective stepped forward, they all took turns giving Geneviève a hug and to congratulate her, with the last person being Hector.

"Thank you for being here," she said, still wiping tears from her cheek.

Hector shrugged his shoulders. "Thank Captain Lemieux; he's the one who called me about today," he replied. "I wish I'd left earlier, though, so I didn't miss your superintendent's speech."

Geneviève looked over at Claude, who nodded in return.

"Now, if you'll allow me, I'd like to take you to dinner tonight," Hector continued.

Geneviève smiled. She could see the sincerity and compassion in his eyes. "I'd like that," she whispered as she kissed him. "But I've still got work to do, and so do you."

Captain Duval made a point to clear his throat loud enough to catch everyone's attention. "Before we get too comfortable, I've got a few things to announce.

"With Detective Benoit's promotion, there will be a change in the department's assignments," Duval stated. "Captain Lemieux is transferring to Internal Affairs effective next Monday. And Detective Juneau will move from his position on the evening watch to days and take Captain Lemieux's place." Duval looked at Berger, and continued. "Detective Berger, you'll work with him until further notice."

"I'll do my best to make him feel at home," Berger replied with a forced smile.

Geneviève looked at her friend and felt a sense of emptiness. She'd just begun to get comfortable with Nicolas at her side as a partner. Now he would be working with another officer.

"Detective Benoit, you'll partner with Detective Vidal," Duval declared.

Geneviève glanced at Aidan and nodded. "I'm sure we'll do fine together." As Captain Duval finished, Geneviève felt her phone vibrate. As she looked at the message, she was shocked to see who had sent it. *Congratulations Detective, your promotion is well deserved*, and it came from Gregory Arsenault. "How did you find out I wonder?" she muttered under breath.

"Something important? Hector asked as he stood by her side.

"No, just someone expressing their well wishes," as she slid her arm through his. "It's nothing to worry about."

As the group began to file out of the conference room, Francine LeBeau walked up to her companion Nicolas Berger and Geneviève. "I just heard about your promotion," she exclaimed while she hugged the detective.

"Thanks, I guess," Geneviève replied.

As she took Berger's hand, Francine glanced over to Aidan. "Did you get the ballistics report I sent yesterday Detective Vidal?"

"Yes, I did," Vidal answered.

Geneviève stopped and looked at Vidal. "Did the gun prove to be a match to the one used to kill Yvette Segal?"

Vidal exchanged looks with Geneviève and the others before he spoke. "It was a perfect match, as far as bullets are concerned," he said. "However, the tests on Ulysse Reno's hands were negative."

"So, he wasn't the killer?" Berger asked.

Vidal shook his head. "No, and neither was her brother, Pierre. It seems Homicide has more to investigate to solve Yvette Segal's murder."

*** THE END ***

Acknowledgements

First and foremost, I'd like to thank my wife, Mary, for letting me scratch this itch called writing and for supporting me with her comments and encouragement, even after I locked myself away for hours at a time. Also, a big thank you to my daughter's Rebekah and Jennifer for letting 'Dad' to his thing without the need to keep asking, "Why'd you decide to write that?"

Next, to my good friend and co-worker, Doretta Burgess, for providing the first level of sanity checks, grammar checks and being that punctuation pundit on all the many pages of my random thoughts and ramblings.

Also, I would be remiss if I did acknowledge my fellow authors and mentors who I turn to more often than necessary when I'm wallowing in mental quicksand.

First, R.L. Merrill (https://www.rlmerrillauthor.com/) for her continued support and encouragement.

Next, Angela Ackermann and Becca Puglisi and the staff at One Stop for Writer's (https://onestopforwriters.com/)for their untiring commitment to the craft by providing the best prompts, references and guidance in character development. They also provide numerous avenues for authors and writers in their publication of the thesaurus's which proved to be invaluable.

My thanks to Jane Cleland (https://janecleland.com/) for taking the time to help me understand how to plot my story using her 'Street and Sidewalk' method to ensure the story kept on track.

About the Author

Anthony is a first generation American and native Californian, the son of Scottish immigrants, and who's fraternal grandparents hailed from Ireland, while his maternal grandparents hailed from Scotland. A product of a mixed education (part parochial and part public schools), he developed a thirst for reading early in his childhood.

He is also a 20-year veteran of the U.S. Navy, and traveled the globe. His assignments allowed him to step foot on four of the seven continents. He's known to boast of walking around the world at one point *(It's true, he did)*.

Anthony's dive into the world of fiction writing came as an escape from his work as an Instructional Systems Designer. When not working on improving his writing, Anthony can be found on the local golf course, honing his game invented by his ancestors.

He is married to his high school sweetheart, Mary, and has two grown children. He continues to reside in Southern California.

Send your comments or feedback to the author at;

mailto:fairwayscribe@gmail.com

www.ingramcontent.com/pod-product-compliance
Lightning Source LLC
Chambersburg PA
CBHW071155100726
47908CB00002B/394

* 9 7 8 1 7 3 2 4 0 8 1 5 9 *